The Reluctant Bride

A Dark Mafia Romance

Arianna Fraser

Copyright © 2021 Arianna Fraser - STC LLC

All rights reserved

The characters and events portrayed in this book are fictitious. Any similarity to real persons, living or dead, is coincidental and not intended by the author.

No part of this book may be reproduced, or stored in a retrieval system, or transmitted in any form or by any means, electronic, mechanical, photocopying, recording, or otherwise, without express written permission of the publisher.

ISBN-13: 9798711661009
ISBN-10: 1477123456

Cover design by: Fantabanner
Library of Congress Control Number: 2018675309
Printed in the United States of America

To Lynda - the best of friends, the dearest of cousins.

And to you...

A sincere and whole-hearted thank you to everyone who has bought The Reluctant Bride or read it on Kindle - proceeds from the book benefit the two crisis nurseries in my city. These facilities are non-profits who exist to serve parents who are overwhelmed and in desperate need of help. Their little people can be safely and lovingly cared for - for up to four days - while the parents get connected with services for anything from housing, to employment, to mental health. These brave folks get the help they need, and when they come back for their little ones, their faces are shining with hope, maybe for the first time. At any given time, there's usually several infants and toddlers, elementary school aged kiddos, even a preteen or two. A friend of mine told me that if there had been a place like this when she was a child, maybe she wouldn't have had to endure what she did, growing up with an alcoholic parent. I think about that every time I volunteer at the nursery. Thanks to your kindness, I've had the chance to purchase much-needed items, like cases of diapers, industrial-sized boxes of goldfish crackers, books, formula, toys, and so much more. And socks. Those kiddos can never hold on to a pair of socks.

Contents

Title Page

Copyright

Dedication

Preface

Chapter 1 – It's Time You Took a Wife, My Boy	1
Chapter 2– The Job Interview	12
Chapter 3 – Crying Doesn't Solve Anything	27
Chapter 4 – I Am All that You Have Right Now	42
Chapter 5 – No Diggety	52
Chapter 6 – The Wedding Night	66
Chapter 7 – The Light of Day	77
Chapter 8 – A Carnal Symphony	89
Chapter 9 – Safe Words and Too Many Cocktails	100
Chapter 10 – Until I Take It Off You	124
Chapter 11 – Everything But Her Freedom, Of Course	136
Chapter 12 – Are You Planning My Death, Darling?	149
Chapter 13 – A Mexican Standoff in Suburban London	158
Chapter 14 – Is My Terrifying Bride Brave, As Well?	175
Chapter 15 - The Team Building Exercise	179
Chapter 16 - Abruptly, As My Passion Now Makes Me…	192

Chapter 17 – There's so Much More at Stake Than Just You, Dear	201
Chapter 18 – The Ladies Who Lunch	216
Chapter 19 – I Promise You, You Will Beg for More	224
Chapter 20 – Yes, Sir	236
Chapter 21 – Food and Conversation	248
Chapter 22 – If I am All You Have, You Will Love Me	259
Chapter 23 – Accepting the Unacceptable	272
Chapter 24 – It Seems I Must Remind You Who You Belong To	280
Chapter 25 – You Are Whatever I Tell You To Be.	292
Chapter 26 – How I Feel Safe	301
Chapter 27 – I Wish We Could be Different People	318
Chapter 28 – What a Conscience Can Bear	328
Chapter 29 – I Fell in Love with the Wrong Guy	343
Chapter 30 – This Merits Correction	354
Chapter 31 – Saint Margaret and the Dragon	370
Chapter 32 – I Won't Forget	386
Chapter 33 – Mine	392
Chapter 34 – In the Belly of the Beast	399
Chapter 35 – New Friends and Old Enemies	408
Chapter 36 – For Better or for Worse	421
Chapter 37 – 'Til Death Do Us Part	432
Chapter 38 – It Was All So Simple When They Planned It	442
Chapter 39 – About 50% of St. Petersburg Seems to Want Us Dead	454
Chapter 40 – I Know the Oddest People	465
Chapter 41 – I am not a good man. But I am in love	475

with you.

Chapter 42 – Taming the Dragon	482
Chapter 43 – Twelve Hours	493
Chapter 44 - If you try to pull out that IV, I will sit on you.	504
Chapter 45 – I Shall Wait, Darling. But I Fully Intend to Ravish You	512
Afterword	527
About The Author	529
Books By This Author	531

Preface

The Reluctant Bride is a story revolving around organized crime, and there are mentions of criminal activity involved such an enterprise, like drugs and violence. There are also scenes of (consensual) explicit sexual activity between a husband and wife, forced marriage and profanity. Oh, so much profanity. If these things offend you, please find something more to your taste. Are you still here? Excellent! Grab a glass of wine or a cup of tea and settle in.

As always, thank you for reading, Arianna

Chapter 1 – It's Time You Took a Wife, My Boy

In which Thomas is compelled to do that which is against his will. And everyone is going to pay for it.

"It's time you took a wife, my boy."

Whatever Thomas Williams had been expecting Number One to say, it was not that. Williams had risen to the second position in one of the most powerful crime organizations in Europe by anticipating every move from not only his rivals but within The Corporation - Jaguar Holdings - as well. He'd thought, perhaps that the man seated across from him and enjoying an excellent glass of scotch would maybe compliment him on the flawless execution of a partnership with the terrifying Russian Solntsevskaya Bratva crime syndicate. Or gloat over the multi-million-dollar agreement that would send The Corporation into Eastern Europe, extending their reach three times farther than their current chokehold in Great Britain and South America.

But... what the *hell* was this nonsense?

One dark, elegant brow rose as Thomas eyed the urbanely smiling monster across from him. Ben Kingston may look like everyone's favorite bald uncle, but he was a terrifying sociopath who took enormous pleasure in the suffering he caused for his many enemies and occasionally, his friends. There were few enough of them, better described as uneasy allies. And for Kingston's wife? Thomas snorted silently. Number One had married a beautiful escort with superb social skills who was just aging out of the most lucrative portion of her career when she turned 30. She was happy enough to leapfrog into the position of Trophy Wife, though ten years later it seemed Arabella Kingston was a shaken, diminished version of her former self who just barely managed not to flinch every time her husband looked at her. But she did deftly handle the many fundraisers and social engagements The Corporation used to keep strong ties to the most powerful in society, the excessively wealthy, politicians, and the like.

Taking another swallow of the scotch and enjoying the warm burn it made sliding down his throat, Thomas shook his head. "I beg your pardon, Number One? Where on earth did that come from?"

Kingston smiled at him in an avuncular fashion. "I was speaking with Ivan Kuznetsov, the head of the смерть Triad branch."

Thomas forced a smile, "I've negotiated mainly with Semion Mogilevich. What did Kuznetsov have to say?" What he wasn't saying to Number One, but was quite clear was that Williams had been dealing with the titular head of the Bratva organization, not one of his lieutenants.

But Number One was not the head of The Corporation without reason. "My dear boy. We will not see Mogilevich again for months, likely years. Unless, of course, The Corporation fucks up." He chuckled mirthlessly and took another sip of his drink. "Kuznetsov will be overseeing our co-interests.

And he discussed his concerns about you tonight."

Feeling the heat rising from his expensive cotton dress shirt, Thomas took a deep breath. "Do enlighten me."

Knowing he had his arrogant Number Two's attention, Kingston relaxed and crossed one leg over the other. "There's to be a rather large party in St. Petersburg in June to celebrate the merger of our combined business interests. Have you been to a Bratva gathering before?"

Brow furrowed; Thomas shook his head. "We've always avoided such large gatherings for a reason."

"That's not how Bratva works," Number One scowled. "It is expected, which is to say it is mandatory. And we've worked too long to lose this now. You'll see that the Russians are very fond of family. All the wives will be there, older sons. And we will be there with our wives."

Thomas was losing his patience, but he forced himself to chuckle lightly. "Did Number Three get married within the last... what? Twenty-four hours?"

Rising to fill his glass, Kingston raised the heavy crystal decanter to Williams, who shook his head. It was clear they were in a bizarre negotiation and he'd prefer to keep a clear head.

"No, Fassell did not marry Clara, but they are engaged, and the key players did see the ring on her finger at dinner. But they expect more from you since you will be our point man on the Bratva project." One corner of his thin mouth turned up at Number Two's incredulous headshake.

"You must be joking. How would being saddled with a wife

make me a better business partner?"

Kingston shrugged, seating himself again. "The Russians equate wife and family with stability. They are violently opposed to homosexuals, and if you're an attractive man in your mid-thirties without a wife and children on the way, they're going to question it. And you. And by extension, The Corporation." His pleasant smile vanished. "And this, I cannot allow. If you do not wish to marry, I will have to assign this partnership to Number Three's handling-" here, Thomas actually choked on his drink- "or take it over myself."

Williams ran his thumb over the scotch on his lower lip. "You must be joking. This is my acquisition. I made the contact; I have handled the entire negotiation since. I do not intend to relinquish control to Fassell. Or you, Ben."

The unspoken threat hung in the suddenly tense room, and finally Number One stirred. "I'd warned Kuznetsov you would react this way. He said you were welcome to contact Mogilevich himself, that he'd be expecting your call. I would strongly suggest making it a call to assure him of your imminent wedding." With that, Kingston finished his drink and left the boardroom, leaving Thomas to stare incredulously into the fireplace.

"What the bloody hell?" He hissed, slamming his glass down and reaching for the phone.

Had he'd been there, Kingston would have taken enormous satisfaction in the look of stupefaction that spread across Number's Two's handsome face, which then transformed into utter fury. Calmly bidding the Bratva head a good evening in flawless Russian, Thomas pushed a button to end the conversation, then lobbed his glass across the room, gritting his teeth as it shattered into a satisfying spray of crystal.

It was only 2 weeks later when Thomas found himself furiously knotting a blue silk tie around his throat, yanking it just a bit tighter to make the sense of a noose tightening around his neck feel more than just symbolic. *How did I end up in this mess?* he raged silently, *How did that bastard Kingston manipulate this without me even guessing?* Thomas knew perfectly well that there was more to this than just the Bratva's insistence of "home and family." Number One had been throwing women at him since he'd risen in rank in his mid-twenties. Kingston liked associates with family. It gave him the ultimate tool to ensure compliance. Wives, children, were valuable collateral. And Thomas's infuriating indifference to either was a problem for Kingston. There was nothing to hold over his slippery vice-president's head. Finally dressed, Williams looked bitterly in the mirror.

"This is a transaction. Like any other. Select the most viable candidate and get this over with. It will be like having a housekeeper with a larger list of duties." With that inspiring assurance, Williams got into his Jaguar - midnight blue this year - and roared off to St. Luke's. Handing his keys to the valet, he straightened his tie and glared at the beautiful building as if it had personally offended him. Entering the restored old church, he chuckled slightly, tapping the toe of one shining Louis Vuitton loafer on the entryway, half expecting to burst into flames. When his first step proved he was unscathed, Thomas strolled in, mildly surprised at his fanciful thought. "Must be deconsecrated," he murmured.

Jerwood Hall inside the building was exquisitely decorated with huge arrangements of spring flowers and expensively dressed men and women, chatting and laughing. Number One's gathering, which he macabrely labeled "Williams's Buy A Bride Bash" was doubling as a fundraiser for the London Symphony Orchestra, who'd supplied the talented string quartet playing on the riser in the center of the room. Accepting a drink from the closest bar, Williams took a sip, letting his polar blue eyes canvass the room. Kingston and his wife had gathered a dozen or so young ladies who would fill all the requirements of being a Corporation wife. Good breeding, well-educated, beautiful, and capable, as he'd disgustingly leered, "Of keeping their mouths shut about The Corporation's business and their legs open." The statement was so appalling that even Number One's wife stared at him, forgetting to laugh.

"Williams!" Sighing inwardly, Thomas turned and plastered a polite smile on his face as Number Three came towards him, hauling his fiancée along by her hand. "Good to see you! No date tonight?" Michael Fassell's slate-grey eyes twinkled. The tall, handsome third in The Corporation knew perfectly well why his partner was dateless. "Eh, knowing your charm, I'm sure you'll be leaving with one. Or maybe three."

Clara giggled, "Never mind him, Thomas. Nice to see you." She would have liked to have kissed his cheek in greeting, but there was a nearly palpable barrier around him that clearly said touching would not be welcome.

All the same, Thomas looked down at the cheerful redhead with a smile. "Clara darling. Are you ready to come to your senses and leave this fool for me?"

Fassell laughed a little too hard, "Now, Number Two. No pouting that I can find someone who adores me, even though that terrifying stare of yours sends sane women screaming."

"Don't you mind him," Clara scolded, "I know you enjoy your freedom. I'm just lucky Michael's ready to settle down." She went up on tiptoe to kiss her fiancé's cheek, and Thomas smothered a grin, remembering there'd been a spray of blood right across the spot she'd kissed, just last week when Number Three had participated in an interrogation. Oh, if only sweet Clara knew what she was marrying into...

That was a good point, Thomas thought morosely, accepting another drink from the bartender. At least the "candidates" about to be thrown before him here knew exactly what he was. What The Corporation did. Not that he would ever discuss even the most mundane detail of his work with a spouse, but at least he wouldn't have to make the effort to hide it. So, when he heard the oily, amused tone of Number One crowing, "Thomas, my boy! There's someone I'd like you to meet..." he turned and forced a less forbidding expression on to his beautiful face.

A nauseating two hours later, the ice-cold Number Two was moments away from drowning himself in the punch bowl. He knew Kingston feared and likely hated him. But surely no one could despise another human being enough to attempt to saddle them with this bevy of harpies.

Carlotta: Italian mafia, fire-engine red hair, and a screeching laugh that sounded like a goose getting buggered.

Wendy: Terrified brunette and the daughter of one of their division heads. Nearly started crying when he looked at her.

Misha: An "administrative assistant" in one of the London-based Bratva outfits. She purred *"Zdravstvuyte,"* and immediately cupped his genitals. She also husked something into his ear while licking it, when trying to decipher it later, Thomas gathered she was telling him she was "free of diseases."

And these were the three top candidates.

Tossing back his sixth drink, Thomas looked around the room, his face set and expressionless. The less ammunition he gave Number One, the better. But the bald-headed bastard would pay for this. His frigid gaze swept the room, landing idly on the string quartet, who were finishing their final number.

After the scatter of appreciative applause, Kingston's wife stepped up. "Thank you all for joining us tonight- these wonderful musicians are here as an example of the fresh blood being pumped into the London Symphony Orchestra. All under thirty. All in first seat positions with LSO this season. Your donations tonight will continue to help promising young students through scholarships to some of the best music schools around the world..." Turning to the four musicians, Arabella Kingston pointed to the young blonde, seated with her cello. "Lauren, dear! Come up for a moment, would you?"

With a shy smile, the girl gracefully set her instrument aside and stood. Thomas's thin mouth curled slightly to see her brush her hands against the full skirt of her black dress, clearly trying to dry her palms and leaving white resin marks against the dark velvet.

"My dear, please introduce yourself and speak a bit about how the scholarship program helped you."

Forcing a smile, the girl nodded. "Hello, and thank you all for your kindness tonight. I'm Lauren Marsh, and I graduated from Juilliard School - that's in New York City - oh, you probably know it's in New York, you're music lovers, right?" She flushed a little under the ripple of laughter, chuckling a little herself. "I was very fortunate to be blessed with a scholarship courtesy of the LSO grants: funded by your generosity. The arts are fading in schools around the world with budget cuts. Most students struggle to attend a fine arts school, so the support from forward-thinking corporations like yours will save the arts."

Thomas was utterly still, glass half raised to his mouth as he watched the blonde girl blossom, her pale cheeks flush and her eyes sparkle - a peculiar shade - lavender? It must be the lights, he mused.

"See, music is the one commonality that serves a global consciousness. It is the one sensory element that lights up all areas of the brain. You hear a song you love, and it brings you back to a particular moment in your life. You can feel where you were, smell and see your surroundings... *practically* taste it." There was something rapturous about her lovely voice that made Thomas's previous disinterest disappear. Arabella took another discreet step back from the mic. She knew a moneymaker when she heard one. And everyone was paying attention to the girl.

"For instance, like... Bob Marley's protest song, *Get Up, Stand Up*, it's immortal! The song's been embraced and re-imagined on every continent in the world- adapted slightly to blend with their musical style and instruments, but the song remains the same. One song, every nation on the planet. That's the power of music. And that's what your donations fund, a chance for communication and a powerful connection with anyone- everyone, really. So, thank you for funding my dream and allowing me to find a home within the LSO. And I hope you'll do the same for the next generation of students." Stepping back from the mic, Lauren actually jumped a little when thunderous applause greeted her finish, everyone in the ballroom flush with the grandeur that a swipe of their credit card was saving the world. Looking around at the beaming faces, Thomas shook his head slightly. If only the girl knew she'd been speaking to members of one of the most brutal crime enterprises in Europe.

Putting his glass on a passing waiter's tray, Thomas ambled closer to the girl, talking in the corner near the exit with her three fellow musicians, who were clearly praising her efforts. The violinist, a pretty African-American girl gave her a hug. "Nice work! You think they might toss you a bonus for hiking the donations? I could use a loan."

Lauren laughed and shook her head. "I don't think it works that way, but I can still spot you a couple of bucks-"

"Pouuunds," drawled her friend in a terrible cockney imitation, "pounds here, dahling, and- wait." Squinting, the girl eyed a man crossing the ballroom. "Lauren, shit! Is that your *dad?*"

Thomas's dark brow rose as he watched Lauren stiffen. "Why would- what the hell! He's supposed to be in- night, guys. I'm gone." With a slippery grace he appreciated, the girl disappeared.

Frowning, he turned back to look at the man who'd nearly reached the remaining three of the musicians, and a mild recognition stirred. *Marsh... hmmm... ah. Frank Marsh. CEO of Atlantic Equities in New York. One of our under-performers.* "Under-performer" was a very bad designation in The Corporation. Very bad. As in, 'the management was about to be shot and fed to the alligators to dispose of any evidence' bad. But Thomas knew the man was wealthy. Extremely so. Yet his daughter worked through a school as rigorous as Juilliard on an LSO scholarship?

"Now, why isn't Daddy dearest paying his angel's way through university?" Thomas murmured. Pulling out his cellphone, he texted a request to an associate with a dark smile on his face.

"Now that's what I wanted to see!" Number One's heavy hand clapped him on the shoulder of his beautifully tailored jacket. Kingston must be drunk, Thomas thought, even he wasn't foolish enough to touch someone as unapproachable as his second in command. "A smile, Williams! Does that mean one of the ladies here tonight has caught your interest?" He couldn't read the strange expression on the younger man's face, but it was almost... avaricious.

"Perhaps," Thomas finally answered. "Goodnight Ben. Arabella, darling." He bent to kiss the woman's cheek and was gone.

Number One's smile disappeared as he looked at his wife, still a little fluttery from the kiss. "Go find out which girl he was interested in." Arabella nodded anxiously and disappeared.

While stripping to take a shower, Thomas leaned over his laptop to type in a passcode. Reading the report compiled within the last hour, he smiled, pleased with his assistant's thoroughness.

Typing a reply, Thomas wrote:

Good work.

Contact Miss Marsh and instruct her to meet me at the office tomorrow at 3 pm. Tell her it is an interview to have her perform at my next event. Begin the usual surveillance.

Williams

Finally showered, he crawled into his sheets naked, putting a forearm across his forehead and looking out his window. Yes. She'd do just fine.

Chapter 2 – The Job Interview

In which Thomas interviews his prospective bride.

The pretty musician Thomas had seen warning Lauren about her father's unfortunate appearance the night before was, in fact, named Macie. And Macie was currently sipping a double espresso at a table in their favorite coffee house, waiting for Lauren to meet her for lunch. Seeing the blonde head of her friend entering the shop, she waved cheerfully, then her eye caught the face of the man trailing just a bit after Lauren. *Was he at the benefit last night?* she thought, trying to remember. He was wearing a good suit, but his broken nose and the hard set to his jaw didn't speak of the wealthy glitterati from the night before. As he seated himself a few tables away, ignoring her, Macie shrugged mentally and turned to smile at her friend.

"I'm kind of relieved to see you! I was worried your asshole Dad caught up with you outside or something." She leaned in, looking at Lauren's tired face. "Hey, you're dressed up! Well, for you this is dressed up anyway. You got a gig?"

Lauren sighed, "Don't call him that."

Macie snorted inelegantly. "What else am I supposed to call a guy who threw you out of the house at seventeen because you wouldn't go to law school? Jesus! Every one of your music teachers called you a prodigy and your dad wants you to turn into a soulless corporate clone?"

"Well, fortunately, I have wonderful friends who helped me," the blonde squeezed her hand and picked up a menu. "Let's not talk about him anymore. I need to be in a good mood, I have an interview this afternoon."

"Yeah? For what?"

Lauren wiggled a little, an excitable habit that she was trying to crush since it made her look like an adolescent. "One of the vice presidents from the company that hosted the fundraiser last night wants to meet with me today about performing at an event. If we get in good with these guys, we could have a steady side income! I got the sense from Arabella- she's the president's wife- that they throw these kinds of parties all the time."

"If the man wants to take you home with him, I expect you to go." Macie's expression was completely serious, but she finally cracked up at the appalled expression on her friend's face. "Really? You won't take one for the team? Selfish bitch!"

Rolling her eyes, Lauren shook her head. "I swear to god, for half a second I thought you were serious."

Still giggling a little, Macie asked, "Now, which one was he?"

"I'm not sure?" Lauren hesitated, "I don't think he ever spoke to us but he's really tall, dark hair, gorgeous eyes? I looked him up on The Corporation website."

"Nice," her friend twisted a long black curl around her finger. "Maybe you *should* go home with him- it's been a long, dry spell for you, honey." Laughing as Lauren covered her face, she asked, "What's his name?"

Swallowing the last gulp of her chai latte, the blonde answered "Thomas. Thomas Williams."

"Mr. Williams will see you now."

Lauren looked up from smoothing the front of her pale green linen dress. Why did she pick linen? It wrinkled the second she put it on. Standing, she smiled at the gorgeous brunette secretary, who looked her up and down like she was reeking of malt liquor and badgering her for a dollar. Sighing, she followed the impeccably suited woman into the interior office.

It was, of course, beautiful and awe-inspiring. Floor to ceiling windows in a corner office with expensive walnut paneling and a gigantic desk. Everything designed to strike terror into a humble visitor. Trying to not let her knees knock together, Lauren stiffened her spine and attempted to look confident.

The man behind the desk was the one she'd seen the night before- *Oh god oh god oh god he's gorgeous!* Lauren chanted internally, trying to keep her composed expression.

"Miss Marsh? Thank you for coming on such short notice. I'm Thomas Williams." He *was* beautiful, and tall, and his suit was surely bespoke, the girl thought dreamily before remembering her manners and taking his hand. Unlike most businessmen she'd met who worked with her father, he didn't try to crush her knuckles in his grip or try to keep her hand in his for an indecently long period of time. But when she looked into those glittering eyes, they were an icy blue, chilling her and making her pull her hand back a little quickly. Fortunately, he didn't seem to notice and gestured for her to sit.

Lauren did, smiling politely and looking around the office.

"Something wrong?" Thomas was leaning back in his chair,

running his finger across his lower lip.

She shook her head, laughing a bit. "Oh, no. Sorry. I was just expecting your events planner to be here."

Thomas nodded, fixing her with his warmest, most reassuring smile. It was traditionally the smile he gave to someone he was about to kill. Or worse. He did so enjoy the look of horror they invariably gave back. But this time, he actually intended to make the girl relax. He could tell she was already apprehensive. He'd been right last night about her eyes- they were lavender. Beautiful. They reminded him of an old Elizabeth Taylor movie his mother used to watch, over and over. Lauren's eyebrows and lashes were dark, setting off a nice contrast with her pale hair, cut shorter with curls just brushing her shoulders. Tall, not slim, more like an athlete's figure and small, shapely breasts. Pity about her hair, he mused. Thomas enjoyed wrapping a woman's hair around his fist and yanking on it as he fucked her. No matter, he'd make the girl grow it out.

"Ah," he smiled easily, "I like to handle the important matters myself. I had one highly recommended planner book a heavy metal band for a retirement party."

He liked the sound of her laugh, pretty and light. "A good cautionary tale! Most 65-year-olds aren't all that into Anthrax or Korn."

They spoke for a few minutes, discussing music and favorite artists. Lauren was pleasantly surprised at his wide range of music interests. Finally, he leaned forward, hands together and she automatically sat up straight like a student with a stern professor, a movement he regarded with a bit of amusement.

"I wanted to interview you personally, Miss Marsh because I am looking for something of a more... durable nature. I need someone responsible who can handle these requirements for me with professionalism. Your career with the London Symphony Orchestra will not be disturbed, of course. But I find myself requiring..." Inside, Thomas was laughing at himself. This was a job interview he'd never anticipated holding. "...requiring someone discreet. Well-versed in social nuance and able to represent me and The Corporation in the best light. I do assure you this can be quite lucrative."

Lauren was thinking of her horrible one-room flat, down an alleyway and within walking distance of St. Luke's. Hot water was optional at best and she'd once found a rat racing across the floor when she came home. She may have had a scholarship to Juilliard, but there were still student loans to repay. Mr. Williams was hinting at a second job! Omigod! To be able to pay her rent *and* her cell phone bill at the same time! Dizzy with the visions of occasionally being able to order takeaway instead of discount ramen, she nodded eagerly. "I see. I do have connections to musicians from many different genres of music. I can certainly help customize the music to your events." She trailed off as she noticed his expression. Did he look almost... hungry?

"That sounds very useful, Miss Marsh. Tell me a bit about yourself. Do you have family here?"

Forcing a smile, she shook her head. "No, I'm an only child, my father lives in New York."

"Your mother?" This was unkind, Thomas knew her mother was dead but he wanted to see how she handled it.

Lauren looked down at her lap. "She passed away from cancer five years ago."

"I'm sorry," he reflexively murmured, not sorry at all and pleased to have one less obstacle. "Have you made new friends here in London?"

"I haven't been here long," she confessed, "but everyone at LSO has been very nice, and I was lucky that one of my closest friends at Juilliard was also hired by the Orchestra. She was the violinist from last night?"

"Hmmm..."

Oddly, he didn't seem pleased by that and Lauren brushed the confusing thought away. "We're still a couple of months away from beginning practice for the new season, so I'm happy to devote as much time as you need to set out your events calendar for the year."

Thomas was looking her over, a slow visual circuit that made Lauren vaguely uneasy. Then, he nodded as if his mind was made up. Rising, he held out his hand again. "I believe we'll work very well together Miss Marsh. I'll be in touch." She gave him a huge smile that made a wave of heat run through his lower half, and he irritably willed it away.

"Wonderful- I mean, that's really great Mr. Williams, I'm really-"

Laughing he shook his head, "Call me Thomas."

"Thank you, Mr. Williams. I mean, Thomas. I mean, thanks, that's great and I'm Lauren and I'm... just going to shut up now. Talk to you soon." Flashing him another happy grin, she turned and left his office.

Pulling out his phone, he texted one of his burlier assistants.

Pick up Frank Marsh and bring him to my office tonight at 6pm.

She ignored her phone for three days. It was a record. Three days of endless, persistent calls from her father, the Darth Vader theme from *Star Wars* blaring ominously every time he tried to reach her.

"It can't be anything but bad news," she reminded herself.

Ring, ring, ring...

"Every time he finally gets to me, it's bad." Lauren recited as she looked at the lit screen at 2am and tossed it back on her bedside table.

Ring, ring, ring...

"He makes you feel like nothing, every time. Every time, Lauren!"

Ring, ring, ring...

"Hello?"

She deliberately chose a coffee house far away from where she lived, not wanting to give her father any hints on how to follow her home. And Lauren was surprised to see he was already seated as she walked in. Frank was never on time. He always kept her waiting, just to remind her that she was the least important thing on his "to-do" list that day. He stood, relief evident on his still-handsome face as he walked over to kiss her on the cheek, not seeming to notice how his daughter flinched back when he leaned in.

"Thank you for meeting me, sweetheart. It's been a long time."

Frank Marsh looked every inch the wealthy CEO- expensive suit, an expensive haircut and expensive Botox designed to keep him looking formidable. But Lauren knew better. The slight inconvenience of his wife dying of cancer hadn't slowed down his drinking and gambling in the slightest. In her most bitter moments, Lauren wondered if he'd ever placed a bet on the time of death. He was disappointed that his only child was a girl. He was disappointed that Lauren was like her mother, loving music and dance and literature. Frank Marsh was most particularly and specifically disappointed when Lauren grew a spine and refused to give up her place at Juilliard when he found her acceptance letter, furiously drunk and shouting at her. She was sure he'd come to his senses when he sobered up the next day, but he'd had her clothing packed up while she was at freshman orientation. When Lauren came home, Frank calmly told her that it was either accept her admission to business school or leave home. She'd chosen the latter.

"Yes. Around four years, to be precise." Lauren looked calm, but her hands were gripping her thighs.

When his eyes turned back to hers, they were suspiciously shiny. "Your beautiful eyes. Just like your mother's, I'd forgotten." Frank chuckled, "Do you remember that Elizabeth Taylor movie she used to make us watch, over and over? *Gone With The Wind-*"

"It was *National Velvet,*" Lauren interrupted. "Vivian Leigh was in *Gone With The Wind.*"

Frank looked at her blankly. "What?" he shook his head, "Never mind. But your violet eyes... you look so much like her."

Lauren took a painful sip of her hot coffee, then soldiered on. "So, what are you doing in London? How did you know I was here?"

He chuckled, leaning back and smiling at her fondly, "I was surprised, sweetie, to be honest. I thought you were still in school back in Manhattan. But I'm here for a board meeting with our parent corporation-"

Her brow furrowed. "You sold the company? When?"

Waving one hand expansively, Frank said, "Oh, a few years ago. It was a wise business move."

Lauren pondered the news. The company was actually founded by her mother's family, Frank took over as CEO when her grandfather died. Ironically, her mother had deeded her shareholder status to Lauren before she passed away- which her father had immediately transferred into his name since she was "A minor and knew nothing about business."

"Well, congratulations, I guess. What did you need to discuss with me? You said it was life or death for you. If it's money, I don't have any- you already spent my college fund, so-"

Reaching over the little table, her father tried to take her hand, but Lauren's fists were still in her lap. "It's not about money, sweetheart- but it is life or death." He looked around the crowded shop anxiously, then back to her. "Take a walk with me? Please?"

Rubbing her forehead and feeling a headache forming, Lauren hedged, "Frank, look, I just-"

"Please, honey. PLEASE?" Frank hastily lowered his tone as she looked up. "Please. Please, just do this one thing for me."

With a sigh, his daughter nodded, and he beamed getting up from the table and beginning to leave. Realizing he wasn't going to pay for their coffee, Lauren angrily pulled out some money and followed him after tossing the bills on the table.

They somehow ended up in Hyde Park, Lauren automatically following along one of her regular running trails. "So, tell me what's going on, Frank." She already knew it was going to be bad. She just had no idea how very bad it could be.

"You must be insane! How could- what were you thinking?"

"Honey," Frank hissed, looking around them anxiously, "please, Lauren, lower your voice! You know I never would have let this happen- I didn't-"

Lauren was so enraged that she was crying. Furiously wiping away her tears, she snarled, "Even after everything you've ever done, Frank, I never thought you'd try to sell me off! I'm not a bunch of your shitty stocks! You can't just-"

"Stop it! Listen to me!" her father grabbed her by the upper arms, turning her to look at him. He was sweating, his eyes wide. "Honey, I know you hate me. And you have every right! But- you must have got on Williams's radar at the fundraiser because there is no negotiating with this man! He wants you, and he will fucking kill me and take what's left of the company if you don't agree to this!"

"Don't touch me! Don't!" Lauren yanked her arm away, stumbling a bit.

"Is there a problem here?" They both turned to see two well-dressed men standing behind them, uncomfortably close. Frank must have recognized them because the blood drained from his face.

"No!" He nearly shouted before collecting himself. Smoothing his jacket and breathing in, Frank continued calmly, "No, just my daughter and I having a-" he attempted to chuckle, and the sound was horrible. "Just my daughter and I having a lively discussion."

Their new acquaintances didn't look convinced, and one- who looked like he'd has his nose broken more than once, said, "Mr. Williams would like to see you." He took Lauren's arm and began walking her briskly towards an exit as she attempted to dig her heels in, looking frantically back at her father. Realizing he was following with docility, head down, she glared back at the man dragging her.

"Let go of me or I swear I'll scream my bloody lungs out!" She tried to sound fierce and authoritative, but she knew her voice was shaking.

Broken Nose Guy only chuckled. "No, you won't." He gestured at her father's back, and Lauren realized the other man had a gun pressing painfully right about where Frank's kidneys would be.

The ride- once they'd been shoved into an anonymous black car was silent, Lauren clenching her shaking hands together, looking out the window and refusing to speak. To her misery, it was clear they were heading for the same building where she'd had her "job interview" earlier that week. It was then, that the sickening reality hit her: Frank wasn't lying. He wasn't drunk, this wasn't some sick figment of his imagination. For whatever completely fucked-up reason, he sincerely intended to give her to the vice president of The Corporation in exchange for not killing him over her grandfather's now-failing company. Which meant... anyone willing to kill over a weak P&L statement had to be involved in organized crime. Which meant- Jesus! Did her dad work for the *Mob?* Arms dealers? The group was still silent, riding up the mirrored lift, Lauren numbly counting the numbers by heart as they reached the top floor, Broken Nose Guy taking her arm again, squeezing cruelly when she angrily tried to yank it away.

It was Deja vu of the worst kind to be entering Mr. Williams's awe-inspiring office again, the floor quieter now that it was evening and after hours. And even worse was to see the man sitting behind his desk, beautifully clad in a severe black suit with a grey and sapphire printed tie. There was no smile this time, no courteous rise to his feet to shake her hand, but Lauren had to try. This was impossible- this shit didn't happen in real life!

"M- Mr. Williams? Um, Thomas? This has to be some kind of mistake, right? This isn't-"

Thomas ignored her for the moment, his beautiful face set in cold lines as he stared at her shaking father. "Frank. I'm very disappointed in you."

Lauren stood silently, dazed as her father stammered out excuses and explanations, apologizing profusely for his daughter's ungrateful and disobedient nature and promising to *bring her to her senses* if only Mr. Williams would give him once more chance to-

Thomas raised his hand, cutting off the flow of begging and pleading as his frigid gaze turned to Lauren. "Do you understand what your father had told you?"

She was amazed at how much could change with this man from one meeting to the next. The vice president she'd met just days before was cool and abrupt, but charming, handsome. This man was terrifying. "Noth- nothing rational, Mr. Williams. This can't be real, you can't want-" She halted as his hand came up again.

"It's quite simple, darling. I require a wife. You fit my requirements. Your father requires your obedience in order to live." Staring at her pale face, Thomas smiled suddenly. "Do you understand?"

His frown returned as Lauren angrily shook her head. "This is insane! What the hell is wrong with you people?"

Thomas made a negligent gesture, and Broken Nose Guy calmly pulled out his gun and shot her father in the thigh. The weapon firing was close enough to the girl to make her ears ring violently, making Frank's shrill scream of pain seem fuzzy, far away. With a sigh, Thomas rose, and abruptly hustled her over to the same chair she'd sat in during her ill-fated interview that week. Cupping his hands over her ears, he watched her terrified violet gaze until the buzzing faded and she was able to draw a full breath without her chest hitching. Coming back to her senses, Lauren whirled to see Frank sobbing as the men swiftly bandaged his leg.

"Stop making such a fuss, Marsh." Thomas's tone was bored and disapproving. "The bullet went straight through. You should be more relieved that you didn't get blood on my rug." Lauren's nausea rose as she realized they'd positioned her father on a sheet of plastic as they'd entered the room to keep the furnishings tidy. Jerking his head, Thomas instructed the men to take him out.

"Where are you taking my father!" Lauren hissed, trying to

stand up. One broad palm went to her shoulder, seating her decisively back down.

Looming over her deliberately, Thomas leaned against his desk. "They're just taking him to be checked over. Not to worry yourself, darling."

"I'm NOT your darling, asshole!" Lauren was instantly sorry for her moment of courage when his hands shot forward, gripping the top of her chair and hemming her in.

"Oh, darling," Thomas purred, "you are anything I choose you to be. And as charming as I find your defiant stance, it ends as of now. I am not permissive, like your father. You will behave. You will keep your mouth shut. You will do as you are told and you will not defy me. And if you do..." he leaned forward as Lauren shrank back, his cold gaze pinning her. "I will kill your father in front of you. And if you still defy me. I will kill you. Are we quite clear, darling?"

There was dead silence in the vast office, nothing but her frantic breathing. Lauren was suddenly aware of how good this monster smelled- crisp notes of his cologne, the warm scent of fine wool and the warmth radiating from his closeness. But he was still a monster.

"Why?" she suddenly asked, not sure what else to say, "Why me?"

Thomas tilted his head thoughtfully, still not moving away from his close scrutiny. "Because... you fit my requirements," he said, a little surprised at his honesty. Leaning back, he offered his hand. "It's late. My driver will take you home. Try to get some rest, the wedding coordinator will call you in the morning. You will answer her call immediately."

Lauren shook her head, unsteadily getting to her feet and refusing to touch his outstretched hand. "A coordinator? Already?"

He was already back in his chair behind the desk, his attention back on a huge computer monitor. "Yes, darling. We don't have much time. We're getting married three weeks from now."

Chapter 3 – Crying Doesn't Solve Anything

In which Lauren discovers there are some things from which there is no escape. Marriage. Bondage. And loss of best friends.

When his office was quiet again, the bloody plastic cleaned and up the sniveling Frank Marsh carted away, Thomas rose and poured himself a drink, looking thoughtfully out on the London cityscape. It was not quite the unveiling he'd planned for his new bride, but Lauren's idiot father had cocked it all up quite solidly. He'd enjoyed the girl even more on their second meeting. How she'd handled the shock of it all - her father's ungraceful punishment - was really quite impressive. No screaming or hysterics. Thomas was always impatient with a new acquisition's stammering pleas or weak explanations, but when the girl realized they weren't working on him, she'd shut up. A slow smile crept across that mobile mouth as he recalled her defiance. His sweet little musician *did* have a backbone. He would enjoy bending it to his desired shape.

Meanwhile, Lauren was trying to open the door to her flat, hands shaking and causing her to drop her keys twice and swearing under her breath. When she'd been dropped off by

Broken Nose Guy, she'd noticed that the black Mercedes did not drive off, instead standing sentry in front of her ratty building. Oddly, she felt embarrassed that the thug - and by extension, Thomas - knew of her feeble living accommodations. She was sure filthy rich lunatics like Thomas never dealt with little inconveniences like student loans and the tiny salary of a new member of the London Symphony Orchestra.

Finally getting the door open, Lauren stepped inside and started clicking all the locks on the inside of the door shut, trying to add a new layer of protection with each chain secured and deadbolt engaged. Finally standing back and wiping her sweaty palms on her jumper the enormity of the situation finally slapped her in the face and she slid down the door to her nice little entry rug, beginning to cry and absently wiping her palms over and over on her jeans.

Waking up in the morning, for one glorious moment it was as if nothing had happened, that she was still Lauren with an indifferent, selfish father and just beginning a promising career with one of the most respected symphonies in the world. Then, the phone rang.

"Noooo," she moaned, burying her face into her pillow. "No, no nononononono..." Surely, if she simply kept denying it, it wouldn't be real, the bizarre meeting with the beautiful and terrifying Vice President of Jaguar Holdings. This didn't happen in the real world. The phone rang, persistently, steadily until she poked "dismiss call" and turned over. Then, it began again. This time, Lauren angrily put it on silent. She was given ten more minutes of blissful oblivion until there was a loud knock on her door. Then, another. Then another until they sped up and the shabby wooden frame was rattling against the blows.

"I'M COMING!" she finally shouted, angrily getting to her feet and grabbing a sweatshirt to go over her sleep pants. "FOR CHRIST'S SAKE! GIVE IT A REST!" Yanking open the door, Lauren's angry diatribe instantly shut off as she observed the unamused expression on Broken Nose Guy's face. He was dressed in a fresh suit and holding out an iPhone.

He thrust the phone towards her. "Take it."

"No," Lauren mumbled childishly, staring at the phone as if waiting for it to turn into a rattlesnake and bite her.

With a sigh, Broken Nose Guy pushed his way into her flat and shut the door, tapping the speaker button so the cold voice of her new fiancé was audible.

"Lauren."

She concealed a shudder. No one this evil should sound so good, Lauren thought despairingly, his beautiful voice was sonorous, deep, his enunciation perfection. And his displeasure, apparent.

"Answer me now, or my associate will *make* you answer me."

"Dude! What!" she snarled, trying not to let her voice shake.

"First," Thomas's tone was measured and calm as if he had all day to train her, "You will address me as Thomas. Secondly, you will eliminate these American vulgarities from your speech."

The grinding of Lauren's teeth was nearly audible.

"Third," he continued as if she'd already acquiesced, "I understand you have not answered the phone call from the wedding planner, as I had instructed last night." She could hear the shifting of papers as if he was conducting Corporation business while handling such a minor inconvenience as forcing another human being to marry him.

"Why do we need a wedding planner?" Lauren finally asked, a little proud that her voice wasn't shaking. "Wouldn't a lunchtime trip to the Registrar's Office do the trick? Doesn't all the pageantry seem a little... vulgar in this case?" She was a little proud of the bite at the end of her question, but her new fiancé squashed that flat.

"Our union is rather high profile, darling." Thomas's unamused voice was deeper, more clipped. "It is expected to garner quite a bit of attention, and we are to celebrate this occasion with much pomp and circumstance. I assure you it is not to my taste either. But neither is getting married, so-" He stopped dead as he realized he'd said more than intended. Unfortunately, Lauren immediately pounced on his lapse.

"You don't want to marry me? Then why is this disastrous thing even happening? You don't seem like the type to do anything you don't want to do."

Thomas ground his teeth. Maybe he should just lock her in a room in his house until the wedding day. With nothing but bread and water. Because this cheeky little bitch was becoming extremely irritating. "I am a businessman, darling," he answered, his tone back to cool and emotionless. "And as I told you last night, you fit my requirements. Now, I have been rather lenient, knowing that you must be a bit in shock over the developments of the last twenty-four hours. My permissiveness ends here. You will answer the call from our wedding planner. You will do what you are told. And if you resist my instructions again, the next bullet goes through your father's heart. Are we quite clear?"

Lauren was frozen, the blood drained from her face, leaving it sheet-white as she remembered Frank's screams from the night before.

"ARE. WE. CLEAR?" The voice that whiplashed through the speaker on the phone was harsh and cold, the voice of a man who would be completely comfortable murdering her father, and then, her. A man who probably had plenty of random, untraceable burial sites already picked out.

"Yesss..." she hissed, trying not to let her voice waver.

"Yes, WHAT?" He was relentless.

"Um, yes, Thomas?"

"Very good." The next sound she heard was a click that signified her psychotic new fiancé was finished with her.

Numbly handing the phone back to Broken Nose Guy, Lauren kept her lavender eyes wide, trying desperately to not cry in front of this corporate thug. Slipping the phone back in his jacket pocket, he made an irritable grunt and produced a box, handing it to her.

"What's this?" she asked, holding it like the box might detonate at any moment.

"A new phone," he replied, "it will be better protected than yours. You are to use it for any calls related to the wedding or Mr. Williams."

Feeling her nose begin to run and wanting desperately to get away from this man before she cried, Lauren nodded rapidly and tried to close the door. His foot slid out and blocked her efforts.

"Miss Marsh," Broken Nose Guy's voice was firm, but not unkind, "it is in your best interests to make this event run smoothly. You are not helping yourself by trying to put up a fight. This will happen. I would suggest you keep your father alive to walk you down the aisle."

That did it. With tears literally springing from her eyes, Lauren nodded rapidly and shut the door.

She was given a full fifteen minutes to weep until her new phone began to ring. Angrily opening the box, Lauren found a shiny new silver iPhone 12 Pro Max, fully charged and buzzing insistently. Clearing her throat and hastily blowing her nose, she answered it.

"H-Hello?"

"Lauren! A pleasure to speak with you, dear! I'm Jessica, your wedding planner." The voice on the other end was warm, gracious, almost as if this was a normal, high-society union.

"Um, hello." Lauren ran a hand through her wildly disordered curls. "Nice to meet you."

There was a respectful silence at the other end of the line that told her this Jessica was quite aware that she was not at all happy to meet her, given the reality of what this would set in motion.

"Well!" Jessica said, "I'm sorry to throw you into the thick of things, but we have exactly twenty days to put everything in order, so-"

"Where am I getting married?" Lauren gave a wet sort of chuckle, trying to not laugh at the bizarre nature of the call with this relentlessly cheerful woman.

"Oh," the planner answered, "the Royal Opera House. The glass atrium is magnificent, I assure you."

"That's nice," Lauren said blankly. She listened obediently, making agreeing sort of noises every time Jessica paused and numbly promised to meet her at Brown's Bridal later that afternoon. For some reason, her first search on her laptop was the Royal Opera House. You could get married at the Royal Opera House? Apparently so, though her search told her they only hosted two weddings a year, and even though hers was set in a mere twenty days, Mr. and Mrs. Williams's would indeed be one of them.

Beginning to cry again, she automatically picked up her own phone, about to press the button to call Macie. Macie would make her laugh - she could talk her down from the completely fucked-up disaster that was now her life and - Lauren's thumb hovered. With a spear of ice running through her stomach, the girl realized she couldn't tell Macie. She couldn't tell anyone. How could she have her best friend as her maid of honor in a group of crime lords? Murderers? God knows what else? She couldn't endanger Macie that way. For the first time, Lauren realized she was utterly and completely on her own. No one was going to rescue her. No one could help her. And she started crying so hard she thought her heart would come out of her throat.

Nonetheless, she showed up at the elaborate bridal shop on time, shifting from foot to foot as the impeccably suited woman at the reception area stared at her. "Do you have an appointment, dear?" she asked in a saccharine tone that indicated she clearly thought the young blonde in the inexpensive sundress, in fact, did not.

"Carolyn." A cool voice Lauren recognized came from behind her, and a firm hand slipped into her elbow, pulling her along. "This is Miss Marsh. We have very little time, and I *do* hope you will be able to handle our requirements."

Automatically cringing at the dreaded word "requirement," Lauren obediently followed the short redhead who was already hauling her through the store's private dressing area. Finally turning to her, Jessica gave her a huge, red-lipsticked smile. "Hello, dear. I'm Jessica, you're Lauren and we have absolutely no time to waste. Now. Do you have any particular vision about how you'd like to look on your wedding day? Any certain style?"

There was something about the older woman's shrewd gaze that told Lauren the planner knew quite well what was going on. So, she numbly shook her head.

"All right!" Jessica said cheerfully. Turning to the cowering saleswoman, she briskly rattled off a list of designers. "Monique Lhuillier, some of the 2018 fall couture line. Vera Wang, spring 2016. Oh, and some of the gauzier versions from the Delphine Manivet Paris Fashion Week collection. Bypassing the assistant, the redhead took the alarmed Lauren's measurements herself. "Very nice..." she murmured approvingly, "I'm so tired of dressing skeletal society types. You've got a lovely, healthy figure. Some of the softer styles would drape so beautifully off that toned back of yours..."

Lauren tried to form her numb lips in the shape of a smile, but she mainly stood silent, allowing them to strip her to her underwear and haul her into various gowns like a mannequin. It was clear the assistant was beginning to be confused by her utter lack of enthusiasm, but finally, Jessica hauled the woman away, murmuring something about "Painfully shy... terribly uncomfortable..." as she sent the fitter out of the room. Turning around and looking at the dispirited blonde standing on the dais in the middle of the room, her expression softened.

"I imagine this is quite overwhelming to you, dear."

Pressing her full lips together, Lauren stared at her. There was nothing she could say. There was nothing to say.

The planner finally decided on an exquisite Delphine Manivet creation, simple lines and a beautiful, sweeping skirt. Turning Lauren this way and that, taking pictures and making notes in her iPad, she nodded. "It's perfect." Pausing to look at the blank expression on the blushing bride's face, she asked, "Would you like to offer an opinion, Lauren? Did you have a preference?"

Staring at the piles of lace and chiffon confections thrown across the couch and dressing room racks, Lauren shrugged and shook her head. Whatever foolish dreams she'd had as a little girl about her dream wedding bore no resemblance whatsoever to the nightmare in which she was currently entangled. There was no frame of reference that she could even access. "This one... seems nice," she finally offered, touching the silk bodice and missing the look of pity in her wedding planner's eyes.

Twenty days became fifteen, then ten. Macie kept calling for lunch, a drink after rehearsal, and a couple of texts that simply read, "What the fuck is up with you, girl?" Lauren excused her pale face and the growing dark circles under her eyes as "Not feeling well, some kind of bug," and explaining she was heading home to sleep. Then five days, and she obediently returned to the bridal salon for her final fitting. The seamstress clucked her tongue disapprovingly.

"You didn't need to lose weight, dear! Why must you girls starve yourself before the wedding? The dress fit perfectly!

I'll need to do some alterations..." Lauren was confused about the woman's disapproval until she looked in the mirror. She'd always been proud of her strong body, lean muscles earned from Lacrosse and running. Her ribs were showing through her skin, and it wasn't particularly attractive. Jessica walked behind her, looking at Lauren's reflection over her shoulder. She refused to look at her. She hated pity. She hated seeing it in the redhead's eyes.

Clearing her throat, the planner returned to her iPad, tapping in some notes. "I'll have some high-protein, high-calorie drinks delivered to your flat," she said calmly, "many of my brides get too excited or anxious to eat. Let's see if we can get you better-nourished before the big day, all right?" Waiting until Lauren forced herself to nod, Jessica continued in a light tone, chattering about the details they needed to attend to in the next couple of days.

By the time Lauren dragged herself home, she couldn't think of anything but a glass of cheap wine and a hot bath. *God,* she thought, *I really hope there's hot water. Please, Mother Mary and all the Saints, let there be hot water.* So consumed with her dream of soaking in a tub and maybe slipping down until the water went over her head and drowned her, Lauren didn't see her angry friend sitting on the stairs in front of her flat until she nearly tripped over her.

"Well, what the hell do we have here?" Macie was pissed, and she wasn't shy about showing it. "It's my best fucking friend. You know, the one where we had slumber parties and talked about our hopes and dreams and shit? And the one who's getting married and never fucking told me?"

Lauren rubbed her throbbing forehead. "What?"

Macie held up a newspaper accusingly, and it took Lauren a

moment to realize it was a copy of *The Times,* open to the wedding announcements page. Taking it from her friend, she read it slowly.

Forthcoming Marriages:

Mr. T.W. Williams and Miss L.M. Marsh

The engagement is announced between Thomas, son of the late James and Diana Williams of London, and Lauren, daughter of Frank and the late Aurelia Marsh of New York City.

"Congratulations," Macie said sarcastically, "they usually don't do wedding announcements for anyone but celebrities and royalty. Like, fucking Benedict Cumberbatch announced his nuptials here. You're so upper crust."

Lauren sat down next to her furious friend on the stairs. "Maze... It's not what you think..."

She couldn't even look at Macie, knowing there were tears in her warm brown eyes and not wanting to feel even lower than she did already.

"Girl, are you kidding me right now? You're fucking engaged to someone I don't even know and you've only been here like two months and you're getting married and- shit! I've never heard of him?" Yep, there were tears because Macie angrily brushed them away. "Who ARE you? What the hell happened to my best girlfriend Lauren? You really were never going to tell me you were getting *married?* Are you shitting me?"

Macie leaned in to look at Lauren's face, staring at the worn riser. "You're not even going to tell me what's going on here?"

If she gets hurt, it will be because of me. It was all Lauren could think of, and she forced herself to concentrate.

"You... He's a friend of my father's, his company bought Frank's company and we met up here-"

"I know who he is, idiot! You were meeting him that day after our coffee date! What I don't know is how he went from a potential gig to your fiancé!"

Fury rose up in Lauren, usually the nice girl, usually the one who worked to make everyone feel at ease. "Goddamnit Macie! Back the fuck off! You really don't think I have enough shit right now that-"

Fuck, she thought bitterly, *shut up, you idiot!*

Macie's fury melted into concern. "What's going on? This isn't you. You look sick, honey, and I've never seen you like-"

"Look, Macie, I'm just really stressed over the wedding, okay? And it's really small, and it's just like... my Dad's friends and Thomas's and it's not really-"

She didn't have to see her friend's face to see the hurt there. "You were never going to tell me. Holy shit. You were going to get married and act like nothing ever happened like you didn't have a husband and a whole other life." Macie drew in a shuddering breath. "Are you ashamed of me?"

Lauren's soul curled like it had been set on fire. Macie was always acutely miserable because of her background, from a mother who was more interested in her career and a non-existent father. "No! Jesus, honey, no! Not at all! I can't-" the blonde drew in a shuddering breath. "You took care of me when my dad threw me out. You've always been there for me. But I am begging you to listen to me!" Turning, she grabbed

Macie's hands, squeezing them. "Please trust me. There is a reason-" she groaned, what could she possibly say?

"What?" snapped Macie, "then what the hell is the reason?" Her eyes narrowed when her friend's teary-eyed violet ones met hers. "You're not going to give me one, are you?" Pulling her hands away, she stood up and dropped the paper on the stairs. "Well, okay. Congratulations, and all that shit. See you later."

Listening to her only friend here in London furiously clomp down the stairs and slam the door shut, Lauren started crying again. Somehow, this was even worse than the realization that there was nothing she could do to escape Thomas's horrific "proposal."

And then, just to make things as depressing as humanly possible, the invitation came from Arabella Kingston and Clara something - another vice president's fiancée? - to a Hen's Night. Staring at the invitation, Lauren chuckled mirthlessly. Of course. Who else was going to celebrate her upcoming hell, aside from other Corporation wives? Did they know what their men did for a living? So, as the moving men sent from Thomas relentlessly packed up the meager belongings of her flat, Lauren sat down to email the women back, politely thanking them for their invitation.

"Have a drink, honey! It's your last night as a free woman!" Clara missed the actual cringe Lauren gave as she raised her glass of champagne, but Number One's wife did not. The three drank a toast, and Lauren carefully smiled as she refused to let the other girl stick a tiara on her head that read: "Fuck me! I'm the Bride!" when Clara trotted off to the loo, Arabella eyed the hollow-eyed blonde keenly.

"I should have been here for you sooner. I'm sorry."

Looking up from her drink, Lauren frowned. "Pardon?"

Checking behind her by habit, the older woman leaned in. "I understand what you're going through. I didn't believe it when my husband first told me. I know this wasn't your choice, and believe me, it wasn't Thomas's plan, either."

Lauren laughed bitterly. "Then why am I here?" She watched the lovely woman across from her hesitate. The Corporation's president's wife was beautiful, exquisitely groomed and wearing a diamond slightly bigger than her head. Sighing, she seemed to come to a decision.

"The Corporation has new... business partners," Arabella offered carefully, "important ones. Dangerous ones. They prefer... settled men. Married men. For Thomas to continue holding this account, he needed to become a married man. To show stability." She smiled sympathetically at the younger girl's rising fury.

"I'm being trapped in this hell because it looks better if Thomas is *married?*"

Arabella squeezed her hand. "You don't understand how important these business partners are. They are deadly. Even more so than our men."

Watching Clara bounce across the crowded bar and heading to their table, Lauren asked, "Does she know?"

Shaking her head sadly, Mrs. Kingston admitted, "No. And we are forbidden to tell her. You're going to learn to keep a lot of secrets, dear. At the cost of your life."

Coming home from her "Hen's Night," just a little drunk and trying not to show it to Broken Nose Guy, who was stolidly waiting outside the club to drive her, Lauren undressed, still quite steady. She'd been terrified to drink too much, ever since the ugly night where her father's bullet wound had sealed her fate. Looking at her exquisite wedding gown, hung neatly on a little rack in her bedroom, she squeezed her lavender eyes shut, trying not to cry. Crying doesn't solve anything.

Chapter 4 – I Am All that You Have Right Now

*In which Thomas and Lauren are married.
And it is as horrible as it is beautiful.*

If she'd been asked later how she'd gotten to the Royal Opera House, Lauren could not have said. She only knew she was sitting in a palatial dressing room with a hairstylist sweeping her blonde curls into an elegant chignon while a makeup artist deftly painted her face. Jessica, clad in an elegant blue suit, was darting this way and that, speaking with someone on her Bluetooth device about flowers, where the Russian vodka was stocked, and whether the musicians were assembled. For a moment, Lauren froze at the mention of musicians and she turned to look at the planner, causing the makeup artist to swear when her eyeliner went awry. Seeing her stricken expression, Jessica pushed her 'mute' button.

"The string quartet is a lovely group I've used many times before," she assured, "but none of them are aligned with the London Symphony Orchestra."

Forcing a smile, Lauren nodded and tried to sit still again for the makeup artist to finish her work. She was suffused with a huge wave of sadness, thinking that if she'd ever really thought about some future wedding, it would have given her great joy to have a group from her friends at the LSO play.

Which then led her to thinking that of course, Macie would have been her maid of honor, which made her realize exactly what she was here for and what was about to happen.

Her heart started pounding as she felt a wild sense of unreality. *This... this really couldn't be happening, right?* she thought, *I mean, this is 2021. People can't just force you to marry them? Maybe I should have gone to the police?* Her common sense kicked in, reminding her that a crime organization at this level likely owned the police- or enough of them to be notified of her efforts. Picturing Frank and herself in a shallow grave and a bullet in the back of their heads made Lauren dizzy, and she gripped the table in front of her, trying to take slow, deep breaths.

"There she is!" The cheerful voice of Arabella broke her concentration and Lauren looked up, earning another curse from the makeup artist. "Oh, my... you look so beautiful, honey. Doesn't she look beautiful, Clara?"

Clara's warm face appeared over Lauren's shoulder in the mirror. "You certainly do, Lauren. Wow, just- wow!" she giggled, clearly happy for the girl before her as she handed Lauren a glass of champagne. "Here, a toast!" Raising her glass, Clara intoned, "To a long and happy marriage. I hope you and Thomas are as in love as Michael and I." Looking at the girl's innocent smile, Lauren felt terrible for her, wondering when Clara's day of reckoning would come.

"Clara, honey, would you go check with Jessica and see how close we are?" Arabella's tone was still calm and sweet, and Lauren envied her unbreakable calm.

Smiling, a little confused, Clara did as she was told.

Kneeling down, the older woman took Lauren's cold hands in

hers. "Honey, are you all right?"

Staring at her, the terrified bride didn't know what to say. That she was trapped in a nightmare that she couldn't possibly comprehend? But Arabella seemed to understand because she plunged onwards. "Here's the thing-" she hesitated, trying to find the words, "Thomas is well-known for enjoying... force."

Lauren's brow furrowed, trying to understand what Number One's wife was telling her.

Squeezing the girl's hands, Arabella plunged on. "I'm concerned that you could get hurt if you try to resist him. I know you don't want this, but don't give Thomas an excuse to force you. Do you understand?"

The new bride shook her head, trying to shake loose the words rattling around her brain.

Arabella leaned in closer, whispering in her ear. "I have some excellent, high-dose Xanax, I'll give you a few, just take one when Thomas brings you home. You won't... mind so much, all right?" She watched as Lauren stared at her blankly, then turned to her right and promptly vomited into the sink.

"I'm sorry," Lauren apologized to the wedding planner, who was at her side in a flash, "I hope I didn't ruin the dress."

"Of course not!" Soothed Jessica, a wide, false comforting smile on her face. "Not at all." After shakily brushing her teeth and taking a tactfully offer breath mint, Lauren forced herself to keep upright on the stool in front of her makeup table. "There you go," soothed her planner. "Now," she continued briskly, "I want you to take this." Her palm opened to show a little blue pill. "Not to worry dear, most of my brides need a nice Xanax for their nerves, and more than one has thrown up from nerves." She chuckled, "I've learned to carry a toothbrush, toothpaste, and some heavy-duty breath mints."

Trying not to smudge her eye makeup, Lauren carefully wiped away the moisture from her eyes. "Xanax? I'm not good with drugs, I don't, uh…"

Arabella leaned in. "It's just to relax you, poppet. It's not like my high-dose candy."

Lauren stared at the pill in Jessica's hand, then remembered the expression on Thomas's face when her father was shot. Nodding, she put the pill in her mouth and washed it down with champagne. A knock on the door sent them all upright, and Arabella cupped her face in her hands. "Don't be afraid. You can do this. Just be sweet and pretty and it will be over soon, all right?"

Nodding obediently, Lauren seated herself to let the makeup artist touch her up. Then, the crew forced her to stand in front of a full-length mirror so they could gush and sigh as the photographer fluttered around her. Staring at her reflection, Lauren was amused. She'd always been pretty enough, even though her father scolded her to "Smarten up! Better makeup and a decent wardrobe, and there would be no one to compare with you!" But Lauren had always been the music geek, wandering around with resin from her bows on her fingertips and hair bound up in a ponytail. But here, she had to admit that Jessica had made her beautiful. Stunning. What a shame it was going to be wasted on a man who cared nothing for her.

By the time she was being led to the doors to the magnificent glass pavilion, Lauren could feel the warmth spreading through her muscles, her arms, and legs, smoother and more coordinated. Her head wasn't pounding anymore and she was even humming a little. Until her father stepped up to her. Reluctantly placing her hand on Frank's offered arm, Lauren took a deep breath, grateful for the effects of the blue pill.

If she'd been less heartbroken and terrified, she would have been amused at the deft way the wedding planner had settled the awkward "bride and groom" sides of the seating. All The Corporation lackeys were seated on the "bride's" side of the room, and a group of stern and ominous men and their wives were settled in the chairs on Thomas's side of the pavilion. For one, terrible moment, all she could hear was the Imperial March theme from *"Star Wars"* as she walked down the aisle, and she tried desperately not to break out into a laugh she was certain she wouldn't recover from. But Lauren focused on raising her chin and not looking at anyone, much less the beautiful, tall, and terrifying man clad perfectly in an Armani tux and waiting for her at the exquisite arch of flowers at the end of the room. Numbly offering her bouquet of baby blush roses and white lilies to Arabella, Lauren turned to Thomas, not even noticing her father slink away to sit in the front row.

Her soon-to-be husband raised one elegant brow to feel how hard her hands were shaking, but he did nothing but squeeze them gently as he turned them towards the priest who was beginning his speech about love and honoring each other. Lauren stared at a fixed point just behind the priest's ear until it was time to say their vows. "With this ring..." Thomas's voice was at its most beautiful, deep and nearly vibrating through her bones as he promised to love and honor her, slipping a huge and beautiful Tiffany diamond ring on to her finger. Lauren floundered for a moment until Arabella shoved a ring box into her hand.

Clearing her throat, Lauren's soft, lovely voice repeated the vows as she slid the plain platinum ring on Thomas's broad finger. She wondered if he's chosen the rings, or if it was something else that the ever-efficient Jessica had put together. But then her new husband's hand was under her chin, raising it so she was forced to look into the polar blue of his gaze, feeling him hold her still as he brushed a slow, light kiss against her lips.

Thanks to her blue pill and another glass of champagne to drink to the several, overly flattering toasts made to the new couple, Lauren was able to stay calm throughout the reception. Nodding and smiling at the correct times, she drank, ate a bite of cake, and sat silently next to the terrifying man who apparently now owned her. No one here knew this, but one of Lauren's best friends from her expensive, exclusive high school in Manhattan was a Russian immigrant, his surgeon father, and professor mother quite happy to welcome a shy young friend of Yuri's at their dinner table. So, she knew that the harsh men shaking Thomas's hand and squeezing hers painfully were telling him what a "sexy piece," he'd captured, that they wished they'd be there to "hear the screams from the marriage bed." No, she was smarter than the desire to tell them they were utter pigs, though the tightness around Williams's mouth made her wonder if he thought the same thing.

Then, finally the moment she'd been dreading most. And the tears in Arabella's eyes and the look of pity she hated in Jessica's expression meant it was time for the "happy bride and groom" to be on their way. To be alone and consummate the marriage. "Don't fight him, remember that!" Arabella whispered, "Don't give him an excuse to hurt you." Lauren eyed the older woman and wondered if that had been her wedding night with the scary as fuck Number One. She nodded and smiled, doing the same as Thomas took her hand and pulled her through the cheering crowd, barely acknowledging the magnificent fireworks exploding outside the Royal Opera House as she and her new husband made their escape.

"You didn't eat anything at the reception. Are you hungry?"

Lauren startled at the sound of Thomas's voice from just behind her as he led her into his gleaming kitchen. His townhouse in North London was of course, beautiful. Four stories high in an exclusive neighborhood in Hampstead Heath, and decorated - of course - with exquisite taste. Standing uneasily in his chef's kitchen, looking at her reflection in the stainless-steel appliances, she shook her head. "No, I'm fine. Thomas!" she hastily added, her tired brain trying to remember his rules.

Thomas was shrugging off his tuxedo jacket and simply nodded. "Very well. Come with me."

Numbly following his perfectly-sculpted ass up the narrow stairs, Lauren tried to hoist her long skirts higher, praying she wouldn't trip over them. On the fourth floor, he opened a beautiful old oak door. "This is your music room." She looked inside to find her plethora of musical instruments carefully displayed on their stands.

"Oh... thank you, Thomas." she wasn't expecting this small kindness and it threw her off balance. But she didn't have a chance to recover her equilibrium before he went down a flight and opened another door.

"This is the master bedroom."

Lauren paused at the door as he walked through, pulling his expensive cufflinks free from his tuxedo shirt and ignoring her. As he stripped off his shirt, displaying his beautiful musculature, he finally looked back, registering with irritation that his blushing bride was frozen in place. "Come here, Lauren."

Ohhhh, that voice! She mourned internally. If only her new husband had the soul to match that beautiful voice, so lovely and deep, brimming with promise. Forcing her pretty Jimmy Choo-shod feet to cross the threshold, the girl walked numbly into the room.

"Turn around, darling."

She did as she was told, trying to repeat Arabella's advice in her mind, over and over as his long, warm fingers began undoing the long line of buttons that held her dress together. The bodice had been very tight, and Lauren breathed a small sigh of relief as she felt it loosen against her constricted ribs. But feeling his warm breath on her neck, those sure hands pulling down her dress, she clamped her arms tight against her sides and tried to hold it together.

Thomas, however, was finally relaxing now that he was in the privacy of his own home and away from those Bratva bastards and the smirking, knowing leers of Numbers One and Three in his own organization. Lauren had performed beautifully today, nodding and smiling at the right times, keeping her mouth shut, He was feeling quite appreciative of her efforts and beginning to notice as he undressed her, how very lovely his new wife was. Really, when she'd walked down the aisle, there had been an audible gasp of appreciation when Lauren passed the guests by on her way to him. He'd selected the perfect girl, after all. Thomas chuckled internally. Number One had been so infuriated when he'd rejected all of his candidates, but he'd still chosen someone with unbreakable ties to The Corporation.

Despite his hatred of being railroaded into this sham, the tall man undressing his new bride like a delicate, invaluable package was feeling his cock rise in interest at the sight of her long spine and the creamy, pale skin of Lauren's back. Bending to place a kiss against the base of her neck, he enjoyed the scent of her sweet, light perfume and the irresistible pheromones of fear and arousal. And then, his hands paused as he realized those slender shoulders were shaking. Lauren was crying soundlessly. Pulling his hands away from her dress, Thomas turned her around to face him.

Lauren was looking at his polished oak floor, but she swallowed hard and managed to whisper, "I can still... if you want to. I won't... I won't fight you." The tears were dripping off her cheeks and splashing on to his bedroom floor.

Thomas recoiled in disgust. Never *once* had he ever tried to force a woman to- "What the bloody hell- do you think I want to *rape* you? I'm quite sure you feel you've married a monster, but I'm not a rapist." Angrily, he stepped away. "Just... get in bed, Lauren. Go to sleep."

He could tell she tried to obey him, moving slowly towards the bed while keeping her arms in a death grip around her beautiful dress, still crying those awful, silent tears. With an irritable sigh, Thomas yanked out his own bathrobe and settled it around his bride's shoulders. "Drop your dress and put your arms through the sleeves, there's a good girl." Tying his robe around her, he helped Lauren into his high, wonderfully plush bed and settled her comfortably, making her drink a glass of water and handing her a tissue, helplessly watching the tears stream silently down her reddened cheeks.

Finally, he groaned and got into bed with his new wife, pulling the fluffy comforter over her and guiding her into his arms. The contact with the skin of his bare chest seemed to galvanize Lauren into pulling away, still crying but turning her face away from him.

Dropping a kiss on the top of her head, Thomas settled Lauren more securely against him as she twisted her shoulders, trying to distance herself without angering him.

"Darling. I know you don't want to accept comfort from the man who is causing you misery," he finally offered, feeling her strain away even more at his words. "But I am all that you have right now, Lauren. So... just pretend I'm someone else. Let me take care of you."

The terrifying Second in Command of Jaguar Holdings knew his bride understood his suggestion when she sagged gratefully against him while she cried herself to sleep. Thomas continued to hold her, rocking Lauren gently as he stared out the window at the streetlights outside.

Chapter 5 – No Diggety

In which Thomas gives quite a spanking. Also, dinner out, sinister Bratva lieutenants and dirty dancing.

When Lauren woke the next morning, she was alone in that sumptuous bed. Sitting up and tying Thomas's robe more firmly around her, she thought for a moment. They'd come here... he'd showed her a room on the fourth floor where he'd had all her instruments set up... and then...

"Ugh!" Lauren buried her face in her hands. And then she'd lost it and started crying. And told him she expected him to rape her. The genuine surprise on his face made her wonder if Arabella knew him as well as she thought. Forehead wrinkling, Lauren wondered why Arabella had told her those things. She'd been quite intent on it, bringing it up twice. Was Kingston's wife being as kind as she'd thought? But what would be the point of scaring Lauren further? Settling more comfortably against the fluffy plethora of pillows, she remembered meeting - what did they call him? Number One? - last night at the wedding. She'd felt a chill shoot up her spine when the president of The Corporation took her hand in his cold one, smiling fondly with his lips while his coal-black eyes examined her like a particularly interesting species of insect. *He* didn't like her, that was quite certain. Then her full lips firmed angrily. Rapist or not, her new husband forced her to marry him by threatening to kill Frank and then her if she didn't behave. Thomas Williams was *not* a good man.

The sound of the front door closing drew Lauren out of her thoughts and with a stifled shriek, she leaped off the bed like a gazelle and tore into the bathroom, grabbing her overnight bag on the way. Hastily showered and dressed, she was buttoning up a pink striped shirt over her jeans when there was a knock on the door.

"Sorry! Coming!" Lauren trilled anxiously. Her hand tightened on the handle; she was dreading seeing Thomas this morning. Would he be scary and cold again? Kind, like last night?

As it turned out, neither. Strolling into the bathroom, he eyed her briefly while pulling off his sweaty shirt. "I'll need to go to the office today," his sonorous voice was calm, slightly indifferent. "I'm sure you'll want the time to unpack and get settled," Thomas was still facing her, talking casually as he toed off his running shoes and began pulling his shorts down. With an alarmed intake of breath, Lauren whirled and scampered from the bathroom, not hearing Thomas's low chuckle as he started the shower.

Lauren was standing in the middle of Thomas's exquisite kitchen, uneasily examining the coffee maker and trying to figure out how to actually coax a cup from it when he entered the room, armored again in a beautifully tailored charcoal gray suit. Stepping up behind her, he reached one arm over her shoulder and pressed a button. Instantly the stainless-steel monstrosity began obligingly percolating a wonderful-smelling brew. As she slid to the right to step away from him and ease towards the door, Thomas's back was to her, opening one of the cherrywood cabinets and pulling down two white mugs.

"Stay here."

His voice halted her instantly, one foot actually lifted to step from the room. Embarrassed that he could make her obey so effortlessly, Lauren gritted her teeth before replying, "I was just-"

"-running away, I know." Thomas turned to her, his polar gaze sweeping over her well-worn jeans. "Do you wear those abominations often?"

Brow furrowed, Lauren looked down, trying to figure out what he was talking about. Her flowered Toms? Her clothes?

"Those ratty jeans," he clarified. "They're inappropriate. I want to see you in dresses and skirts. Leggings and yoga pants only for actual physical exercise." His lovely new wife was staring at him, her mouth open in what was clearly infuriated surprise. Thomas refrained from chuckling, but he was, admittedly, enjoying breaking in his bride, just a bit.

"You're actually trying to dictate what I *wear?*" Lauren burst out angrily and unwisely. She realized the unwise element when Thomas straightened, strolling casually to her and edging her back against the wall by his proximity. Deliberately placing one hand, then the other against the wall behind her, her terrifying new spouse pressed his suited chest against hers. *He smells so good,* the girl thought, dazed and trying to hide that he scared the hell out of her. Thomas's chest was firm, and she could still smell his body wash from the shower.

"Look at me."

When she did, her eyes had darkened to a furious violet, and Lauren's chest was heaving angrily.

"This is where you say, 'Yes, Thomas?' Go ahead." Williams was relentless. He knew the slightest softness now might make her think she actually had a say in this partnership- it was still so odd to say the word, marriage.

"Yesss, Thomas?" Lauren not-quite hissed.

One big hand left the wall by her head and took her chin between his fingers. "Perhaps, darling, you are under the illusion that our union is a regular one, with bickering and disagreements and endless wrangling to get what you want. I will disabuse you of this notion immediately. You are a Corporation wife. You are here to be clever and pretty and act as a gracious hostess while keeping your mouth shut about anything related to Corporation business. I have a standard I expect you to uphold as my wife. Foolish or bad behavior from you reflects on me. And The Corporation. And more to the point- decisively reflects poorly on your father's continued good health." Thomas could see his warning was hitting home. Her cheeks had been prettily flushed pink by her anger, and now they were white, her huge purple eyes gazing into his. "So, little one, when I give you an instruction, you are to listen and implement it without argument and with no pouting. Are we clear?"

Lauren's hands were clenched in fists so tight that her knuckles were white and her nails cut into her palm. She wasn't a particularly meek person. She was shy, not always comfortable with scrutiny from others, but her mother at least had raised her to speak up for herself. But here…

She jumped when Thomas suddenly shouted, "ARE. WE. CLEAR?"

"Yes!" Lauren yelled back. "YES, Thomas!" He was so close to her, his beautiful eyes the color of a frozen sea and glaring into hers, his warm, hard body pressing her so firmly into the expensive paint that she expected it to be embedded in her shirt. She instantly recognized that shouting back was a mistake when her new husband's mouth firmed into a straight line and he took her by her upper arms and led her to a chair. Seating himself, Thomas immediately pulled his rigid bride over his lap, one hand quickly gathering her wrists behind her back and holding them immobile while his other hand rested on her ass, keeping her down when she tried to rise.

"What are you- what do you think you're DOING, Thomas!" Despite her furious growling, it never occurred to Lauren that this horrible man would actually attempt to spank her like she was an eight-year-old throwing a tantrum! In fact, she had never been spanked or slapped. Her mother Aurelia despised corporal punishment and Frank wasn't around enough to really care.

"You're not going to-"

Thomas yanked down her jeans with one firm jerk at the cloth and then ran his rough palm appreciatively over her lace panties. Lauren snarled and tried to wiggle again as she felt the warmth of his hand over her buttocks. In fact, his palm was so big it easily cupped one cheek while his long fingers stroked the other.

"Yes, darling. I am," Thomas commented, still enjoying her pert ass and rather looking forward to turning it red. He pulled her pretty undies down her thighs despite his wife's furious struggles, "You are a bad girl. I do not tolerate bad girls, and this is what happens when you require correction." To Lauren's horror, he suddenly chuckled as he stroked the smooth skin of her ass. "Though correction is not always what will earn you a spanking. Sometimes, being a very good girl will have the same result. Just not as painful."

Lauren was livid with anger and embarrassment. This horrible man had her over his lap and he was staring at her bare butt! He was touching it! She hated this smug, insufferable bastard!

"You smug, insufferable ba- OW, Thomas! Stop it!" His hand came down again, this time on her other cheek. "STOP IT! I'm not a child!"

Thomas's next strike was a resounding slap, managing to nail both soft globes with one harsh swat. "No," he agreed amiably, "even a child wouldn't be this spoiled and obstinate. This spanking will continue for as long as you fight me. Then, when you stop, you will receive twenty more. You will also count them, and thank me for each strike on this luscious arse of yours."

"Like HELL I will! You're- OW! Thomas will you cut this shit out- OW!"

Sliding his hand appreciatively over the rosy color of her bottom, Thomas kept his voice level. "Yes, baby. You will. And in addition, you will receive five more strikes for cursing. That is another vulgar habit you will end immediately." His voice was even and calm, but his focus was entirely on the feel of her- the warmth radiating off her insulted bottom, the corresponding sting on his palm. Thomas had always preferred to administer a spanking with his hand- enjoying the intensity of his flesh striking that of his submissive. How the pain on his hand from striking the flesh resonated with their agony. And Lauren - his stubborn, infuriating bride - *it must be the American in her,* he thought, *never stopping her yowling and struggling.* His lips curved in what could be considered a fond smile as he slapped her ass again, enjoying Lauren's enraged shriek. She was still kicking those strong legs furiously, trying to dislodge herself from his lap and adamantly refusing to give in.

Finally losing his patience, Thomas pulled her legs apart and landed a harsh blow on her nether lips, enjoying her strangled scream. Putting a hand in her blonde curls, he took a fistful and turned her shocked face to meet his. "Perhaps harsher methods are required here. Very well. I shall commence slapping your tender, slick cunt instead of your arse until you comply. Would you prefer that?"

Lauren was so stunned she couldn't speak- her horrified brain couldn't even form a complete sentence. No one, NO ONE had EVER touched her there, much less slapping her- that, uh, part of her! And calling it the C-word like she was some sort of slut? This son of a- "AAAH!" she screamed this time, the slickness of her making her horrible, awful, vile husband's smack on her girl parts sting even worse.

Instantly abandoning her furious intent to not give into him, Lauren sobbed, "O- One, th- th- thankyouThomas!"

Raising one elegant brow, Thomas smiled darkly. Excellent. Now he knew at least one of this stubborn creature's breaking points. "Very good, darling." His hand moved up to safer, but sorer territory and landed another slap on her crimson ass.

"Two!" Lauren gritted tearfully, hate radiating so strongly from her that he could almost taste it. "Uh- thank you, Thomas!"

"Three!"

"Four!"

And it went on until her ass was an excruciating shade of

purple and she could no longer feel anything other than the impact on her brutalized skin.

"No!" Lauren sobbed when her evil spouse finally leaned her on one hip in his lap and pulled her arms around his neck. "Don't! I hate you and you can't-" Thomas ignored her as she felt his long arms around her, enveloping her and humming low in his throat as he rocked her. "You don't get to try to comfort m-me!" she wept, still so overwhelmed that she couldn't move her head from his shoulder. "You don't care and you did this so it's sick to pretend- I can't-" Lauren finally gave up and sagged against him, weeping helplessly. She didn't understand why she was clinging to this horrible man. She didn't understand why he was pretending to be comforting after setting her ass on fire. And she most particularly didn't understand why her center was even slicker after he'd slapped her there.

For his part, Thomas was fighting an unpleasantly alien sense of confusion. He hadn't experienced that emotion for years. After all, his entire focus was always centered on calculating every possible outcome, every move, and counterstrike by both enemies and allies. He never failed to predict the result of any action. So, why was he feeling a sudden sense of anxiety for his stubborn, ridiculous bride, crying like her heart was breaking? That if he didn't convince her to behave more carefully, more obediently, that her life could be in danger? Of course, the formidable Number Two could not say any of these things - not yet - so he simply sighed and held his puzzling new wife more tightly, rocking her as she cried for the second day in a row.

When Lauren was finally calm, she tried to pull away from the strangely comforting grasp of her husband and hissed in pain as her abused ass met his lap. Standing up like he'd set her on fire, she backed away from him, clumsily trying to pull up her undies and jeans at the same time. Thomas didn't move or try to correct her, he simply sat comfortably as he watched her awkward efforts, which of course made Lauren hate him even more. He waited until his rebellious bride was clothed again and had furiously scrubbed all the tears off her cheeks before speaking.

"As I've said, I'm heading into the office. I require you to be dressed properly for a dinner out, something suitable to meet some of our most important clients by 7 pm. I will send a car for you. Your role tonight is to be demure and pretty- my blushing bride." Thomas stood and straightened his jacket, idly brushing a couple of her blonde hairs off his shoulder. "Our clients would expect us to be on our honeymoon." He watched as she flushed angrily, turning her head away from him. "Lauren. Look at me." Her wet gaze met his immediately, and without thinking, Thomas murmured, "Good girl..." noting with interest that she sucked in a breath harshly, flushing at his words. "These clients can be..." he seemed to be searching for the right words, and she watched him curiously, "...they can be coarse. Ignore them, blush sweetly and be my lovely wife. Can you do this?"

For her part, Lauren tried to force down the hysterical laugh trying to bubble up from her throat and come shrieking out of her mouth. *Do* this? Be a monster's bride and giggle and blush like a complete idiot? Swallowing heavily, she paused for a moment before answering him. "I'll be ready," she answered levelly. "I'll make sure I don't embarrass you." When her gaze rose to his, it was empty of the kaleidoscope of emotion she usually radiated when around him. Strangely, Thomas felt the lack of it.

Clearing his throat, he nodded. "Very good. I'll see you this evening." He turned and left the house, pretending he didn't hear her begin to cry again as he shut the front door.

Mechanically painting her face that night, Lauren tried to avoid thinking about how this had ever happened- trying to stop the hurricane of terror and confusion that had swamped her ever since this beautiful maniac had invaded her life. Her ability to power through what would have been her breaking point was honed after her mother died and falling apart was no longer an option. When Frank couldn't "handle" planning her funeral and an 18-year-old Lauren had to pick out a casket for her dead mother.

You just had to pretend none of it really involved you- like it was a stranger experiencing these awful things and you were just a spectator. Finally zipping up an elegant black dress with sheer panels just above her breasts and around the hem of the flared skirt, she adjusted the neckline, her blank expression catching the light reflecting off her suitably large Tiffany diamond. Thinking of her time pinned on the lap of her terrifying and beautiful husband that morning, Lauren wondered again why she'd been so wet and slick down... there when he'd finished.

"*Ypa!*" roared the burly man at the head of the table, and Thomas and Lauren repeated the phrase, raising their glasses for a toast. If it hadn't been for the unfortunate reality of her present company, she would have been thrilled to be here. The Social Eating House was a brainchild of Gordon Ramsay's protege Jason Atherton, the most sought-after restaurant in London. But their Corporation guests were not known for their nuance. She had learned this when her dark husband had smoothly reintroduced her to their Russian wedding guests. "Why are you not on your honeymoon?" leered Karl Romanoff, one of the more brutal of the Bratva lieutenants, "You have such a lovely bride."

"Ah," chuckled Thomas easily, "my sweet wife understands that I have obligations to our new, valued associates."

Tossing back another drink, Romanoff looked Lauren up and down, insultingly lingering near her breasts. "Is this true, *malen'kaya nevesta*? You will sit and wait for your husband to service you?"

Time seemed to stand still for Number Two and the rest of the table as his new wife hesitated. But then Lauren turned to look at Thomas, simpering adoringly. "Mr. Romanoff, I am sure a man of your responsibilities understands that business must sometimes take precedence over... um... pleasure. But I have faith my dear husband will more than make up for the delay in our honeymoon." Smiling blandly during the harsh laughter that followed, she pressed further, "But you- I am sure there are little ones that miss their Papa?"

There was dead silence for a moment. No one had ever thought to inquire after anything related to any human emotion with the lieutenant responsible for melting informants in a bathtub full of acid. But, there Karl was, pulling out his wallet in a careless gesture that made The Corporation operatives slide their hands into their jackets, just touching their shoulder holster. But he was only flipping it open to show Lauren pictures of his three sons and a baby girl, while she praised their attractiveness and obvious strength. Thomas exchanged a glance with Kingston, who'd been watching the interaction with great interest. Number One nodded to him, raised his glass of wine in a little toast to his Number Two, and continued watching the bizarre photo session.

But the warm little moment was the only one of the evening, and after a while, Lauren found she was taking a gulp of wine every time one of the Bratva men made a lascivious "joke" about the newlyweds in Russian. Three glasses later, she realized this was a drinking game she couldn't win. And Thomas's mouth was tightening as well. He'd been watching his new wife flush and look down when the men talked about her in their language, and he began to suspect that she was quite aware of what they were saying. Which meant his slinky little minx could speak at least some Russian.

Clever girl.

When the laughing and toasts got too loud for the elegant restaurant, Thomas smoothly piled everyone into discreet black Mercedes' and brought them to a loud dance club where they could drink to boisterous toasts and roar with inappropriate laughter all they liked. Lauren and Number Three's fiancée sat together for moral support, and Clara eyed the men. While Thomas graciously ignored the vilest commentary from the Bratva operatives, Fassell reveled in it, laughing just as loudly while getting discreet translations. "Most of the business dinners I've gone to haven't been like this," Clara volunteered.

Lauren looked at her, squeezing her hand. "I guess some groups are just bigger partiers than others." For the first time, she felt the stirrings of concern for Clara, already feeling more world-weary and in the thick of The Corporation's dealings, like Arabella. The two chatted together and tried to ignore most of the conversation and shouting, until one of the older men slid across the couch, his thigh boldly touching Lauren's.

"We should dance, you and I," he leered, attempting to look down the neckline of her dress.

Suddenly, Thomas was there, his hand taking Lauren's and lifting her up. "Ah, my apologies, *moy drook*, but the first dance with my lovely bride belongs to me."

As Thomas pulled her to the dance floor, Lauren was rigid and as brittle as a cube of ice, visibly flinching when he ran one hand around her waist to the small of her back, pressing her into his body. One thick, muscled leg slid between her slimmer ones, easily resting her suddenly heated pelvis against his thigh and rubbing it gently with the elegant sway of his hips. Lauren groaned internally, the music was slow, sultry, and worse- it was a singer she loved- Chet Faker with the cover of a hip-hop song.

He could *dance?* There was no god, Lauren thought despairingly, proven by the fact that her horrid husband could actually move those lean hips with all the grace of Maksim Chmerkovskiy. The slow roll of his pelvis against her suddenly heated one made her breath hitch in her chest, feeling the coiled grace of all that lean muscle and controlled strength around her.

Then, it was as if the horrid, knowing chuckles of their Bratva guests melted away, along with the stares of Numbers One and Three from The Corporation. They were alone on that shadowy dance floor, feeling the throb and pulse of the music seep through her feet and tingle up her legs to her spine.

This time, Lauren's groan was audible. The way his hips thrust so seamlessly with the chorus, winding, and twirling and carrying her suddenly loose body along with his. Her hands went to Thomas's lean waist, gripping him and one sliding up his back to try to stabilize herself, to get herself to focus again. But Lauren couldn't - her scary new husband simply felt so good - moving her gracefully along with him as they swirled and dipped among the anonymous, ghostly dancers around them. When the song faded away, she suddenly felt his mouth on hers, their second kiss ever and it was hot and slow and delicious, just like the music. Thomas continued exploring her mouth with lips and tongue until her legs felt shaky and she was pretty sure his arm was the only thing holding her up. Lauren gasped as he lifted his head, staring at her. His eyes were blazing, and cobalt blue. Taking her by the hand, Thomas pulled her off the floor and headed for the exit.

"Where- wher'we going?" Lauren managed, following him and trying to keep up in her sky-high heels.

Hustling her back to the Mercedes as the driver hastened to open the door, Thomas looked down at Lauren, kissing the girl until she was breathless. "Going? To my bed, little girl."

Chapter 6 – The Wedding Night

In which Lauren is deflowered. And enjoys every moment of it.

She should be stopping him.

Lauren knew that - she *did* - but Thomas had yanked her onto his lap the moment the door shut behind them, the privacy screen already tactfully raised and her thighs straddling his waist, her skirt rucked up to a scandalous degree and exposing her pretty black satin panties. Ironically, the gorgeous underwear was a gift from Arabella from her grim "Hen's Night," but Lauren had to admit, Number One's wife had spectacular taste in lingerie. She'd never expected Thomas to get a look at it since he assured her he was no rapist and there was not a chance in the blazing pit of HELL that she would give herself willingly. But, there she was, finding her back arched as she rubbed shamelessly against the wool of Thomas's trousers and the hard cock beneath it.

Moaning a little, Lauren was pleased that his warm hands were sliding up her thighs, growling as he discovered the gossamer-thin stockings, held to her legs by lacy garters. There was something about the way his rough thumbs stroked appreciatively over the strip of bare skin between Lauren's stockings and panties that made her shudder.

"Why, darling girl," Thomas purred, "you're wrapped up so

prettily for me."

Suddenly, Lauren felt herself twist and land on her back, her new husband looming over her and sliding down her body. Thomas bent his head and breathed against the wet panel of her fancy undies, enjoying her shudder as the warm air pushed against her pussy. Her little sigh ended in a startled yelp as her diabolical husband nipped one silky lip, just a bit, and the thin skin of her inner thigh.

She tensed, suddenly remembering who this dark, beautiful bastard was and that he was drawing down that scrap of silk that protected her from his scrutiny. She hated this man! He threatened her, he said he would kill- "Oh! Oh, my GOD what are you DOING?" She could feel his shoulders shake with laughter against her thighs, spread wide suddenly, and her lean muscles tensing as he placed his mouth on her. After pointing his tongue and sliding it between her swelling lips, Thomas circled her channel, making Lauren gasp and twitch when he suddenly pressed it up inside her. Halfway coming to her senses, she put her hands in his thick hair, disordered into the beginning of what would be lovely curls if the man didn't keep his hair so short.

"Wh- wait- I..." She'd had several drinks, Lauren thought dazedly - well over her usual limit - but if she let him do this... she *knew* what was happening, she would never be able to pretend she didn't agree because Thomas said he wasn't a rapist so if she said "no" he'd stop and then... Her wild thoughts began swirling sluggishly when her husband removed his face from her pussy - an action Lauren noted with some regret - and looked up at her with a devilish glint in his beautiful eyes. Not cold and pale as always, Thomas's eyes were cobalt. Like the sea just before a storm.

Those eyes were knowing, damn him. Thomas rested his wet

chin on her pubic bone and looked up at her in amusement. "Why baby, aren't you enjoying yourself? Do let me take care of you. I'll make you feel so." He placed a kiss at the top of her wet slit, grinning at Lauren's squeal. "Much." This kiss was lower and included his tongue, which swirled around her hard, little clitoris. Then, his voice lowered to a growl as he purred, "Better..." then fastening his lips around the little nub and sucking.

Lauren could feel the darkness creeping in from the sides of her vision, making her gaze on the top of her husband's head with laser precision. The light shining off his dark hair, the pleased little groan he made with the utterly scandalous slurping sounds of his lips and tongue invading all the secret parts of her - closed off and hidden away from other men - the boys, really that she'd dated in high school and college. How had this man- this terrible man had so easily demolished her defenses and swept them away as easily as her panties?

"Oh! Oh, GOD! Please don't... um..." Damn him! Lauren could feel her orgasm start at the base of her spine, in her legs, shaking as they tried to tighten against the barrier of this man with his face buried between them. She'd never come before, aside from her own hand, nervous and uncomfortable but loving the warmth and how her muscles twisted and twitched under his hateful, certain mouth. It wasn't a shock to her that this beautiful, terrifying man knew his way around a woman's private parts. And she was so close- just let him and maybe later she could ask him questions about-

"Mr. Williams?" The driver's voice was calm, carefully neutral, "We've arrived, sir."

Easily pulling down her skirt and helping his dazed bride upright, Thomas regally answered, "Very well. Thank you,

Stevens."

He looked his usual self, the handsome, urbane Number Two, graciously escorting his unsteady bride out of the Mercedes and sending The Corporation driver on his way. But as Thomas hustled Lauren up the stairs and through his decorous, shiny black front door, his mind was seething with scenarios and trying to plot out the evening. *Let's be honest,* he thought, looking at her flushed cheeks with wry amusement, *the girl is a wild card.* Even the "good girls" had thrown themselves at Thomas over the years. But he rarely wasted time on a woman who didn't know exactly what she was in for when she said 'yes' to him. And he'd promised Lauren he wouldn't force her, even though the more feral part of him was beginning to regret that assurance.

So it was, perhaps, a bit out of character for Thomas to shut the door and then pin his bride against it with the hard length of his body, pulling her arms above her head and holding them in his long fingers. Forcing himself to be still for a moment, he noted her wide lavender eyes and rapid heartbeat. And also, with great satisfaction, that she didn't look away from his intent gaze or flinch when his mouth descended on hers again. In fact, Lauren moaned quite sweetly when his free hand traveled down to take hold of her thigh and hoist her aggressively against his hips and the hard press of his cock.

"So lovely, darling..." Thomas crooned, kissing along her jawline and luxuriously moving his pelvis against his wife's damp center. "I want to see you in our bed, hair spread out across the pillows, coming for me and as beautiful as you were that night, playing your cello and speaking so passionately of Bob Marley." For one, terrible second he thought he'd miscalculated and reminded his sweet captive of their arrangement. Lauren pulled back searching his face with her mouth wet and open. He thought she was beautiful when she *played?*

Men had often complimented Lauren, aware of her father's sizeable wealth or aroused by her lovely face. So, she'd heard most of the lines about her "knockout eyes," or her "sweet ass," or the worst: "That beautiful mouth would look even better wrapped around my dick!" But her secret truth was that the deepest part of her shined brightest when she played, when her hands translated the language of the universe and it flowed through her and into her instrument. And that was how her terrifying new husband viewed her beauty? Through her music? With a needy little moan, Lairen pushed against him, arching her breasts into his hard chest and sucking his tongue back into her mouth.

Eye briefly rolling back in his head, Thomas absently thanked whatever force in the cosmos that granted him this favor. As much as he wanted to yank down his zipper and plunge into his delicious little bride, he knew she was a virgin. Treating her crudely for her first time would not make for a good morning after. And he already knew he would want her again. Many times. Lifting her and wrapping Lauren's legs around him, Thomas fisted a hand in her hair and pulled her mouth to his as he swiftly climbed the stairs to the third floor. *Why the fuck,* he thought dimly, *did I ever agree to anything other than a ground floor master bedroom? Idiot!* Still, the man wasn't even breathing heavily when he shoved open his bedroom door and more or less flung Lauren on to her back on his comfortable bed. Flipping up her skirt again, Thomas paused to look at the girl's wide eyes.

"Just one more taste, darling. Then I'll take care of my girl."

The words should not have aroused her the way they did, Lauren groaned internally. For heaven's sake, she was a grown-up! She had a college degree and she- oh, sweetbaby-jesus he was doing that thing with his tongue again, and- Thomas raised above her, licking his lips and laughing as she hid her face in her hands. When she peeked between her fingers, her scary new husband was already naked and sliding the zipper down the back of her dress. For a moment, her elbows instinctively clamped against her sides again, holding the dress immobile the way she had the night before. Her husband's hands stilled, his long fingers stroking along the bare skin of her back. He took a deep breath and licked his lips again.

"Do you want me to stop?"

"I..." she did, right? The terrifying Number Two who made her marry him? The one whose sure hands were stroking and caressing her skin appreciatively, but not pulling at her dress? Lauren shook her head. "I don't... I'm..."

And then he said the magic words. Leaning closer, Thomas groaned internally, then spoke calmly, evenly. "This is your choice, Lauren. I will not take it from you."

He had her. It was maybe the only thing in her new life where she had any choice, and Lauren knew it. And yet, her dark and beautiful husband gave it to her. Sighing, she leaned in and kissed his firm mouth again, enjoying the faint scrape of his five o'clock shadow and that sleek, sinuous tongue that rewarded her for letting her dress fall by stroking along her jaw and into that embarrassingly sensitive spot under her ear. He chuckled, low and a bit smug, at her shudder, tickling the skin again before biting down her neck as he put her back against the pillows.

She *was* such a pretty package, Thomas thought as he finished undressing his new wife. Beautiful, spirited, intelligent. Falling into his hands at just the perfect moment and crushing Number One's plans while fulfilling his own. He would make their first time as romantic and satisfying as he could. It had been so long since he'd been gentle with a woman... Angling his hips along the soft skin of her thighs, he enjoyed her little groan as his uncomfortably stiff cock stroked along her, leaving a cool trail of slick behind. His mouth was hot- fastening greedily on to one breast and then the other, sweet, slow sucks and then a sharp nip or two. Lauren tensed and relaxed, then tensed again, trying to participate and barely keeping track of where his hands and mouth were on her body.

And then, Lauren discovered her new husband's most deadly weapon. His voice. The Voice, if she needed to be descriptive, as he chuckled into her ear. "Hmmmm..." his moan purred along her nerve endings, sending up a shock of goosebumps and making her desperately stifle a whimper. "Such a lovely surprise you've turned out to be, darling. Sweet and delicious..." he bent his head and ran his patrician nose along her collarbone. "Who knew that such a very good girl could be so irresistible? I am using all my self-control to keep from plunging into that tender pussy, trying to be a *gentleman.*" Thomas laughed a little unkindly as his bride shook her head with a frown. "I am not a gentleman, this is true..." He leaned back to enjoy her rapid pulse and the sweet, pink flush spreading over her chest and up her throat. Taking her hand, he put it around his cock, groaning again as Lauren gasped and stiffened. "Shhh... be my good girl and I will make it all better. You want to come, don't you? You need to come." Stopping all movement, Thomas hovered over her like a murky and dangerous angel until his bride reluctantly opened her eyes to look at him.

"Tell me what you want. Be my good girl."

Frustrated beyond reason, equal parts terrified and aroused by this stunning man, Lauren's eyes filled with helpless tears, turning them an exquisite shade of lilac. She watched Thomas take a deep breath, almost a groan as he watched her. "I don't have any... I don't know if I'm any good," she finally managed, too overcome to be anything but honest.

Impossibly, the thick organ she was still holding on to seemed to grow harder, and his dark head dipped to kiss her breast again before recovering. "Such a sweet, good girl for me," Thomas praised hoarsely. "Let me do all the work." Settling more comfortably between her thighs, his hand moved his cock from his wife's shaking fingers to her wet center, idly running it up and down her slippery opening. When he circled her clit, Lauren yelped, making him grin and do it again, and again until his innocent bride was the one to raise her hips and try to guide him inside her. "Ah- ah!" Thomas chided, making her groan with frustration. "Such an impatient little thing..." Nonetheless, he was at the end of his rope as well, so he carefully positioned the broad head of his cock at her entrance and paused, surprising himself. The moment seemed to contain a significance he'd not felt before, this first breaching of his wife. The only man to have her. The only man who would *ever* have her.

Wildly aroused by the realization, Thomas pushed his agile hips forward, slowly and enjoying the look of surprise and then shock in Lauren's eyes as her silky walls stubbornly resisted him, only to finally spread open slowly and allow him passage. "Such a good girl," he gritted, "let me in..." Thomas used his deepest, most persuasive tone, "Let me in now, and I'll make it all better." His bride's eyes squeezed shut, but he couldn't stop watching the expressions run across her mobile features as he braced his feet against the walnut footboard of his bed and pushed deeper, taking her so much more slowly than he'd like. There was a vaguely feral undercurrent urging him to shove into his property- mark her- fuck her! But Thomas managed to keep his leisurely pace, stroking along her until a quick push shoved him past the thin tissue barrier that kept her from being his. Aside from a pained gasp, Lauren didn't make a sound as he moved up inside her, using the strength of his hips to widen her. One hand moved down to her clitoris, gently stroking and teasing along the bit of flesh and nerves to distract her. Thomas was rewarded with another gush of slick, and he leaned down to kiss her cheek, murmuring how beautiful she was- how lovely and perfect his bride- how dearly he wanted to pound into her like a greedy bastard.

Lauren's eyes were still tightly shut until she felt his warm hand caress the skin just under her belly button.

"Can you feel me, sweet wife? I'm in you all the way. To the hilt." Thomas pressed his fingers against her abdomen, and her breath left her in a rush, feeling the hot press of him inside and the carnal push of him without. As his hips began moving, Lauren's eyes opened and stared into his intent gaze, as shy as it made her to watch him carefully categorize her response, the embarrassingly eager moisture that eased the way for his thick shaft to push faster along her, even enjoying how the painful tingling along her hamstrings drew her knees up against his ribs and pressing tight, toes actually pointing like a ballerina's from the sensations sending up fireworks along her nerve endings.

As one hand slid to the small of her back to arch her against the slide of his cock, Thomas kept his other hand on her abdomen, grinning darkly as he gloated, "Ah. I can feel you, sweet girl. Here-" he pushed down on her stomach and Lauren gasped as her spine arched even tighter, which made her uncomfortably stretched pussy tighten involuntarily. Part of her enjoyed the sudden groan from her husband, who began pistoning faster inside her, striking like a match along nerve endings and lighting sparks that made her hips rise and try to help him. "And here," he managed, swirling his hips to push against the tender tip of her cervix. "No further, darling, not tonight. But someday you will enjoy the pain of me pushing past and into your womb. You have no idea-" Lauren cried out as her dark husband's cock suddenly pulsed against her, "-how very deep I can be inside you."

Feeling his bride's fingers dig into the muscles in his back, Thomas chuckled and moved faster, dipping his hips to drive into Lauren's pussy and scoop luxuriously out, pushing the head of him along her painfully swollen nerves. "You want to let go, don't you, baby? All this sweet slick around me..." She dimly felt his fingers bracket the thickness of his cock breaching her, sliding along her painfully stretched entry and stroking her wetness along their joining.

This loosened a desperate whimper from his bride's clenched lips, hearing Thomas continue to torment her with his heated cock and his words, making her certain she could come solely from that guttural, knowing tone. "Wouldn't you like to come, sweet Lauren? Wouldn't you like to flood me, make us all damp and filthy? Now, baby, come for me now-" The last was delivered between clenched teeth, and her frightening husband's gentleness was suddenly gone, rearing above her and driving greedily through the tense squeeze of her silky walls and fucking into her- sealing them with sweat and slick and suddenly with a scream as Lauren almost scared herself by hearing the wail come out of her good girl mouth as she loudly joined Thomas in a finish so intense that it was actually painful- but she still squeezed against his spurting cock and clung to his broad back, holding on as tightly as she could as they came and flooded and slid along each other in a greedy gush of arousal and satisfaction.

Thomas cruelly continued to stroke inside her quaking walls to keep her orgasm going until Lauren groaned pitifully and begged him to stop. This time, his voice didn't sound as calculated, as assured as he moaned into her ear, "Such a very good girl. Your Sir is so pleased with you."

Lauren puzzled over what that meant as he gently pulled from her, kissing her as she whimpered and returning with a warm cloth to wipe gently along all the wet places on her, drying her and making her drink one of those always-available bottles of water before curling up behind her and letting her settle into his arm, possessively draped over her waist. Vaguely promising herself to think this whole mess over in the morning, Lauren wiggled her still-sore buttocks comfortably into the hollow of his groin and fell asleep.

Chapter 7 – The Light of Day

*In which Lauren questions who she has become.
And Thomas is infuriatingly indifferent
to her moral dilemma.*

If Lauren had been in any shape to think about the following morning during her post-coital bliss, it would have ruined it for her. So, it was fortunate for the happy sex buzz that she fell asleep before anticipating having to face her terrifying husband in the light of day.

When the sun slanted across her face the next morning, Lauren stretched sleepily, halting the movement in a hurry when she felt the pull and the soreness in her lower half. Even her thighs hurt, and her pelvis was on fire. Why was she so-

Oh, my god! Her eyes flew open. *I had sex with Thomas!* she thought. *I had sex and I enjoyed it! What kind of a sleazy human being has an orgasm with the organized crime monster who made her marry him?* Burying her face in her hands, she wished she could disappear. Reappear somewhere else. Anywhere else. Far away, though. Far enough away that the terrible knowing gaze of Thomas Williams couldn't find her. Knowing this was sadly unrealistic, she finally took a deep breath, holding it for a moment. The breath expelled from her in a rush when she spotted a note leaning against the lamp on her bedside table in Thomas's distinctive handwriting.

"*Lovely.*

I headed into the office for an early meeting. I will require you at a dinner meeting before our Russian guests fly out. Romanoff, in particular, was keen to say goodbye. You were very charming last night.

And at dinner as well.

T."

Her face flaming at his suggestive praise, Lauren angrily kicked the rest of the covers off the bed. Great. Wasn't *she* a "full-service" wife? Then, just to make the mortification of her morning complete, she was greeted with the red smears of her virginity staining Thomas's expensive sheets.

"Mom would be *so* proud," she mumbled before beginning to cry. She missed her mother so much. Aurelia was always the parent Frank never was- caring and kind. Even as a snotty teenager, Lauren always knew her mother loved her, always knew her advice about her adolescent drama was sound. And now she was gone and Lauren had no one to talk to. No one she could trust, anyway.

Angrily gathering up the sheets, she threw them into the dirty clothes hamper, finding the linen closet and re-making the bed with fresh sheets. "Let's not give Thomas any more ammunition to use against me," she hissed bitterly. "The fact that he just deflowered like, the last virgin in England over the age of sixteen? That should make me just about as pathetic as humanly possible."

Lauren angrily practiced her cello and violin, and finally played her beloved bass guitar turned up as high as she dared, enjoying the windows actually rattling in the fourth-floor conservatory that her confusing spouse had set up for her. It was a surprisingly thoughtful move- a private space to practice and all her many instruments laid out respectfully. It was something only a musician - or someone who understood the power of music - would even think to do.

Hardening her heart, Lauren decided to step out and go for a run. It was a good time to get to know her new neighborhood, where to get coffee in the morning, maybe a nice park... To her fury, Broken Nose Guy stepped out of a sedan as she did some quick stretches in front of Thomas's beautiful house.

"Mrs. Williams," he said calmly. "Good morning."

"Don't call me that!" Lauren snapped at him instinctively before recoiling. She was a nice girl, a kind person, and she was being rude to another "employee" who was just doing his job.

Like her.

Forcing herself not to cry, she nodded stiffly. "I'm... going for a run. I'll stay on the street where you can follow me."

Broken Nose Guy was carefully expressionless. "Very well. We'll be just behind you, should you need assistance."

Lauren frowned. "There's more than one of you? What exactly do you think I'll do?"

This time, the well-dressed thug's eyes met hers with just a hint of a smirk. "That is the problem, Mrs. Williams- ah, Miss Lauren. We have no idea."

She snorted inelegantly. "I'm the wild card. In a 'corporate structure' such as this..." she made the mocking quotation gesture with her fingers, "I'm the thing you can't predict." Without waiting for his answer, Lauren angrily turned up the music on her phone and began pounding the pavement with her running shoes as if the cement had insulted her personally. She ran and ran, trying to outpace her thoughts, her fear and embarrassment, and the humiliation of having been even more vulnerable in front of this terrifying, beautiful man. Finally succumbing to the raw ache between her legs, Lauren sullenly slowed down outside a small coffee house. It looked very pleasant and low-key, and she could see trays of delightfully massive baked goods behind the glass counter. Exactly her sort of place.

It was darker and cool inside the little shop and Lauren breathed in the lovely scent of caffeine and the freshly baked muffins. Closing her eyes and settling her jangled nerves, she looked at the chalk-drawn menu before turning around and walking to the black BMW that followed her all morning. Tapping on the heavily-shaded window, she waited for a moment before it drew down slowly. The carefully expressionless face of Broken Nose Guy gazed out at her.

"Yes, Miss Lauren?"

She couldn't see the man in the passenger seat, shrouded in the shadowed side of the car, and she chose to ignore him. One professional shooter at a time. "I want you to come… um… have coffee with me." The polite expression of incredulity on his battered face was similar to the one he would have offered if his boss's wife has suggested he juggle a passel of cats, but he nodded slowly. With a meaningful glare at the other man in the car, Broken Nose Guy exited the BMW and looked at the determined girl. Watching him stare down at her with a vague expression of discomfort, Lauren finally ventured, "So, what do you drink?"

Of course, she was not surprised when he said firmly, "Coffee. Black. No cream or sugar. Just… coffee."

Finally making the bulky man sit down at the ridiculously little cafe table outside on the deck, Lauren watched with some amusement as the waitress brought him a gigantic muffin. Her unwilling bodyguard poked at it carefully with a fork for a moment as she drank her chai tea latte. "It won't explode, you know," she finally offered, "it's just a crumpet."

The man, of course, was not mollified by her assurance. Sighing, Lauren took a bite of her own, chewing ostentatiously. She swallowed down the first smile of the morning watching this terrifying creature nibble a corner of the sweet as if it might blow up in his face.

Finally gathering up her courage, she finally asked, "Am I the first... uh... I dunno, 'responsibility' that Mr. Williams saddled you with?"

Not a flicker of expression crossed the man's face. "I am not at liberty to comment, Mrs. W- Miss Lauren."

Rolling her eyes, the girl sighed. "Of course." Taking a sip of her chai latte, she pondered what she could ask this man. "So, are you stuck with me?"

Her Corporation shadow looked at her quizzically. "I beg your pardon?"

Gesturing uselessly with her long, graceful hands, Lauren struggled for the right questions. "Instead of doing exotic, uh, Corporation-based things, are you going to be stuck following me around so I don't do anything stupid?"

He was turning his coffee cup- black, no cream or sugar- around in his blocky hands. "You are a valued asset of The Corporation, Miss Lauren. You are also an innocent. You may not be aware of the... uh... complications of corporate life. My assignment is to be certain of your safety."

Lauren's brow furrowed. "So, you have to be my babysitter? Sorry, dude."

For the first time, she saw something other than stoic irritation on Broken Nose Guy's face. His tight features relaxed slightly. "I volunteered for this position, Miss Lauren."

She had to admit, she was shocked. "Why?" Lauren blurted, "Why would you do that? I'm going to bore you half to death." She leaned forward earnestly, "I'm incredibly not exciting, seriously."

There was a small cough from the man that might possibly be characterized as a rusty little chuckle. "And I would like to keep it that way." He looked at her confused face. "You don't belong in this world. Mr. Williams is decisively interested in keeping you as apart from it as possible. As am I."

There was more. Broken Nose Guy used to have children. Three of them. He hadn't seen them for years. The wife had up and left without a trace, even with his more advantageous search skills. He thought of them all the time, missed them desperately. And just as desperately grateful they weren't here to see what he'd become. Not that he would ever say any of this to Number Two's new wife. What on earth had possessed the man to marry someone so ridiculously naive and inexperienced?

Pursing her lips thoughtfully, Lauren stared at him as she finished her muffin. "What's your name?" she asked suddenly.

Broken Nose Guy stared at her for a moment. "Charles," he admitted finally, "Charles Straker."

"Can I call you Chuck?" his new charge asked.

Finishing his coffee, Broken Nose Guy said, "No."

The new Mrs. Thomas Williams ran home, absently keeping to central streets so the BMW following her could keep pace easily. Finally pausing in front of Thomas's (not hers, she reminded herself sternly, the Crime Lord's house) she nodded to the car idling alongside her. "Bye, Chuck!" she called, "I'm in for the rest of the day!"

The man in the passenger side of the car looked at Broken Nose Guy. "Did she just call you Chuck?"

Putting the car in park and turning it off, Charles settled himself more comfortably. "No."

It was late afternoon when Lauren's shiny new iPhone 'pinged' with a text from her groom. *"Be ready by 7. Straker will be waiting for you in front of the house. Wear something elegant, similar to last night. T."* Holding the phone, Lauren squeezed it a little too hard, putting a ripple in the screen. Thumbs finally moving over the buttons, she gritted her teeth against everything she wanted to say to this arrogant British asshole.

"Fine."

Pausing for a moment, she knew it could be read as churlish. And Lauren did not want another spanking. Though... her treacherous thighs tightened against a tingle in her lower parts, remembering being over Thomas's lap. Sighing, she added to the text, *"I'll be ready."*

Getting ready in the gleaming white of the master bathroom, Lauren kept looking at the big bed, neatly made up with fresh sheets and looking completely innocent. She was still utterly confounded by her nearly instant capitulation to that horrible man. The man who terrified her and shot her father - admittedly, not really an emotionally scarring moment - to force her to do what he wanted. But even being terrifying, he had shown her kindness when she'd broken down. Gave her the choice to sleep with him or not. He'd even pulled back - and most flatteringly, made it look like an effort - when she'd hesitated. "It is your choice," he'd said to her, "I will not take it from you."

Her hand paused over one cheekbone with a brush laden with bronzer. What did that make her? To give her virginity to this man? To *enjoy* it? Finally not able to spend one more brain-frying moment trying to understand herself, Lauren sighed and finished getting dressed. This time, she was wearing a strappy red silk dress with a long, swishing skirt that went just over her knees. She left her hair down, suddenly remembering vividly how it felt to have his big fist in her blonde curls, moving her head back and forth to meet his lips. She'd struggled over what she wore underneath the dress for longer than anything else. If she wore more of that flossy lingerie from her hellish "Hen Party," it was admitting she wanted more of what they'd shared the night before. But if she didn't... did it make her look weak? Scared of Thomas? Unable to bear one more moment of questioning herself, Lauren went bare-legged, skipping the hose and garters, but pulled on the racy red and black bra and panty set. There. Not a message one way or another. Sort of.

To her surprise, her scary new husband was actually waiting outside for her as The Corporation car pulled up to the restaurant. It was one of the clever new creations from a chef raised in his youth on going to raves in random warehouses, who insisted on catering a new location every week. Gingerly taking the broad hand presented to pull her from the car,

Lauren eyed the old shoe factory perched on the Thames. "Let me guess. Chef Gustav?"

His brow rose with the barest hint of surprise and respect, but Thomas nodded. "Several of the Russians are terrible food snobs- I was quite surprised as well. There are constant mentions of *"Фарм на стол,"* and *"блюда местной кухни."* Lauren burst out laughing before suddenly realizing Thomas had spoken the phrases in perfect Russian. A language she would not be expected to understand. Trying to stifle her chuckles, she shrugged innocently.

"Sorry... I don't know what you said, but it sounded so funny. Especially following the vision of the Bratva as "food sno-"

Thomas's arm was suddenly a cruel vise around her waist and he yanked her into an alcove. Lauren began shuddering when his mouth pressed against her ear. "You will *never* say that word again. Simply speaking it out loud is enough to have you killed." He felt her body trembling violently, but he forced himself to continue. Shaking her roughly, Thomas snarled, "Do you *understand?* Answer me!" Some unfamiliar part of him cringed a bit when he heard her swallow a terrified sob.

"Y- yes." Lauren drew in a deep breath, trying not to pull away from his painful grip on her body. "I understand. Not a word."

Forcing down the uncomfortable feeling of regret, knowing that all the ground they'd made the night before was suddenly demolished, Thomas drew in a breath and loosened his grip. "Very good. Now be a good girl and behave nicely." He could feel his bride pull away from him in an almost visceral way, though she didn't move a muscle.

"Of course." It was the last thing she said to him for the rest of the evening. Lauren smiled, nodded, even laughed on occasion at a joke in their guests' accented English.

This was, after all, not unfamiliar to her. She'd been raised attending her grandfather's- then her father's boring-as-shit corporate dinners, expected to be a delightful little prodigy designed to make Frank look even more impressive. She went back into the old motions of keeping her hands in her lap, ankles crossed prettily and appearing to listen intently to the guest next to her and remembering small details that would make them feel special, make them feel important. This made her unfortunately excellent memory travel back to other times when this charming trait was misunderstood, but Lauren shoved the ugly images down and mechanically played her part. Her life depended on it.

To her surprise, Romanoff wasn't the problem tonight. Her interest in his children the night before had suddenly relegated her to "honored wife and daughter" status, and his conversation was nothing but fatherly. In fact, when a younger, brash lieutenant took advantage of Thomas's absence from the table to take a call as a moment to leer at Lauren with a few suggestive phrases, it was the older Russian who snarled at the man to "Shut the fuck up- or I shall cut your dick off and choke you with it!" To his approval, Thomas's new wife simply turned to him and deftly changed the subject. He nodded, answering her questions and getting the strained atmosphere of the table back to normal. This girl- she was young, but she was a good fit for the murderous Number Two. Thomas may be an arrogant *Мудак*, but he was a smart one.

So, Thomas knew nothing of the ugly moment with the younger Russian. He simply returned to the table to see his lovely wife deep in conversation with the blood-soaked Romanoff as Number One regarded both of them with mild surprise. His pride in his beautiful choice of a bride rose higher. Clever girl.

There was no dancing that night to soften Lauren's rage and terror. No sudden surge of protectiveness to send Thomas out of his urbane, controlled self. So when the young couple bid goodnight to Romanoff and the rest of the terrifying Bratva and were ferried home, Lauren pressed herself as tightly as she could to her car door and her dark husband observed the movement expressionlessly. Very well. His bride was sulking after her correction for her loose lips. No matter. He was quite confident of his ability to loosen her thighs as easily as her mouth. But back in Hampstead Heath, Lauren swiftly exited the BMW and went for the stairs.

She paused and stiffened as Thomas's rough fingers trailed down her back. "Ready for bed so soon, little girl?"

Thomas knew it was the worst possible thing to say when it was clear that Lauren stifled a shudder. "No, I'm not... sleepy. We have our first big dress rehearsal next week. I'm going to practice. But I'll be quiet, okay?" He leaned in, trying to look at her face, lowered and turned away from him. When Lauren refused his fingers on her chin to turn and look at him, he dropped his hand.

"Very well. Do not stay up all night."

But Lauren was already rapidly climbing the stairs, not looking back. "Of course. I'll be quiet. Goodnight."

Nonetheless, Thomas laid awake for several hours longer, listening to her fierce movements in "Toccata and Fugue in D Minor." He recognized the piece from Bach, and vaguely admired the way his reluctant bride attacked the piece, over and over until she conquered its complexity and forced it into a ribbon of perfection, streaming from her cello. Finally rubbing his throbbing temples and groaning, he fell asleep.

Фарм на стол - "farm to table"

блюда местной кухни - "locally sourced cusine"

Мудак - asshole

Chapter 8 – A Carnal Symphony

In which Lauren discovers hoping Thomas will just roll over and fall asleep is inadequate protection from his delicious and filthy intent. Also, muffins and coffee, just not with Chuck.

When Thomas opened his eyes again, he knew two things at once. First, it was early morning- 2:15 by the glow of his stainless-steel Rolex, and secondly, he was still alone in his suddenly oversized bed. His dark brows drew together. Did his sweet bride panic and run? Did he terrify her enough to flee, thinking her utterly useless father's life was no longer worth sacrificing her freedom? Briefly, he was filled with respect for her. Frank Marsh *was* worthless. He'd given up his only child in a heartbeat. He should be fucked over in the most heartless possible way. Still, Thomas sat up, putting his feet on the floor and rubbing his eyes. Number Two was not a betting man. He was too obsessed with the odds and the outcomes and the probabilities of any given situation to do something as ludicrous as guessing what might have happened. His lovely new wife would be upstairs, sleeping uncomfortably in the only chair in her new conservatory, rather than getting into bed with her monstrous spouse. In fact, Thomas chuckled as he climbed the stairs to the fourth floor of his house, she would lie half-awake all night, rather than be in the same room as the man who'd given her three orgasms the night before, no matter how much he frightened or infuriated her. His Lauren- his pace slowed for a moment, when did she become *his* Lauren? Nonetheless, she was his. His Lauren was a good girl. She'd agreed to this unfortunate transaction to save the old man's life in the first place. His Lauren was the kind of good girl who kept her promises.

Of course, Thomas was correct. His bride was curled in an awkward little bundle, one hand still holding her cello's bow. He towered over her for a moment, looking over the graceful lines of her, even contorted to fit in the leather club chair. Something twinged in his chest, seeing the dried tear tracks on her cheek.

Even while terrifying her after her foolish "Bratva" comment, Lauren had kept her composure. He'd disliked feeling her curl away from him, the terror in her lavender gaze... Thomas idly smoothed her blonde hair off her forehead. He'd seen a lavender field in Provence, France once... not anywhere as beautiful as his new wife's eyes. As much as he appreciated her courage, he couldn't allow her to spout off about the Bratva. She belonged to him now. Lauren was his responsibility and no one- NO ONE would be allowed to hurt her. Leaning down, Thomas picked her up, holding her to his chest as he walked back down to their bedroom.

Perversely, he wanted to stain his snowy-white sheets with her again, take his bride's virginity twice. Thomas had actually chuckled unkindly when he'd pulled back his down comforter that night to see the linens changed. As if he wouldn't know she'd been untouched. As if he wouldn't know everything there was to know about this beautiful, excellent selection as his wife.

Thomas carefully undressed Lauren, unsurprised that she didn't awaken. The combination of the freefall from adrenalin, her anger, and four glasses of wine had made sturdier souls than her sleep like the dead. (There were one or two that specifically ended up that way at his hand, he thought, but that was a memory for another time.) His beautiful mouth shaped into a knowing grin when Thomas slipped off her dress, seeing the pretty matching undies. They looked delicious, like something he'd like to remove from her with his teeth. In fact, all that smooth skin was luscious and tempting.

Bending over her on the bed, the man ran his cool mouth over one collarbone, and then the other, his tongue dipping into the hollows above them- tasting his bride's warm skin. She smelled of peppermint from the soap she loved, with a dash of rosin from her bow, the rosemary scent of her shampoo, and the faintest fruity tones of the good wine they'd had with dinner in the old shoe factory.

Groaning just slightly, Thomas was struck with the desire to lick her all over, like a big cat. Instead, he settled for gently nudging her breast up and free from the red and black bra, suckling her pink nipple into his mouth, toying with it with the tip of his tongue. His warm mouth was the first thing that made her stir, her head turning unconsciously toward him, letting out a sigh.

Lauren knew musical instruments- her long fingers and clever hands knew how to coax the melody from them. Thomas however, knew women. He understood how to draw out a gasp or a moan, what made one girl shriek and another pass out with a soundless gasp. But he was still finding his way around his bride and quite interested in learning everything that would pull the music from her.

So, while she hovered, half-asleep, he toyed with each breast, keeping them trussed in her bra, stroking one finger over the wet lace lining of her undies. He ran his tongue up the silky skin of the inside of her arm and bit lightly on the throbbing cord in her neck. His cock grew uncomfortably hard at the symphony he was creating with Lauren, enjoying her soft moans and the louder, sharper gasps.

It was when his mouth was placing a long, cat-like lick along her wet slit that he heard a little trill- a high-pitched sound like a bird's. Fascinated, he licked his wife's center again, dividing her lips and sliding the tip of his tongue between them. The musical hitch came again as her back arched, pushing her wet pussy against his mouth.

When Thomas pursed his lips around her stiff clitoris and sucked, Lauren came awake with a scream. Her hands flew down to grab at her husband's hair, maybe to grip those almost-curls and yank him away, or... It was too late, she felt the orgasm barrel up her legs, making them shake and cycle through her pussy like a series of electrical shocks, the cycle beginning cruelly again when he slid one, then two fingers inside her, swirling, pumping up and down, scissoring- no movement long enough for her to concentrate and try to regain some semblance of control. After finding a couple of different spots inside her that made Lauren wail and try to slam her thighs together, her diabolical groom slid up her body, taking her hands from his hair and crossing them over her head, holding them with one hand while the other turned her face to kiss him. He grinned against her mouth when Lauren tasted herself and stiffened.

"Ah, ah!" he scolded gently, "You have been utterly delicious tonight. You must taste what I have been enjoying." Bending to kiss her again, Thomas ran his tongue over her full lips and slipped inside again, delicately tracing her teeth and then her tongue, before sucking it into his mouth. Purring against her ear, he enjoyed her corresponding shudder. "I've been making music with your lovely little body tonight. Would you like to hear it?"

Her eyes were wide, but not frightened, and the girl didn't even try to pull her hands from his grip. Lauren was utterly confounded, falling asleep in that miserably uncomfortable chair and suddenly waking up under her husband's long body. "I- what are- oh, GOD!" Lauren's voice swooped up a few registers when his white teeth landed in her neck, worrying the flesh like a lion, just barely not breaking the skin. One hand was plucking lightly from one nipple to the other while the other hand's fingers resumed their insidious play inside her. Staring back at Thomas's intent gaze, she tried to remember the words to make him stop- to tell him that is NOT what she wanted and certainly NOT from an asshole who shoved her up against a brick wall and scared the shit out of her because she said the "B" word.

But then, she felt the broad head of her husband's cock circling her opening, sliding in teasingly enough to allow his puffy tip to pop in and out of the tight seal of her entrance. In her dazed brain, she could hear the percussive sounds of her gasping and moaning, every now and then the high-pitched keen when the horrible man's cock almost pushed inside her. And finally, the shameful melody of her inviting whines, escaping her clenched teeth when Thomas finally smoothly shoved himself up her passage, his corresponding growls rumbling in tandem with Lauren's moaning.

Fortunately, Lauren's infernal spouse slowed halfway inside her, wrapping her legs around his waist and moving his hips sinuously, back and forth, playing with her without violently forcing his way inside. It was the taunting, slow play of his granite cock inside her that broke her determination to remain silent. "You are a horrible person," she noted in a small voice. Pausing long enough to raise up on his elbow to look at her, Thomas suddenly smiled. It was terrifying. It was arousing. It was murderously confident that she would not say 'no' to him, no matter what he chose to do to her.

"I am," he agreed and bent to kiss her as his shaft made its way up inside her again. When he finally felt some of the rigid tension leave the strong adductor muscles in her thighs, Thomas began sliding in and out faster, steadily pushing to the top of her and pausing for a moment, rotating his hips and gloating a bit about how very deep he could bury himself inside his wife.

Staring up at him, Lauren was struck with the beauty of this bizarre and terrifying man. Thomas's head was thrown back in bliss, eyes closed and thick lashes resting on his cheekbones. His mouth was slightly open and he was groaning helplessly as he circled inside her again.

She was suddenly struck with an inexplicable pride that she could bring this seamless, urbane bastard to his metaphorical knees, moaning and growling like a big cat inside her, no longer in control of everything. She *owned* some part of him- and Lauren was filled with a strange sense of power, tightening down on his shaft and enjoying the corresponding hiss- half pleasure, half discomfort as her wet walls halted his movement for a moment. Dropping his forehead to the collarbone he'd lavished so much time on earlier, Thomas managed to groan, "Lovely, I fear that if you do not release me from this utterly enticing grip, I will finish immediately and leave you unsatisfied. Let your Sir take care of you first."

Sir? Lauren thought, a little distracted, he'd said that the other night when she came. What did the title mean to him- oh, sweet Jesus that felt good! He'd arched his hips to push roughly against the silky front of her pussy, using the hairy base of his cock to tickle and irritate her clit, making it itchy somehow, needing something to feel less... or more something... that-

Suddenly his mouth was at her ear again and Thomas

was hoarsely whispering the filthiest, most complimentary things. Dirty praises about her "sweet cunt," and "how wet and silky she was inside," and how he'd "twist her clit until his good girl came and he'd let her rest, and-"

And, Lauren did, gripping her thighs against his waist and crossing her ankles just over the swell of his perfect ass, feeling it clench and unclench under the press of her heels, and the feeling of it along with his nasty talk sent her skyrocketing. She was being so *loud*, she thought vaguely as she wailed and gasped her aria, her little moans of pleasure as her relentless husband made her come once, then again. And as he surged and filled her with liquid heat, she shocked herself by coming again with him. Lauren buried her face in his neck, confused and exhausted and deeply satisfied, and asleep before Thomas gently pulled his cock from her and enjoyed the slick rush of fluid seeping from her tender opening. Putting his head on his wife's abdomen, he ran his long fingers in the wet, sliding it along her swollen lips and pushing it back inside her. Something feral part of his brain made Thomas want to make sure Lauren took all of him. Every drop.

Waking that morning - quite a bit later that morning - Lauren opened her eyes to the sight of her husband's dark head resting comfortably between her quite unclothed breasts, his hips holding her legs open and one big, warm palm cupping her still slightly sore ass. And apparently her unconscious self was just as debauched, one hand on his head and the other on the smooth skin of his back. In fact, her sensitive fingertips were lightly stroking along the beautifully defined muscles there. The handsome bastard worked out, that was clear, she thought resentfully, wondering how he found the time in between raping and pillaging the business world and defiling his bride. Her wandering fingers suddenly crossed over a patch of rough, scarred tissue and Lauren raised her head from the pillow.

Just above Thomas's kidneys and alarmingly close to his spine was a thick scar. It was wide but clean- clearly a precision cut and not something as clumsy as a bullet wound. Her lips tightened, suddenly furious at whoever tried to mutilate her husband so, forgetting for the moment of the irony, if not hypocrisy of her indignation.

As if he'd felt her fingers wandering on uncomfortable territory, Thomas's cerulean eyes suddenly opened, making her jump. How did he *do* that? She thought crossly, coming instantly awake, like a snake or something. He was so abruptly alert that it made her paranoid that he'd ever been asleep at all.

"Good morning, lovely."

Lauren groaned internally. That man and his voice. That beautiful, infernal voice.

He was watching her with some amusement, as Thomas gracefully twisted to his side and onto his elbow, looking down at her. "You came to bed quite late," he scolded smoothly, leaning in to breathe her warm skin. "We really must work on your bedtime, darling." He enjoyed watching his bride actually grind her teeth.

"I'm not a child, Thomas," Lauren managed a polite tone, "I get plenty of sleep."

"Hmmm..." he agreed, tracing his fingers along those lovely collarbones of hers again, ignoring how his bride stiffened. "But your responsibilities will start stacking up once the LSO season begins, along with your Corporation duties." Thomas stifled a grin as Lauren's mouth dropped open in horror.

"But- I- I mean, I thought I was already-"

Even her stutter was musical, he thought fondly, softened from a surprisingly powerful orgasm that morning and the pleasure of giving his sweet innocent several of her own. "You've been dressing up nicely and going to dinner," he corrected. "There is more, of course. Arabella will help you." He noted how Lauren went rigid again. *Really,* he thought absently, *I might need to work with her on her tells. My darling wife would be a terrible poker player.* Still, intrigued he leaned up over her, neatly caging her in between his arms and looking into her eyes. "What concerns you about Number One's wife, darling?" *Ah,* he thought, watching her gaze dart away, *there is something.*

"Thomas, I need to get up," Lauren pleaded, "I need to go to... I need the bathroom, please."

He was quite certain she was avoiding his question, but it was hard to doubt a morning bladder, so he simply nodded and rolled over, allowing her freedom. He nearly chuckled as his sweet bride sat up, the white sheets sliding down to settle against her hips, just obscuring the line of her buttocks. She was looking for a robe or something to cover herself, and Thomas let her stew for a moment before calmly assuring her, "I shall close my eyes, lovely. You are free to scamper to the ensuite without scrutiny."

Lauren thought she heard him leave the bedroom, so she sighed with relief and opened the bathroom door to discover her horrible husband dressed for running and pulling out her workout gear from the dresser assigned to her. Stepping behind the door again, she looked at him pleadingly.

"There you are," he was apparently not in the mood to be merciful, because Thomas stepped into her space, gently pushing her away from the door and under his scrutiny. "Beautiful..." he drew out the word appreciatively, looking her body over as Lauren tried not to squirm. "Here," thrusting her spandex shorts at her, he smiled maliciously, "I thought you'd like to stretch your legs a bit and go running with me." He watched as her pink mouth opened helplessly, then his bride shut it with a snap.

"Fine..." Looking up at his cooling expression, she hastily added, "uh, Thomas."

Stepping out of the house, Lauren followed her new husband down the stairs, noting Chuck already parked discreetly at the curb and starting up the car to follow them. Thomas started them out in the opposite direction from her travels yesterday, but they looped around the little park and still ended up at the bakery Lauren had embraced.

"Nice to see you again!" yelped the cheerful young man at the counter, smiling at Lauren. His beaming expression wilted under Thomas's thoughtful stare. "Uh, hi, Mr. Williams. What can I get you?"

"My wife and I," Thomas inserted smoothly, enjoying the look of shock on the boy's face, "would like a Columbian dark with cream and a hot chai tea latte." He ignored Lauren staring up at him. Of course, he would know what his new bride ordered for her caffeine fix. The same way he knew she'd been a virgin. That her pretty little friend from America wasn't speaking to her. That Lauren had made cautious friendship overtures to her new bodyguard, Straker. The same way he'd specifically selected the man because he knew Straker missed his own daughters. And that his volunteering to look after Lauren was somehow a kind of redemption for the man. Which meant he would give his life for Thomas's sweet new bride. Because Thomas Williams was not a man who let anything to chance.

Anything.

Chapter 9 – Safe Words and Too Many Cocktails

In which Lauren samples new cocktails.
And new sex positions.

Thomas could see that it unnerved her.

That he knew she liked hot chai tea lattes. That she'd been here before. That he felt the need to brutally shut down any mild hopes the nice young man at the counter might have had towards his (once again, that infuriating designation as "his") might have had towards his Lauren. As they accepted their drinks, the light smell of her heated skin from running together made his nostrils flare appreciatively as they found a place to sit. Thomas watched his new wife curl inside herself.

"So..." she finally ventured. "Is there anyone in my life now that doesn't report back to you?"

Frowning just slightly behind his RayBans, Thomas watched the drooping head of his bride, not looking at him as she examined her paper cup with an unnecessary degree of interest. "It's my job to keep you safe, darling," he said calmly.

He was unprepared for the level of rage he encountered when Lauren's furious gaze met his. "Keep me safe?" she hissed, at least attempting to keep her anger at a manageable level. "Keep me *safe?* You stole my life, you-"

"Mr. Williams, what a pleasure!"

Lauren gritted her teeth and looked down at her chai.

"...congratulations, of course, on your happy news!" The supercilious creature still fawning over Thomas was beginning to strain the fine lines around his mouth, a "tell" that Lauren was coming to recognize as, "I'm going to be polite because we're in public but if you don't shut the fuck up, I'll kill you."

"Hello, I'm 'the wife,' I guess," Lauren chuckled humorlessly, "what's your name?" She pointedly extended her hand, hating the look of subtle amusement on her horrible husband's face.

"Oh!" The creature assaulting her husband stilled, perhaps in shock as she turned towards 'The Bride.' "Ah... Maryanne Harding, from the Berkshire Harding's? We're neighbors, you know- oh, you're new to the neighborhood, so of course-" The effusive creature's narrative died off as she examined Thomas's mysterious and lovely new bride up close. Bloody *hell*, the girl was beautiful, of course. A forced social smile was spreading across those pretty pink lips of hers.

"It's a pleasure, Mrs. uh, Harding. I hope you'll forgive

my cluelessness, I'm still learning about the neighborhood," Lauren lied with a warm smile and an equally ignorant understanding of who this woman was and if Mrs. Harding even mattered. For instance, if her new husband didn't like this officious woman, *would* he kill her? Like, if this person that Lauren did not know was annoying enough to murder, would Thomas just... make it happen? In the woman's expensive stainless-steel kitchen? Driving home from the spa to find her brake lines cut a little too late? Lauren didn't know who her scary new spouse murdered, or why. And the enormity of this realization stopped her dead in her tracks, no matter how desperately she tried to pretend everything was "normal."

Eyeing his wife's sudden pallor, Thomas's brow creased and he smoothly cut off Maryanne Harding's (from the Berkshire Harding's) patter mid-sentence and rose, leaning over to take Lauren's arm and helping her to her feet. "Excuse us, Maryanne, we have an appointment."

Watching them walk rapidly in the direction of Thomas's house, the woman called after them hopefully, "We must have dinner soon!"

Slowing once they turned a corner, Thomas slid his arm around Lauren's waist, steadying her with a squeeze. "What has you so upset, darling? You looked like you might faint for a moment."

"I just..." she wasn't foolish enough to discuss something as incendiary as her spouse killing people out in the open, so Lauren shook her head and forced a smile. "Nothing important." Her fury from before was gone, and now the full enormity of what she'd married into what truly sinking in. How did Arabella stand it? How was she still sane? "Can we run back, now?"

Eyeing her speculatively, Thomas finally gave a nod, taking off in a smooth run to match hers.

Back at the house, Tom casually began stripping off his sweaty clothes in front of her, just the way he had that first morning. It was when he smiled devilishly and purred, "Come share a shower, little girl," that Lauren made some garbled excuse and not-quite scampered from the room. She was in the huge kitchen, pressing a cool cloth against her face when he appeared behind her soundlessly, making his poor bride jump and almost shriek.

"Why do you *do* that?" Lauren gasped, dropping the wet washcloth and having to bend down to pick it up. She froze when her beautifully suited husband stepped right behind her, hands going to her hips to "support" her as she picked up the fabric. Lauren could feel his hardening cock press against her ass as she stood up, and mumbled, "I can pick up something off the floor without help, thank you." She tried to step away, but Thomas's big hands tightened against her waist as he pulled her against his chest.

"I want to know why you turned sheet-white when meeting the officious Maryanne Harding." His voice was colder. Crisp. There was none of the subtle humor or playfulness from the morning.

"How many people have you killed?"

The horrifying question burst out of Lauren's mouth before she could even think and she gasped in horror, slapping her hand against her mouth. Thomas abruptly yanked her around to meet his eyes, blazing and his mouth in a flat line.

"What are you talking about?" If she'd thought his tone was cold before, it was polar now, and terror rose up and nearly choked her. She was going to die. Her husband was going to kill her, right in his gourmet kitchen.

"I'm sorry!" Lauren gasped, "I don't- I don't know what made me ask that I'm sorry I don't want to know and I apologize for asking and-"

He gave her a quick, brisk shake that nearly separated her head from her body. "What does that have to do with this morning?"

Shrugging while she tried to force her trembling mouth to form words again, his young wife finally forced out, "You sh-shot Frank and said you would kill me and I knew that women- Harding of the Berkshire Harding's-" here, Lauren gave a hysterical little giggle and mumbled, "I've never heard someone say something so stupid, outside of the movies."

Sighing impatiently, Thomas filled a glass with water and sat down on the same chair where he'd spanked her the other day. Lauren dug in her heels as he pulled her towards his lap. Not another spanking! She moaned internally and shook her head.

"This isn't punitive," he said impatiently, "come sit down before you faint or say anything else so deeply foolish."

That worked, pissing her off made Lauren's shaking disappear as her eyes narrowed, but she perched bitterly on his knee and took the glass of water.

"Drink it." The expression on his beautiful face told her Thomas was losing his granite hold on his self-control and she hastily did as he told her. "Now," his gaze was polar blue again and Lauren sat very still. "You have some idea of what you have married into. I corrected you rather harshly when you mentioned the Bratva out in public-something that will never happen again, will it darling?" Thomas paused and gazed at her coldly until his bride nodded in a jerking fashion, like a marionette. "Today you showed the wisdom and restraint of not saying anything until we returned home, which is very good."

Briefly, Lauren hated herself as she felt a sudden surge of warmth at his praise.

Thomas's hold around her waist loosened a bit and his thumb began stroking the strip of skin visible between her tank top and shorts. "I do not kill people for being annoying, or half the population of London would be dead by now." Her wide, horrified eyes told him that Lauren did not appreciate his little joke. "In fact, I very rarely take a life, or order someone else to do it. I would make every possible effort to avoid it." The slight hope she felt was abruptly crushed by his cool, indifferent tone. "It is messy. These events require a great deal of... cleaning up and backtracking."

Lauren simply stared at his beautiful, indifferent face. Her unspeakable husband avoided murder simply because it was inconvenient?

"It's too late to pretend that you've married a man who simply goes to the office every day and attends to stocks and bonds- though you would be surprised how much more of my time is taken by financial dealings than anything else. But you will never be involved in anything so... serious. There are secrets you're required to carry for the rest of your life." Thomas watched as her huge purple eyes filled with tears, "I am sorry. But your silence and your obedience keep you safe. Your father alive. And because you're a smart girl, your friends like Macie-" Horrified, Lauren tried to pull away from him again, but he tightened his grip until she was still. "-like

Macie will never know a thing. There is a reason The Corporation wives spend quite a bit of time together, because no one else can understand your position." Thomas watched her closely as his bride turned her face away from him. "You did the right thing by pushing Macie away," he added gently.

She finally seemed to collect herself and looked back at him, studying the translucent blue of his eyes in the morning sun coming through the window, his dark hair and sharply defined cheekbones and jaw. How strong his hands were, holding her down. The feel of his muscled thighs under her own.

"You're a monster," Lauren said tonelessly, and simply stared at Thomas until his hands loosened and he let her rise from his lap.

She was alone in Thomas's beautiful house after he left for The Corporation's offices without speaking to her again. A look out the front window showed that Chuck was waiting patiently at the curb. Lauren was grateful that she had a rehearsal for the season debut in a couple of weeks and just needed to burn off a couple of hours before it was time to leave. She'd already practiced, worked out, cleaned the huge kitchen of her insignificant mess from lunch, and now... absently wiping her sweaty hands on her jeans (Thomas wasn't home and she'd damn well wear jeans if she wanted to- until, you know, he was home, and stuff...) Lauren was standing in front of his office door. Her new husband had given her a brisk (and short) tour of the home, calmly explaining that any room with a locked door was logically not meant to be entered by her. This included the room on the second floor that he referred to as his office, and the room next to their bedroom on the third.

She'd been happy to see the beautifully remodeled home had

a third-floor laundry room which meant she didn't have to enter the basement, which she found creepy. Along with walking her through the suspiciously elaborate security system which looked closer to something Buckingham Palace might require, Thomas introduced her to the Panic Room, "Once the locks are set, darling they do not open for twelve hours" the alarm button in each room that went directly to The Corporation security, and incongruously, the lovely butler's pantry off the kitchen that was filled with endless amounts of sweets of every kind and a rather impressive wine selection.

Damn him, Lauren had thought bitterly, *"my two biggest weaknesses!*

But here she was, in front of The Room She Was Not To Enter, and of course, dying to do so. What would he have? Knives and guns in the desk drawers? A wall full of spikes and swords? A live leopard, like the pets some of the Colombian drug lords thought made them look terrifying? Reaching out one hand, she tried the door handle. You never knew. Thomas might have forgotten to lock it. But the solid oak door didn't even more under her determined rattle, so Lauren sighed and got on her knees, laying her head down on the polished floor to look under the door. Other than the nicely polished legs of some chairs and an expansive desk, she could see nothing, so she crossly sat up, leaning against the door and drawing up her knees to rest her arms on them, thinking. Which was the sight Thomas viewed on his home security camera as he sat in a board meeting, looking at his iPad and keeping a smile from creeping across his face.

He knew his Lauren would not be quelled for long. Settling back and listening to Number One drone, he thought back to the only other locked room in his house, next to their bedroom. Perhaps he would accidentally leave that door unlocked. He was looking forward to seeing her expression when she opened *that* door.

Lauren was grateful when it came time to put her cello in its case and head out the door to rehearsal. Thomas had made it immediately clear that her new bodyguard would be driving her everywhere. "For your security, darling." When she'd glared at him, he'd chuckled infuriatingly as he stroked her cheek. "You're new to London, you wouldn't want to be lost or in an emergency without assistance, would you?"

Translate that to- 'I intend to keep an eye on you every goddamned second of the day,' Lauren thought bitterly as she hauled her gigantic instrument out the front door and suddenly into the capable hands of Chuck.

"Let me get that for you, Miss Lauren," he assured blandly, easily swinging the heavy instrument in one hand as he opened the car door with the other.

Being back into the crowd of musicians laughing, chatting, and catching up made Lauren feel - for the first time since that terrible night in Thomas's office - that her life was normal again. Laughing and nodding as she listened to one of the violinist's memories of his trip to Greece with his wife and children, she stiffened when she heard Macie's pretty laugh from across the room. When Lauren's friend turned to see her staring with a faint, hopeful smile, her own dropped and Macie turned away. Then reality came back like a slap in the face, and the new Mrs. Williams numbly found her seat and began tuning her cello.

The misery of her dearest friend's dismissal ate steadily away at Lauren during the rehearsal, forcing her to pay closer attention. In the past, she could always lose herself in the music, no matter what concerns or worries nagged at her in real life. But the cyclic feelings of loss, fear, fury, and frustration grew until she was a veritable cyclone of emotion by the end of the rehearsal. So, when she checked her phone and there was a message from Number One's wife informing her The Corporation men would be late in a meeting that night and would Lauren like to join her for a drink? Lauren was happy to type back, *"Yes! When and where?"*

"So..." Arabella waited until their obviously flirty waiter left their table before she leaned in, cradling her cocktail between her hands. "How are you? How is it going? Are you..." her shrewd brown eyes roved over Lauren's face, "is everything, you know, all right between you two?"

Delaying as she took an appreciative sip of the cocktail Arabella ordered for her - a Sritangtini? - Lauren tried to decide what to say. She'd paid the price for trusting people who were nice to her in the past, and she still didn't know what Arabella's motivations were.

Finally forcing a smile, Lauren looked up and shrugged. "Well. It's all going well. I mean, all things considered, it's going well, and so..." she died off, having run out of anything she felt comfortable saying.

The older woman laughed, her head thrown back and looking very lovely, proven by the several admiring stares of the men around them. In fact, Lauren thought the selection of the Connaught Bar was a little surprising. It was beautiful, elegant, very "old-school" London, but they seemed to be the only women in a sea of expensively suited men relaxing after a long day of fucking each other over in the business world. Even Chuck had raised one discreet brow as he'd seated himself a couple of tables away, giving them their privacy.

"I know, dearie. It's difficult to say anything, especially in public." Arabella took another swig of her cocktail and raised a hand to their waiter for another.

"Oh, I don't-" Lauren tried to protest when his white-gloved hand placed another full glass next to her half-finished one.

"Live a little!" her friend gently urged her glass to her lips, "It is delicious, right? And you look like you could use some girl talk."

Idly twisting the glass in her fingers, Lauren chuckled humorlessly. "Thomas said-" she was looking at the glass and at not Arabella, not seeing the woman lean forward avidly. "He said that's why Corporation wives hang out together so much because no one else can understand our position."

Shrugging, Arabella made a noise of agreement, finishing cocktail number two. "He is completely correct, your Thomas. I feel guilty being so happy that you married Number Two and that you're so sweet and fun to be with-" Like magic, another glass appeared before the woman and she took a long, somewhat inelegant gulp, Lauren joining her and finishing her first.

This thing really was delicious, she thought, savoring the lemongrass and Kaffir lime juice.

"-but it's such a relief to have someone to talk to."

Lauren nodded a little vehemently. She was feeling more relaxed now, that tightness in her neck and chest from rehearsal not so noticeable. "Exactly. Never knowing what I can say or what I can't. I mean, even today with Thomas's neighbor, I-" She took another swallow, "-I never know what he's going to do. What he *could* do. And that's the scariest part."

The waiter was back with a third drink for her and a fourth for Arabella. When he left, Arabella's voice dropped to a whisper. "Has he hurt you, honey?"

"What?" Unaccountably, Lauren was insulted for Thomas. "Me? No!"

"Good, you didn't fight him," Arabella nodded knowingly, "I'm relieved. I was so worried he'd hurt you quite badly if you put up a fuss."

Thinking of the spanking her new husband had given her in the kitchen a couple of days ago, Lauren squirmed uncomfortably. But she knew that wasn't what Arabella meant, and the woman actually looked a little disappointed. "Why do you think Thomas likes to uh, hurt women?"

"Not just women," Number One's wife began to giggle, a little shrill and a titch sloppy. She was finishing her fourth drink and gestured at a man pushing an elegant little martini cart around the room. "Let's try something new."

"And maybe some food?" Lauren asked hopefully, she was starving, but she thought getting some food into this woman would be a good idea. The dark, mean-faced man sitting with Chuck was undoubtedly Arabella's minder and neither of them looked happy right now.

Following her nervous glance at their bodyguards, the older woman immediately pulled back. "Just some water please, and your small plates menu," she ordered, and Lauren relaxed a little. Arabella was flushed, her platinum blonde hair just slightly out of its elegant chignon and her tanned skin too ruddy. Stabilizing the blood alcohol level of her (maybe?) friend was a good idea.

The one thing she was quite certain of was that the horrible Number One was not a man to displease. She could tell Arabella was desperate to let loose but this was *not* the place. Lauren felt an odd sort of protectiveness for the woman, even knowing she probably couldn't trust her and that at more than fifteen years older and over a decade in The Corporation, Arabella should definitely know better. Even so, she persisted. "Why do you think Thomas likes to hurt women?"

Arabella laughed incredulously, then stopped as she looked at Lauren's puzzled face. "You mean, he hasn't?" abandoning the small plates menu, she leaned forward again. "Thomas hasn't you know-" she drunkenly waved her hands around, "safe words and the titles and all that?"

"Lauren. Hello, darling. I see the two of you are having a little Hen's Night?"

Lauren's heart froze. Thomas was *right behind her,* his hand on her chair and his body heat radiating through the thin cotton of her sundress. His voice was low and beautifully composed, the tender and slightly indulgent tone of a husband here to collect his wife after one too many cocktails with a friend. Swallowing against the lump in her throat, she croaked, "Yes? I mean, Arabella told me the board was meeting tonight, so we thought we'd-" Lauren looked at the other woman who suddenly looked terrified. Was this an unauthorized outing? Feeling the need to cover for Number One's wife, she forced a smile, "So we thought we'd have dinner and catch up while we waited for you all to... uh... finish?"

Looking up, she couldn't quite gauge his expression. Thomas had his urbane smile in place, but his grip on her shoulder was slightly too firm and he hovered over her, almost protectively. "Of course, darling. I'm glad the two of you kept busy while we finished up some boring details." He chuckled in a charming fashion, his eyes crinkling and white teeth flashing. The "Board meeting" was actually an execution list of underperforming employees, of which Frank Marsh was spared because of his new familial association with the Vice-President of Jaguar Holdings. The other three men would not be so fortunate.

His Lauren's eyes were wide and anxious, but her smile was sweet and her voice calm as she stood, putting her napkin on the table and leaning over to shakily air-kiss Arabella's cheek. "Thanks again for the night out, it was so nice to chat."

"You, too!" her friend shrilled, smiling widely as her bodyguard stepped up behind her.

Being escorted out of the bar, Lauren resentfully eyed Chuck's placid expression. He obviously had called Thomas, reporting on her like an adult calling out an underage partygoer. She was too upset to notice the eyes of most of the men in the bar watching her leave, though the suited arm of her husband possessively sliding around her waist was quite clear.

"Goodnight, Straker."

Lauren could feel the dull rumble of Thomas's deep voice along her spine as Chuck politely bid them both good night, then sheared off as she was helped into her husband's Jaguar. Her fingers clenched the fabric of her dress when he suddenly leaned over her, then relaxed as Thomas simply clicked her seat belt. His low chuckle as he withdrew from her side of the car and shut the door made her hiss like a cat. They drove in silence for a while, until he suddenly commented, "Next time, I expect you to contact me first if you intend to deviate from your schedule."

It was such an odd way to put it that Lauren turned to stare at his cold, beautiful profile, more confused than afraid. "My what, my schedule? I went to practice and then Arabella texted me and told me you were all in a late meeting and that we should meet for drinks? I thought you knew?" She didn't want to say that she assumed he'd approved the outing because that really did sound completely pathetic. Though, she did, indeed, assume that.

He looked at her briefly as he shifted gears. "No. I was not aware of the change in plans until Straker contacted me."

It took Lauren a moment to realize he meant her new bodyguard because he was already cemented as "Chuck" in her mind. "Okay..." she said cautiously, "I guess I thought... you'd just said today that The Corporation wives stuck together because..." They were pulling into the driveway of their townhouse and the garage door closing behind them when Thomas took her chin firmly between his long fingers.

"No, darling. I was unaware. And I do. Not. Wish. To be unaware of your whereabouts. Ever again." Thomas could see by the sudden terror in Lauren's eyes that his tone was fiercer than he'd planned. Drawing in a calming breath, he forced himself to relax. "I know Arabella texted you, it's not your fault. But you must check with me first. She may be a Corporation wife, but that doesn't mean I trust her. Nor should you."

Puzzling over his warning, Lauren absently allowed Thomas to help her out of the car and through the door to their kitchen.

"You haven't eaten, have you?" She looked up, startled to see he'd spoken again, opening the huge stainless-steel refrigerator.

"Um... no. We were just about to order when you showed up," Lauren admitted, watching her new husband pull out a series of items; eggs, bacon, cheese, and mushrooms.

Thomas slipped out of his jacket, laying it over a chair and rolling up his sleeves. Despite herself, she shivered, watching his long, capable fingers fold up the fine cotton of his shirt. His forearms were broad and strongly muscled, and unbidden the vision of how easily he'd manhandled her in bed that early morning made Lauren shiver. She scowled to see a slight smile cross his lips, but her infuriating new spouse said nothing. He asked her a few calming questions about how the rehearsal went, what she did that day, as he cooked a beautiful-looking omelet, slicing some fresh fruit and putting in some toast to brown.

Setting the kitchen table as he finished, Lauren was struck with a moment of Deja vu. Looking up to catch her glistening eyes, Thomas asked, "What are you thinking?"

Shaking her head and smiling with somewhat forced cheer, Lauren took the plate he offered her. "Oh, it's just... my mom used to make this for me sometimes, 'breakfast for dinner,' she'd say." To her gratitude, he simply smiled and pulled out her chair. She wouldn't cry about her mom in front of him. Not *him*.

"Ironic," Thomas mused, seating himself and offering her the fruit plate. "My mother did the same."

Lauren's fork froze over the omelet. Her mysterious spouse was offering *information?* Freely? Unfortunately, even though she kept silent, he didn't offer anything else and the conversation went back to safer, duller things. When they were nearly finished, he leaned back and eyed her speculatively. "You looked uncomfortable when I showed up," he finally said, "and Arabella looked a bit worse for wear."

Shrugging awkwardly, she tried to brush it off. "I think she just wanted to let her hair down, have a little fun. That's all."

Thomas was watching her, and that beautiful blue gaze of his was piercing. "You seemed uncomfortable with some of the things Arabella had said to you when we spoke yesterday. What in particular, darling?"

She felt like a butterfly pinned to one of those long display boards in the Natural History Museum in London. Lauren had toured through the museum on a school trip in high school, her first trip to Europe. Rubbing her hand over a suddenly aching forehead, she tried to decide what to say.

Finally, exhausted, she blurted, "Arabella keeps asking me if you've hurt me yet." She looked up to see the same look of surprise and disgust he'd worn when she'd timidly offered herself, sobbing, on their wedding night. Plowing on uncomfortably, she persisted, "When she was uh, when she was helping me get ready before the wedding ceremony, she told me to..." the unreality of the conversation caught up with her. There was nothing in her life thus far that prepared her for such a bizarre conversation such as this, and with a man such as this.

"Yes?" Thomas's voice was cold but controlled. "She told you what, darling?"

"She told me that if I resisted you, you would- uh, you would like to- to hurt me, so she said to not say 'no' and just... let you." Lauren couldn't even look up from her plate. She could feel the chill of his rage and just gripped her napkin in her lap, wishing she'd never opened her mouth.

"Lauren." His resonant, deep voice was suddenly calm, almost caressing. "Look at me, lovely."

Swallowing against the whimper that wanted to escape from her throat, she looked up at her confusing, beautiful, terrifying husband. His eyes seemed to soften when he watched her bite into her lower lip.

"Baby," he said gently, "have I ever forced you into bed?" Her blonde head dropped, but she shook it back and forth.

"No."

"Have I ever hurt you in bed?"

"No." Lauren's head was still bowed, so she only heard Thomas's sigh as he pushed away his plate and hers, rising and walking around to her side of the table.

"Look at me." Unwillingly, her eyes rose to see him bending over her, helping her rise to her feet and then briskly hoisting her onto the long farm table. "Lauren. Darling. Look at me."

They were nearly eye to eye now, thanks to the extra height of the antique oak table and Lauren forced herself to meet his gaze. "Arabella was trying to scare you. I don't know why..." his brow briefly creased, then Thomas smiled at her, a warm, reassuring smile that almost made her relax until she remembered who she was dealing with. "This explains so much about our wedding night," he chuckled ruefully. "I am sorry she frightened you, darling."

Lauren was startled to hear that he almost did sound regretful. "So, um, what was that stuff, I mean, what did she mean about safe words and titles and-" she died off again as she watched a flash of fury go through his polar gaze.

Breathing in, Thomas seemed to calm himself and when he looked at her again, his eyes were the warm color of the Caribbean. "My darling, part of what Arabella said was true," his jaw tensed for a moment, "but it was my right to discuss it with you." His fingers were sliding over the smooth skin of her thighs, bared from her new position on the table, the rasp of his calloused hands feeling oddly soothing. "I do enjoy dominating you in bed. I do enjoy being your Sir."

Brow creased, Lauren remembered him referring to himself as "Sir" as she was shaking from an orgasm, more than once. "What does that mean?"

Briefly, Thomas looked incredulous before he recalled who he was speaking to. His new wife's guileless eyes watched him apprehensively. "Do you know what a dominant-submissive relationship is?"

Entertainingly, her expression twisted into one of disgust. "Like those shitty *Shades of Grey* books? God! Ugh!"

Thomas laughed uproariously before he stopped himself. "Not quite, lovely. Tell me, why did those disgust you?"

Lauren leaned back and stared at him judgmentally, "Seriously? They were shit! I tried to read the first one and had to give it up- god, her pitiful characters and that insipid dialogue?" She shuddered, suddenly making him adore her even more. "Ugh! No one talks like that. I mean, I may have been-" He watched with amusement as his bride shut her mouth abruptly. ('I might have been a virgin,' was what she'd been about to say, and his barely concealed smirk told her he knew it.) "Anyway. They sucked. I may not be an expert in Dom/sub relationships, but I can't picture anyone talking like that with a straight face-"

She was cut off abruptly as Thomas suddenly kissed her greedily, all tongue and teeth until the girl was gasping and flat on her back. "My clever girl," he crooned approvingly, "such a good girl." He watched as she shivered involuntarily. "You are, of course, correct. It was utter shite." Kissing her again with a certain arousing degree of savagery, he smiled against her mouth as Lauren went limp. "But in a true relationship between a Sir and his beautiful girl..." his hands were moving again, spreading her thighs as he slipped between them and stroking up her neck, down her arms and suddenly unbuttoning the front of her sundress.

"In a true relationship, it is the submissive, darling, who has the control. Just as I gave you the first time we were together." His hands were tickling lightly around the cups of her bra until it somehow disappeared and then circled her nipples, his eyes suddenly dark and intent as he watched her reaction. "It is a Sir's responsibility to take care of his beautiful." Here, his lips pressed against one stiff nipple, and then the other. "Perfect." Kiss and a flick of his tongue, enjoying watching her startled gasp and how his wife's back arched. "Darling."

Lauren's eyes were closed, but she could feel his mouth against her breast, the feel of the words his lips were shaping against the painfully sensitive nerves in her nipples. "So, you are a Dom and you want me to-" To her consternation, Thomas pulled his warm mouth away from her breasts as she whined involuntarily.

"I will never force you to do anything, lovely," he was leaning over her, hands stroking along her thighs and pushing her skirt higher, carefully not looking at her bare breasts, pink nipples gleaming wet from his mouth. "But, yes. I intend to be your Sir. To care for you and pamper you. I will give you all sorts of delicious new experiences if you will trust me to guide you." To Lauren's embarrassed relief, he bent his dark head to kiss along her neck and back to her breasts again.

Without even thinking about what she was doing, her hands came up to cradle his head as Thomas toyed with her breasts again, running his tongue over her skin and his sharp teeth making her yelp. "Do you want to, you know, hurt me? Like she said?" Her voice came out smaller than she preferred, and Lauren's eyes were pleading with him to... what?

With an effort, he pulled back, stroking her skin as he smiled at her. "Not in the way she means. Do you remember me sliding my cock up you the first time? Rubbing against the top of you?" Thomas patiently pulled her hands away from her beet-red face. "It's like that, baby. It can hurt, just as much as it feels good. I will never give too much of one without the other, and you will come like the good girl you are. Every time."

He could already feel the strong muscles in her thighs loosen, the tight abdominals relax against his roaming hands. Lauren wasn't trying to pull away, she seemed more transfixed by his words. Gritting his teeth against the need to rip off her panties and shove himself inside her, Thomas forced himself to calm down. "Would you like your Sir to take care of you? You needn't decide anything tonight, darling. Just... let me make you feel good. Can you do that?"

Could she? Lauren watched the shades of blue sweep through his gaze. Her mysterious husband was far too good at schooling his expressions, she had no way of truly knowing how he felt. But his eyes... furiously cold, sometimes warm and almost caring, and now an alluring calm that made her want to bathe in him, in his vision of what they could be.

"Just," she stopped and licked her suddenly dry lips, "just for tonight? Nothing is written in stone?"

His rough hand ran down her cheek, making her close her eyes. "Nothing that you don't want."

Lauren sat up, holding onto his shirt with sweaty hands and took a deep breath. "Okay."

She was surprised by the sudden ferocity of his kiss, but then Thomas pulled back. "If you want me to stop, you will say 'red.' If you would prefer I slow down, you will say 'yellow.' Like, stoplights. Do you understand?"

That's what Arabella meant about 'safe words,' Lauren realized. She may have been a virgin, but that didn't make her clueless. "Okay," she managed, trying to nod decisively.

Thomas stepped back. "Unbutton my shirt."

Tongue slightly between her teeth, Lauren did as he told her.

"Good girl, now take it off." Her hands smoothed away the fine cotton and pulled his shirt away from his broad shoulders. He was beautiful in the light from the kitchen's warm glow, and she sighed a little in appreciation. "Touch me."

No hesitation, her fingers slid over his biceps, his sculpted pectorals and abdominal muscle firm, but without the overly sculpted look from endless, self-indulgent hours in the weight room.

"Now, I'm going to touch you, darling." Lauren's eyes closed and she shivered a little as he pulled her to her feet, letting her unbuttoned dress slide down her body along with her bra, leaving her in a pair of white undies. Plain cotton ones, not the fancy bits The Corporation Wives had given her. "So sweet, " he approved, kneeling to run his mouth along them, puffing warm breaths of air and finally making her shriek in surprise his lips and teeth fastened over the fabric shielding her hard clitoris. It felt like nothing was there to stop him and Lauren was shocked and embarrassed to realize how close she was to coming.

"Hold on to the table, baby..." she yelped again as Thomas slung a leg over each shoulder and attacked her pussy, throwing her off balance and forced to grasp wildly at the wood surface to steady herself as he yanked her panties aside and ran his tongue along her and then pointed it, jabbing it into her opening. She felt the vibration of his chuckles against her center as her husband soothed, "That's all right, lovely girl. I'm going to make you come now. Go ahead as soon as you're ready, but-" here, his hands tightened down on the soft skin of her thighs and Lauren froze. "I want to hear every single sound, baby. Every whimper. Every moan. Can you do that for your Sir?" His mouth was attacking her again by then and all she could do was nod helplessly as she squeezed her thighs against his head, gasping at the feeling of his lips, tongue, and teeth all moving against, inside and around her. And when two thick fingers slid up and inside her, Lauren let out a very unladylike yelp.

"OH! Oh, my GOD that feels-" her flailing hands were seized and held over her head as her beautiful and frightening husband rose and loomed over her.

He looked her over, mouth still wet from her pussy. "I'm going to make you scream, little girl," he promised in a husky tone. Before her dazed senses could register the unzipping of his trousers and the smooth rasp of the fine wool down his thick thighs, Thomas had shoved his entire cock up inside her, making Lauren's entire body stiffen like she'd grabbed a live wire and she shrieked in surprise and pleasure and relief as she came screaming, just as he'd ordered. And again, hearing Thomas groan as he braced his feet to push up into her harder against the convulsing walls of her channel, enjoying her body's slick efforts to push him out and clutch his cock at the same time.

His arms slipped under her knees and pulled her wider, making Lauren grasp vaguely for the edges of the table, looking up at his eyes, narrowed and vaguely feral, a hard set to his jaw. She was reminded of their dance together when his hips slipped into a sinuous rhythm, sliding and slipping his cock in and out of her as his thumb moved from her leg to her clit, drumming it lightly as he began pushing into her harder. "I do believe," he said, just a bit breathlessly, "that you have one more orgasm inside this tight little cunt for your Sir, don't you?"

"I..." she was still staring at him, watching the cords in his neck tighten as he seemed to fight against his own finish. After his thumb pressed down and began moving in a more determined, circular pattern Lauren grabbed at his arms.

Thomas bent lower, purring as he smiled devilishly against her mouth. "One. More."

"Yes Sir!" his wife gasped as she mindlessly obeyed him and came, clamping down so hard that his head fell backward, then dropped to her chest. Lauren's hands looped around his shoulders as Thomas buried his face between her breasts, growling harshly as he shoved once, then again, and one more time until she felt the heat of him finish through her, warming her lower half as she shook against all her nerve endings below her waist firing off, all at once.

"Such a good girl," Thomas praised hoarsely against the soft skin of her chest. "Such a very, good girl. Your Sir is so pleased."

Chapter 10 – Until I Take It Off You

In which Lauren finds it increasingly difficult to say "no" to Thomas, even if she knows she should.

Had Lauren been given a moment to consider what she might think a Dom/sub sexual encounter might include, it wasn't being held immobile in Thomas's huge walk-in shower as he easily kept her legs open, resting his chin on her shoulder and enjoying the sight of the showerhead spurting water in a staccato rhythm against her bare and defenseless clitoris. He'd lifted her up by her thighs, resting her back against his broad chest and then spreading her legs wide. Naturally, Lauren immediately attempted to close them, embarrassed, but Thomas refused to budge, having angled one of the showerheads just so. She'd not noticed at the time until her diabolical spouse turned the water on.

"T- Thomas?" she gasped, hand flying back to slide through his hair, "This is really inten- AH! -Intense and I'm- AH! GOD!" She could feel his chest shake with laughter as she writhed in his grip, trying to close her legs against the implacable spray of the water against really, what was a decisively overworked portion of her body.

After the wild episode on the table, Thomas had stayed inside Lauren as he carried her up the stairs to their bedroom, the curl and stretch of her walls around him hardening his cock again. He'd made her sit upright, chests pressed together so he could feel the arch of her back, hear her moan as he easily bounced her up and down on his shaft. But back to the present. This was round three- did it count as three if Thomas just used his fingers and the shower head?- and Lauren was fairly certain she'd be walking with a limp in the morning.

His dark head bent closer, enjoying Lauren's pretty face, made lovely and carnal from her orgasm, mouth wet and open, lashes fluttering as she fought to hold on to her sanity.

"So beautiful," Thomas mused, "so beautiful for your Sir." He could tell by the desperate movements of her once-strong legs, muscles now slack and shaking, that his lovely new wife was quite finished. His darker, more greedy side wanted to push her lithe body harder, force her to come again and again until she couldn't remember how to beg him to stop. *She's new to this,* he reluctantly reminded himself. Groaning internally, Thomas gently rinsed her slickened thighs and pussy and closed her legs, shifting Lauren to carry her bridal style out into the bedroom and wrapping her in a big terrycloth robe.

Gingerly shifting her hips and trying to find a more comfortable position for her sore and throbbing center, Lauren sleepily opened her eyes as she felt her head lifted and put on her mysterious and scary husband's long thigh. He was holding a brush- one of those fancy silver ones, broad with a raised "W" on the back.

"That's a pretty brush," she mumbled, feeling slow and clumsy as she tried to make her lips move properly.

"It's quite useful," Thomas said oddly, a hint of mirth in his voice. Lauren's brows drew together in confusion, but it seemed like too much effort to appear puzzled and she made a vague affirmative-sounding noise. "I'm going to brush your hair, little girl. Just relax. You've been so very good for your Sir."

"Sirrrr...?" Lauren groaned in frustration. Why couldn't she form a coherent sentence?

Running the bristles gently through her blonde curls, Thomas grinned, just a bit. "You're frustrated because you're sleepy and confused, aren't you? Having trouble trying to talk?" Her head nodded and she hummed in agreement. Running the brush through the next section of hair, he soothed, "You're in subspace, baby. When you've had a particularly intense evening, your body produces endorphins and enkephalins, which can make you feel a bit like you're having an out of body experience."

He waited, continuing to use the elegant silver brush on her hair until Lauren stirred enough to mumble, "Oh. Okay."

Thomas knew she was too intelligent to not want to know more about what he'd done to her, but his bride was exhausted and she needed rest. Another dark smile crossed his lips. She was going to have trouble getting out of bed in the morning. "It's time to sleep, lovely," he soothed, brushing his mouth on her forehead. "Be a good girl and close your eyes. I have you safe." Lauren was out like a light, most likely before he even finished the sentence, but The Corporation's terrifying Number Two carried on brushing her hair, looking forward to the time he'd be using the other side on her shapely little ass.

Thomas was shaving in the gleaming master bath when he heard the pathetic whimper the following morning. Grinning, he ambled out into the bedroom, wiping the shaving cream off his face as he surveyed the limp form of his bride attempting to get out of bed. She was making a sort of pitiful paddling motion with her hands, much like baby turtles trying to get into the surf before the seagulls caught them. When her resentful gaze met his, Thomas schooled his features into something resembling concern.

"Ah, good morning darling. I suspected you might be a bit uncomfortable today." He leaned over her, clad only in a white towel wrapped around his waist and a slightly lecherous smile.

Pushing a handful of hair out of her eyes, Lauren tried to control her embarrassment and fury over having given in so easily to this terrible man. Clearing her throat, she finally managed, "Yes... this should be uh... challenging. Uh. Walking. Today." Looking up, she could see nothing but care and concern on Thomas's beautiful face, which instantly put her on guard.

"Shall I help you move past this discomfort, lovely?" he chuckled at the look of suspicion on Lauren's face. She knew him so well, already. "Since you won't be running this morning-" pausing as she made a choked sound as she tried to sit up, he stroked her cheek tenderly. "I can assist you in not thinking about your sore, tender kitty-" Lauren gave a high-pitched noise when his broad palm cupped her center, and he continued on as if he hadn't heard her, "-I think you'll be quite surprised to see how quickly you can forget."

If Lauren had had more than three hours of sleep, or her drunken hormone hangover wasn't confusing her, she might have caught on to Thomas's wording and scooted away. But as it was, his warm hand actually felt rather nice on her desperately sore pussy and his sweet tone of concern was lulling her into a false sense of security. He could see it - see the moment her resistance and suspicious waned - and Number Two almost felt a pang of guilt about manipulating his sweet, just-broken virginal bride.

Almost.

"First..."

Lauren gave another high-pitched yelp when his hand cupping her center was suddenly smoothing cream over her still-swollen lips. The lotion was cool and vaguely comforting as she felt the worst of the soreness and over-sensitivity fade away. Her face flamed as Thomas pulled fresh undies up her legs.

"Better?" Thomas leaned closer to her red face; eyes determined to stare at her lap until his hand moved to her chin to force his bride to look at him. "Better?" he repeated firmly.

"Yes, thank you," Lauren's gaze tried to flutter away like an anxious butterfly but he shook her chin lightly.

Bending in to kiss her lips, he smiled, just on this side of smug. "Very good. Now, for the second part. Why don't you tidy up in the bathroom and then come back out to me?" Thomas phrased it in the form of a question, but the girl had no such illusions, nodding and getting up slowly. Refusing to look back at him, Lauren hobbled her way into the pristine master bath and sat down on the toilet with a sigh of relief.

Last night had been much, much harder on the lower half of her body than even losing her virginity to her... that... to Thomas on what she still mentally referred to as the "No Diggity" night in honor of the song that apparently made every one of her morals go flying out the window of his Jaguar. Staring blankly at the greenery outside the paned windows, she edged around their discussion the night before.

Dom/sub. Huh.

Lauren had never heard it put like that, but she was assuming it was part of the wider BDSM world, but what part, she was uncertain. Thomas had waited for her agreement before doing anything with her sexually, which was deeply reassuring, even though the man HAD forced to her marry him. Flushing the toilet and washing her hands, she looked at her flushed cheeks, hair flying everywhere. Thomas Williams, the Terrible Number Two of Jaguar Holdings radiated danger, even before she knew what he was. So it shouldn't surprise her that the man was into exotic sex. Her hands slowed under the water; soap forgotten in her hand. If she didn't agree to be a sub, would he go somewhere else for it? Wouldn't that actually be a good thing? Lauren's eyes widened as she felt a sudden flush of fury sweep under her skin like a brush fire. *Hell, no!* she snarled internally, *He's my husband and-* Suddenly sitting down on the window seat, she stared out into the elegant little backyard garden.

What did that even mean? Did fidelity have any part of a hellish union like this? A marriage she was dragged into under pain of death to a- what did they call these people nowadays? Was Thomas a mobster or was that just a New York thing? Kingpin? No, too old-school. Shadowy organized crime lord? Burying her face in her still-wet hands, Lauren was torn between laughing and crying. Here she was, hiding in her husband's luxurious master bath and trying to figure out what kind of criminal she was married to?

A knock on the door made Lauren shoot upright. "Darling? I'm waiting for you." The composed tone of her scary-ass husband was still meant to convey she'd been hiding quite long enough. With a sigh, she ran her hands through her hair and then opened the door. Satan was standing there, in the form of the handsome Thomas Williams, well-groomed and already dressed in another expensive suit. He looked her up and down with a sardonic smile. "Much better." Taking her hand, he led her over to their huge walk-in closet slash dressing room. When she'd first seen it, Lauren had squee'ed internally. A dressing room! And all those cool dressers and storage bits and elaborate closet space! And, a huge, well-lit mirror in front of a table for her jewelry, makeup, and such. There was pitifully little there, she didn't wear much makeup and her only jewelry aside from her wedding rings were the few, treasured pieces passed down from her mother that she'd managed to hide from Frank.

"Stand right here," Thomas's hands were pulling her robe from her and then her bra, which made his shy bride's hands fly to cover her bare chest. "Ah, ah, ah." he chided, "You cannot hide your lovely body from me." He pushed his chest against her back, feeling the warmth of her bare skin seep through his dress shirt. "And why would you?" he murmured into her ear, enjoying Lauren's corresponding shiver. Pulling her hands away, he spoke lower, a darkly persuasive tone that she could *feel* as well as hear. "Why would you want to hide these beautiful breasts? Hmm?" Holding her wrists together with one hand he stroked the other over her pink nipples, enjoying watching them stiffen.

"Gorgeous, darling. A perfect size for holding... and squeezing..." he did both, hearing the little moan escape between her clenched teeth. "Firm enough not to need a bra, and these delightfully sensitive nipples, such a pretty color." Her diabolical spouse blew a warm breath on the aforementioned item and watched her shiver. Pulling back with a sigh, he smothered a grin as her eyes opened, looking mildly indignant that his attentions had ceased. "I have something for you."

Lauren's head was swimming a little between her dark husband toying with her breasts and the potent alchemy of his voice, but she managed, "Oh?" Looking down as he pulled something from a drawer, her brows rose. Thomas was holding a rather beautiful corset. The first one she'd ever worn was under her wedding dress, but she had really liked the sculpted waist it gave her. She had more of a swimmer's build - straight up and down instead of curves, and it made her feel rather luscious during the final fitting.

Before she remembered why she was wearing it.

"Now, darling. Raise your arms." Thomas was behind her again, close enough to feel his breath on her bare shoulder as he held the garment in front of her, shielding her breasts. Simply because it was covering that part of her from his amused gaze was reason enough to obey him, so she did. "I remembered how beautiful you looked in your corset under that lovely wedding dress," he began conversationally, settling the corset straight and taking the strings in his hands.

Lauren smiled with a little chuckle. "That's just what I was thinking of."

"Oh?" His beautiful cerulean gaze met hers in the mirror.

"Mmm-hmm," she nodded, "it was the first one I've ever worn, and- OH!" Thomas had taken the moment to yank the laces at her waist quite tightly. She could feel his practiced fingers rapidly tightening the laces downward towards her hips, the compression getting more aggressive as he went.

"Did you enjoy how lovely you looked in that white lace corset? Your tiny waist?" His gaze was on her back, but she could see a bit of a smile hovering around his mobile lips.

Lauren's hands were holding the top part of the corset to her breasts. It was a lovely pale green, satin, no itchy lace and wonderfully sleek. The cups were ruffled silk and felt smooth on her skin. "Yes?"

His eyes met hers again in the mirror as he gave another brisk tug, this time moving from the center upwards. "You don't sound certain, little girl."

She flushed, edging from one foot to the other. "How um- how do you know how to lace a corset, anyway? I doubt they had a course in this at Cambridge." He burst into laughter, those long fingers still moving the laces expertly up her spine.

"Have you been researching me, darling?"

Lauren shrugged one shoulder. "It's on The Corporation website. I looked you up before you called me in that day to..." Remembering suddenly that the whole meeting was a miserable sham, her voice died off.

Thomas tugged silently for a moment, harshly enough for Lauren's hands to fly from her front to hold on to the table for support. She could feel her ribs compressing in a bit, like the foldable legs on a card table but he was working so quickly she hadn't had a chance to notice.

"I learned the art of lacing a lady's corset," he murmured, "in New Orleans. In a boutique devoted to the means of shaping the female form. Corsets and waist-trainers, heels and hosiery..." she wheezed as he yanked the laces through the eyes just behind her breasts, and when Lauren could draw a breath, she could see her modest bosom heave in a somewhat buxom fashion, all flushed and pretty and swelling alluringly over the ruffled silk of the corset's cups. "It's quite precise, you see," her strange spouse continued, "one begins at the middle- because shaping the hips is quite different than the curve of the waist, or how the ribs sweep up to the breasts." He finished the lacing, tying off the cords with one last, deliberate jerk that pulled Lauren's grip loose from the table, making her fall back against him again.

"Beautiful," he growled, his resonant voice deepening, thickening as his hands followed the curve of her corseted waist, up her torso and stroking over the silk hiding her peaking nipples from him. Very gently, Thomas reached in to adjust her breasts to their best position, swelling alluringly over the confines of steel boning and satin. His hand went to her chin again. "Look at yourself. How beautiful, how arousingly perfect you are." One hand slid down her back and Lauren shivered. "Your posture is magnificent, proud and straight," he made a pleased noise and dropped a kiss on her bare shoulder.

Trying to draw in a deep breath, Lauren spoiled the moment by wheezing. "It's a little..." she gave a hiccup of air, "this is really tight. Can we-"

"No." Thomas refused, still placing kisses on her skin. "You'll get used to it, I assure you. The beauty is worth the discomfort. And the self-discipline will help you."

"For what?" Lauren asked, "How will it help me?" Her dark husband was looking at her reflection in the mirror, a slow visual pass over every curve, every line of her body. Then he looked into her eyes and smiled. Not reassuringly. It was a terrible smile full of all kinds of murky, troubling promises.

"You'll see."

A sudden burst of courage made her spine stiffen. "You said it was my choice," Lauren managed, "you said I had the power to say yes or no."

Thomas was distracted by the swell of her breasts again, calloused fingers stroking over the skin. "It is your choice," he agreed finally, and then his eyes met hers again and Lauren's knees nearly buckled. They were on fire- blazing with his need to fuck her, control her, own her. "And you will agree."

A few moments later, he brought out a silky dress for her- a simple wrap style that he solicitously helped Lauren step into and then slowly, deliberately drew the zipper up her spine, his long fingers straightening the fabric around her waist, smoothing it over her hips. Finally stepping back from her his heated gaze went over her, then Thomas nodded his head. "Lovely. Why don't you finish up and meet me downstairs? You'll be coming with me today." He watched her eyes widen with alarm and chuckled lightly. "Only a business lunch, darling. The wives are joining us for some photographs for the LSO charity. He watched Lauren's face fall. "Surely," he purred, "you're still grateful for your scholarship? You want to help other deserving students?"

Lauren rubbed her forehead, "Of course I do. It's just... it's different now."

"Now that you're the wife of a monster?" Thomas didn't look angry, but his voice was frigid. Smiling humorlessly, he checked his watch. "You have thirty minutes to get ready."

Trying to get another breath and failing against the corset's iron grip, his bride managed to call, "Wait!" As he turned toward her again, Lauren nearly lost her nerve. "How long do I have to wear this?"

Stepping back, he brushed his lips over hers. "Until I take it off you."

Chapter 11 – Everything But Her Freedom, Of Course

In which Lauren finds that saying "yes" to her terrifying new husband is never as simple as it might seem. There's always a price to pay.

She had to admit, Lauren thought grimly, the fiend she'd been forced to marry was quite accurate in his promise to make her forget how sore and tender her undercarriage was. Because the iron grip of the corset currently compressing all her internal organs was doing a fine job of capturing all her attention. Thomas hadn't spoken to her once, other than to subtly give her more assistance in and out of his low-slung sports car and then whispering how lovely and elegant she looked, pointedly running his hand down the laces under her dress as he ushered her into Jerwood Hall, where a fund-raising luncheon would also act as a photo session for *The Daily Mail*.

To Lauren's horror, she recognized the quartet on the stage as hers- well, the other three that made up the original quartet with her, along with a new cello player. Thomas, who had his hand on the small of her back, felt his wife stumble slightly. His gaze followed hers to the musicians and his hand squeezed her waist. Leaning in, he murmured, "They had to replace you, of course. While I am quite happy and proud to see you perform with the full orchestra, you no longer have time for these little engagements." The look of fury she gave him turned her eyes a chilly purple-grey. It was not a pleasant color or a pleasant expression.

Lauren's heart was hammering in its constrictive cage of steel boning and satin, and she formed a ghastly attempt at a smile on her face as the two clueless members of the quarter raised their bows to her in greeting as Macie looked away, expression stony. Waving back weakly, she numbly followed her monstrous spouse's guiding hand to their table. *Act normally, don't show it, don't show anything!* she repeated the furious mantra over and over, trying to recover her shallow breath before she passed out. There was a part to be played, after all. A somewhat hungover-looking Arabella and her vile husband were seated at their table, along with the handsome Number Three and his sweet Clara.

"Ah, our dear Lauren." Number One's voice was fond and avuncular, and it was all Lauren could do to keep from launching across the table at him. Instead, she bit the inside of her cheek until she could taste the soothing coppery sensation of her little wound. She learned the habit when her mother died and Frank would be drunkenly crashing around their expensive brownstone in Manhattan, railing against the injustice of fate leaving him with a daughter instead of a wife. "How lovely to see you here, instead of laboring as the entertainment today."

Lauren could feel Thomas's hand tighten on the rigid satin and steel compressing her waist, his long fingers still leaving their warning squeeze. "I loved playing with the quartet, Mr. Kingston-"

"Ben, dear. Do call me Ben, we're family now." Gaze darting between a pale and silent Arabella and the insectile stare of her husband, Lauren forced another facsimile of a smile.

"But I know working on the fundraising side with Arabella will be so..." Lauren almost choked on the words, and she could feel her husband's long fingers tighten again. "Will be so meaningful."

The black, beetle-like leer of The Corporation's president made her want to shudder, but she kept her set, bland smile until his sinister attention turned elsewhere. "Very good, little girl." Lauren shuddered involuntarily as Thomas's rich, sonorous tone stroked along her sensitive ear. "There's my happy, content bride." Looking down to see her knuckles turn white as she gripped her linen napkin, he growled low in his throat. "No naughtiness, darling. I can feel you wanting to make a scene. But you know better, don't you?"

At that moment, his bride was trying to catch her breath again. Every time she started getting angry and breathing more heavily, the implacable strength of the corset would curtail anything but the lightest of gasps. When a photographer from the *Fail* - as her friends here called it - came over, Lauren angled herself as nudged by Thomas to lean against him gracefully and smile as if she was the happiest newlywed in the world. Because if the reporter didn't believe it, her miserable father could die. Or maybe her vile husband would just cut to the chase and take her out instead. So Lauren pictured herself standing in the corner, watching the table laugh and exchange clever quips for the benefit of the reporter while dining on pheasant and salmon. Like it was someone else. Like it wasn't happening to her at all.

Finally sent home with Chuck as Thomas returned to The Corporation's offices to finish the day, Lauren tore out of the car the moment it stopped, hustling up the stairs and jamming her keys in the lock and disarming the security system. In a moment she was in the ground floor bathroom and wiggling like a demented eel, tearing off the pretty dress given to her by her new husband and clever fingers frantically searching for the bottom or top of the laces on the corset, wanting to get the fucking thing *off*.

"Goddamnit!" she hissed, "How the hell do I get- fuck!!" The symbolism of trying to get free from her beautiful restraints couldn't be more obvious, and Lauren knew it. But her entire focus shrank to tearing this thing from her body- but when her fingertips finally reached the end of the lacings, she felt something strange, metallic. Frowning, she twisted, angling her body to look behind her.

"Are you FUCKING KIDDING ME?" Lauren screamed, or tried to, with the limited amount of breath offered to her. There was the tiniest of padlocks at the top of the corset. At the bottom, and a third in the middle, so even if she tried to cut the laces loose, she was not getting free from this infernal contraption.

The sun was angling over the tops of the slate roofs around the house when she wearily heard the door open and close, calm, measured footsteps coming through the entryway and into the kitchen. Lauren could hear a soft shuffling that told her Thomas was looking through the mail that she would pick up from the floor under the mail slot every day and then leave on the little mahogany table near the door where he kept his keys. Her full lips twisted bitterly. He had her trained like a faithful dog in only a matter of days. Though, today she was more like a show poodle, standing adorably on her hind legs and "arfing" on cue.

"Darling?" Despite herself, Lauren shuddered. The Voice...

She heard the footsteps move into the hallway, pausing between the great room and the wide stairway. "Where are you, little girl? Don't you know it's naughty to hide from your Sir?" Still, Lauren folded her arms over the monstrous device that had confined her all day, angrily refusing to answer him. To her alarm, she could feel her thighs press together as his footsteps paused, then turned in the direction of the bathroom where she was still sprawled on the pristine white tile floor. Breathing growing even lighter, she was horrified to feel her center heat up. It sounded like he was... hunting her? Thomas was silent now, the only sound in the quiet house the light 'click' of his A Diciannoveventitre loafers. Lauren suddenly wanted to get up - to run or hide or do something - but it was too late and the door opened, blinding her momentarily as the setting sun glanced off the bathroom mirror.

"There you are."

Shivering in spite of herself, Lauren could feel the cool tones of disappointment in her fearsome husband's beautiful voice. Thomas stood over her, hands plunged into his pockets as he examined her. "And why are you sprawled on the floor of the bathroom, little one?" When she refused to answer, he gave a sigh and elegantly hitched his trousers as he squatted closer, examining her. "You've been such a good girl," he murmured, disapproval clear. "And now I find my sweet bride sulking on the floor like a child?"

Taking a deep breath that seemed to cut off mid-inhalation, Lauren gritted her teeth. "You locked me into this infernal device."

"Yes," Thomas agreed, eyeing the torn dress resting on the sink. "And?"

Lauren was so enraged that she coughed as she tried to

gather the breath to shriek at him. Thomas propped his chin on one hand, elbow resting on his knee as he waited for her. There was so much she wanted to spit at him, venomous, hateful, and cruel. The nerve of this fucking dick, and - and she wanted to beg him to put himself inside her again as he cut this miserable contraption away from her body, let her draw a full breath and come screaming on his cock, and - okay, seriously, what the fuck was wrong with her? Also, she had never said 'fuck' so many times within one 24-hour period.

"Hmmm..." Thomas settled himself comfortably on the floor next to her the warmth of his skin suddenly feeling comforting against her chilled skin, because really, this tile was fucking freezing, and there was another 'fuck.' "Let me extrapolate from the poignant scene I find before me." He enjoyed the look of hate his bride gave him from her watery, bloodshot eyes. "You attempted to be a bad girl and remove your corset without my permission."

Lauren breathed heavily, coughed at the effort and looked away.

"Then," he continued, "you realized the discipline garment you are wearing cannot be removed without taking out the padlocks first?" He cocked his head at her inquiringly, as if waiting for her confession. Instead, he enjoyed her slitted-eyed glare. "Then," Thomas continued casually, one finger beginning to idly stroke along the sumptuous swell of her breasts, heaving so delightfully over the satin confines of her corset, "being the stubborn creature that you are, you still fought against the corset until you ran out of breath, and ended up here on the floor of our bathroom?" Lauren made an abbreviated noise of fury and tried to pull away from his wandering hand, only to be held in place by the other. "Such a face," he scolded indulgently, enjoying how his bride was simply seething with helpless rage.

She was a *good* girl - she'd *always* been a good girl - but Lauren was so angry! At herself, at him, at the whole bizarre, twisted mess that landed her here on the elegantly tiled floor of Thomas's ground floor bathroom. And she wanted to kill someone- but her furiously rotating thoughts made it difficult to specify whom. "I hate this!" she hissed; common sense overridden by her ferocity. "I hate *you*! I don't deserve-"

Within a second or two, she was off the floor and straddling her formidable spouse. "You will not speak to me in such a way, little girl." Thomas's tone could have been chiseled from ice, and Lauren shivered accordingly. "I decide what you deserve. I decide how you will handle these challenges." His grip tightened unconsciously, and Lauren gritted her teeth. She wouldn't show a thing to this man! "I have made every effort to give you as much choice as I can within the confines of..." for a moment, the unflappable exterior of Thomas faltered, then his mouth tightened again. "...of who and what we are. But you *belong* to me." He watched her mouth open, hateful words ready to spill from those full lips and shook her lightly. "You want to be good, sweetness, I can feel it. You know that life with me will be so much more pleasant as a good girl, don't you?" The last query was nearly a whisper as Thomas leaned into her, mouth moving against her reddened cheeks. His hands were moving now, sliding soothingly up and down her bare arms, tickling along the top of the monstrous satin device and settling her thighs more comfortably over his lap.

"Why be angry and rail against the little things, when you know..." here, his agile tongue slipped out, tracing a delicate line down her throat and circling her collarbones. "...you *know* how good I can make you feel? Hmmm?" Lauren's lashes were fluttering frantically, trying to keep her eyes open against the feel of his hot mouth on her skin. "Darling," he purred against her neck, enjoying the way his new wife's hips would twist against his groin, "you are such an intelligent girl. Such a strong girl- you've had to be. This is not the hardest thing you've had to do."

Lauren yanked away from him, her legs trying to push free from her confines on his lap. "Don't you dare- don't you talk about my mother!" She gritted her teeth, refusing to let herself cry. He knew about her friendship with Macie. He knew she'd been a virgin. And aside from the odd interview in his office when they spoke about her mother passing from cancer, she suspected her horrible husband knew quite well how much she'd had to shoulder after losing Aurelia. This man had violated every part of her life, even the parts she held sacred. And yet she'd still played his games! Did she have any decency- any backbone at *all*?

Thomas refused to let her loose, calmly holding her wrists together and simply letting her bat furiously at his chest until she was tired. Lauren's struggle wasn't a long one- the goddamned contraption she was locked into cutting off any vigorous rebellion. And when she was finished, he simply sighed and moved his long arms around her heaving body to hold her. "I have you, Lauren. Go ahead and be angry, or sad. it's all right to hate me."

These kind words, of course, had the opposite effect, and his infuriated and exhausted bride began crying as if her heart was breaking, arms wrapping around his neck and hot tears staining his shirt. And the terrifying Number Two of Jaguar Holdings simply held Lauren as she cried, rocking her calmly. Though part of him wondered if there would be a time she would stop... crying. He knew why she cried. It was understandable. But there'd been quite a bit of tears in the short week they'd been married, and his cold heart was cracking around the edges.

And this would never do.

Finally feeling Lauren's sobs reduce in volume and frequency, he stirred and gently readjusted her again, trying to keep her away from the inevitable swelling of his cock. Really, Thomas thought crossly, it was as if he had no self-control at all, anymore. "Would you like me to take this corset off you now, little one?" She couldn't talk yet, but he could feel her head nod against his shoulder. Pulling the tiny key out of his trouser pocket, he swiftly freed the tiny padlocks from the corset and began to unlace her as elegantly as he'd bound his wife in the first place. Enjoying the little groans of relief as her ribs were freed and breath restored to his wife, Williams hummed a bit against the delicate skin where her neck met her shoulder. He could feel the warmth of blood rushing back into her torso, enjoying the pretty flush of her skin.

"Lovely..." he crooned against her back, gently massaging her constricted flesh, hearing Lauren actually groan in pleasure as he finally finished unlacing her and freed her from the confining garment. "I do wish you could see how beautiful you are, sweetness. The lovely line of your spine to the narrow curve of your waist. I could span it, you know," and Thomas broke off his carnal appreciation to wrap his hands around the still-tight confines of his wife's waist, enjoying how his thumbs met together. "How your sweet curves shape to align in such an exquisite way." Chuckling against the soft skin of her back, Thomas began placing slow, sucking kisses against it, feeling her breath catch. "Let me take care of you." He could feel his reluctant bride's body give a full shudder against the potency of his beautiful voice. "Let me make this good for you, pleasurable. Your Sir..." Thomas's lids fluttered closed abruptly as he felt her whimper, "...can give you so many things, darling, that you never thought possible."

He watched as her long fingers clenched against the fluffy bath mat, knowing his clever captive was battling her hurt and fury at being trapped against how very good her new husband could make her feel. Rough hands sliding up again to cup her breasts, Thomas grinned as Lauren stiffened against his hold but didn't try to break free. Restlessly trying to shift his hips and his uncomfortably erect cock away from her, he drew in a deep breath.

"I have you," he purred, and this was the sentence that began slicing through her defenses, he could feel it with the sag of her tense spine against him. "You are mine, baby. But as your Sir, I will show you such delicious, dirty things. Experiences that will make you come screaming on my cock. Places you could never imagine. And you will love them all. Accept our life."

Lauren's spine stiffened again; he was breaking her. She could feel it.

"Accept what I can give you." There was something that changed in Thomas's deep, and persuasively sonorous tone then, and his long fingers began stroking and pulling at her nipples. "Marriages, unions, have begun on less, darling. Think if I were the husband your parents promised you to- a King, perhaps..."

Nonononono! she groaned internally; *I will not let him do this again! Not the Voice.* But it was too late, and Lauren knew it. It wasn't just hearing his beautiful, measured speech, it was feeling it vibrate against her spine, tickle along her skin and make her shiver. And worse, she could picture it. Every word.

Picking her up and carrying her to the drawing-room, Thomas diabolically refused to stop the story he'd spun for her, putting her down on the wide and comfortable suede couch. "On the wedding night, so uncomfortable, not knowing what to feel?" After removing the infernal corset, his sweet bride was left only in her undies, and he pulled them down her thighs, kissing the thin skin there appreciatively. "But I would still treat you with the same care, darling. I would not force you. But that bride- in whatever time or place- would know the reality of her new life."

He could feel Lauren stiffen, but he kissed her persuasively, sweetly, enjoying the hitch in her breath when his tongue slipped between her lips. "That Lauren - that wife - would know what she could fight against, and what to accept..." A stifled sob broke from her throat, and Thomas enjoyed kissing along her heaving chest, stroking her sides until she calmed and allowed him to kiss her again. "Why not be that Lauren, my lovely girl? Why fight what I can give you?"

She was trying to gather her senses, gritting her teeth against the delicious alchemy of her husband's voice, the terribly persuasive tone that made everything he said seem so reasonable- so logical. But then Lauren made the mistake of opening her eyes and seeing his beautiful face hovering over hers, a tender smile gracing his mouth and the gentle feel of his hands on her. There was something so filthily dominant of being laid out naked under his fully-dressed body, bare and open for him. "You..." Lauren swallowed, trying to form her words into something that made sense. "You terrify me."

Her husband's ministrations paused then, and he rose over her, blocking the light behind him in the room, face darkened in shadow and pale eyes making him look even more like the fallen angel she already pictured him to be. "I know," he said honestly, knowing the truth could be even more devastating, more compelling, "but that doesn't mean everything I've said here isn't true." Watching the sweep of emotion across his wife's lovely, mobile features, Thomas was suddenly struck with a desperate need to be inside her - to stop all this silly indecision and turmoil. If he could just force his sweet wife to accept it - all the pleasurable, filthy, delicious things he'd been planning could be put into play. He could show her how very good life as Mrs. Thomas Williams could be. "Let me comfort you, Lauren," he soothed, "let me show you." Her eyes were huge, he noted, that pretty lavender that made his bride look even more innocent.

Slowly, her fingers slid into his hair, and Thomas bit back a triumphant chuckle. He could imagine a thousand ways to debauch that innocence from her.

It was some time later when Lauren was barely coming back to an understanding of where she was as she felt the heat of Thomas spurt inside her, warming her stiff pelvis and loosening the tight tendons of her legs gripping around his waist. Her scary new husband had swiftly bound her wrists with his belt and somehow lifted her onto a hook she'd never seen near the doorway of his hallway. He'd enjoyed watching her teeter on tiptoe as he'd toyed with her wet and silky pussy, sliding those damnably long and knowing fingers inside her, slicking along her tender, swelling lips and embarrassingly stiff clitoris. First throwing her thighs over his suited shoulders and gleefully eating her out until she came, he'd started again until he felt her tell-tale stiffening, then leisurely pulled back to remove his clothing- the expensive jacket, then trousers, watching her desperate gaze travel over each part of new skin bared to her. His belt was already binding her wrists, and Thomas grinned in a filthy, terrifying way as he pulled his tie free to wrap over her eyes, blocking her view as he finished stripping and enjoying her frustrated little whine at being denied the view of his lovely, hard body and sculpted musculature.

He'd bitten her then, harder than she liked and he knew that because her body would jolt and she'd moan softly, but Lauren didn't pull away, especially when he settled her on his cock and moved smoothly along her channel, strumming her oversensitive clit and whispering the devil's promises in her ear- how beautiful his sweet girl was, how very good she was for her Sir. How good he would make her feel and how much he wanted to fuck up inside her until she couldn't think of anything but the weight of him inside her. And when Thomas paused just long enough for his innocent bride to make confused, anxious noises and arch against his stilled cock- he chuckled into her ear and promised she would never have come as hard as this. And she did. Limp against the leather bond holding her to the hook and the grip of his fingers hard on her thighs around his waist, Lauren moaned and shuddered and came again as he groaned against her and came hard, just as he'd promised.

"Your Sir is so very proud of you. I will give you everything, my sweet Lauren."

Dimly feeling him loosen the belt and free her from the hook, all she could think in the middle of the tremors from her pussy and the slack, helpless feeling of her body, was that he could. Thomas could give her everything.

But her freedom, of course.

Chapter 12 – Are You Planning My Death, Darling?

In which Thomas discovers it is not as easy to manage a wife as it is terrified employees, and Lauren discovers that despite her best intentions, lust, need and hate can all co-exist.

Lauren woke as the first line of sunlight escaped between the thick curtains on the bedroom windows, and she held very still. Her mother used to tease her when she tried to hide in bed, calling it "playing possum," like the irritable white creatures from her home state of Louisiana that would pretend to be asleep or dead when confronted with a predator. Swallowing hard, she pushed the memory away, analyzing where she was and what she could remember. Thomas freed her from that horrible contraption. That was *never* happening again. That fucker was a fucking *red*. A hard limit red. Also, she had discovered that she could use the "F" word several times in one sentence. He'd seduced her with his voice, comforted her - though it was his fucking fault she needed comforting! - and there's the "F" word again. Flushing a bit, she remembered him angling his hard cock uncomfortably away from her as he cared for her, a move she found oddly respectful. And the weird, almost "Arabian Nights" kind of tale about arranged marriages and how she should accept theirs.

And then the sex. She'd hated him so much when she'd been writhing like a demented eel on the floor of the bathroom yesterday that there would never have been a time she could have imagined agreeing to let him tie her up and have sex with her again, but she had. And, with another hot flush under her fair skin, Lauren remembered she'd come three times. And then aftercare - she knew that word now - understood that's what Thomas did when he bathed her and brought her dinner in bed and rubbed her back and feet with that almond-scented cream. That part was wonderful.

Then, Lauren's mouth tightened furiously, remembering that hellish luncheon. Letting her walk in on her own quartet, realizing she no longer belonged there? Having to wave to her own replacement? Who *does* that? It was such a dick move! And he was so condescending, chuckling in his indulgent, stupid, condescending, stupid way.

Settling more comfortably into her pillow, Lauren let herself furiously dream. How to rid herself of this monstrous keeper?

One day, having realized that he has security cameras everywhere, she has secretly slipped a knife inside of her blouse sleeve while cooking and secreted it into a bedside table. That night, while he's sleeping, she cuts his throat. And that is that. She then goes to the safe, for which she has learned its combination, cleans it out, puts on her beloved jeans and hoodie, erases the security camera's feed, and exits the house through a side service door and disappears into the night.

Taking a bus or walking, she keeps to the shadows to avoid CCTV cameras and gets herself to a bus station and heads west. She gets off as soon as she's outside the greater London area. She finds a small mom and pop drugstore that won't have a security camera connected to a larger system and buys hair dye and a cheap hoodie in another color, and a different duffle bag. She finds a gas station restroom and cuts and dyes her hair. Changes into the new hoodie. Dumps her old one and the original duffle into a dumpster. Knowing that everyone will expect her to make for Europe, she heads North, traveling cheaply and unobtrusively as a student with mousy brown hair and getting brown cosmetic contact lenses (paying cash all the way), and loses herself in the Wilds of the Scottish Highlands before making her way up to Orkney and the Faroe Islands and up to Scandinavia. She could keep moving in any number of ways before ending up somewhere outside of The Corporation's power even if it is a small hut in Thailand somewhere.

And what of her father? Well... She's done what she could for him. At this point, he has to save himself. Enough is enough.

Lauren was so immersed in the intricate fantasy that she gave a huge, savage grin.

It was, unfortunately, the moment that Thomas awakened beside her, and his clear gaze watched the play of emotion over his wife's expressive features. Fury. Hurt. Hate. Spite. These were all emotions he'd seen, many times before. It twinged him somewhere internally to see them on her lovely face.

"Are you planning my death, darling?"

Lauren actually jumped and shrieked simultaneously, shocked out of her fantasy into the terrible reality of her new husband's unpleasantly knowing grin. He caught her just as she was about to flop awkwardly off the bed. Lifting her over him, Thomas settled her on his lap, the down comforter acting as a flimsy barrier between them. Lightly stroking his fingertips down her thighs, he watched her thoughtfully. "What upset you most from yesterday, sweet Lauren?"

She pressed her lips together, trying to stem the furious flow of hate and hurt. He continued smoothing his hands along the thin skin of her legs, waiting for an answer.

"Perhaps..." he mused, "being unable to free yourself from the corset?" Thomas paused long enough that his bride gave a stiff nod. "And then, finding you'd been replaced in the quartet?" That was pushing her too far, because Lauren hissed like a cat and slapped him across the face with all of her strength, then gasped in shock, scrambling off the bed and racing for the door to the bathroom. With the unfair agility of those long legs, he was on her in a moment. Lauren was shuddering in terror and he caged her into the corner with his arms. "You will never. Hit. Me. Again." His voice was glacial, terrifying. It reminded her of that night in his office when he'd had Chuck shoot her father in the leg.

But his timid wife was no more. Between gritted teeth, she managed, "You could have killed me yesterday, just to get off on your Dom fantasies. I couldn't breathe. What I hyperventilated? I would have died, right there on your pristine bathroom floor."

Thomas's polar gaze was steady. He wasn't going to tell her he'd been watching her on his well-placed security cameras. That if he'd seen her going into distress he would have called her to tell her where the other key was. Or Straker of course, if she seemed too panicked to handle it herself. Though the vision of his employee seeing his bride in her corset and panties made his fists tighten. There was always another key. Only a fool would rely on one means of escape. That watching her force herself to dial down every time she started to scream and didn't have the breath made him proud of her. That he was very much looking forward to one day making her come whilst wearing a corset and actually enjoying the sight of her losing consciousness upon orgasm. But he wasn't foolish or cruel enough to bait her further. "I always have ways," she eyed his hesitation speculatively, "of making certain such a thing does not happen. And you underestimate yourself. Your magnificent breath control- you use it for playing your instruments, especially the most vigorous and robust pieces. And you never tire. I've watched you with some admiration. It made me think of how lovely you would look, forcing your fears away in that corset."

His soothing words didn't comfort her this time, Thomas could see that. His sweet bride's natural need to be loved couldn't overcompensate for her misery and betrayal. "I have practice this morning," Lauren finally said. "May I get ready?" Thomas watched her for an excruciatingly uncomfortable amount of time, then finally nodded, stepping aside to allow her into the bathroom.

If she thought back, Lauren would have seen much later that it started when the orchestra was served a surprise champagne brunch after rehearsal. The season tickets - wildly over-priced in her humble opinion - were already sold out and the new photo session in the *Daily Mail* ("Fail," Lauren mumbled) had brought a flattering amount of attention on the LSO. Knowing she didn't have to drive since Chuck was parked calmly and illegally right outside the door, she accepted a second glass, then a third, and when no one seemed to be paying attention, she poured herself a fourth round of the really lovely beverage, so fizzy...

Concentrating, Lauren carried her cello out the door perfectly, knowing her grim-faced shadow would be there to take it from her with a muttered, "Allow me." And the terrifying sharp eyes of her captor/spouse were gone, along with the rest of him when she came home, so the girl helped herself to a big package of chocolate biscuits and a lovely Riesling, which she drank straight from the bottle. Why waste a glass? This led to a long nap, woken finally by the buzzing of a text on her phone from Thomas.

"We have a dinner meeting with some French clients. Be ready by 7 pm. I know you speak fluent French. Do not do so during this meeting."

His curt and mysterious instructions made her angry, but Lauren dragged herself out of bed and pushed her short blonde curls out of her face. Heartless bastard. She could be heartless, too.

Meanwhile, Thomas was in a meeting regarding a delicate negotiation of arms sales between two equally unlikeable parties. Really, why did he allow The Corporation to stay in such a distasteful side of the business? Too many sloppy and stupid clients. Too many needless deaths. But his mind kept returning to the blank misery of his new bride as she'd escaped into the bathroom that morning.

No matter what she'd expected, he thought with some chagrin, this was an equal surprise to him. He'd planned on getting the girl settled as Mrs. Thomas Williams, fucking her a few times - she was beautiful, of course, he would - then ignoring his sweet virgin and heading back to the dark and murky pleasures he'd sunk into so long ago. He'd intended to keep Lauren happy by keeping her vile father alive and giving her space for her music and social interaction with the other wives as he moved her into a bedroom on the fourth floor by her beloved instruments. The cold-hearted Number Two never expected the odd pleasure of waking up beside her warm little body, running with her in the park, how good she felt writhing on his lap as he spanked her into a near-orgasm...

"-the second shipment arrives via- Thomas, which port

would that be?"

His suddenly alert cobalt gaze found everyone else at the long table looking at him inquiringly, though the pitch-black gaze of Number One showed a mix of amusement and warning.

"The Port of Marseille-Fos, of course," he answered crisply. "Two weeks exactly upon receipt of your final payment." The rest of the men at the table nodded and continued negotiations, but Thomas was quite aware of the insectile gaze of Kingston, lingering on him for several uncomfortable moments before returning back to the conversation.

Even he'd been surprised by the words flowing from him last night, trying to convince this puzzling and arousing girl that even an arranged marriage - *their* marriage - could be something deeply satisfying to both of them. It had been a long time since Thomas had needed to woo a woman- court her. Women in his circles... they already knew what he wanted and were quite happy to give it to him. But Lauren was different. In every possible way different, and he would need to adjust his course of persuasion accordingly.

This was never clearer than when Chuck delivered Lauren to him that evening. The dinner party was held in an old, beautiful estate home, cooked by a magnificent chef, and served gracefully by waiters from some surely five-star restaurant. Lauren never caught which one, exactly, but it didn't matter. She was still a bit tipsy from her permissive afternoon and spending most of her time behaving as the demure bride of The Corporation's scary second in command.

"And you, Mrs. Williams, have you ever been to Florence?"

Lifting her head with an automatic smile, Lauren found the

inquiring gaze of the grey-haired man across the table. He was pleasantly rotund with a kind, wrinkled face. *He looked like someone's grandpa,* she thought distantly, *if someone's grandpa killed people. A lot.* "I have, Monsieur Boucher," she paused for a second. Boucher. Butcher. Her stomach twisted alarmingly and she took a hasty gulp of her Caymus Napa Valley Cabernet Sauvignon, which made her feel vaguely guilty. Really, it was too lovely a vintage to treat so harshly, but she continued. "We stayed at the Suoro Oblate Della Spirito Santo-"

"I know it," the man answered slowly, "why would you pick a humble room in a convent?"

Lauren shrugged, the first real smile of the evening crossing her face. "It was simple, but it was beautiful monsieur. We heard the evening prayers as the sun set, and the nuns baked bread every morning to go with the honey from the convent beehives. It's one of my best memories of Florence." After a short, polite silence from the table, the conversation continued to eddy around them, but Thomas watched his bride and the man who was about to buy six million pounds worth of surface to air missiles continue to talk about something as innocuous as the nun's beekeeping.

"You did beautifully tonight, darling."

Closing her eyes in a misguided attempt to block out her husband's beautiful, potent voice, Lauren nodded in a noncommittal fashion. "Thank you," she answered politely. He could hear the dull tone in her voice, but Thomas chose to ignore it.

It was impossible to ignore the painfully stiff posture of his pretty bride when they were finally safely behind the doors of their home, however. Looking longingly at the stairs, Lauren managed, "I'm really tired, I'm going to take a bath and just... you know." Leaning deliberately against the doorway leading to the stairs, Thomas crossed his arms over his beautifully fitted suit,

"Are you." His resonant, sculpted voice was cool, but Lauren hardened her heart against it.

"Yes," she gritted out. "So, if you'll excuse me—"

His hand caught her arm as Lauren's foot rose for the first step. "We've been doing so well, little girl." Her frightening husband's voice was composed, even as a chill was sweeping across each crisply enunciated word. "Are you going to take a step back from all our progress? Something you have, darling, enjoyed quite a bit."

Her back was to him, but his wife paused obediently. "You told me it was my choice," she answered flatly. Lauren closed her eyes, doing everything she could not to cringe.

"I did," Thomas answered thoughtfully. Another pause and she knew he was looking her over. "Very well. Goodnight." He moved behind her as she walked up the stairs and for a panicked moment, Lauren was still frightened he'd push her into the bedroom, make her give in... But he didn't, stepping off onto the second floor, punching a complicated code into his office security system, and shutting the door behind him.

Lauren was relieved enough to take a hot bath, wrapping her arms around her drawn-up legs and sobbing in relief. And frustration. And some hurt. And Thomas watched it on his in-home surveillance system, index finger thoughtfully moving across his upper lip.

Chapter 13 – A Mexican Standoff in Suburban London

In which Thomas and Lauren hate each other's guts. Until they don't.

Mexican standoff: a confrontation amongst two parties in which no strategy exists that allows either party to achieve victory. Thus, all participants must maintain their strategic position which will remain without change until some outside influence resolves it.

The bitter standoff between the new Mr. and Mrs. Thomas Williams continued for a week. Lauren practiced for several hours a day, only leaving her fourth-floor conservatory when she knew Thomas was gone. He would fall asleep at night hearing her furious movements over and over on her cello. Sometimes when he was in his office and the surveillance cameras were on, Thomas would unconsciously relax, leaning back against his leather chair as he watched his wife play her violin, or grinning slightly when she amped up her bass guitar. God... his head lolled back on the padded seat, a vision of his demure bride in leather pants and wailing out something by Paramore... angrily pushing down his sudden erection, Thomas rolled his head, making his neck crack and getting back to work.

Coming home later one night after a "meeting" that Numbers One and Three had insisted be conducted at a Corporation brothel, Thomas strolled into his house, a little drunk and unreasonably furious at his elusive Lauren. How could the stupid girl not appreciate what he'd done? Saving her worthless father, keeping her from having to select yet another coffin for a parent... He strolled into the living room and poured himself another drink, idly loosening his tie and hearing her viciously saw through "Orlando Furioso" by Vivaldi. Smiling sardonically, he soundlessly walked the stairs to the third floor, deliberately letting the bedroom door bang open, hearing the music abruptly stop.

"Come out, come out, wherever you are..."

Lauren's head dropped back, shuddering suddenly as the music of her husband's beautiful voice poured through her. She could almost not miss the melody he played on her body if she didn't have to see him. Or better, not hear him. She'd stayed hidden on the fourth floor for most of the week, even curled uncomfortably in that damnable chair, knowing her husband better now she was quite certain had been selected for its supreme discomfort.

"Lauren. You will answer me." The light humor was gone from his tone, the commanding chill spreading through her spine.

Clearing her throat, she realized she'd not spoken for a couple of days. "Yes?" Looking around her, Lauren attempted to tidy up a couple of empty wine bottles and a half-gnawed wedge of Camembert.

"Come down here."

Groaning under her breath, she blew a loose strand of hair out of her eyes and wiped her damp palms on her skirt, ascending the stairs as ordered. Stiffening her spine and lingering on the landing of the third floor, Lauren eyed the cold, beautiful face of her husband. He was leaning against the doorway to their bedroom, arms folded as he watched her. When she attempted to raise an inquiring eyebrow, he angrily gestured her closer with two beckoning fingers. Lauren tried to obey without actually getting close enough for Thomas to grab her.

"You called?" Her attempt at light and breezy came out in an anxious croak.

He stepped forward, looking down at her, the dim light from the bedroom slanting across his sharp cheekbones. "I believe you've hidden upstairs, sulking long enough. You will put your instrument away and come to bed." Her eyes were wide, the violet shade that showed that his bride was anxious. Thomas had enjoyed learning her moods more than he'd anticipated. But then Lauren stiffened, her nostrils flaring.

"Why?" she seethed, "It's clear you've been finding alternative entertainment. Whoever she is, maybe suggest she doesn't hose on that godawful perfume next time." Thomas's brow rose as he registered hurt and fury fighting for prominence on Lauren's pretty face.

Despite himself, a cold grin curled his lips. "I don't believe that's a concern of yours, darling. Particularly when you find your marital duties so distasteful." Thomas was surprised to see Lauren stumble back a step, pain twisting her full mouth.

She was humiliated to feel how much his admission hurt her. That she felt stupid for feeling... special? Like Thomas might have been as aroused by her as he'd... well, what he'd made her feel? "Whatever," Lauren finally hissed. She tried moving past him into the bedroom, but her confusing new husband grabbed her arm.

"Another American vulgarity you will remove from your speech," Williams snarled. Leaning in to sniff her neck, he chuckled coldly. "And go wash off the stink of all that wine. Do I need to put a lock on the pantry?" Her hand came up so quickly that Lauren didn't even register it until he gripped her wrist harshly. "I told you, you will *never* hit me again." Without another word, he pulled her closer with an arm around her waist and carried his stunned bride to the bed. Lauren suddenly gathered her senses and began kicking and struggling against him. He laughed harshly, seating himself on the mattress and throwing her over his lap. "Not to worry," Thomas sneered, "I have no interest in your tasty little pussy tonight. It's your ass that requires my attention."

Lauren struggled harder as she felt the cool air of the room on her suddenly bare bottom as he flung up her skirt and ripped her panties down her legs. "Don't you dare, Thomas! You- OW! Stop it!" But she felt one muscled forearm come down hard over the small of her back as one leg pinned her two kicking ones under it. And then the next slap across the unprotected skin of her ass. There were three more before her horrible spouse paused for a moment, lean muscles in his thighs shifting as he reached for something on the table next to his side of the bed.

"I will not require you to count these strikes," Thomas said with terrible, good humor in his voice. "You won't have the presence of mind this time. But in the future..."

The next impact made Lauren scream in shock. It was not as if this hit against her already red ass was more painful, but the chill and the wideness of the instrument he was using against her was overwhelming. It took another blow for her to recognize it was the silver-backed brush Thomas had used on her hair in a more tender, comforting time. And that was what made her heart break. And made her fight even harder until the next swat made her scream again.

"Hold still, little girl." The sonorous voice of the monster she'd married still poured over her shattered nerve endings like a balm, even though the brush came down again. And again, and again, until he'd spanked her ten times, enjoying how the raised "W" engraving on the back made such an enticing corresponding mark on Lauren's pale bottom. "Lovely..." he mused, running a cool hand over the heat of her, tracing the marks with one long finger. Feeling her body heave against his legs as his bride wept, Thomas sighed and lifted her upright and against one shoulder, rocking her until she stopped feebly swatting at him and allowed his comfort against her will. His stubborn, beautiful girl refused to say another word, even as he bathed her, gently rubbed a cooling lotion into the bright red skin of her ass, and pulled her into his long arms back on the bed, feeling her breath even out as she fell asleep. Thomas stayed awake until dawn began lightening the horizon, trying to understand this confusing, infuriating creature.

Giving up on going to sleep, Thomas went running that morning, unreasonably angry at Lauren for not being there, running alongside him. Of course, she wouldn't be, even if they were back on good terms, her shapely ass would be in no condition to do so. But she *should* be. He'd enjoyed the few times they'd run together before the Mexican Standoff that kept his bride hidden on their fourth floor. Then, of course, Thomas was angry for being angry. *God!* he thought furiously, picking up his pace, *Why does anyone get married? This is ridiculous!*

Meanwhile, his exhausted wife was dragging herself out of their sumptuous bed, equally furious at Thomas. Raising her nightie to look at her reddened ass, Lauren gritted her teeth in rage. Her first season performance with the symphony was tonight- she'd been practicing obsessively and now simply sitting down would be a challenge, much less concentrating on playing her best.

"Bastard!" she snarled, "Selfish, horrible, condescending son of a bitch-" Pausing for a moment, Lauren's fair brow raised. Speaking of family - though certainly in the most disrespectful way - she realized that she didn't know a single thing about Thomas's family. For Christ's sake, the man couldn't have been hatched from an egg! They certainly weren't at their wedding, but did Thomas have parents? Human beings he called "mom," and "dad?" Cautiously, she went through his exquisite closet, gingerly opening drawers and looking for photos and kind of memorabilia. She'd not seen any photos anywhere in the house. Hands slowing as she closed the last drawer, Lauren slumped against the wall. Did gangsters just not have a family? Cutting down on the potential liability of loved ones? So... what was she? Her upper lip hovered between a sneer and a tremble. Someone that wouldn't cause much of a stir if she disappeared? Idly walking through the house, Lauren poked through books in the crowded shelves in the living room, looking for photos. Kitchen drawers, the pantry. Nothing. Leaning against the beautiful stone counter in defeat, she finally shook off her curiosity and fetched another bottle of Chardonnay from the pantry, making herself a sandwich to accompany it. Hearing her phone buzz in her purse, Lauren sighed and defiantly took another swig of the rather nice white wine. It would be Thomas. Because no one else called her anymore. The phone buzzed angrily again as if her horrid husband somehow knew she was ignoring him.

Finally, Lauren stalked over and yanked her shiny new phone out. A text. Curt and to the point.

"There is a season opener soiree The Corporation is hosting before the performance tonight. You will be required to mingle and chat

with our more prominent donors before going backstage. I'll pick you up at 6 pm. Be ready."

Lauren's fist tightened on the phone, wanting to throw it across the room and hear the satisfying shatter as it hit some no doubt expensive item in Thomas's high-tech kitchen. Bastard. Autocratic asshole! Looking at the time, the new Mrs. Williams growled as she realized she only had an hour to get ready. Abandoning her sandwich but dragging along the wine bottle, Lauren angrily stomped up the stairs like a child, trying to make as much noise as possible.

Nonetheless, Lauren was ready at 6:02 pm, hair up in an elegant twist and looking calm and collected in her off-shoulder black, velvet dress. Fortunately, the costumer for the LSO had excellent taste, so the female musicians had a universally flattering dress- full, sweeping skirt, tight bodice, and a v-cut neckline that gracefully showed off a woman's collarbones and not too much of the bosom. Sweeping majestically out the door after keeping Thomas waiting for exactly three minutes, she handed her cello case to him to stow in the back of his Jaguar, which took a bit of effort in the sportscar, Lauren noticed with some malice, and seated herself, stiffening as he bent over her as usual to fasten her seatbelt. They drove in silence for a short time until Thomas used his most infuriating, condescending drawl. "Do you understand your responsibilities tonight?"

Lauren rolled her eyes, "Of cour-"

"That's one." His eyes were still on the road, but there was a certain set to his jaw that spelled trouble.

"One, what?" she asked in spite of herself.

This time, her dark husband side-eyed her briefly before

turning his attention back to the road. "Your insolence will be dealt with after the performance tonight."

"My insolence?" Lauren protested angrily, "You- dude, you couldn't even see me roll my eyes, so-"

"That's two," he interrupted calmly, "insolence, arguing with me- ah, really, that's three for the gratuitous American slang. I've told you to stop using it."

It was entirely possible that the girl's next move was to fling herself over the gear shift and attempt to strangle the horrible man who'd ruined her life- as evidenced by her raised arms and fingers curled into claws. It was, however, also the exact moment that the rear window of the Jaguar shattered and they heard the screech of crumpled metal as another car slammed into the BMW driven by Chuck, tailing them as always. Thomas instantly yanked Lauren down by one arm to keep her out of the line of fire and jammed one foot on the brakes while hauling the steering wheel to the right, spinning them into a neat circle that ended up with the car facing the damaged one of his employee, whose face was bloody, but based on his coldly furious expression, not badly injured.

Thomas's car door was ripped open and he instantly seized the head of the invader and slammed it viciously against his dashboard, knocking the man out. Unfortunately, Lauren's door was opened simultaneously and she was yanked out by another man, a gun placed and pressing hard into her abdomen. Stepping out of the Jaguar with his hands up, Thomas eyed his wife. Lauren was pale, but she was calm and her mouth in a tight furious line, looking between him and her bodyguard to make sure they were both alive.

"Heeey, Tommy! How's it hanging, motherfucker?" The idiot currently training his Glock on her husband apparently knew him, and this theory was solidified by his expression of well-bred contempt.

"I believe you've been sniffing too much of your own product, you imbecile." Thomas leaned against the car in a deliberately casual fashion. To Lauren's relief, the thug jamming the gun into her ribcage must have decided she wasn't a threat, because he pulled the weapon back, at least enough for her to draw a breath.

The man taunting Thomas turned to look at her with a grin. "Well, well, honey. Aren't you just pretty as a peach? Did Tommy here pick you up in one of The Corporation whorehouses, like Kingston did?" *His accent was American*, Lauren thought absently, *maybe Texan?*

Admittedly, she didn't exactly think before she spoke, but the new Mrs. Williams snarled, "Unlike *you,* cowboy, my husband doesn't have to pay someone to sleep with him." Out of the corner of her eye, she could see an actual expression of surprise cross her stoic husband's face before a corner of his mouth turned up in a smile and he focused on the suddenly infuriated American again.

"Coleson, how desperate can you be to try something this stupid?" Thomas's voice was ice. "What can you possibly think will happen after pulling a gun on me? On my *wife?*" There was a sudden fury in his voice that made even Lauren take a step back. "I will burn your pitiful group of fuckwits into ash."

Growling, Coleson raised his pistol, ready to slam it against Thomas's head and incongruously, all Lauren could think was, *Don't hurt his face!* Eyes darting back to Chuck, she saw him nod slightly to the right, where the second man who always accompanied him was edging behind the chase car driver holding a gun to his head.

Letting out a shrill shriek, Lauren sobbed, "Don't hurt Thomas! Don't! We- we just got married!" She was struggling to give a convincing wail, but it was at least enough to get both Coleson and her husband to stare at her as Chuck's partner bashed in the head of the man holding him hostage, giving Chuck room to grab the gun and let off a shot that nailed the American in the shoulder. Which, then gave Lauren the (rather impressive, she thought) strength to yank out her cello case and smash it against the head and upper torso of the man holding her hostage, who had, admittedly, lost his focus during all the shooting. But it was enough to drop him like a bag of dirt, and while her husband drove his fist into the face of Coleson, both Lauren and the cello were put abruptly back in the car as Chuck not-quite yelled at Thomas to do the same.

The Jaguar took off like a meteor, streaking down the roadway with the only sound being Thomas's curt order to "Fasten your seatbelt, darling."

"What the *hell?* What the hell was- seriously, what the hell was *that*, Thomas? Who were those assholes?" Lauren's shaking hands struggled to do as she was told, even while trying to demand some answers.

"Language," he chided automatically while keeping an eye on the rearview mirror. At her outraged hiss, Thomas unbent to explain, "Coleson is a coke-addled simpleton who's furious that I stopped The Corporation from dealing with his idiot drug ring in America. Apparently, he's taken it rather badly."

His wife's next question was cut off by the scream of metal grinding against metal and the rather painful snap of her head back from the impact of another car hitting theirs from behind.

"Take the wheel."

"WHAT?" gasped Lauren, "Are you nu-" she swallowed back a scream as Thomas's hand yanked hers to the Jaguar's steering wheel.

"Keep us steady if you want to live." With this deeply unhelpful advice, her husband pulled an alarmingly large firearm from the car's center console and turned to fire rapidly out his window, one polished shoe firmly holding the gas pedal down as Lauren clutched the steering wheel in a death grip, ignoring her chattering teeth and forcing herself to keep her eyes on the road in front of her.

The first blisteringly loud "pop!" of the handgun shattered the windshield of the remaining car in pursuit, and after the third shot, she could barely hear the wild screech of the tires over the loud ringing in her ears as the grey SUV behind them veered violently and then flipped off the road. Thomas's dark head pulled back into the car and he handed the gun to a horrified Lauren, handle first.

"Take this," Thomas was pleased to see his wife didn't say a word, eyes alarmingly huge as she took the firearm and relinquished hold of the wheel. His foot pressed harder on the accelerator and they shot down the road.

It took Lauren a moment to recover the ability to speak. "Don't you ha..." she paused, then tried again. "Don't you have to check and see if they're..." Thomas forced himself not to smile as his poor wife licked her lips, attempting to string together a coherent sentence.

"The Corporation's backup was right behind us, they've already signaled they've reached the crash. It would be unwise of us to linger." Williams side-eyed Lauren's set, pale face. She hadn't screamed, nor cried. It was possible she was in shock, but he didn't think so. He gently put on hand on hers, limp on her lap. "Are you all right?" He expected crying, hysterics maybe. Possibly unhinged laughter. Instead, Lauren started singing.

"Ninety-nine red balloons
fly... uh... float and da da dah..."

"Darling, what the hell are-" Thomas stopped, then gentled his tone. "What are you singing?"

Now, Lauren started to laugh, "Oh! *Grosse Pointe Blank,* when he takes out the East German assassin with a ballpoint pen to the ear at his high school reunion? Remember? And then his friend the real estate guy helps him stuff the corpse in a locker? Or was that the boiler in the basement?" Williams was silent as he drove, hands gripping the steering wheel, listening to his wife absently hum the rest of the song as she tried to remember the murder sequence. Finally pulling herself together a bit, she sucked in a shaky breath and smoothed her hair. "You know, John Cusack? The movie? This isn't like, required viewing for gangsters and hitmen?"

Williams found himself letting out a deep sigh as he patted her hands again. "You did well, darling. Magnificently, in fact." Looking over, he gazed at her slack jaw doubtfully. "I don't believe you'll be able to play tonight, however. It's a bit much after-"

Absently flapping her hand in a dismissive way, Lauren answered blankly, "Don't be silly. I'll just need to change- this dress has blood all over the skirt." It took her another minute to gather her thoughts, and then she tried to sound firm as she added, "You're gonna... you know, the whole thing with The Corporation whorehouse and the Texas drug ring... thing... you're gonna have to explain that stuff. Later, though. Okay?"

Simply nodding, her dark husband turned towards Hampstead Heath, listening to her sing.

"Wegen 99 Luftballons..."

Thomas deftly stripped Lauren back at the house and helped her shower quickly. It was the first non-sexual touch they'd had in some time, and he was irritably forcing his cock back down at the sight of her lovely, pale body. It didn't help that he'd been sporting a constant erection since running those imbeciles off the road. And remembering his sweet, virginal bride crack that bastard American over the head with her cello case? Magnificent.

She seemed to start coming back to herself as Thomas briskly dried her off, laying out (with an inward smirk) his choice of a lacy pile of ebony undies and bra to wear under her other orchestra gown. Fully dressed, Lauren hastily re-applied her stage makeup as her curiously kind spouse zipped her up, pulling her hair free of the collar and straightening the skirt. Hands over the bare skin of her shoulders, Williams stroked her collarbones with long fingers as he watched her.

"How do you feel?"

Lauren's eyelids fluttered a bit, just the way that always did when he used the Voice, this time deep, compelling, and with a rather startling note of sincerity. "M'okay," she mumbled, before shaking her head and standing straighter. "Surprisingly good, in fact." She felt absurdly grateful for the warm, approving smile her beautiful husband/captor/savior/assassin gave her in return.

"Good," he kissed the top of her head and led her from the bedroom. "Did you check your instrument for any damage from finishing off that oaf with the case?"

A bit of a laugh escaped from Lauren before she realized she was chuckling at someone's imminent demise, even if it appeared he'd certainly planned on killing *her*. "I did," she agreed, "that case is like titanium, I swear."

Back downstairs and opening the door to their connected garage, Lauren stopped short. "Your Jaguar turned into... another Jaguar. That's the best fairy godmother ever."

Thomas laughed as he carefully stowed her instrument and opened her door, helping Lauren into the new car. "This is the F-type R Coupe, matte black and capable of 289 kilometers per hour on an open roadway. A crew from The Corporation's vehicles division retrieved the other car." He was just rounding the corner of the park that separated the elegant section they lived in from the more busy, crowded part of the area when Lauren's hand landed on his thigh.

"Stop the car."

He looked down, concern on his beautiful face. "Are you all right, darling? Are you sick?" With a sudden movement, his formerly shy wife was straddling him, hitching up her sweeping velvet skirt to rub her lace-covered mound against him. Hands sliding up to bracket his face, Lauren put her mouth on his, kissing him feverishly, hard sucks and licks along his lips until they opened and for the first time, she slid her tongue into his mouth with a sigh of pleasure.

Thomas groaned. He knew she was simply feeling the giddy

arousal that comes with survival, with violence and triumph. But her agile hips felt so good swirling against his crotch and good Lord, he'd been hard for the last hour. Still... "Lauren- sweetheart-" with an effort, Thomas pulled his head back. "I don't want to take advantage of you after such an intense-" His delightful little trollop cut off his rather gallant effort by fastening her lips over his again and unzipping his fine wool trousers, yanking open the belt and making a guttural sound of delight in her throat when she realized her wildly arousing husband hadn't bothered with underwear that day. Thomas helped her by yanking aside her flimsy panties and holding his cock steady, his other hand on her hip and helping her center herself over him.

"Oh..." it was barely an exhalation from her open mouth, but Lauren's dreamy smile gave it away, her pleasure in sliding down, pushing herself over her husband's thick shaft. She had *missed* this. Not that she would ever admit it, but god, Thomas felt so- A stifled chuckle from the man she was riding made her freeze in horror, which pulled a corresponding groan from him as she unconsciously gripped down on his cock at the same time. Dropping her face into his neck, Lauren mumbled, "I said that out loud, didn't I?"

Sliding his fingers into her hair, Thomas pulled her head up and looked at her, grinning, but his cobalt eyes warm, reassuring. "Well, yes, darling." He grinned again at her pleasurable shriek as he drove his hips up sharply against her, shoving himself deeper inside her. "But I promise never to tell a soul. But as we're being so open with each other..." his hands gripped her waist and began moving her up and down on his shaft, pulling up quickly to hover just inside her opening, then brutally yanking her down on him, groaning against the pull and resistance of all that heat and wet inside his bride. "I quite agree. It has been far too long since I've been inside you." One of her hands gripped the shoulder of his suit, the other slid to the back of his neck as she tried to balance herself and kiss him at the same time. As his arms flexed, moving her faster, Thomas enjoyed watching the lovely bounce of Lauren's breasts, wishing he could rip the dress off of her and really enjoy this pretty body, this lovely, tight pussy that belonged to him. But instead, he settled for sliding his hands under her skirt and gripping the globes of her ass harshly, continuing to move his bride brutally fast, enjoying hearing her moan each time he bottomed out inside her.

Feeling the first of those tempting flutters from inside her pussy, a flexing that rippled in tighter and tighter movements up and down his cock, Thomas groaned and tried to focus. "I can feel you, sweet girl, you're tensing against me, ready to come. You want to come, don't you?" One long finger slicked against the lovely mix of her arousal and slid to the pucker of her ass, idly circling it as she stiffened. Which made Lauren clench down against his cock again.

"As much as I adore the strength of your warm little pussy, if you keep clutching against me, I fear you're going to rip my cock right off my body."

Lauren bit her husband's earlobe quite a bit harder than she'd planned. It was something she couldn't defend against- his deep, nearly guttural groan, the dark rasp of those filthy words in her ear, and the strength of him. Even arching her hips away from that damnable finger of his just drove her clit harder against the coarse hair on his pelvis. So really, there was nothing left for her to do but come. So, Lauren did, with a scream that startled even her, still pushing up and down on his spurting cock and rubbing her slickened ass against his scrotum. It was greedy, it was wanton, and she'd never come harder. Panting with her face buried in his neck again, she could hear her dark husband murmur, "How beautiful you are, how sweet my good girl is, how delicious." He was stroking his hands soothingly up and down her back and kissing along the pale column of her neck. Lauren found she was shaking- she wasn't certain why. Thomas felt it, and wrapped his arms around her for a moment, feeling her chilly skin warm against his embrace and the shivering stop. "You're coming down from all that adrenaline," he soothed, kissing her again.

With a regretful sigh, he helped her off his softening cock and pulled out the pocket square from his suit to help tidy her before straightening her panties back into place. Lauren was still silent, he noted, but Thomas didn't push her, simply settled her back in the low-slung leather seat and putting the car back into gear with a single, salacious wink.

Settling into her chair onstage and rapidly making sure her cello was still in tune, Lauren couldn't keep the silly, little smile off her face. She must be insane. She must be just as immoral and evil as her crime-lord husband. But she'd never felt so alive, almost fierce. So when she caught Macie looking over at her with a puzzled expression, she couldn't stop herself from giving her old friend a huge grin before leaning into the neck of the cello, bow poised and ready.

In the audience, Number One looked at the composed expression on the handsome face of his second in command, noting calmly that the fool's trousers bore blatant evidence of exactly why the new Mr. and Mrs. Williams missed the season-opening soiree.

Chapter 14 – Is My Terrifying Bride Brave, As Well?

In which Lauren is rewarded for being a complete badass by her doting spouse.

Part of Lauren sat somewhere outside herself for the next few hours, just watching in amazement at what had become of her. Not in the coping way she was used to - separating herself from misery or trauma - more like… astonishment.

Astonished at how she played beautifully in her first formal performance in the soaring hall of St. Luke's. How she kept her gaze from The Corporation's private box but bit back a smile, knowing her husband was watching her with a knowing gaze. How she graciously laughed and spoke with everyone afterward, hugging her fellow musicians. How she finally walked out the door to find Thomas waiting for her, leaning against a pillar with his arms folded. He leaned down to kiss her cheek, whispering in a voice so sinfully pleased, "Such beautiful work. I have never enjoyed a concert more, darling." Lauren bit back a groan, knowing she was flushing a mottled red and hearing his low chuckle as he took her cello case.

There was silence for a moment as Thomas's new matte black Jaguar turned for home.

A giggle erupted from Lauren before she put a hand over her mouth. As her husband looked over at her, brow raised, she finally offered, "Well, that was a full afternoon."

A fleeting smile went over his thin lips. "Quite. Are you all right?"

Shrugging, Lauren was about to go into her patented "I'm always fine!" response, then stopped and thought for a moment. "I'm... actually really calm. I probably should be more upset, huh?"

Thomas's warm hand slid over her thigh. "You were magnificent. I knew you were intelligent and resourceful, but really, darling, you exceed my expectations."

But the moment to really question her sanity began as Thomas took her hand and led her rapidly up to their bedroom. "Thomas..."

"Shhhh," he whispered, rapidly unzipping the back of her dress, "where did my magnificent Valkyrie learn to crush a villain's skull with her cello case?"

Despite the really distracting - and painfully arousing - feeling of her husband's lips moving down her spine, Lauren laughed, embarrassed. "Uh, some guy tried to mug me in Manhattan when I was attending Julliard. I was turning to try and run away from him when my arm swung out with my case and clocked the bastard. Knocked him right out." To her belated relief, Thomas did not admonish her for her language and merely gave a low, savage chuckle that made her shudder against his mouth.

"Clever girl," he soothed, "you didn't fall into hysterics, you were magnificent." Thomas was mildly irritated as his bride pulled away from his efforts to strip her of her gown and turned to him.

"Soooo..." she drew out the question, knowing it would irritate him. "Will these random fender-benders be a part of life as a Corporation wife?" Lauren realized the question was ill-advised when a shadow fell over Thomas's beautiful face, like a cloud passing over the moon.

Harshly yanking down the black velvet clinging to her hips, he snarled, "I shall make quite certain we never hear from this particular brand of idiots again. Now..." his ocean blue eyes were traveling lazily up and down her body, appreciating her black, strapless bra and the little undies he'd slipped up her legs personally earlier that evening. "Perhaps you will allow me to focus on something far more interesting than those pathetic coke fiends. Your lovely breasts in particular."

Lauren allowed him to tumble them both on the bed and even wrapped her legs firmly around his narrow hips. Incongruously, however, she burst into laughter.

Irritably lifting his dark head, her husband fixed her with a steely glare. "You're distracting me, darling."

Smoothing her hands over his sculpted shoulders, the blonde simply continued giggling. "You know during the Prohibition in the early 1900s in America, the gangsters would hide their guns in violin cases and carve an opening at the top of the case." Smiling devilishly at his speculative expression, Lauren ventured, "Imagine what we could conceal in my cello case, like a surface to air rocket launcher, or someth-"

Growling, his lean body arched over hers and stopped her with a kiss. "You will never be in that position again, little girl. I shall make quite sure of it." Thomas tried to bend in and kiss her again, but with a rather loud grunt of effort Lauren managed to flip them, hovering over him with a dark smile.

"You can't make sure of it, Thomas. But you can teach me more about defending myself." Giving a deliberate, long roll of her hips, she enjoyed the involuntary groan from her husband's perfect lips. "You don't want some pathetic little wimp for a wife. You like that I could maybe kick some ass."

Tightening his thighs against her, he flipped them again, biting down on the throbbing artery in her neck as he growled, "Maybe, my arse. My sweet." He kissed her soundly, "Little. Demure. Wife." She was breathless when he finished the assault on her lips, and he growled a little, the sound rippling through the thin skin of her throat and making Lauren let out an embarrassing whimper. "You took out a contract killer with a vicious swing from an improvised weapon. I find you to be a bit... terrifying." Thomas found he loved the way she felt when his surprising bride laughed, breasts jolting and teasing along his chest, legs tightening and loosening, the look in her eyes when Lauren gazed up at him without fear, for a change.

"Terrifying? That is a word," she giggled, "that has never been used to describe me. But it's kind of flattering, to be honest."

Her husband was smiling down at her, a strangely tender expression that surprised her for its rare appearance in her life. "I am going to order in from that Thai restaurant you like. Why don't you go find a film you like?"

Brightening, Lauren asked, "Can we eat in bed?" This was a forbidden activity, so she enjoyed the pained smile on Thomas' face even more.

"Of course, darling."

Chapter 15 - The Team Building Exercise

In which Lauren is forced to participate in Bratva's bizarre form of "hospitality."

Lauren woke to the sound of Thomas's cell phone on the bedside table. Sighing, he picked it up, rubbing his eyes.

"Yes?" She couldn't hear what was being said on the other end of the line, but she could feel the big body next to hers grow still. "Very well. We'll be there."

"What's up?" Lauren tried to sound like her brain was fully functioning, but when she looked at Thomas as he rose from the bed, her heart sank. His face was set and composed; his voice indifferent.

"Be ready at 8 pm," he answered, "wear one of your more sophisticated black dresses. We have a dinner meeting with the head of Bratva. He's in town," he added ominously, "this is a surprise."

Clutching the sheet to her chest, Lauren could feel her breath hitch. "Oh, *shit*," she mumbled.

"Stop staring at me. That side-eye is going to give you a headache."

Thomas's eyes hadn't diverted from the road, Lauren thought resentfully, but of course, he caught her effort to watch him while trying to be inconspicuous about it. She wanted to ask just how bad this was going to be. This dinner had surprised Thomas, and she knew without asking that her scary husband did not like to be surprised.

"Sorry."

They stopped for a red light, and he looked over. His bride looked beautiful- sleek, shiny updo and a pair of pretty diamond studs in her ears. Simple, elegant. The cold Number Two of Jaguar Holdings knew Lauren felt awkward many times- well, most of the time when it came to her confusing and often terrifying new life. But he'd been taken with how gracefully she'd handled so many sticky situations. Internally groaning as he thought again of Lauren knocking the seven bells out of that Texas thug with her cello case, Thomas irritably willed his swelling cock to stand down. Taking pity on her, he took her warm hand and squeezed it gently. "I know you're too clever to think this is a relaxed social occasion," Thomas said calmly. "Semion Mogilevich is an important business partner."

Lauren looked down at their loosely clasped hands. Semion Mogilevich was, in fact, the head of the murderous Bratva empire. She was quite capable of using a search engine. She knew exactly the kind of monsters The Corporation was in bed with. Which made her wonder just how monstrous *they* were as well. What was her husband capable of, this man who tied her up and taunted her into multiple orgasms, who held her hand and curled behind her and soothed her when she was shaken by just how far he'd brought her into this dark and alluring world of his? He was capable of kindness, her husband, even if he had forced her into a life she never would have chosen for herself.

Her mouth twisted unattractively. Of course, it could be said that Frank forced her into this life by leaving them wide open to his coercion. If her father had been a valuable member of the Jaguar Holdings empire, Thomas could not have demanded her hand in marriage. Rubbing her forehead, Lauren vowed to stop thinking about it. These thoughts would swirl round and round in her brain until she stilled them with enough glasses of wine and hopefully, sleep. She had the luxury of neither tonight since she needed to be at her most alert.

"His arrival seems to be a surprise to you," Lauren ventured, "I'm guessing a surprise visit from the Bratva is not a good thing."

Thomas looked at her sharply then, those frost blue eyes keener than she liked. "You would be correct," he allowed, "which is why we listen and watch. And in your case, say nothing." Rolling his eyes as Lauren's narrowed, he impatiently added, "Not because you are not an excellent conversationalist with an astonishing ability to draw out stories from the most tight-lipped men I know. Because you are, of course. But because I want no attention drawn to you. This is a man to whom I want you to be invisible."

"Kind of like Moses painting lamb's blood on the doors in Egypt to make Death pass them by?" Lauren meant it in a somewhat sarcastic aside, but the image suddenly chilled her.

"Something like that," he agreed grimly. "Listen and watch. Be my clever girl."

Lauren was humiliated to feel herself shiver a little at his words, how his tone dipped as he called her his "clever girl." God. She was such a pushover for the Voice.

"Просить милостыню и умолять. Ужасный ублюдок." Thomas chuckled politely along with the few others at the table who spoke Russian, an assistant leaning over to Number One and subtly translating the conversation. Mogilevich continued, hands waving expansively, spilling a bit of his excellent vodka. *"Поэтому мы взяли его детей вместо этого!"*

Lauren's fingers curled into claws in her linen napkin looking down at her plate and counting her breaths. She'd always loved to learn, her mother fondly called her "my clever bookworm" since she was old enough to sneak a flashlight and a book into bed. But at this moment Lauren deeply regretted ever learning Russian. Deeply. She didn't want to hear these things. Even the French "butcher," or the Bratva captain with three kids and a penchant for melting his victims into sludge with acid, they couldn't possibly be as horrible as this man, every word he spoke was violating any sense of decency left within her.

Looking over at a puzzled but pleasantly smiling Clara, Lauren gave a little shrug with one shoulder, indicating confusion but with a "Let the men tell their stories," gesture. When Number Three's fiancée nodded back, Lauren could see her jaw was trembling, like Clara was gritting her teeth. With a rising sense of concern, she realized the sweet girl was smarter than she'd thought.

As dessert was served and tiny cups of coffee consumed,

THE RELUCTANT BRIDE

Lauren allowed herself to relax. Just a little. That meant this hellish dinner party was nearly at an end, right? To her horror, the Russian stood up and spread out his arms grandly. *"Я отвезу вас к моему новому бизнесу здесь, в Лондоне. Думаю, вам это очень понравится."* Lavender eyes darting to her husband's pleadingly, Lauren was quite sure she would not enjoy this "new business." Not at all. Unfortunately, Thomas looked at her expressionlessly and simply nodded his head.

"Where *are* we going?" Unfortunately, Mr. and the soon to be Mrs. Fassell had joined them in their car, and what Lauren was really dying to ask was severely curtailed. She watched as Thomas's sculpted jaw clenched, not a good sign.

"We will graciously accept Mogilevich's hospitality-" Thomas paused at a chuckle quickly turned into a cough from that idiot Fassell in the backseat, then calmly continued, "-for an appropriate amount of time, then we shall leave." He was turning into a brightly lit parking lot and when Lauren caught the name on the sign her blood turned to ice.

"He's taking us to a STRIP CLUB?" Lauren wasn't a prude, *The last few days certainly burned, salted and scorched the earth of* that *theory,* snarked her spiteful inner voice, but the concept of having to spend an evening with an overpriced drink and her husband staring at naked women with likely much, much better bodies than hers was the last possible thing she would have expected Thomas to ever make her do.

Clara was clearly of the same mind, "Michael? I don't want to go in there." Her voice was shaky and it made Lauren twinge internally.

Number Three was all that was soothing, "Baby, I'm sorry. I know this is a little, uh, off, but we'll just have a drink and leave, all right?" There was silence in the back seat, and

Michael tried again. "Where's your sense of adventure? One to check off the bucket list?"

Turning back to Thomas, Lauren was alarmed to see the tight set to his jaw didn't soften. Steeling herself, she asked, "Could you at least let me drive Clara home? We could wait at your house- I mean our hou-"

"No."

Her cold husband exited the car, moving gracefully around it to cut off the valet as he attempted to open the passenger door. Leaning in to offer his hand to Lauren, he kept it steady as she stared at it. She knew this was the Russian's idea, not Thomas's. But why would he allow something so disrespectful to her and the other wives? A low growl disguised as clearing his throat made her realize she was taking too long, and with a sigh, she swung her legs out and attempted to rise from the low-slung sports car as gracefully as possible. Sliding his arm around her waist, Thomas leaned in close. "This is a common Bratva move," he murmured so quietly that she could barely hear him over the street noise. "They like to test new business relationships under the guise of 'hospitality,' and unless this endangers you in some way, we are required to go through with it." His grip tightened around her waist, but Lauren knew it was from fury at their host, not her. "So, you will be my gracious bride and handle this with some sophistication. Have you ever been to a gentleman's club before?"

Snorting at the dignified euphemism, she shook her blonde head. "No."

The first tinge of humor entered his deep voice as Thomas answered her, "I didn't think so. You've seen naked women before. Other than that, it's a standard bar. Try to be a little bored, polite, but not shocked. He would enjoy that."

Lauren tried to tell herself it was the blast of air conditioning from the front door opening that made her shudder, but she knew better. Looking back, she watched an uncomfortable-looking Clara being more or less dragged along by Number Three, who was eagerly looking around. Rolling her eyes, Lauren gave her friend what she hoped was a reassuring smile. Number One and their vile host were striding a bit ahead of the others, their bodyguards surrounding them and Arabella left walking behind, forgotten. Lauren reached out to link her arm with the older woman's, and Arabella gave her a grateful smile. The VIP lounge was suitably beautiful, secluded and filled with expensive furniture and a private bar. Lauren was actually grateful for the harsh vodka shot they were all demanded to drink, and for the one after. She tried to focus only on their little group, but there was no getting around the completely naked women, *Except for those clear Lucite heels,* she thought, *why those see-through shoes? Why?* who were hovering over the men, offering a shoulder massage or another drink. When a stacked redhead started slinking up to Thomas, she fixed her with a glare that should have turned the waitress to stone, but the redhead was made of stronger stuff. *She probably has plenty of experience with pissed-off dates,* Lauren snarled internally. However, Thomas looked up briefly as the waitress/geisha/whatever started cooing and impatiently waved her off mid-sentence. He did notice his bride smiled a bit malevolently and put her hand on his thigh. As the men drew into a deeper discussion, The Corporation spouses found themselves focusing on each other. Only Arabella looked around comfortably, long legs crossed and arms stretched across the back of the sofa, drink in hand.

"Ah, see there?" Arabella said, gesturing with her drink, "I was considering that girl's tits. Perfect!"

Unwittingly, Lauren and Clara turned to look at a voluptuous girl with lovely milk chocolate-colored skin and magnificently full breasts. Gaze going to Arabella's chest, Lauren laughed. "I think you got them, 'Bella." All three began to giggle, feeling less awkward. Looking around, Lauren didn't see anything particularly shocking. She thought strippers wore those- the things for the nipples? Oh, pasties and a G-string- but she wasn't seeing anything she didn't see in the dressing room at the "Y" where she used to take yoga. It was the men at the club that made her uncomfortable, the things they were shouting, how they spoke to the girls. Taking a healthy swallow of her wine, she let herself relax a little. She could do this.

"Это твой выбор. Шлюха или жена." (*"It's your choice. Whore or wife."*) Feeling like she'd just been punched in the stomach, Lauren's gaze flew back to the knot of expensively suited men. For some reason, the head of Bratva was looking at her as he said the ugly words.

What the hell- what could that possibly mean? she fumed internally, trying not to let her rising fury show on her face. This dickhead must not know *she* knew what he just said. After a few more moments of discussion, Number One stood up and buttoned his jacket, nodding at one of the blondes, who came forward to take his arm and lead him away. He didn't look at his wife as he left, and Arabella pretended not to notice.

Thomas rose as well, holding out his hand to Lauren with the same cold expression he'd worn that night in his office when he told her she'd be marrying him, one way or another. It was the face of a man who would order another to be shot right in front of her. Her father, in fact. So, without a single word, she put her ice-cold hand in his and rose stiffly. Following him down a hallway, she didn't speak until a smirking "hostess" opened a door and Thomas abruptly ushered her into a blandly furnished room, a bit like a medium level hotel room, though instead of prints of landscapes, there was glossy framed porn.

"What is-"

He abruptly moved her a bit to the left and cut off her question with a harsh kiss. Pulling out his phone, he pushed a button and scanned the room.

"Not a word," Thomas breathed into her ear, ignoring the way Lauren was beginning to shake. "This room is wired for sound, no cameras. We're in here to fuck." Anticipating her sudden attempt to get loose, he pushed his struggling bride harder against the wall. "Listen to me," he enunciated coldly, "our host insists that we accept the hospitality of the club: which means making use of a woman before we leave."

"I'm n-not a whore," Lauren gritted out, trying to be quiet and choke down the scream of rage building in her throat.

Thomas growled slightly, "It's either you or a club whore. Which do you prefer I fuck?"

She wanted to throw up. She wanted to run screaming from the room. She wanted to crack that fucking bottle of vodka over that bastard Mogilevich's head. But Lauren made her numb lips move. "You want to have sex with me while they... while they listen to us?" To her humiliation, there was a sob at the end of her whisper.

Feeling his big, warm body sigh, she drew in a breath as he leaned back a bit. "We have to do this. Can you keep quiet?"

"I don't want to do this," Lauren hissed, a little childishly. "Who the fuck has to *do* shit like this? What the hell kind of fucked-up corporate retreat was this?"

Thomas's voice dipped, lowering into that soothing, persuasive tone that always made her capitulate. "I know, baby. As your Sir, I would not ask this of you unless I thought you were ready. But as your husband, I must insist. Be a good girl, quiet and sweet and we'll get this over with." He didn't wait for her agreement, simply unzipping her dress and pushing it off of her, pausing to appreciate the lacy black bustier (thank you, Hen Party) and matching undies. Rough fingertips slipped over the skin of her thighs as he deliberately stepped on her dress, marking it as he pulled off his jacket.

"Loosen my tie." His voice was louder this time, easily overhead. Brow furrowed, Lauren did as she was told and unbuttoned the top buttons of his shirt as Thomas pulled his belt loose and unzipped his trousers. "Take me out," he ordered, and pressing her lips tighter, his bride did, unconsciously stroking its generous length once, twice, before realizing what she was doing and pulled her hand away like his dick was on fire. Chuckling smugly, Thomas drew his hands to her ass and squeezed, suddenly hoisting her up as Lauren gave an undignified yelp before gritting her teeth again.

Her thighs tightened harshly against his waist as her dark husband began sliding her down, beginning to impale her until Lauren stiffened and gave a tight-lipped whimper of discomfort. *Of course,* Thomas thought, *dry as the Sahara and no surprise.* Balancing her with his hips and one hand, he raised his other palm and spat into it, watching her look of shock at the crude gesture and the flaming red of her cheeks as he smeared it on the head of his cock. Lauren made an abortive effort to move away, but his grip tightened and he began thrusting again, slower and more gentle than usual. Thomas's angry grip on her ass spoke otherwise, but Lauren knew he was trying to not hurt her.

"Relax," he murmured in her ear.

"I can't," Lauren gulped, "I hate this. I don't want to be here."

Those lean hips of his began moving against her, smoothly, persuasively swirling and rubbing against all those secret spots he'd found inside her. "I know," his voice was sin, deep and just barely loud enough to understand him. "Picture instead some shadowy hallway at a club, where we've been dancing. Do you remember that night on the dance floor? The first night we-"

"The 'No Diggity' night," Lauren agreed without thinking. She heard Thomas choke back a laugh and cringed.

Picking up the thread again, he purred, "We can't wait to have each other, you want me fucking up into you right then. My good girl turned naughty." He felt her bite into his shirt to stay quiet and his hips moved faster. "So I take you by the hand and we find a quiet place like this, those clever hands of yours unzipping me while I grab the back of your thighs, just like this-" Her savage little teeth were *really* digging into the muscle of his shoulder, but Thomas let it go, smugly pleased to feel shoving into his wife was turning into a delicious glide, her sudden slick smoothing his path and letting him push into her higher. "It's quick and greedy, both of us needing the other too much. The heels on your shoes digging into my back rather uncomfortably..."

To her embarrassment, Lauren realized he was right, but it was from anxiety, not arousal. Thomas was hoisting her up and down on his cock, it was inelegant, messy, and vaguely humiliating, but she was aroused enough from his filthy narrative that it didn't hurt as much as when he first entered her. Removing her teeth from his shoulder, she finally managed to whisper, "Please just... you know, just finish, okay? I can't... here. I'm sorry."

Her scary husband merely kissed her and with a few more hard thrusts, came inside her, his knees buckling just slightly before pulling from her gently and pressing the pocket square from his jacket over her wet center. Lauren felt for her underwear and found they'd been torn. *Great,* she thought bleakly, *perfect.* Quickly tucking himself away and zipping up, Thomas bent for her dress and helped her into it. Lauren looked at its rumpled appearance and knew it was meant to show off what they'd been doing. Extra proof, or something. She'd never thought sex with Thomas was anything other than amazing, wonderful, delicious. But now Number Two's new bride felt... disgusting.

Tidying her as well as he could, Thomas looped his tie loosely around his neck and shrugged back into his jacket. Taking her chin and raising it, he nodded. "You were very brave. My good girl. We'll leave this room with flushed cheeks, looking as if we'd just had the fuck of a lifetime and heads held high. I will take you home immediately."

Lauren could feel their combined spend trickling down her thigh and clenched her legs together. "Yeah, okay."

They did exactly as Thomas described, and Lauren refused to look at anyone, knowing her furiously flushed cheeks spoke for her but just focused on the exit to this shitty hellhole and the end of this vile "team-building exercise." Clara and Number Three were nowhere to be found, so she assumed they were still fulfilling their host's required "hospitality," and Arabella was still on the couch, idly swishing her drink and staring at nothing. "Goodnight Arabella," Lauren managed as they passed her, and the woman looked up and smiled blankly.

"Bye, honey. Hopefully Ben doesn't make this an all-nighter, I'm getting bored."

Nodding back with an equally blank smile, Lauren let Thomas lead her to the car and away from there.

"Просить милостыню и умолять. Ужасный ублюдок." - "He begged and pleaded."

"Поэтому мы взяли его детей вместо этого!" - "So we took his children instead!"

"Я отвезу вас к моему новому бизнесу здесь, в Лондоне. Думаю, вам это очень понравится." - "I'm taking you to my newest business here in London. I think you will enjoy it very much."

Chapter 16 - Abruptly, As My Passion Now Makes Me...

In which Thomas outdoes himself. As he should.

Thomas was not in bed by the time Lauren woke the next morning.

Not that it surprised her. Sighing and sitting up a little gingerly, she noted the aches and pains from their rough coupling the night before making themselves known. When they'd arrived home, she'd headed straight for the shower, and her Crime Lord husband was smart enough to not offer to scrub her back. Nor was he in their bed when she came out, skin bright red from a vigorous scrubbing and her most unattractive jammies covering her like a sea of Avengers-themed flannel. She did feel Thomas slide into bed much later, putting one long arm over her waist and kissing the back of her head gently, nuzzling in her clean hair. Taking in a deep sigh, Lauren was angry to feel tears well up in her eyes.

"Well, you can just cut that shit out," she counseled herself, "no crying over spilt milk, or spilt come, or-" For some reason, this struck her as hilarious and when Thomas came in, perfectly groomed in a dark blue suit, one brow raised to see his bride giggling uncontrollably.

"Good morning," he intoned, watching her sober immediately.

"I see you've dressed for work already," Lauren said a little stiffly.

Thomas made an agreeing sort of noise and sat next to her, watching her defensive body language. "How do you feel?"

Watching her fingers twist until he put one big hand over them to still her nervous movements, Lauren cleared her throat. "About, what? Do I feel physically okay? How do I feel about our little Team Building Exercise From Hell from last night, or-"

"Our team what?" he interrupted, fighting the smile that wanted to erupt.

"You know," Lauren mumbled, "like when you do the Trust Fall or walking over hot coals or... you know, that stuff." She refused to look up at him. Part shyness, but part feeling gross.

Somehow, he seemed to have a sense of what she was feeling. Thomas could feel himself slide into autocratic Number Two persona, but he forced himself to slow his irritation. "Tell me, darling. If I had wanted to fuck you- in a filthy, delicious way- in some dark corner in no way related to Bratva or Mogilevich, you would have enjoyed it, wouldn't you?" It was the wrong thing to say. His bride stiffened, looking up at him in hurt, humiliation, and fury.

"Yeah, well, it wasn't that. We, you know, did it against the wall of some sleazy room in a strip club. And I'm pretty sure that psycho Russian was right outside with his hand down his pants while he listened. Is this my- our life?" Thomas absently noticed her tears made her lavender eyes a dark violet, always beautiful. "Do you always let business partners push you around like this? Make you do weird stuff?" Her rant stopped abruptly when she saw the cold fury in his expression.

"No. One." he gritted, "Tells me what to do."

His big hand slid up her chest, long fingers settling around her throat. Lauren drew in a deep breath just in case it was her last and continued. "You married me to please them. You go to their little dinner parties and their strip clubs and you make me feel like nothing-" humiliated that her voice broke, she paused for a moment, refusing to look at him, "-using me just the way he told you to. Did you leave my ripped-up undies for them to find? A little souvenir to-"

"STOP!" Thomas watched her flinch, feeling vaguely disgusted with himself. The only person in his life he was relentlessly honest with, was of course himself. He was angry at Lauren because she was absolutely correct, not because she was being disobedient or disrespectful.

Drawing in a deep breath, he slid his hand down from her throat and smoothed his long fingers along her shoulder blades. "I've done you a disservice darling, both as your husband and your Sir. I should have paid closer attention to Mogilevich's intentions, and kept you at home and out of harm's way." Thomas leaned closer and Lauren cursed herself for instinctively swaying into him, smelling the crisp notes of his cologne, and the warmth of his skin. "Poor baby," he soothed, "I've treated my sweet girl terribly." His lips ghosted along her jawline and his tongue dipped out to suck on her ear lobe, enjoying her helpless shiver. "I owe you something lovely for that, don't I? You don't have a rehearsal today, correct?"

Lauren cleared her throat nervously. *Smooth bastard,* she

thought, how could he pull her from her outrage in *seconds* like this? And even more surprising, why wasn't he doing something terrible to her for talking back to him? "Uh..." she stumbled, "no?" She felt him grin against her neck feeling oddly aroused and still terrified, picturing him as that panther again, ready to sink his teeth into her throat.

"Then I am going to change," he said calmly, "and I suggest you do too." Casting a jaundiced eye over her voluminous jammies, "Something not as... squishy as these."

"Wait!" Laura called out after him, "What am I dressing for?"

Thomas turned and gave her what was unmistakably a leer. "For everything, darling," he said before disappearing into their dressing room. After tidying up in the bathroom, Lauren peeked in to look at what Thomas was wearing and dressed in something similar- a comfortable flowing sundress that matched his black jeans and pale blue shirt. She almost never saw him dressed down like this, so it was with a little bit of a thrill that she realized they looked more like just a normal newlywed couple. The thought warmed her and she eagerly took his outstretched hand.

"Where are we?" Lauren's eyes widened after Thomas took his hands away from covering them. They were surrounded by an unspeakably lush garden with stately columns dripping with wisteria. There were fluttering butterflies and hummingbirds, the sun filtering just so through the green branches above them. She started laughing in delight. "Seriously? There's like swans over there on that pond. All these animals are straight out of Central Casting, I swear."

Thomas took a basket handed to him by an expressionless

Chuck and ordered the bodyguards to trail at a discreet distance. "Hampstead Hill Garden," he answered, pulling her along the slate path, "very private, very quiet."

"Really," agreed Lauren, "it feels like we're the only people in here, not a lot of tourists stop by, I'm guessing."

Thomas merely gave her his most arousing half smile and continued on the path. No need to tell his bride that he'd arranged to close the gardens for the afternoon, to everyone but them. Rounding a corner, they were greeted by a stunning pergola, exquisitely hued peacocks strutting back and forth. He started laughing at Lauren's eye roll. "Yes, darling. The peacocks did cost extra." Dashingly pulling out a chilled bottle of champagne and two flutes, he opened the bottle with an impressive "pop!' of the cork and poured them both a glass with the experience of a sommelier.

"Is there anything you don't know how to do perfectly?" Lauren accepted a glass and shook her head in amazement.

"Apparently, being a husband," Thomas answered with honesty that shocked them both. With a devilish gleam, he leaned in. "But I do intend to improve my performance." Tapping his glass to hers, he murmured, "To a perfect day."

A little dazed, Lauren nodded, "A perfect day."

"Really," she persisted, her head on Thomas's lap, enjoying the surprising warmth of the autumn sun on her face, "I don't think I've seen one person since we arrived, have you? It's like *The Secret Garden.*"

"The children's book?" Thomas said lazily, "I never read it."

"Mmmm," Lauren wiggled a little on his hard thighs, getting

comfortable, "Frances Burnett wrote the story of a lonely little girl who was sent to live in her uncle's big, scary fancy house near London. No friends or family, no one to talk to."

Thomas shifted uneasily, some of the parallels not lost on him, even if she was unaware.

"So, Mary - the little girl - finds the key to a secret garden, no one's been in there for years and it's wildly overgrown. She begins to clear it and make the garden bloom again. She discovers she has a cousin – Colin - who's been shut away in the scary mansion and more or less ignored by everyone because of his illness, no one even caring that he was in pain!" Her lips firmed angrily, and her husband hid a smile. So empathetic, this girl. "So, Mary brings him into the garden, and as they restore the trees and the flowers, the garden heals them both. It was my favorite book as a child," she confessed, "I must've read it a hundred times." She felt his rough fingertips brush back and forth across her forehead, very gently. Looking up at him, she grinned. "So sentimental, huh? Unrealistic?"

He forced a smile, "I'm sure it's an uplifting message for children."

Lauren started laughing, daringly rising to straddle him, hands on his shoulders. "And what did Thomas Williams the... uh... what are you, like the fifth? Thomas Williams the-"

"First." Thomas answered firmly. She drew her hands away nervously at his tone, but he caught them, kissing the soft skin of one and then the other. "Thomas Williams the first, a new bloodline from an old one."

She nodded, treading carefully on this unstable new ground. "And what did young Thomas read? Edgar Allen Poe? Maybe a little George Orwell? Who was the guy who wrote *Lord of the*

Flies? Or maybe-"

"Shakespeare."

Lauren's mouth dropped open. "Ooooo... Will you please recite something for me? Maybe from *Much Ado About Nothing*, or- or *As You Like It?*" Watching his cobalt eyes cool a bit, she backtracked, "I mean, don't worry about it, I just-" With an alarmed squeal, she suddenly found herself on her back on the cushioned seating staring up at the dark beauty of her husband.

Running one long finger over his lips, Thomas pondered her flushed face.

Wooing, wedding, and repenting is as a Scotch jig, a measure, and a cinque-pace: the first suit is hot and hasty like a Scotch jig--and full as fantastical; the wedding, mannerly modest, as a measure, full of state and ancientry; and then comes repentance and with his bad legs falls into the cinque-pace faster and faster, till he sink into his grave.

Though it was certainly one of the most cynical passages from *Much Ado About Nothing*, delivered in Thomas's spine-meltingly beautiful voice, the rich elocution of his accent... Lauren could feel an uncomfortable warmth developing south, a certain weakness of the knees that made her question if she could stand up again. He smiled suddenly, subtle lines spreading from those penetrating eyes.

I have marked
A thousand blushing apparitions
To start into her face, a thousand innocent shames
In angel whiteness beat away those blushes;
And in her eye there hath appeared a fire,
To burn the errors that these Princes hold

Against her Maiden truth.

"Ooooo... that's..." Lauren was trying to form a full sentence, but the feeling of his mouth on her neck and sliding downwards made putting thought together more than she was capable of.

Oh, thou did'st then ne'er love so heartily.
If thou rememb'rest not the slightest folly
That ever love did make thee run inot,
Thou has not loved.
Of if thou has't not sat as I do now,
Wearying they hearer in thy mistress's praise,
Thou has not loved.
Of if thou hast not broke from company
Abruptly, as my passion now makes me,
Thou has not loved.

Her fingers slid through his thick hair, his mouth currently traveling from one breast to the other, the backless sundress having been an excellent choice since she couldn't wear a bra with it. When his teeth delicately bit one nipple as his tongue teased its tip, Lauren moaned. Yes, this was her favorite dress. Ever.

"Beautiful," she finally gasped, "you're so beautiful. This is perfect. So perfect." When he slid lower and his warm hands spread her thighs, Lauren tried to force her brain cells back together. "T-Thomas? We shouldn't-"

"No one will see us, darling," his dark head rose and he gave her a diabolical smile, "do you want your Sir to wipe away those ugly memories from last night?" He was very gently nibbling on the thin skin of her inner thigh, and Lauren's toes twitched, feeling her nerve endings spike under his teeth. The vibration of his chuckle against her center made her back arch. "Here we are, in the most perfect spot in England, and I have *never* wanted you more, little girl." He was actually *growling* now, and Lauren's hands flew to her hair, almost yanking the blonde curls out by the roots to keep from screaming in anticipation...

...And after, her favorite even more than coming together, was when he praised her for being his good, good girl and caring for her tenderly as he re-dressed her and carried her to the car, her face buried in his neck and not even seeing Chuck and Aimes carefully looking in the other direction.

Chapter 17 – There's so Much More at Stake Than Just You, Dear

In which Lauren discovers sex with Thomas is totally worth walking with a limp. Also, that she might have a backbone. Which comes as a surprise to both her and someone extremely unpleasant.

If Lauren had been a cartoon character, little heart emojis would have been following her for the next week. Thomas could not have been more charming, and even though she felt like she was walking bowlegged after days of glorious sex, it was worth the awkward gait to take the sure off her sore girl parts. Not that she limped in front of Thomas, of course. She had some dignity after all. So, she didn't catch her spouse watching her hobble to the bathroom one morning after a particularly acrobatic night, a fond smile on his face and a vague sense of irritation that his dick was getting hard again, just watching the effect his more prized possession had had on his wife. But Lauren had been so very, very good. So flexible. And willing. With a growl, he pulled off his running gear and followed his darling into the shower.

But as it inevitably does, Real Life and Organized Crime made their unwelcome appearance.

Lauren was just carefully putting her cello in its indestructible case as Macie walked over, not actually looking in her old friend's direction but sort of angling by her.

"Hey."

Looking up, startled, Lauren froze to see Macie gazing just over her head. "Hi, Macie," she said cautiously, "your section sounded amazing on the *Brandenburg Concerto No. 2,* are you all meeting up separately from the regular practice?"

"We've practiced in the quartet," Macie said a little sharply, but when her gaze briefly met Lauren's there was hurt in her brown eyes.

Lauren nodded, looking down. "Oh. Well... it sounded good." If she'd been looking up, she would have seen Macie's mouth open again, a hopeful expression that was instantly silenced by the cool voice of Chuck behind her.

"Miss Lauren, Mr. Williams has asked you to ring him, please."

Macie snorted. "Your master calls..." and walked away.

Biting the corner of her lip to keep from snapping at her former best friend, Lauren could taste the coppery feel of blood in her mouth. Biting her lip - literally - was becoming more and more of a habit. Then she raised her phone to her ear and the cool, sonorous voice of her husband soothed her instantly.

"Darling."

Gritting her teeth against a giggle, Lauren managed some dignity. "Hi, Thomas, Chuck said you needed me?" She groaned internally at his unfairly carnal chuckle.

"Well, yes little one, I always seem to need you these days..." he paused for a moment and she was humiliated to hear a faint whimper escape her clenched jaw. Thomas heard it, of course. "Oh, sweet girl, are you needing your Sir as well?"

"Please," Lauren groaned, "you know I can't keep a straight face when you talk to me like that. Everyone in this orchestra already thinks I'm nuts!"

He chuckled again, the low rumble feeling like it was vibrating straight up her spine. "Well then why don't you come by the office, and I shall, ah, talk to you like this in person."

"What- really?" Lauren was genuinely startled. She'd never been by the tall, ominous granite office building that housed Jaguar Holdings in downtown London since her second, disastrous meeting and her father's messy gunshot wound. Thomas had never suggested her visiting him there again. "Um, sure. What are we doing?"

Daaamn, that Voice... "What do you mean, my lovely bride?" She could picture him, sitting at his big, expensive desk and looking out an improbably huge window as he purred into the phone.

"I mean," Lauren groaned, trying to regain her composure, "are you taking me to a business dinner? Some reception at the office? Is this business or pleasure?" She could hear Thomas's sudden need in his tone, greedy, possessive.

"Both. Be here as quickly as you can, little girl." There was a small whimper on her end of the line as he said goodbye. With an unholy grin, Thomas looked out his window, absently rubbing the swelling front of his trousers. That his sweet bride could get him hard at the most inopportune of times... This was immediately reinforced when, with a brief tap on his door, Ben walked in.

"Thomas, we'll need to be ready for-" looking up, Number One's brow creased, "what are you grinning at?"

His Number Two irritably cleared his throat. "Nothing at all, Ben. Tell me your concerns over the Paris agreement." Despite his best efforts to pay attention, his thoughts drifted back to the blushing blonde that would soon be walking through his door.

Despite her internal pep talk to remain cool and calm, Lauren was nervously wiping her sweaty palms on the pleated skirt of her kilt when Chuck pulled into the underground parking of her husband's office building. She looked a little young - her family tartan, expensive black riding boots, and a lavender silk sweater - but she tilted her chin and put her game face on. She couldn't embarrass Thomas. Not here. Riding up the lift, she and Chuck kept their gaze on the rising numbers on the display. "Mr. Williams has asked me to make you comfortable in his office," he volunteered suddenly, "Mr. Kingston called him into a last-minute meeting, but he assured me he would not keep you waiting long and sends his apologies." Lauren eyed the big man and chewed on the corner of her mouth again. Thomas could have texted her, she was holding her fancy new iPhone quite literally in her hand at the moment. But if the insectile Number One was involved, there was probably a good reason for it. But she wouldn't have to see that freak, he was in the meeting with Thomas and she'd just hang out in his office until...

Unfortunately, luck was not on their side.

"Lauren!" She cringed a little to hear the booming voice of

Michael behind her. The loud third in command at The Corporation seemed too happy to see her. "What are you doing here, love? An early dinner with Williams? Lucky bastard." He smiled, but it didn't reach his oddly tinged grey-blue eyes.

Looking around her, she could see the top floor - of course - of the huge building housed only three offices and a gigantic board room. "Hey, Michael- I'm just here to see Thomas. Is Clara here, too? Do we have a business thing, tonight?" She was trying to avoid his speculative gaze, suddenly remembering his fiancée's anxious request to go home that night at the strip club.

Putting his hands in the pockets of his expensive suit, Number Three eyed her more closely. "No. Thomas must have special plans for you."

Lauren's brows drew together. Thomas's partner had never spoken to her like this before, that sort of hateful, knowing way and eyeing her like... a thing. He'd always been perfectly polite with Clara by his side. She pasted together a false smile. "Well, Thomas is really romantic. Lucky me," she barely kept on the non-sarcastic side of a simper and eyed the smirking Fassell. "Like how I'm sure you are with Clara, right? Such a perfect girl, you're so lucky, huh, Michael?" His sudden frown raised her flagging self-confidence and she smiled, batting her eyelashes. "With a crazy schedule like you all have here, it takes the right woman to have the... understanding to put up with all of that, right?" Fassell was no longer smiling, instead looking her over with a set, angry mouth.

"Why, it's Thomas's sweet little bride. What a pleasure to see you, dear." Lauren's eyes closed, wondering which god she'd managed to offend to encounter both the murderous One and Three in Thomas's organization without the protection of her terrifying spouse.

Chuck, bless his heart, was apparently feeling both protective and suicidal that day, because he spoke before she could. "I've been instructed by Mr. Williams to take Mrs. Williams *directly* to his office to wait-"

Kingston cut him off. "No need. We'll be happy to entertain the lovely bride while she waits for Thomas, won't we, Michael?" Lauren narrowed her eyes at his black gaze, not sophisticated enough to hide her dislike and instinctive disgust of this man. She just barely managed to avoid yanking her arm away when he took a grip on her elbow. "Come into my office, dear," he said with barely controlled malice, "we're quite happy to keep you entertained while Number Two finishes his meeting."

"I was told to-" Chuck made a valiant effort to stop them, but Lauren cut him off. She knew the vile husband of Arabella would be all too happy to do something to her bodyguard if he put up too much of a fuss.

"No worries," she interrupted, "why don't you just text Thomas and let him know where you and I are while he finishes up, okay?" She could feel the disapproval radiating off Straker's stolid frame, but she'd rather have him mad at her than... dead? Would they kill her Chuck for disagreeing with Kingston? The feeling of helplessness and anxiety that nearly crushed her that day at the coffee house with Thomas's society neighbor hit hard again, and Lauren took a deep breath. She couldn't embarrass Thomas, and she had to keep Chuck safe. The irony of keeping her bodyguard alive was lost on her as Number One escorted her into his office and tried to shut the door. Lauren dug in her heels. Number One looked down at her, irritated. "I'm not allowed to go anywhere without Chuck. Thomas is very specific about that."

Kingston lost his patience. "Who is Chuck?"

Lauren had a wild urge to giggle, knowing her bodyguard was dreaming of murdering her at that moment. Pointing at the large, angry man, she clarified, "Mr. Straker. Chuck."

Michael looked surprised. "Your name is Chuck?" He looked at Straker who definitely wore the expression of a man who wanted to murder someone.

Chuck cleared his throat. "No."

Once when she was more or less shoved into sitting on a leather couch in Number One's office - Lauren tried not to gag on the reek of expensive cologne, fine scotch and Smug. "Would you like a drink, dear?" Kingston offered with false solicitude, "I fear I don't have any wine here." He held up one of the bottles of amber liquid, and her stomach twisted. Who knows what this psycho doctored these drinks with? Did he have a special "murder bottle?" Scotch meant to make one bleed from every pore? So paranoid. She was beginning to think like Thomas did.

Unaccountably pleased by that realization, Lauren reached out and took the glass away from Number Three, who was just returning to the couch. They wouldn't have poisoned his drink, anyway. "Thanks, Michael. This looks great. I love bourbon."

Number One snarled, "That's a 12-year-old Royal Lochnagar, young lady."

"Even better," she lied, having no idea what he was talking about. The first gulp surprised her. Lauren hated hard liquor, the sense that she was really just drinking flavored rubbing alcohol was something that never left her, but this was pretty tasty. Taking another big swallow, she sighed happily, balancing the glass on her crossed knee and smiling brightly at her husband's murderous partners. "Thanks, this is pretty good."

Kingston looked like she'd just spat into the bottle, but he rallied and smiled down on her in an avuncular fashion. "How are you enjoying married life to our Thomas, dear?"

She fluttered her eyelashes elaborately. "It's even better than I imagined." This was technically true, since Lauren had grimly expected to crack at some point and provoke her chilly husband into murdering her. This expectation had faded over the last few weeks, but...

"I'm surprised we didn't hear more about you before the wedding," he continued, still staring at her with his creepy black gaze. "You were quite the surprise."

Lauren had swigged down the last of her drink and handed the empty glass to Chuck, smiling at him meaningfully. With a barely concealed sigh, he went to the bar to make her another one. This part, she had down. Thomas had brusquely told her in the very beginning what to say when questioned about their sudden engagement. "Well, we met that night at the LSO scholarship fundraiser. Thomas isn't a man to hesitate when he knows what he wants," she smiled blandly, "and what girl could resist him? I'm so lucky."

As Chuck bent down to hand her the new drink, Lauren was certain she heard him snort derisively.

But Number One wasn't finished. "That's very sweet, dear. Really. But far more important than your infatuation with your shiny new wedding ring is your understanding of what is required of you as a Corporation wife. You're young. Youngsters can be reckless." He was leaning forward now, shifting the expensive crystal glass in his hands looking like he wanted to crush it while picturing her head instead. "We don't tolerate recklessness here."

The moment seemed to slow down, Kingston's voice almost going into a cartoonish slow-motion slur as Lauren stared at him. She sort of expected to be wetting herself right now in sheer terror and was mildly impressed that she wasn't. Out of the corner of her eye, she could see Chuck's hand inch towards his shoulder holster under his jacket. Taking another deep breath, Lauren drank half her glass in one gulp, enjoying the involuntary flinch on Number One's face for abusing his expensive scotch. "Since Thomas has never um... punished me for acting badly during any Corporation event, I think that means I'm behaving properly. I'm quite aware," she stilled herself, trying to stop the hiss that wanted to spurt out with her words, "quite aware of what's at stake. And your uh, kind attempt to warn me could not possibly make me more aware of this than my husband has already managed to do."

Number Three, at least seemed convinced, laughing loudly, he got up to get another drink. "Well done, love! Quite a backbone, who knew?"

The head of Jaguar Holdings, unfortunately, was not willing to let the moment pass. "How fortunate," he sneered. "Because there's so much more at stake than just you, or even your father, isn't there, dear?"

At that moment, Lauren understood exactly why Thomas pushed her to move away from any close connections in the orchestra, here in London. Anywhere, really. She wanted to scream. She wanted to claw at Kingston's face. But instead, she shakily took another drink of his insanely expensive scotch and forced herself to smile. "I'm sure you can express your concerns to my husband, *Ben*," spitefully popping the "B," she forced herself to not look away from his cruel, nasty face. "I listen to every single thing he says. He's so good at this..." Lauren floundered, wondering what anyone would call "this," her current, bizarre universe. "This." She finished the thought and her drink at the same time.

"Ah. There you are, darling."

Lauren had never been so happy to hear the cool, resonant tone of her husband, currently speaking in her ear, hovering just over her right shoulder. "Hi, honey," she batted her eyelashes again, looking up, "we've just been waiting for you to finish up. How was your meeting?"

Thomas chuckled insincerely, she was a little surprised that she could tell, that she could "read" her mysterious spouse. "Just fine, darling. Gentlemen-" he fixed a steely gaze at his partners, "thank you for taking such good care of my wife." The threat behind his tone was clear. With shaky legs, Lauren rose with help from his offered hand and quickly escorted from the office.

After thanking Chuck in low tones, Thomas sent him away, pulling her into his office, placing her on the couch before shutting and locking the door.

"Are you all right?" He was in front of her again, running his long fingers over her face, tilting up her chin so he could force Lauren to look at him.

Lauren made her lips shape into a smile. "Of course. Believe it or not, I've has creepier conversations than that one. Not by much, but..."

Effortlessly hitching his trousers, her husband knelt in front of her. "What did he say?"

"Number One?" Lauren asked, gazing longingly at his bar set across the room. *Did every big executive have a full bar these days?* she thought vaguely, *Is that the new symbol of a crime boss, instead of like, a live tiger or an alligator?* Looking back at Thomas, she watched him sigh and rise to pour her a glass of wine from a bottle in his small fridge. Noting that it was her favorite Riesling, she felt unaccountably warmed that he'd noticed, taking a grateful sip. "He uh, was warning me, I guess." She chuckled suddenly, "Like he could scare me worse than you di- Um..." rapidly changing course at her husband's chilly expression, she amended, "like, telling me to keep my mouth shut, don't be reckless, the usual." Suddenly, her jaw clenched and Lauren felt unaccountably furious. "He told me that there was more at stake than just me and Frank." Looking up, she nearly quailed at the expression of ice-cold fury on Thomas's beautiful face, but for the first time, she realized it was *for* her, not *at* her.

"I am sorry, darling," her husband sounded remarkably sincere, "I should have been there to meet you." Noticing her glass was already empty, Thomas raised a dark brow but rose and poured her another one. "And Michael?" he asked, handing her the new drink.

Lauren was feeling much, much better after the application of two tumblers of scotch and now moving on to her second glass of Riesling. "He was a dick," she answered bluntly, "totally like a frat boy drunk and hanging out with his buddies. He's a different guy with Clara, huh?"

Thomas shifted to sit beside her, pulling his wife on to his lap and feeling the alien notion of... not guilt, certainly, but a certain... discomfort that Michael was luring the sweet Clara into this world with no understanding of what she was getting into. "Hmmm," he mused, turning his attention back Lauren, who really did look rather fetching in this sweet schoolgirlish outfit. "I'm sure you will be a great help to her, darling." Lifting her lightly and turning the girl to face him, straddling his lap, he gave her his most delicious, carnal smile. "I fear this ugly encounter has ruined my plans for this evening."

After four drinks on a relatively empty stomach, Lauren was feeling pleasantly buzzed and a little daring. Leaning into his neck, she breathed in the scent of this beautiful man, the feel of his arms surrounding her, hands stroking up her tights-clad thighs. "What did you have in mind, Sir?" She felt his hands briefly still at the use of his title, then squeeze and smooth along her legs again.

"Oh, my good girl..." Thomas purred, "I'd thought of perching you on my desk..." he bent to kiss along her throat, moving her hair out of the way. "Then... putting your heels pressed to the edge, spreading your knees..." he felt her gulp, no doubt trying to hold back the whimper trying to escape her. God, he loved those little noises from her. "Then, tearing a hole in those tights, pulling your knickers aside and..." This time, the groan escaped her before Lauren could choke it back, and she felt his chest jolt as he chuckled into her neck. He pulled her into his body tightly, putting one hand on the bottom of her spine to push his sweet wife's center rather harshly into his already swollen crotch. After feeling her hips move against him a bit, Thomas cruelly moved back, sighing ostentatiously. "But, of course, darling, if that unpleasant encounter has put you out of the mood..."

Lauren hated him when he was like this, her beautiful, manipulative Sir. He knew damn good and well that anything short of a grenade launching right down her cleavage couldn't put her out of the mood when he talked to her like this, rubbing that lovely, thick part of him against her. Damn him. Clearing her throat, she managed, "Well we haven't tried 'throwing everything off your expensive fancy desk and putting me on top of it' sex yet, so... um..."

Thomas looked up at her, his eyes clear and honest as he laughed. "So, just in the interests of a thorough examination of all the sexual basics?"

Her heart twisted painfully. Lauren couldn't remember a moment when her husband had looked at her, so unguarded and delighted. "Precisely, Professor Williams."

The bit of humor evaporated from his face and she suddenly found herself flat on her back on the polished expanse of his desk and legs yanked up and into the position he'd described.

They were driving home - much later - in the dark when Lauren suddenly remembered something he'd said that day in the pergola in Kensington Gardens. Before he nearly made her pass out from coming so hard. "Thomas?"

"Hmmm?" His profile was beautiful as always, lit by the Jaguar's dashboard as he focused on the road.

"Remember when you said that you should have kept me home that night when we had to, uh, do it at Mogilevich's strip club?" Lauren watched him nod slowly, a frown creasing his forehead. "But you said that night you had to have sex with someone for his creepy brand of hospitality?" She looked down at her hands, twisting in her lap. "So, if I wasn't there, would you have had done it with one of the club girls?"

Thomas slowed the car as the light ahead of them turned red, then looked at her. "No." he answered, "I would have made my excuses and left."

"Even if it offended him and threatened your deal with the Brat-" she remembered the night he'd terrified her for saying the word out loud. Lauren realized she'd not spoken it since. "With the Bratva?"

Looking back to the road as the light turned green, Thomas answered shortly, "I would have found a way to smooth over the insult."

"Oh." Her voice was smaller this time, but Lauren persisted. "Thomas?"

He sighed heavily. "Yes?"

"When you came home that night from your business meeting and stinking of perfume, did you sleep... Did you sleep with one of the girls at the- uh, do you call it a brothel or is that old-fashioned?" Lauren cringed to see him bite back a grin.

"The Corporation brothel. No."

She leaned in, trying to get a look at his face, "No, you didn't, or no, it's not old-fashioned to call it a brothel, or-"

"No," Thomas said firmly, softly covering her hands with his big, warm one. "I didn't sleep with anyone. I haven't. Since we married."

"That's good," Lauren said, a little dazed and kind of hating the spark of hope in her chest. Gathering her thoughts, she offered, "I haven't, either." She didn't have to look at her husband's self-satisfied face to know he was trying not to chuckle.

"That's good, too," he finally offered, squeezing her hand as he turned onto their street.

"So, what do you think?" Michael was a bit distracted, trying to picture exactly what Williams was doing to that tasty little bitch in his office.

Kingston frowned the unpleasant set to his jaw making him look even more frightening. "I don't like her."

Number Three shrugged, "You don't like anyone. Anything specific?"

The most terrifying man he knew turned to look at Michael fully. "She's too confident that Thomas can save her," he spat. "If she makes a mistake, there is no one on this planet who can save her from me."

Chapter 18 – The Ladies Who Lunch

In which Lauren is forced to face the most terrifying predators at The Corporation. Also, drunken revelations.

"Darling, you're just planning a fundraiser, not mucking out a hog trough."

Lauren's mouth was set in a small, mutinous frown, and she barely kept from rolling her eyes at her husband's amused, indulgent tone. She *hated* his amused, indulgent tone, especially when it was directed at her. But since she hated a spanking more, the rolling the eyes thing was off the table. "I know," she mumbled, "I just..." she thought about it. What was worse? Planning it with the confusing Arabella or doing it poorly and making Thomas look bad? She was now quite acutely aware of how important Number Two's image was within The Corporation- the right blend of respect and utter terror of the man- and it was crucial she did nothing to alter that. "I don't want to... Ugh!" she leaned down to pull on her riding boots, and when she straightened up, Thomas was standing in front of her, close enough to feel the heat radiate off his freshly shaved face.

"What?" Looking down at his wife's lovely face, Thomas enjoyed how her lashes would flutter when he spoke in his sweetest, most compelling voice. And he did so love compelling Lauren. "What don't you want to do?"

"Idon'twanttoscrewthisupand... make you look bad," it came out in a rush, and Lauren cringed a little. She sounded like a six-year-old.

Thomas laughed, putting those long arms around her and squeezing her lightly. "You told me you would help your mother when she did these sorts of things, and you handled a fundraiser or two at Julliard, correct?"

"Yes," she agreed, "but-"

Raising her chin for a kiss, Thomas rose one haughty brow, "Then I am certain you will do a spectacular job. Some new ideas are needed, these recent events have been a bit stale. You'll breathe some new life and new ideas into The Corporation's charity division."

Thinking of the bizarre irony of a ruthless organized crime syndicate having a charity division, Lauren forced a smile and nodded. She didn't realize something until after her dark and beautiful husband had left for work. "I never told him about those fundraisers in college," she said out loud to the quiet house, "how did he...?" Her heart settled back in the pit of her stomach, wondering if there was any detail Thomas hadn't stripped ruthlessly from her past.

So, her mood was still glum when she arrived at the restaurant where the other Ladies Who Lunch (as she secretly called The Corporation spouses) were beginning to plan the next fundraiser designed to make Jaguar Holdings look like a beneficent and generous company and not the horrifying entity of fear and death it actually was. *You're being dramatic,* Lauren lectured herself, *paste on that fake smile that got you through all of Dad's shitty dinners.* Chuck opened her door and stood back respectfully, waiting. After a couple of minutes, he cleared his throat. Still, no Lauren emerged from the darkened interior of the car.

"Miss Lauren?"

She jumped a little, not quite noticing that her bodyguard had opened her door some time ago. "I'm sorry, Chuck. I was... uh. I was thinking."

With a sigh that teetered on the side of aggrieved, Chuck slid in next to her in the back seat and shut the door. "Aimes," he looked at his generously armed co-worker. "Go out and hold the perimeter." Once the other man was outside, he turned to Lauren. "What's the problem?" Chuck's tone was more brusque than usual, but she didn't take offense.

Lauren rested her head on the padded leather of her headrest. "I'm a little freaked out. I don't know any of these women, aside from Arabella and Clara. I'm supposed to be scary Number Two's... I dunno, scary bride. I met some of these women at the wedding. They give me the creeps."

Chuck pursed his lips. "I recall you trying to kick me while I held your father at gunpoint. You did not seem unduly intimidated." Watching her roll her eyes, he folded his hands and continued, calm and urbane. "Or the occasion you steered Mr. Williams's Jaguar at a considerable rate of speed while he was shooting out the back window?"

Snorting in a way that she knew would get a reprimand from her stern spouse, Lauren asked, "Is this your British understatement teaching me a life lesson about keeping a cool head with the Ladies Who Lunch if I can do it while being shot at?"

Straightening his cuff, Chuck shook his head. "No. It wasn't required. You just managed that for yourself." Leaving the car to hold the door for her, the man's expression didn't twitch as Lauren shook her head.

"You'd make an astounding life coach. If life coaches carried firearms and ran crazed Texan drug dealers off the road."

"And here she is, the new Mrs. Thomas Williams!"

Lauren cringed to hear the overly loud voice of Arabella, which meant the woman was already a couple of cocktails ahead of everyone, which of course she could relate to. If Thomas hadn't been in the house right to the point she'd had to leave, she would have picked out another bottle from his excellent wine cellar to take the edge off her anxiety. Several well-coiffed heads turned to look, a few women she remembered from her dreadful wedding and to her amusement, a few men as well. Every spouse of upper-level management at Jaguar Holdings was expected to serve on one board or another. Two of the men were partners to males on Thomas's team, a couple of others were husbands to high-ranking women in The Corporation, including the head of Pacific Acquisitions, a red-headed woman so terrifying that even Thomas, formidable as he was, rarely found it "necessary" to speak to her. Forcing a smile, she nodded to everyone and slipped into her chair with an apology. "So sorry to be late, it's a pleasure to see you all again." Looking down at her napkin to avoid some of the more avid stares, Lauren forced herself to remember Chuck's implacable expression. *It couldn't be worse than having a gun jammed in my side, right?*

She was reconsidering that assumption after another round of drinks was ordered and desserts finished. Looking longingly down where a meek Clara sat next to Arabella, Lauren wished she'd been early enough to snag a seat next to her only two allies. The woman next to her was just finishing the story of the "effort" required to get her son back into his college after being caught in a cheating scandal. The man on the other side was earnestly comparing the merits of an early face-lift with the woman next to him.

"Let's get started, shall we?" Number One's wife might be slightly past tipsy and slurring into drunk, but she could command a room. The vaguely malicious smile she wore as she pointed down the table to Lauren made her stiffen. "It's time to set up our latest fundraiser," Arabella commented, "and as agreed by the board we want to continue with a music focus. Since our new Mrs. Williams is a professional musician with the London Symphony Orchestra, I've decided to turn the planning for the concept over to her. Lauren darling, after seeing our last charity effort, how would you change the direction of this next one?"

She briefly considered throwing her napkin over her head and pretending she was invisible, but since that didn't seem like a viable escape attempt, Lauren forced a smile and leaned forward, clearing her throat. "I don't think the last fundraiser on behalf of the LSO scholarship could possibly have been more successful," she said with a polite nod towards Arabella, who preened a little under the praise as she ordered another Cosmopolitan. "But I was thinking..." Lauren smiled as she warmed to her subject. "This time, what if we take a more hands-on approach with some of the local schools here in London? While college - I mean University here, of course - scholarships are critical towards helping a professional musician move on, think of the children who never have an opportunity to learn music- it's a terrible loss of potential for the future."

The same woman who'd complained about getting her son

back into Eton after he paid someone to hack the school's computer system and altered his grades (and several others for money) sniffed. "There is a perfectly lovely music program at my son's school," she said, "they don't need any help, heaven knows I write a large enough tuition check every year."

Lauren pasted on her insincere social smile and continued, "Well actually Evelyn, I was thinking of neighborhood schools with limited or no funding for the arts. Imagine how many talented children we're losing? What if this next fundraiser sponsored several of those schools with a music program and a yearly scholarship that would grow over the years to be a full university scholarship by the time the child turns 18? We could go in and talk about the arts, invite musicians in to play..." her eager voice died off as she realized half the table was looking at her with blank expressions and the other half looked almost offended.

"Go into those schools?" a well-coiffed blonde sniffed, "With those *people?*"

Lauren was struck with a sudden desire to laugh uproariously. The blonde reminded her so much of Thomas's officious neighbor, "of the Berkshire Harding's?"

"I promise," she said in a deeply saccharine tone, "that you won't catch a single cootie by mingling with children from the lower-income areas." She actually did have to choke down a chortle when she caught one woman mouthing the word "Cootie?" to another. "With new some of the new online crowdfunding resources," she continued eagerly, "we could pay for teachers as well as provide instruments. This is just the sort of program that would get donors outside of Corporation circles interested in helping. We could exponentially magnify our reach-"

Arabella's voice cut her off. "Lauren, my dear," she said with an edge of steel under her well-bred tone, "we do not allow outsiders into The Corporation charity efforts. Ever."

There was an awkward silence around the table and Lauren was about to grab the tumbler of whiskey from the man sitting next to her and down it in one gulp when Clara's small voice spoke up. "I think it's a wonderful idea," she said, cringing only slightly when all the mascara'ed and botoxed eyes turned to her, "we don't have to involve outsiders, but these fundraisers certainly net enough funds to start the programs Lauren is suggesting. And the kind of press coverage The Corporation would receive for this kind of hands-on outreach program is much more favorable than just reporting another society luncheon. It's an excellent way to foster goodwill in the business community."

While Number Three's fiancé took another shaky sip of water, Lauren had to remind herself to close her dropped jaw. *Holy shit!* she thought, *Who knew little Clara had it in her?* With a warm smile, she thanked Clara and after another round of drinks, laid out some of the basic ideas she was thinking of and promised to type them into a memo for everyone as the meeting came to a slightly drunken close.

"Well done," murmured Arabella, slipping her arm through Lauren's as they exited the restaurant. "I didn't mean to cut you off so quickly, but we can never open a Corporation charity effort to outsiders, it's crucial you understand."

The new Mrs. Williams shrugged with a wry twist to her mouth, "Oh please," she scoffed, "thank *you*. What kind of an idiot am I? Outside scrutiny is the last thing we would want!" Mildly shocked, Lauren realized that she had now included herself in this vast conspiracy. *When did that happen?* she wondered.

"I already know what Ben will say," Arabella mused, leaning a little more heavily on Lauren for support than she was aware, "he'll say 'that's far too visible! You idiots! What made you agree to something so stupid?'" she cut off rapidly when she caught her friend's shocked gaze. "Oh no darling," she said hastily, "he wouldn't say any of that to *you*. Just me." With a harsh giggle, she continued their meandering towards the exit. "At any rate," she said casually, "it's not as if much would be going to the children anyway, so-"

"What do you mean?" Lauren interrupted, slowing her down to look at the suddenly pale face of Number One's wife.

"Nothing dearie," Arabella said hastily, "I think I've just had too many cocktails; I don't know what I'm saying."

Nodding, Lauren wrapped her arm around the other woman's waist more firmly. While Arabella was certainly drunk, she suspected the woman was quite aware of what she was saying, even if she didn't mean to say it out loud.

Chapter 19 – I Promise You, You Will Beg for More

In which Lauren discovers that sometimes, it's better that locked doors stay locked.

After one particularly passionate evening and when Lauren's sex-drunk haze receded, she remembered - to her horror – that she'd agreed to participate in a "scene" with Thomas. *The big... scene-y thing? Probably at home, right?* she thought, sawing through a round of Joseph Haydn's *Symphony No. 60 ('Il distratto')* which was living up to its name by being just as impossible to get through perfectly in 2021 as it had been performed in 1775. Groaning as her bow clanged off her C string, snapping the horsehair of the bow loose as the string ripped free of the cello's neck, Lauren tossed her bow aside and let the instrument slump against her shoulder as she pondered her extremely poorly thought-out agreement. Eyeing her ruined bow, the fine strands of horsehair spreading across the beautiful oriental rug, Lauren sighed and set the cello aside, rising to pace through the room, eyeing the afternoon sun and pondering her fate. She heard her scary husband's Jaguar enter their garage, and then his footsteps, stately against the slate of the kitchen floor.

"Darling? I thought I'd take you out to dinner."

His damned, compelling voice... Lauren's eyes closed and she shuddered, a little blissfully. Thomas's voice was like music to her, following along the line of some exquisite melody that always made her long to hear the finish, the cadenza that would crush any resistance her sane self had built up to the mysterious, beautiful killer she was married to.

"Lauren?"

She could hear his footsteps on the oak stairs now, pausing at the third landing and ascending to the fourth floor, getting closer and closer to her. Like he was stalking her, like a jungle cat. Unaware that the same image had sent a violent bolt of arousal down the spine of her darkly beautiful spouse, Lauren felt the same heat shoot to her center, making her groan a little bit and rise hastily to her feet. "I'm up in my practice room, Thomas! I'll be right down."

Pressing his lips together in amusement as he heard the rapid patter of her feet across the wooden floor, Thomas idly loosened his tie and leaned against the banister, waiting for his pretty bride to appear. "Ah, there you are," he purred approvingly, watching her flushed face and that little delighted smile, looking almost guilty to be so pleased to see him. "Are you finished practicing for the day?" He was idly sorting through the mail she'd left on the hall table, a slight smile curling his mouth.

He's totally fucking with me, Lauren thought bleakly. "Yes?"

Her husband looked up at her, one elegant brow arched. "You sound uncertain." Climbing the final flight of stairs to where she stood, shifting her feet from side to side, Thomas leaned down to her, hands braced on the railing and breathing her in. "Are you finished, baby..." she stifled a whimper as his nose teased hers lightly, "or are you not?"

"Wh- why?" she managed to croak, feeling herself lean into him. His hands slid up her torso, thumbs idly caressing her ribs and stroking just under her breasts.

"Well, if you're done, darling, I can..." here, Thomas choked back a grin as his pretty wife actually whimpered, "I can..." he put a slow, sucking kiss just under her ear, "...take you to dinner."

The hitch of her breath was like music. "Oh. Okay. That would be good."

Lauren braced herself all through dinner - at a rustic little place a few blocks from their house that served small plates that were based nearly completely on what was growing in their garden - to see when Thomas would remind her of her promise. He asked about the next couple of performances for the LSO- one in Manchester, the other in Brighton- and ordered more of the bucatini with black truffles. Thomas reminded her of a business dinner with The Butcher (as she'd taken to calling him) when the Frenchman returned that week. He remarked on the excellent photos The Corporation's marketing department had released for her new direction for the charity. And when he took her home, he slipped between their crisp, white sheets, gathering her in his arms and falling asleep.

Feeling his arm resting around her, one big hand firmly cupping her breast in his sleep, Lauren watched the shadows of the trees outside reflected against the pale walls of their bedroom. Really? No sex? No mention of... stuff? *He's fucking with me*, she concluded bleakly before falling asleep.

This continued for another week, Thomas working late or Lauren busy with performances. There were business dinners. Charity luncheons. And no sex. She'd taken to running longer and faster every morning, desperate to burn off her rising sexual frustration and anxiety. It's not like he forgot, she thought grimly. Thomas Williams, Jaguar Holding's terrible Number Two never forgot *anything*.

"AH!" Lauren jumped a foot when one of the musicians in the cello section tapped her on the shoulder.

"What on earth is going on with you?" Michael chuckled, but she could read a little concern in his gaze. He was one of the younger members of LSO, having joined just a couple of years before Lauren. He'd always been good about quietly explaining procedures when she wasn't certain about what to do. "You've been so jumpy for the last few days."

"I'm sorry," she groaned, taking the sheet music from him with a nod, "I dunno... just on pins and needles for some reason."

Michael laughed, picking up his cello case and heading for the exit with her. "Something at home? You're a newlywed, right?"

Forcing a bland smile, Lauren nodded. No way in hell could she mention a word about her life outside of the orchestra. This was her safe place, where things made sense and she felt confident. She tried not to think about Thomas, The Corporation when she was here. At all. "So are you staying the night here in Brighton?" Most of the musicians were being put up at a couple of local hotels.

"I was planning to," he agreed, "but I'm sure you're eager to get home. Are you at least staying for the afterparty?"

Lauren groaned internally. She desperately wanted to, one of her greatest idols was the guest conductor for the week -

Riccardo Chailly from the Berlin Philharmonic, and she was dying to hear him talk. He was brilliant and fascinating. "I'd like to," she admitted, "but..."

It was then of course that Chuck made his appearance. "Are you ready to leave, Miss Lauren?" Her ever-present well-suited shadow reached for her cello case. His dispassionate gaze alternated between her and a suddenly nervous Michael.

Suddenly making up her mind, Lauren lifted her chin a little. "I'd really like to stay for the afterparty. I'm just going to call Thomas." She watched her bodyguard's brow raise as if she'd suggested tearing off her clothes and running screaming through the orchestra pit, but he nodded stiffly. Dialing her husband, Lauren frowned when it went to voicemail. "Hi, Thomas, um, there's an afterparty tonight to honor Conductor Chailly, and I'd really like to go. I um..." she sighed, feeling like a 17-year-old asking to stay out till midnight. "Anyway, I'll be home late, unless you have a problem with- unless there's a problem, just let me know, okay? Thanks. L-" Lauren stopped short. She'd been about to say "Love you."

Omigod what's wrong with you? she chastised herself, she was used to signing off in such a way with good friends. But to Thomas? Omigod. What would he even do if she said such a thing? This was a business arrangement! Besides, she didn't love him, so... With a sigh, Lauren went to change out of her stage dress.

Lounging in the backseat while Chuck and Aimes spoke quietly in the front, Lauren was pleasantly drunk without falling into loud and sloppy. Without quite letting herself see the seriousness of it, she knew her day drinking from

Thomas's excellent wine cellar was teaching her how to hold her liquor, more careful about how she spoke and moved. Tonight had been fun. She'd had a chance to stand with the little group listening to Herr Chailly speak- of the flow of the seasons, the movement of time and the rotation of the earth and how music ruled them all and played through nature and the sky and the oceans. When he got very excited, he'd lapse into German, so a bit was lost in the translation but it was so beautiful, his animated face and it made Lauren feel like she was part of something larger, grander.

It had been such a long time since she'd felt she belonged. Belonged to anything but Thomas, anyway.

As they pulled into the driveway, the stately house was dark, save a couple of lights on the third floor. Getting out, Lauren eyed them curiously. She recognized the elegant drapes of their bedroom, but the dim light from the window next to it... she'd never been in that room. Thomas dismissed it once as "storage," but it was locked like several other doors in the mansion she shared with her mysterious husband. The light went out as she unlocked the door, and she wondered what Thomas had been doing in there. Suddenly picturing Blackbeard's wives, hanging from hooks by their hair and surrounded by chests filled with gold, she shuddered a little and went inside. Thomas was standing just inside their dressing room, removing the cuff links from his dress shirt. The pale blue shirt was unbuttoned, and Lauren shivered a little as she looked at the muscled lines of his abdomen. Just drunk enough to throw caution to the winds, she attempted a sexy stroll across the bedroom. It didn't look too bad until she tripped on the ottoman near the bed and fell on it, rapidly adjusting herself to pose seductively. God, she missed his...

"I hear the performance went well, darling," her beautiful and exasperating husband had the slightest smile on his face.

Lauren wasn't sure if he'd seen her stumble over the furniture. It was never clear with him because Thomas's usual expression was one of urbane amusement.

"It was wonderful," Lauren gushed a little, "I felt like we were finally performing Herr Chailly's vision."

He glanced over, casually stripping out of his trousers, tight ass perfectly encased in his black boxer briefs. *At least he's wearing underwear today,* Lauren thought dimly. The sight of that gigantic dick that had been denied her for eight straight days would have been almost too much to bear. She hated needing him like this, craving the feel of him inside her, on top of her.

"...was enjoyable?"

Lauren tore her stare from his crotch, looking up at his amused expression. Definitely amused, now. "Um, I'm sorry?"

Thomas chuckled now, striding to the bed and pulling the cream-colored comforter down. "Did you enjoy the party?"

Flushing, she nodded rapidly. "Yes, thank you, it was so fun to hear the conductor talk about his experiences. Such a life!"

Looking at her bright smile, Thomas was startled to feel two things, tenderness at his bride's sweet, excited face and resentment that it not there because of him. Shoving down the odd feeling, he smiled blandly and let her finish describing her evening. "To bed now, darling," he urged, "we have so much to do tomorrow."

"Oh?" Lauren felt like she suddenly went on point, like one of those hunting dogs. A clue? A hint from Thomas? But he was already asleep when she returned from brushing her teeth. With a sigh, she curled around a pillow, knowing perfectly well she'd be wrapped around her dark and beautiful Sir in a tangle of arms and legs by the time they woke in the morning.

She felt a little more settled because Thomas woke her to run with him, he was amused at her sleepy whining to stay in bed and simply pulled her from her blanket nest anyway. Despite his comment the evening before about "So much to do," Number Two left the house with his Brunello Cucinelli briefcase without another word. Irritably swallowing some aspirin to tone down her hangover from the night before, Lauren practiced, feeling responsible and then went down for a salad and a bottle of wine.

It was ironic, she mused, it was surprisingly easy to keep the huge house clean. Thomas was terrifyingly tidy and expected the same from her. Add in a grim Polish housekeeper who came twice a week to clean the house top to bottom while giving Lauren a mean-looking side-eye, and the place was perfection. Granted, she mused, pouring another glass of Conte Fini Pinot Grigio, there were certain rooms the intimidating Mrs. Kowalczyk did not enter. The basement. Lauren had tried almost daily to see if Thomas had somehow left that door unlocked, but no. His office, the woman cleaned but if she growled if the new Mrs. Williams tried to put a toe over the threshold. But not the room next to the master bedroom suite. Thinking back over her ill-advised agreement from that particularly passionate night, Lauren's glass froze halfway to her mouth. She'd agreed to all those ropes and spankings and buzzing toys, as long as they were alone.

"Shiiit," she groaned. "He's got a sex dungeon. Oh, shit! Shit!"

Suddenly frantic to find this terrifying lair and see what her wicked Sir had in mind for her, Lauren put down the wine and wiped her damp palms on her thin jersey dress. "Basement?" she mumbled, "That's a good place for a sex dungeon, right?" Naturally, the only door leading to the basement remained stubbornly locked. Absently trying a couple of other rooms, "Really, who needs four floors worth of rooms?" she mumbled crossly, but Lauren checked them all until she stood before the door of the chamber next to Thomas's bedroom. There was only the one door leading in or out, no attached entrance from the master suite. Nervously chewing on her lower lip, Lauren reached out a hand. "It'll be locked," she mumbled, "just like always but at least I checked, so-" The knob turned easily under her hand and the heavy door swung open.

At first glance, it was simply a beautiful guest bedroom. Slightly darker gray walls, heavy, elegant drapes drawn back from the floor to ceiling windows. A huge fireplace and the bed. A gigantic four-poster bed made from carved black ironwood. "Olea capensis," Lauren mused, remembering Thomas telling her about an African tree species that was said to be nearly impossible to break because of its iron-like durability. It looked like a normal, albeit huge and intimidating piece of furniture. The comforter was silk, a heavy burgundy and green brocade throw. Many pillows... she eyed them nervously. Some round, so different shapes that made her question their use. Walking closer, she could see the nearly hidden hooks seemingly everywhere- similar to the few Thomas had immobilized her from in his bedroom. There were crossbeams at the top, half-covered by the elegant pale drapes. And, her lips twisted, a round, comfortable cushion on the floor on the left side, the side Thomas slept on. There was an antique trunk at the foot of the bed, Lauren reached out to open it, then pulled back her hand. She was this close to losing her nerve. A beautifully designed armoire in the same wood as the bed. An elegant leather couch in a weathered brown. Two large wingback chairs in the same leather but designed in a slightly different shape than usual. A long ottoman between them, at least five feet long. And two cabinets inset into the wall with antique iron latches. It looked like an elegantly designed bedroom, fit for a prince. But everything was just... slightly off. Perhaps it was her paranoia? But the room was the only one in Thomas's house with a thick, lush carpet underneath, rather than hardwood. Her steps were soundless in the thick plush. Looking up, Lauren could see more subtly placed hooks in the ceiling, and as her heart started pounding, others inset into the walls. Silently padding over to the windows, she pulled the heavy curtain back to see the windows were double-paned, blocking out any sound from the distant traffic outside. And blocking any sounds made inside from reaching the street.

"Ah." Lauren froze in place like a rabbit suddenly spotted by a hawk. "I see you've found my playroom." Stiffly turning around, she found Thomas, still gorgeous and intimidating in his navy-blue bespoke suit. His dark eyes were watching her closely, traveling in a leisurely way up and down her body and watching how his bride kept nervously wiping her sweaty palms on the skirt of her dark pink dress. Straightening and walking inside the room, he paused for a moment as Lauren took a step back. "Are you afraid, little one?"

"Yes," she answered honestly, far past nervous and rapidly approaching terror.

"Hmmm..." he pondered, hands behind his back as he walked around her, leaning in to smell the luscious mixture of her fear and some arousal. "I have so been looking forward to introducing you to this room. Do you remember your promise to me?"

"Wh- was that a promise?" Lauren managed. Why wasn't she

running? Why wasn't she bolting from this room? Down the three flights of stairs and screaming out the front door?

Thomas laughed, a gorgeous sound in the room, thudding off the sound dampening walls. "I believe so, baby. And a good girl like you always keeps her promises, yes?" He could see her feet shift restlessly, could practically hear the thoughts shrieking in her head. "I know you're quite alarmed right now. But I believe part of you has been looking for this room for some time, haven't you?"

Lauren stilled. Had she? She knew Thomas kept all manner of secrets from her. But since introducing her into his private, dark acts, she'd felt oddly closer to him. Like he trusted her enough to show these mysteries. To make her enjoy them. Thomas watched her pretty mouth try to shape words, try to explain or ask or whatever was still racing around that clever brain of hers. He'd always enjoyed her quick mind, how fast his lovely bride could leap to the right conclusion, given enough information. "I..." she paused, trying to think of what to say. "I knew there was, more with you. More here."

"Ah," his tall form was circling her again, long, elegant fingers trailing across her bare arms, the thin skin of her neck and collarbones. "Such an intelligent girl. What did you think was behind this door?"

Her screech of nervous amusement was a little too high-pitched, bordering more on the edge of terror. "Blackbeard's wives?"

Thomas's laugh was genuine, and she stared a little resentfully at his sharp profile, the slash of his high cheekbones and those vivid ocean blue eyes closed as he enjoyed her admission. "No. No other wives. But I believe you will enjoy all the mysteries here, even if they frighten you." His warm hand was suddenly cupping her cheek, raising her face to look at his. "Have I always given you more pleasure in return for your pain?"

Her pink tongue darted out to wet her dry lips, "Yes."

"We will talk about the rules," he soothed, in the same calming tone he used on men he'd been torturing, interrogating, those finally broken enough to be grateful to tell him anything. "You will use your safe words if needed and they will be honored immediately. But I expect you to be brave. I know you are. If you are naughty or disobedient, I will punish you. It will not be as simple as a few swats on that juicy behind. You will know you were punished. You will feel it. You will not wish to be naughty or disobedient again. When we are in this room, I am your Sir. You are my submissive. Sometimes my princess. Sometimes my slave. And I can promise you..." Lauren swallowed back a whimper as he paused behind her, her tall husband's body pressing against hers, the heat of his cock throbbing eagerly against the small of her back. "I promise you that you will beg for more."

Cadenza: *A point near the end of a movement in a work such as a concerto where the orchestra will stop playing and the soloist will perform an elaborate passage showing his or her virtuosity on the instrument.*

Chapter 20 – Yes, Sir

In which Thomas introduces his bride to the dark and murky delights of his "playroom."

For a few moments, the room seemed utterly silent to Lauren, the only audible sound was her breathing, rapid, a little harsh. Thomas was staring down at her, quite at ease but shrewdly gauging her reaction. "Do you understand the rules, darling?"

"Mmmmm, hmmm..." his bride managed, still frozen in place, eyes huge.

"You will need to speak when spoken to, little one," he corrected her, tone cooler.

Lauren cleared her thrust. "Yes, Sir," she whispered.

His cool expression cleared slightly, his polar blue eyes warming to a Mediterranean shade. "There's my good girl," he approved, one big hand coming up to cup her cheek. His thumb slid along her throat, feeling his bride's pulse speed up, her carotid artery throbbing. Stepping back, Thomas gestured at her cotton dress. "Take that off." He seated himself in one of the wingback chairs, long legs spread with his usual arrogance. Lauren was still frozen in place, and she jumped a little when his beautiful voice deepened, enunciation sharper. "You will always answer 'Yes, Sir' when I give you an order in this room."

Head bobbing like a marionette's, Lauren raised her hand to the zipper of her dress. "Yes, Sir."

Voice softening slightly, her dark husband asked, "Do you remember your safe words?"

"Yes, Sir," Lauren's voice was clearer this time. Idly crossing one leg over the other, Thomas was struck by his wife's courage. Forced to marry a complete stranger - he knew he essentially kidnapped her into this union though he preferred to believe it was a positive turn of events for her - but to handle his terrifying lifestyle so well? Her nervous eyes, the color of a lavender field, rose to his. In his careful analysis of all things Lauren, Thomas knew this meant she was anxious, frightened, but her long spine was straight, and after a nervous flutter of hands, they stayed clasped together. "Lovely girl..." that resonant voice was back to soothing again, and Thomas smiled approvingly. "Now your bra. Slowly." Hands rising to obey him, Lauren cringed internally. She knew exactly nothing about undressing in a sexy manner and to be frank- in the past, her scary husband usually had her clothes off before she knew what was happening. "Ah." Lauren froze. Thomas was still seated, but the thin tip of a rattan cane was sliding up the skin of her abdomen. "Slowly. Look at me, no hiding." When his bride unclasped her strap, the top of the cane slapped her left nipple sharply, the fabric doing little to lessen the sting.

"Ow! Wh- why-"

The cool, cultured drawl of Thomas's voice interrupted her. "When I give you an instruction in this room, you always answer me with, 'Yes, Sir,' forgetting this again will merit a sharper correction." Fuming internally, Lauren tried to keep her expression neutral. She failed, of course, she had no idea how open and expressive her features were. And for Thomas, she was the loveliest of open books. The tip of his cane smartly slapped the right nipple this time, a little harder, enjoying his bride's yelp. "And no pouting, little girl."

Gritting her teeth and clutching her bra Lauren nodded. "Yes, Sir."

Thomas settled back, tapping the cane on one polished shoe. "You may continue."

"Yes, Sir." she murmured and slid one strap, then the other down her toned arms and let the fabric slide off on to the carpet. Lauren was infuriated to see her nipples were already peaked, pink tips straining towards the dark, suited figure before her.

"Run your hands up your stomach, darling, and over your breasts, cupping them." That damnable cane was still resting on his leg, her husband's gaze fixed on her.

"Yes, Sir." Lauren was acutely uncomfortable. She didn't know what to expect when she found this room, but she assumed it would involve like... tying her up or something. But standing here in front of him, beginning to obey him was excruciating. And his half-smile told her he knew it. But as her fingertips circled her nipples, palms cradling her breasts, Lauren was surprised to hear the little sigh escape her.

"Such a good girl," Thomas said approvingly. "Now, put two fingers in your mouth, get them wet."

Watching her obey him with a little puzzled frown, he was about to bring that cane down on the plump mound of her pussy when his clever bride hastily added, "Yes, Sir." His cock was beginning to swell, Lauren could see it pressing against those well-tailored trousers of his, but Thomas ignored his erection, still focused on her.

"Run those long fingers of yours down to your knickers, slip them over your tender little pearl and stroke it." He watched the red flush start on his innocent bride's chest and rose up her neck and turning her cheeks crimson. "So shy..." he muses, pensively running his forefinger over his upper lip. "Come here."

"Yes, Sir." Another barely audible response, but Lauren obeyed him.

Putting two long fingers to her lips, Thomas ordered, "Suck these, little girl. Make them slick." That might have been a whimper as she opened her mouth, but his bride did as she was told, round, apprehensive eyes on his.

Plucking them from her mouth with an audible pop, he smiled devilishly as his fingers slipped down between the lace and her skin, running lightly - *Too lightly, damnit!* she thought disjointedly - and slicked along her wet lips.

Lauren cringed when her terrible Sir chuckled. "And here I thought you might need some assistance, so shy and blushing. Only to find you quite sleek and wet all on your own, aren't you, baby? Hmmm?" Thomas pushed harder on her slick center and she went up on tiptoe.

"Yes, Sir!" Lauren gulped. With a sudden movement, he had her on his lap, erection pressing into her back and her legs flung over his, splayed open, exposed.

Tucking his chin on her shoulder, Thomas nudged her. "Look

down, baby. You're going to be doing this all on your own next time." Watching his thick fingers sink into her made Lauren want to die of embarrassment and also greedily thrust her hips up at the same time, wanting to drive him deeper. "Now, every woman has her own secret places," her diabolical Sir commented, "not found in some boring anatomy book. One must study the ways she moves-" Thomas pressed hard on one spot inside his wife and tapped her clit with his thumb. Lauren's back snapped into a very satisfying arch and she let out a breathless shriek, trying to close her legs against his straying digits and held open all the same. She was tingling and if he would just touch her one more- "Ah, yes. So lovely and responsive," Thomas approved, "and here's another..." Two fingers drove ruthlessly up her channel and pressed hard, just under her cervix, putting his other warm hand over the spot from the outside.

"Oh, god-" Lauren choked, grabbing fistfuls of his suit jacket and burying her face in his neck.

To her consternation, he smoothly withdrew both hands and briskly slapped the top of her slit with two wet fingers, enjoying her pained yelp. "Not yet. Did your Sir give you permission to come?"

"No, but you-"

One big hand suddenly gripped her pussy hard enough to make Lauren reach down and grab his wrist, trying to pry him loose. "Remove your hand."

A cold flush went down her spine, making the girl's interest in her orgasm dissipate instantly. "Yes, Sir," Lauren managed.

Thomas nuzzled tenderly against her neck, the gentle move at odds with his newly frigid tone. "For the rest of your time in this room today," he not-quite snarled, "you will say only 'yes, Sir' or 'no, Sir.' Do you understand?"

Watching his hand raise threateningly over her flushed, swollen lips again, Lauren managed to get "Yes, Sir!" past the screech strangling in her throat.

Turning her face to his, Thomas gave her a sweet kiss. "There's my good girl. Now, off my lap, kneel on the cushion next to the bed." He knew her hesitation was from fear, but a low growl got his darling up and moving. Opening the large chest next to her, he grinned, watching her eyes dart to the open lid and back again. The first thing he removed was a neatly coiled rope. Running a length of it down one stiffened nipple, Thomas spoke again, "This is Shibari rope, little one. No harsh fibers to scratch your pretty skin." Suddenly it was wrapped over each shoulder and outlining both breasts tightly. "Put your hands behind your back, each hand holding your other arm."

She was shaking as she did it, but Lauren obeyed, managing to whisper, "Y-yes, Sir." She felt him smooth her hair, resting her cheek against the hard length of his cock, still fully dressed in his expensive suit.

"Such a good girl..." Thomas purred, his voice so deep she could feel it vibrate against her. "Spread your legs, sitting on your heels." Another rapid looping motion had her arms bound in position, pushing her small breasts out quite shamelessly and then each thigh tied to the shin under it, effectively immobilizing her and keeping her on her widely spread knees. Hitching his trousers gracefully, Thomas knelt and rested on his heels, his expressionless gaze searching hers. "You know, darling, not being able to see what is being done to you, how I am playing with your lovely little body heightens the sensations, desperately trying to understand what is happening to you... it's utterly delicious to watch." Lifting one hand, Thomas held up a vibrating wand. "But occasionally I do enjoy the look of shock on your innocent face."

Helpless to move from her lewdly displayed position, Lauren could only watch this dark, deadly man who owned her begin stroking the wand over her center, dipping shallowly into her passage to slick up the buzzing torture device and move it up towards her hopeful clit, circling without touching it. "Oh..." it was an exhale of breath that was suddenly gasped back in when the wand pressed firmly against the little button.

Thomas felt his cock impossibly harden more, hearing his sweet girl's little gasps and moans. "Does that feel good, baby?" he purred solicitously.

"Yes, Sir," Lauren moaned, her hips unconsciously pushing forward, trying to get more pressure. Her eyes popped open as he pulled the wand away, gazing up at him reproachfully.

His brows drew together and she was suddenly hiked off the cushion and on her back on the bed. "Pouting?" he said sternly, "Acting like a little brat? Your Sir is disappointed with you." The cane was suddenly back and there were three red stripes on the inside of both her spread thighs, but Thomas counteracted the fiery sting by putting his mouth over her pussy in an open-mouthed kiss, slurping greedily. When he could feel her pulse against his tongue, he pulled away again, enjoying her choked-off groan of protest. "I can see I must assist you in being good," he was his most terrifying Number Two, rising above her with a frown. Lifting her head, the man slipped a stretchy band over Lauren's eyes. "No more sulking, hmmm?"

Next were two little vibrating, egg-shaped devices slipped inside her, making his sweet little bride clench her hands into fists, determined not to beg. His warm mouth was suddenly on her left breast, gently toying with the soft skin while his fingers viciously pinched her right nipple, the combination painfully arousing, leaving Lauren confused but wildly turned on. Then his mouth and fingers switched sides and it began again.

This time as she started feeling the tremors that meant her sadistic Sir was about to bring her to orgasm, Lauren bit her lip harshly. She wasn't going to give him the satisfaction. She wasn't going to beg him just so the horrible man could just edge her off again, she wasn't going to give HIM the satisfaction of- "Oh, god! Please, Sir!" This was cut off in a scream as the cane snapped another six blows in rapid succession on her ass. The vibration of the toys inside her intensified, counteracting the searing heat of the new strikes, turning her behind a dark rose.

"What phrases did I give you to use here, little one?"

Lauren didn't know whether to moan or cry. "Yes, Sir a- and AH!" Apparently, there was a higher speed on those goddamn eggs. "And no, mmmmm... no, Sir."

"Very good, remembering that will keep you from another caning." But Thomas continued to torment her, playing with toys and his fingers and tongue, bringing her to the brink and taking her back down with another permutation of pain. After an hour, or twenty, maybe it was a week she was past knowing, Lauren was sobbing, it was at the point that becoming aroused was acutely uncomfortable, adding to the strikes and stings and swats on her sensitive parts. The goddamn rope her satanic spouse had bound her with tormenting her by rubbing against her breasts, between her legs. Thomas had removed the bindings holding her arms back and legs apart, only to put her on one of those leather chairs-she knew they were weird! The big comfy chair had nearly invisible bindings for her hands, and the leather footrest rose as the chair was angled back and split into two pieces, perfect for holding her legs wide apart again.

Thomas sat on the leather ottoman between her legs, currently smoothing his hands up and down her shaking legs and murmuring soothingly. Reaching up, he removed her blindfold. "Do you know why your Sir has kept you from your release for so long?"

Lauren's teary eyes focused on him. "I... no, Sir." she managed, still sniffling.

"Two reasons, baby," the feel of his big, warm hand still sliding up and down her spread thighs was oddly comforting, but she forced herself to focus. "First, you will learn how to control yourself, you will not orgasm until I've given you permission. I will help you until you can develop the discipline. Secondly..." Thomas's beautiful face turned sly, knowing as his eyes narrowed and he bent closer to her swollen and sore pussy. "And secondly, I will teach you how you can experience pain at the same time as pleasure. How one can heighten the other." Lauren moaned and almost started crying again as his dark head dipped to kiss her tenderly on her stubbornly swollen clitoris, apparently indifferent to the harsh treatment visited upon it.

Thomas was still dressed for the office, perfectly put together while she was covered in marks, sweaty and her hair a snarled mess. And naked, something that always seemed so much more acute when he was not. "Do you wish to come now, sweetest girl?" Her mouth was open, but Thomas could tell Lauren didn't know how to answer him after such a lengthy bout of edging. He pulled open his belt and unzipped his pants. His cock was hugely hard, he'd borne the discomfort of no relief for the entire session as well, it made him feel closer to her misery, to understanding his pet. "I will make you come now baby, as many times as you like. Just say, 'I beg you to allow me to come.' And then thank me for your education today."

THANK him? Lauren was rigidly furious. Thank him for everything she'd been put through? Her cruel Sir wasn't waiting for her required speech, putting the head of his cock at her entrance and circling it slowly. "This poor, tender cunt is trying to pull me in, darling," he purred. "Be a good girl now. Beg..." he gave a little push, just barely breaching her with the thick head of his cock, "...me, and your Sir will make it all better."

Lauren couldn't think of a time she'd hated him more, but she stared at the gorgeous man who was currently torturing her with that wide, heavy cock. He'd made her love it. Crave it. And that need had her suddenly speaking rapidly, "Please Sir, I beg you to allow me to come!"

Thomas pushed his cock in halfway. She was so swollen from his various ways of tormenting her softest parts that she felt even tighter than usual, and he closed his eyes against the beauty of his bride's gaze fixed on his and mouth open and gasping. "Such a good girl," he smiled approvingly, circling his hips a bit and enjoying her moan. "Now, baby. Thank me for your instruction and I will fuck you senseless." He enjoyed watching her struggle, not yet grateful, not understanding the dynamic he was creating for her. But she would. "Now, thank your Sir..."

Lauren's thighs were shaking and she felt herself rubbing against the thin line of hair leading down to his cock. Suddenly her feet were lifted and the crop delivered a sharp slap to the soles of both. Her corresponding shriek was quite satisfying, Thomas thought. Another sharp slap delivered to her pinked ass made his sweet girl blurt, "Thank you... thank-youformyinstruction! Sir!" With a satisfying push, Thomas seated himself inside her fully and enjoying the fluttering of all that soft tissue clutching his shaft. Waiting for Lauren's galloping heart rate to slow, he kissed along her neck, whispering filthy endearments until she was calm enough to begin sliding in and out. They watched each other, Lauren with hopeful suspicion and he with dark intent. As his darling's breathing became heavier, Thomas rubbed the coarse hair at the base of his cock against her. And as she began climbing the hill he'd been building for her, the one that guaranteed a sharp and wildly satisfying plunge into orgasm, he lightly bit her earlobe. "You may come, sweetness." But just as she nearly fell over the edge, her diabolical Sir slapped her ass- hard.

Thomas groaned as she shrieked and jolted, her cunt clenching down on him in shock. "B- but you said-" Lauren was pulling mindlessly against her bonds, ready to cry again with frustration. Another slap. And shriek. Another tightening down on his thrusting cock.

"You may come, and I will help you come harder than ever..." Another slap on her fiery red ass. Another wail. Clenching down so tightly that Thomas's cock stilled. "You will come from both your need and your agony." Lauren's entire body felt painfully exposed, excruciatingly sensitive and each new strike on her ass hurt just as much. But her Sir's generous cock driving up inside her was still hurtling her into orgasm, she could feel it looming, even as his hands still caused pain. Licking two fingers, Thomas began patting her clitoris, swirling his hips and burrowing inside her deeper. And as her feet began twitching and pointing, he smacked his broad palm on her abused ass and murmured in his deepest, most commanding tone, that lovely accent so persuasive. "We shall come together, sweetness. On the third strike of my hand."

"One.

Two.

Three."

As his hand landed for the final time, the flare of misery from her skin somehow setting off the orgasm he'd threatened her with. Lauren felt it burn through her cunt, her legs, up her spine and jolting back down in a white-hot flash that hurt so fucking much but felt so powerfully good and she would take another three hundred slaps on her bruised ass to feel something so pleasurable that every muscle in her body was rigid but she didn't know that. All she knew was her beautiful, cruel, terrifying god gave her more and more waves of an orgasm so powerful that it tore through her. And Thomas groaned and continued thrusting into her spasming cunt, feeling it not so gently squeeze the come from him. The two cried out, shaking and groaning until the waves finally stopped crashing over them. Lauren dimly felt Thomas's head lift from her shoulder, removing her bonds and gently massaging her wrists and ankles. "Such a very good, brave girl. Your Sir is so pleased with you."

Chapter 21 – Food and Conversation

In which Lauren has a Girl's Night. Which turns out badly. Of course. Because that happens a lot as a Corporation Wife.

"Just one or two days without The Corporation fucking everything up," thought Lauren long after. "Just a couple of days. Was it really too much to ask?"

When one is the spouse of the terrifying Number Two from Jaguar Holdings, apparently so.

Lauren was humming a strain from Debussy's *Nocturnes*, smiling in a vaguely loose-lipped fashion that in no way imbued her youthful countenance with any dignity as she gathered up her sheet music after practice a few days later. She was fairly certain she would be walking bowlegged for the rest of her life because Thomas couldn't leave her alone long enough to heal up, and if he'd tried, she wouldn't have let him. They didn't go into Thomas's "Fun Dungeon" every night, the name she'd settled on when Sex Dungeon sounded too grim and her husband's term "Play Room" was just ridiculous. Lauren was young, very healthy and possessed a delightfully sturdy constitution, but given all the delightfully dark and sordid things Thomas did to her in there as her Sir, she wasn't certain she'd survive the week. But the very discovery of the room and all its alarming accessories and her willingness to submit turned their heated sex life into an inferno.

"How've you been?"

Yanked out of her salacious meanderings, Lauren looked up, flushing as she focused on the slightly amused face of her friend. "I'm good," she managed, "how are you, Macie? I love that new sweater." Macie forced a smile in return, which made Lauren a little sad. But at least her (former) best friend was talking to her.

"It's been a really long time," she finally managed, "I thought we could have lunch? There's a killer kebab place I found a couple of streets over."

Lauren instantly wanted to blurt, "Yes! Hell, yes!" It had been so long since she and Macie spoke since her (former) best friend could look at her with anything other than hurt or disgust. But what did lunch mean in her scary, uncertain new universe? Would a simple lunch expose Macie to any danger? Any scrutiny? Half of her stood back and shook her head in disbelief that she found herself in a place in her life where considerations such as grabbing a kebab with her (former) best friend could mean life or death. *It's just a kebab,* she scolded her sensible half, *no one's dying over a kebab!* Looking up, Lauren smiled more naturally, "I'd love that."

Two lamb kebabs in with a mess of rice and lemon sauce, the girls kept wiping their greasy fingers and giggling. Lauren marveled that after a few uncomfortable sentences she and Macie were chatting away again as if the past few months had never happened, feeling just as close as they had, flying into Heathrow airport and ready to begin their new lives as Professional Musicians.

"...so, this wanker looked down my sweater and said 'I wanna slap those baps,' and it took me a minute to realize the son of a bitch was talking about my boobs!" Macie was waving her stick of oily lamb and laughing over the encounter. "First, I wanted to throw my beer in his face- but it was a really good beer, you know, and then I was slightly impressed because he got his shitty pickup line to actually rhyme, so that was good..."

"What did you do?" Lauren prompted.

Macie shrugged. "I threw *his* beer in his face." The two girls were silent for a moment before bursting into uncontrollable laughter. Lauren was giddy with the relief and the sheer joy of being with her best (perhaps still?) friend again. Finally, their laughter turned into wheezing, which turned into a comfortable silence as they finished their lunch. Walking slowly back to the practice hall, Lauren smiled as her friend carelessly linked their arms together, the way they used to. "So, you ever get a night off from being Mrs. Thomas Williams?"

Lauren's brow furrowed, "What do you mean?"

"I mean," Macie drawled, "could we have a girl's night? Maybe Friday or Saturday? We could hang out at my place and eat crap food- I bought Flaming Hot Cheetos off Amazon! And maybe watch *Pretty in Pink* again."

Sniffling a little, Lauren said, "Remember when she took the thrift store dress and made it amazing and then they were making out in the parking lot by his BMW because he really loved her?"

"Yeah," Macie agreed, a little weepily, "I love that scene."

Lauren was torn. Thomas had made it clear that The Corporation Wives only hung out with Other Corporation Wives, but... he didn't trust Arabella either. What could it harm to just have one evening? Nothing big. Just two members of the same orchestra having a girl's night?

Her voice a little harder, Macie persisted. "Just one night. Does he let you off the leash ever?" She realized her mistake when Lauren stopped, staring at her angrily. "Shit, girl. I didn't mean... not like that. I just wanted to see you, I guess."

Sighing, Lauren rubbed her forehead. "I'd like to hang out, too. But don't be mean, all right? Thomas is really sweet to me." She could tell by the blank expression on her (probably former) best friend's face that Macie did not get it, but she persisted. "He *is.* Thomas is. I think I could do Friday; can I text you tonight?"

Macie made an agreeing sort of noise, looking behind them at Chuck, who was following them at a discreet distance. "Do you think you could leave your boy back there at home for one evening?"

Startled into laughing, Lauren gave her a little shove with her shoulder. "Chuck is super charming, dude. You would be blessed to witness that man's charm."

Thomas had arrived home a little early that day, so he was pulling off his tie by the time Lauren walked through the door. "Ah, there you are, lovely. I want to take you out for dinner tonight. Nora's, across the park. They have magnificent American food."

Still thinking about Macie actually shipping Flaming Hot Cheetos from the states made Lauren smile. If only Thomas knew what real American food could entail. "Thank you," she answered, "I would love that."

Sitting across from her beautiful husband and enjoying a rare warm evening that allowed them to eat out on the little patio behind the restaurant, Lauren circled mentally around how to ask for permission for her girl's night. In the rare times she'd ever thought about being married, she had always assumed that she and her spouse would both have outside interests, other friends that would enrich their lives and give them new things to talk about and keep them from being the Boring Couple That Did Everything Together Because They Were Surgically Attached At The Hip. The reality of her unusual marriage and knowing she would have to ask for permission to see Macie surprised her and made her a little sad.

"Lauren? Come back to me, darling."

Looking up from her pork chop sandwich, she flushed, "Sorry, Thomas. I was just thinking about Macie. You know, the girl who attended Julliard with me? We were in the-" Lauren stumbled a little, thinking about her abrupt departure from the quartet, "we played in the quartet together?"

Thomas had pushed his plate away and was giving her his full attention, toying with the stem of his wine glass. "Yes?"

"She invited me over for a junk food feast on Friday at her flat." Lauren was sweating, *Why am I sweating?* she thought crossly and gave him a hopeful smile. "You mentioned having a late meeting that night, so I thought maybe I could... hang out with her? If you don't mind?" *Stop talking!* she scolded herself. "Unless you've got something you need me to do, or-"

"That's fine." Thomas was back to cutting into his ribeye and gave her a distracted smile. "No need for you to sit at home."

Lauren's jaw dropped at his instant capitulation, but she recovered quickly. "Thank you, that would be great." Hastily changing the subject before he could change his mind; she felt a little warmth in her chest. An evening with a friend.

And at first, it was wonderful, everything Lauren had hoped for: vile junk food from the states, like the aforementioned Cheetos, beef jerky and Twinkies. "Mmmm..." she sighed rapturously, "why is it the rest of the world does not understand the sacred nature of Twinkies? They should be grateful that they have a never-ending shelf life!"

"Right?" Macie said thickly through a mouthful of Cheetos, which were staining her mouth orange, "They have no idea what they're missing."

There was a selection of cheesy '80's movies and Lauren began to feel that frozen part in the center of her start to unthaw just a bit- the part that kept her upright, alert, cautious. It was so nice to be with Macie again, the girl who'd let Lauren sleep on her couch when her dad threw her out and she still had a month before the dorms opened up. The girl she'd nursed back to health after constant alcohol binges and even went to Macie's first few AA meetings with her because she was scared to go alone. Remembering those AA meetings, Lauren squirmed uncomfortably. She'd been longing for a glass (bottle) of wine all night and of course, there was no alcohol here. *I'm missing the wine too much,* she thought briefly before starting the next movie.

It was halfway through *Grosse Pointe Blank* when Macie rose, returning to the couch with a folder and a determined expression on her face. Lauren's heart sank. She knew that expression, the one that meant her bull-headed friend had something to say, and there was no stopping her, by god, until Macie had said it.

"Lauren." She seated herself on the lumpy couch next to the suddenly miserable girl next to her, turning to face her, knees touching. "I've been doing some research, and-"

Oh, fuck! Lauren screamed internally, looking at the folder. Of course, the concept of what Jaguar Holdings might include was there for anyone determined enough to dig for it, no matter how many politicians, celebrities and the wealthy flocked to The Corporation events. Power was more magnetic than distrust. *Don't, Macie,* she pleaded internally, *please don't-*

"-you have to know there's something wrong there," the girl was saying and Lauren forced herself to pay attention. "There's so much here, honey, just look-" Macie proffered a pile of copies from news stories. "These guys are sick fuckers, and I *know* you," putting her hand on Lauren's knee, she didn't quite recognize that her friend was stiffening under her hand, "I know you know it! Why are you married to this guy? He's a murderer!"

The vision of Thomas calmly shooting a gun out the back window of the Jaguar while she steering surged up, and Lauren pressed a hand against her mouth to keep back a hysterical little titter. That would not be helpful here. "Maze, you have to stop. You have to shut up now before you say another word." Of course, Macie's mouth immediately opened and Lauren grabbed her shoulders, shaking her. "Listen. To. Me," she enunciated sharply. "Not another word. You never speak of this again, not ever. We burn these papers and you erase the history on your laptop-"

"But, Lauren, you're not-"

"MACIE!" Lauren shouted with frustration that her well-intentioned friend was not paying attention, suddenly terrified for her well-being, angry that Macie could just not *leave it the fuck alone*. "You have to fucking listen to me! You can't talk about this ever again. Not to anyone, do you hear me?"

"Oh, I already have," Macie interrupted earnestly, big, brown eyes so sincere, "a police investigator from the local precinct, he-"

Lauren shot up abruptly, backing away in horror. Macie was going to die. She was probably going to die, too, but that still wasn't as horrifying as knowing she'd just killed her best friend. "You have no fucking idea what you've done, Maze," she managed to whisper, "call this guy, tell him you were wrong. Don't ever speak to him again. Don't ever speak to me again. You can't imagine- Jesus, please fucking listen to me! Get rid of anything you've investigated."

Her friend, her good-hearted friend who always stood up for her, yelled back. "You're married to a fucking murderer, an arms dealer, probably human trafficking and all kinds of sick shit and that's all you can say? Lauren honey, what-"

Gathering up her jacket and messenger bag, Lauren began frantically stuffing her items back into it, texting Chuck with one hand to come to pick her up. Turning back to look at Macie, who was clearly shocked and now had disappointment crossing that pretty face, she blinked back tears. "I'm trying to keep you alive, Maze. Never fucking talk to me again. I'm trying to- just don't. Drop this now. Never talk about it again." Without waiting for a response, she fumbled with the locks on the door, struggling to get out and slam the door behind her. On the stairwell, she paused for a moment to press her hands - hard - against her welling eyes. It hurt and made her stop crying. She had to look normal. Chuck had fucking eyes like a hawk and he'd hone in on emotion like she was a trembling rabbit.

"A good evening, Miss Lauren?"

She stretched ostentatiously, yawning as she got in the back seat. "Yeah, Chuck, junk food heaven, thanks."

She'd not been home long by the time Thomas returned from his meetings, but Lauren was three glasses of wine in and just beginning to think she could face her husband without bursting into terrified sobs. She was pouring the fourth glass with a shaking hand when she heard the Voice.

"Lauren, little girl, your Sir is home. Where are you, lovely?" Thomas's deep voice purred, it soothed and aroused her at the same time. It was the tone that told Lauren that her Sir was ready to play.

Hastily smoothing her hair and making sure her mascara wasn't smeared, she attempted to walk sensually through the great room to where Thomas was pulling off his jacket and tie. "Hello, Sir," Lauren lowered her voice, trying to sound as compelling as her dark spouse.

Thomas looked up, fine lines around his eyes crinkling as he smiled, cobalt gaze sweeping up and down her body. "Hello, baby. Did you have a good time tonight?"

Forcing herself to shrug casually, Lauren held up a glass. "Can I make you a drink?" At his nod, she gritted her teeth, focusing on pouring the scotch without her hand shaking and spilling it. "It was okay... it's just. I dunno, it seems like we don't really have anything to talk about anymore. We're different people, not much in common, you know?"

"Hmmm..." Thomas took the glass from her, kissing her hand lingeringly. "A pity. But it happens. Once you don't have school in common, it can be hard to keep in touch."

Lauren nodded rapidly, acutely aware that his tongue was sliding between his lips on her skin, the tip stroking across nerve endings and setting them sparking. "You're right. It's just a shame, she was my only friend from home, here." She didn't think her voice broke, but Thomas looked up from her hand. Pulling her closer, he set down his drink, an arm going around her waist, the other caressing the back of her neck.

Leaning down so close that she could see the bits of emerald swirling in the sea of his eyes, Thomas spoke slowly, carefully. "I would very much like to hear you call here, 'home.' This is your home now, Lauren." His expression softened at her expression of surprise, followed by Lauren's traditional shyness and a sudden, hopeful smile.

"That would be..." she paused for a moment, how to answer this sweetly-issued request as a Crime Lord's captive bride? But it wasn't exactly captivity when she'd settled happily into her cage, now was it? And this beautiful, confusing, often terrifying man had been so very good to her. Most of the time. "It would be nice to have a real home. I haven't had one really, not since my mom died."

There was the oddest moment then, where Thomas's usual expression of urbane amusement shifted into sorrow, tenderness, perhaps even regret. Placing a big hand on each cheek, he gently cupped her face and drew her mouth to his in the most exquisite of kisses, lips shifting and sliding against each other, soft swipes of his tongue while his thumbs caressed her cheekbones. Moving his mouth to her ear, Thomas whispered, "Welcome home."

Lauren pulled him closer by his dress shirt, grabbing handfuls of starched cotton to press against him, kissing him a little needily, sliding her arms around his back and hugging him. Her eyelashes fluttered at his soothing endearments, whispered into her ear as he slid his hands to her bottom and lifted her, grunting as she wrapped her legs tightly around his waist. Carrying her up the stairs and to their bedroom- *How does he do that without even breaking a sweat?* Lauren marveled as always. She knew she was not light. She was compact. Sturdy. Not willowy. But nonetheless, she was on her back and stripped of her pretty jersey dress in moments.

The following morning, he parted from her at the front door, dressed for battle in his bespoke blue suit and Lauren ready for orchestra practice in the softest of cotton sweaters and a long skirt. Slumping against the wood as he kissed her with some ferocity, Lauren giggled with embarrassment as his gloved hand lifted her chin. "I'll see you tonight, you tasty little darling." Smiling back up at him, Lauren's brow wrinkled, a little confused. There was a look in his eyes. Regret?

Limping into practice, Lauren gratefully seated herself, testing the strings on her cello, listening for the tone as her eyes swept the hall, looking for Macie. There was a thick knot of anxiety that refused to dissolve. Macie was a smart girl. She'd drop this. She was gone forever as a friend, but... Feeling her breath hitch, Lauren gnawed on the inside of her cheek, forcing herself to remain calm. Crying didn't do anything.

Tapping his baton, the conductor spoke. "We're opening auditions for the violin section, Macie Emerson emailed in her resignation today. Do let those who might be qualified know about our opening."

Chapter 22 – If I am All You Have, You Will Love Me

In which we find out whether Macie lives, or dies. Because it's like that in The Corporation. No matter who your best friend is.

The house was dark, but it didn't occur to Lauren to turn on any lights. Instead, she paced. Her cello was still sitting in the entry where Chuck had placed it for her, the man eyeing her carefully like she was about to detonate and send shrapnel of hysterical tears at him. "Is there anything I can get for you, Miss Lauren?" he'd asked, feeling as if he was somehow failing his duty by not "fixing" his shaking charge.

"Uh..." Lauren had tried to concentrate, "no, it's all good. Thanks, Chuck. Goodnight." Aside from flinching slightly when she called him 'Chuck,' the man remained impassive as he left, carefully shutting the door and waiting for the 'click' of the lock. Standing in the dark hall for a while, staring at nothing, Lauren's thoughts flew around her head like frightened birds.

Did Thomas kill Macie? Would he- could he be that fucking evil?

She couldn't think of anything else to do, so Lauren started pacing the living room. It was exactly ten steps to the big, leaded-glass windows. Seven steps to the fireplace. Twenty-one steps to the front entryway again. Absently counting out loud as she paced her erratic triangle, Lauren kept going over the options.

Was Macie appropriately terrified and chose to run?

Was her former best friend's flat was bugged? By Thomas or The Corporation? Did they have someone following Macie?

What if it's The Corporation? Lauren gave an ugly, convulsive sob and slapped her hand over her mouth, trying to not let the silent house hear her. If it's The Corporation, that sick fuck Number One, Macie was dead for sure. *Jesus... they wouldn't... but they have a bordello,* she thought wildly, *do they get girls like that? Would they SELL Macie?*

"Oh, fuck. Oh, fuck oh fuck oh fuck!" Lauren keened. This was all her fault, all her fucking fault. Remembering Thomas's cold, indifferent face when he'd nodded to Chuck to shoot her dad- this was not a merciful organization. She was not married to a merciful man. It didn't matter how he treated her. He was a monster. But he wouldn't kill Macie. "Thirty-three, thirty-four, thirty-five... I bet Macie cut and run. That's it. Macie's somewhere safe." But she couldn't stop shaking.

Lauren was on the 3,075th step when she heard Thomas's key in the door and her trembling turned into a full-body shudder. *Cut this shit out!* she angrily ordered herself, gritting her teeth.

"Darling?" It was the Voice, Thomas's damnable, rich tones that made her melt, made her cave like a cheap souffle, every time. But not tonight. "Why are you standing in the dark?"

Blinking as the light suddenly switched on, Lauren rubbed

her eyes with the heel of her hand and wondered if she was next. Trying to drag out the plan she'd made from her exhausted brain, she tried to remember if she was going to fake ignorance for a while, lure him into a sense of false security with a nice dinner and a bottle of wine, and then: strike like a snake? Trick him into answering? Watching her husband calmly shed his cashmere topcoat and hang it in the entryway closet, Lauren knew that was ridiculous.

"Macie, she's... Macie's gone." she suddenly blurted, her heart pounding hard enough to choke her. Shuffling through the mail, that smooth bastard didn't even bother to look up, the same calm expression undisturbed on his beautiful, stupid, evil, stupid, stupid face.

"Oh?" asked Thomas indifferently, "Gone where?"

Watching his big hands flicking envelopes open, Lauren shuddered, picturing them around her neck. Were they around Macie's neck last night? *Oh, right,* she thought bitterly, *Thomas never kills himself, too messy.* Clearing her throat, she spoke up. "She's gone, Thomas. Did you- Is she dead?" An ugly sob broke through her hard-won demeanor, humiliating Lauren.

Her husband looked up sharply, eyes cooling to a frost blue as he looked her over. "What did you just say to me, little girl?"

Voice rising, Lauren couldn't stop herself, still walking in her strange little triangle. "Is she dead, Thomas? Did you kill my best friend? Did you hurt her? I've been so careful to follow your *rules*-" she spat the last and suddenly he was in front of her, his tall body blocking the way around him. To escape.

"You will need to stop talking. Right. Now." he snarled, leaning down to crowd her into the mantel of the fireplace.

"Think very carefully about what you're blurting out like a little fool. Think about what's at stake before you open your mouth again."

Staring into the chillingly beautiful face of the demon she was bound to; Lauren could feel her heart hitch and miss a beat before reluctantly getting back into rhythm. Licking her lips, she ducked under his suited arm and began her pacing again. "Thirteen... fourteen... fifteen..." Brows furrowed, Thomas leaned against the fireplace and watched his distraught wife conduct her circuit of the great room. Two more paces of thirty each and Lauren was composed enough to speak again. "Macie's gone," she began lamely.

"So I hear," Thomas answered dryly, taking off his jacket and tie, rolling up the sleeves of his shirt as he found himself mentally counting off his bride's steps before irritably stopping himself.

"It's NOT FUNNY!" Lauren shouted before she could stop herself, trying to back up and nearly falling over the couch as her terrifying spouse stalked over to her, grabbing her upper arms and giving her a brisk shake.

"Lower your voice and calm yourself," he hissed, absently loosening his hands against her arms. Lauren bruised so easily, there were purple marks he very much enjoyed watching sprout the next day after an active session. But the bruises marring her pale skin like handcuffs would give him an unpleasant sensation, they had before. Hustling her into the kitchen, Thomas flipped on the light and started the kettle as he roughly seated her in a chair. The fight seemed to go out of his wife then, hands resting limply on her lap. He cracked his neck absently, remembering her blushing goodbye kiss that morning. The last one he'd be receiving (willingly) for a while, he supposed. "Before you speak another word, you will drink this and take a moment before you blurt out any more accusations." Pouring her a cup of tea, he was somehow irritable with himself for knowing she preferred peppermint when she was sad and upset and like a little drizzle of the honey she'd picked up from the farmer's market in the nearby park. She'd begged him to come with her last Thursday, darting between the booths like a dragonfly and showing him new items with an eager, happy face, looking up to him for his approval with a bright smile. Remembering the outing while he watched her numbly drink the scalding tea, Thomas stopped himself from groaning. When she'd had most of the tea and her hands had stopped shaking, he started again. "How was your 'girl's night' with Macie, darling?" his voice was cold, but composed, "Anything you left out from our chat?"

When his sweet wife looked up at him, her expression was cold, bitter. Something he'd never seen before from her. "I think you know, Thomas. And if you do-" her voice broke, but Lauren angrily composed herself. "-you know I did everything I could to stop her. I tried to scare her, just the way you did to me."

Leaning back against the counter, Thomas folded his arms, his polar gaze intent on her. "What did she say to you?" He slipped into the soul-chilling stare he used on the disloyal or the foolish. Making certain he'd lulled them into a false sense of hopefulness that if only they told him everything- he would *surely* let them live. He would see they were *so* sorry for their mistake. They died, of course. Every time. But this was his wife and he had to make damned certain he knew everything in order to protect her. *But for now,* the cold part of his brain reasserted itself. For now, let her wonder if she might die. To be certain he had not missed a single detail.

"Thomas, Macie's- she's-" Lauren was floundering, wondering if she was only signing her friend's death warrant by saying anything at all. He was silent, still giving her that ghastly stare. "She's so loyal," she choked back a sob, knowing tears would only irritate him. "She would do anything for her friends, she let me stay on her couch when Frank kicked me out of the house, and-"

"What. Did. She. *Tell* you, darling?" Thomas was relentless.

"She was just trying to save me!" Lauren pleaded, looking at his cold, immobile expression, "She did a lot of research online, I guess, and-" her husband's forbidding countenance did not soften, and she swallowed heavily. "The Corporation can't keep everything hidden. But she took... she took." her throat closed and she swallowed convulsively, trying not to scream.

"Yes?"

It was one word, but it was laced with so much barely-contained fury that Lauren started shaking. "Macie said she t-talked to a detective at- at the precinct by her flat. Is that what you call it here a precinct or something else but she said he was a detective and-"

Thomas's hand slammed down on the counter and she nearly jumped off her chair. "Did she give you a name?"

Lauren shook her head adamantly, her watery eyes wide and sincere. "No. I don't know if the detective even believed her. I told her then to forget about it and never talk about The Corporation again. That w- we couldn't ever talk again and she had to keep her mouth shut and we had to burn everything she printed and delete the history on her laptop." Despite her best efforts, her chest hitched and she began to cry. "I told her I was trying to save her life." Looking up at the forbidding figure looming over her, Lauren forced herself to ask again. "Did you kill her, Thomas?"

He had never looked more polar, more indifferent to her desperation. "We had a business engagement tonight. You are clearly in no shape to attend." After checking his stainless-steel Philippe Patel, Thomas looked her over again, like she was yet another problem begging for her life. He'd never killed a woman... Irritated that his thoughts drifted, Williams began rolling down his sleeves again, smoothing his hair. "Straker will be here in the house to keep an eye on you. I expect you to behave. Be my quiet, good girl." Pulling on his jacket, he leaned down to place a chaste kiss on his wife's cheek, ignoring how she visibly shuddered at the touch of his mouth.

Just as his hand touched the front door, Lauren's desperate voice stopped him. "You didn't tell me. Please, Thomas? Please?" Without answering her, Thomas left, ignoring her sobs echoing from the kitchen.

Thomas Williams, the unflappable Number Two of Jaguar Holdings, sat and amiably conversed with their guests at dinner, chuckling at a particularly gruesome story from their Caribbean partners, who were so very excellent at laundering money. Until someone gets greedy, of course, which is what made this little dinner chat so exceptionally horrifying. To the average person. To the group of dark and hardened souls around the table, it was simply in a day's work. Williams continued to chuckle at the right times, lead them in a toast and brush off the efforts of a particularly attentive hostess at the private Japanese house where they had dinner. And dessert. Thomas watched Michael eagerly take the hand of another alluring girl and head off upstairs. Number Three had never been faithful to Clara, so really, it was business as usual as Ben stood and buttoned his suit jacket, heading in the same direction with another girl.

But Number One paused at the first step, turning to look at his second in command. "Thomas!" he called with his false joviality, "Surely there is one lovely thing here that meets your high standards?"

It was a test. Thomas knew Ben was gauging just how attached he was to his reluctant bride. Summoning a leer, he answered easily. "You forget that I'm a newlywed, Ben. So many things left to do to break her in." It was the perfect thing to say. His partner lit up with a nauseating glee.

"Hah, ha!" Ben chuckled fondly. "Off you go then."

Smoothing his tie and leaving, Thomas shook off a feeling of being coated in filth.

The house was dimly lit as he returned home, nodding to Straker and questioning him about the evening. Lauren's bodyguard sat in an uncomfortable chair pulled from the dining table and placed at the bottom of the stairs, where he could see and hear anything going on in the house. Thomas was impressed by the man's deft placement. "How is my wife?" he asked casually, eyeing the darkened hallway leading to the bedroom.

Straker shrugged carefully. "Mrs. Williams chose to retire early," he stated calmly, "she appeared fatigued."

The master of understatement, Thomas thought with a certain sense of respect. He'd chosen well for Lauren's personal security. "Very well," he said out loud, "Lauren will need more careful scrutiny over the next few days. Her anxiety may make her careless. I expect you to head off any unfortunate situations."

Putting away his phone and returning the chair to the table, Chuck nodded. "Of course, Mr. Williams. She will have my complete attention."

Thomas almost softened, hearing the man's certainty and devotion. "Excellent. I know you will. Good night."

"Good night," Straker returned politely as he left, closing the door quietly behind him. Setting the home's security system, Thomas let out an almost soundless sigh and began to climb the stairs to the third floor.

The master bedroom was dark, but Thomas could see the shape of his wife under the down comforter. He'd almost expected her to try to sleep in her music conservatory but suspected she'd be too heartsick to think clearly. He correctly predicted her actions. Lauren was huddled on her side, in a frail-looking fetal position with her knees drawn up to her chest, as if trying to make herself as small as possible. It was not her usual position, Thomas noted, his Lauren slept on her back, arms and legs tossed carelessly over the mattress. He'd woken up more than once with her hand flung over his face or her leg wedged in between his. Mildly irritated at himself for the fond smile he wore at the memory of his wife's random cuddling, Thomas undressed silently for bed. He could tell the moment Lauren awoke, the tell-tale stiffening of her body before she forced herself to breathe evenly again. Pulling down the comforter enough to slide into bed next to her, the cold heart of Thomas Williams thawed just a tad as he watched her body, protectively curved into a tight little huddle.

"Lauren."

There was no answer, and with a sigh, he gently pulled her over to face him. But she stubbornly kept her chin tucked into her chest. "Look at me, little one." She resisted until his hand went under her jaw, lifting her head to look into his eyes. "Macie is alive." Lauren gave a convulsive little sob, but slapped her hand over her mouth, trying to keep quiet as her heartbroken gaze met his. "I've had her under surveillance since you and I became engaged. She did not seem like the sort to let go of a close friendship," Thomas said wryly.

"I tried to keep away from her-" she began, but he hushed her.

"I know Lauren, I know you did," he assured her, soothing her and brushing her hair back from her face. "But it is my job as your husband to make certain of your safety. Macie's irritating, determined nature was bound to surface as a threat to The Corporation at some point. I intended to put a halt to it before it came to the attention of Ben." She nodded shakily, still staring up at him with those huge violet eyes. His voice turned sterner. "Your friend has taken a position with the Berlin Philharmonic. She was moved there overnight by two of my men. I have made it very clear to her that her life, as well as yours, depends on her keeping her mouth shut and never speaking of you, or The Corporation ever again." Tears filled her eyes, overflowing silently onto her cheeks but Lauren nodded again.

The night before...

Thomas was seated in the only decent piece of furniture in the girl's flat, watching Macie frantically throw clothing into a suitcase. "Do you understand what I have told you?" His voice was ice, almost inhuman and it made her cringe.

"Y-yes," she managed, trying to swallow her tears. Macie had crumbled almost instantly when Thomas had arrived at her door ten minutes after the frantic departure of her (former) best friend. He calmly produced copies of her online activities, photos of her meetings with the unfortunate detective and a cruel closeup of his staring, sightless eyes with a bullet hole between them, in painfully crisp, clear focus.

"You've already murdered one person with your stupidity and your arrogant do-gooder insistence," he'd snarled, "your 'holier than thou' idiocy that sent you stumbling through something that anyone with an IQ higher than that of a goldfish would know was certain death. But you just had to, didn't you?" Lauren's friend was sobbing and terrified, huddled in a corner of her little flat and slumped on the floor, the pictures scattered in front of her. "I should have you killed tonight," Thomas's voice was more terrifying by its indifference. "A quick finish for a stupid little girl. If my partners had discovered this first, they would have sold you into a whorehouse, Mexico, perhaps, or Saudi Arabia. Stupid little girls are quite popular there, they so enjoy breaking them."

Macie's horrified weeping was louder now, and Thomas irritably straightened his cuffs. "You care so little for my wife that you'd sign her death warrant as well?" Her desperate brown eyes were wide, owlish as she couldn't break his contemptuous stare. Leaning back, he narrowed his eyes. "What do you think I should do with you, Macie? A foolish creature like you, thinking you could damage us? Expose The Corporation?" he chuckled humorously, "The only reason that poor sod-" he nodded to the dead man's photo, "-had to die was because he was too low-level for us to have bothered to own him." Leaning closer, Thomas watched Macie shrink back, still sobbing and shaking her head. "What should I do with you?"

Macie managed to get a few sentences out through her weeping. "...Never tell anyone... go away... never see me again... swear..."

Rising, Number Two of Jaguar Holdings made his way over to her, pulling a gun from a shoulder holster. "Now, why would I believe that? You didn't care enough about your life or my *wife's-*" taking in a deep breath, Thomas forced himself to be calm, "-to shut up and leave it alone when it was clear what you were dealing with. Why should I trust you now?" He lifted the gun, watching Macie try to crab-walk away from him, tears and snot running down her face, shaking her head over and over, promising him anything if he would just-. Blinking, Williams forced himself back into the moment. This was his Lauren's foolish but well-intentioned best friend. She thought she was saving Lauren from *him*. "Because I find I have a dangerous softness for my bride," he spat, "I will spare your life. There is an opening in the Berlin Philharmonic. They have accepted you. You have a flat in the city by the rehearsal hall." She was shuddering with the effort to stop crying, he noted dispassionately. "You will never return here. You will never speak of The Corporation. You will never speak of, or to my wife again. Is this all quite clear?" She was nodding frantically, as if a single nod would change his mind and the gun would come back out. Thomas thrust the photo of the dead detective into her face again, almost enjoying her stifled shriek. "If you do not learn from this, the next picture you see before I put a bullet in your brain will be the dead body of your dear best friend Lauren." Macie was looking at him with horror now, as if this mess was somehow of his making, rather than hers. "Do you understand?" She nodded again, as fast as she could. "DO YOU!" Thomas shouted into her tear-soaked face.

This time the girl nearly screamed, "Yes! Yes, I swear! I swear!"

Bringing himself back to the present and the warm body of

his wife, Thomas realized with some surprise that she was clinging to him, arms around his neck and thanking him repeatedly in her sweet, tremulous voice. His arms automatically went around her, feeling her body shake. Of course. It was more than just gratitude, he thought, Lauren was made to love. And if he was all she had; she would love him.

"Shhh..." he soothed tenderly, kissing her cheeks, cradling her wet face in his palms, "everything's all right now. Your friend is safe." As he expected (hoped?) his bride covered his face with kisses, thanking him between each one. And when Lauren shyly lifted one leg to wrap over his waist, Thomas hid his smile.

Chapter 23 – Accepting the Unacceptable

In which Lauren is inspired.

When Lauren woke the next morning, Thomas was knotting his tie in the mirror, and he glanced over with a smile. "Why don't you go back to sleep?" he suggested, dressing in a suit. "There's no reason to rise so early."

"Oh..." her disappointed little voice came from under the mountain of pale linen, "you're going into work?" It was a Sunday, but in The Corporation's world, days of the week meant nothing.

Smiling gently, Thomas leaned down to kiss her. "Only for a short meeting or two. If you're not sleepy, why don't you head down to Selfridge's and look at the gowns the personal shopper selected for you? The gala for the fundraiser is less than a month away. When I come home, we'll make dinner together and watch a movie."

Lauren brightened instantly, as he knew she would. They rarely had quiet evenings at home alone. "Can I pick the movie?" He groaned, but agreed, knowing he'd be watching some vile Romcom but it would be worth it to see her happy.

So, Lauren went to the legendary department store and went

through some of the ridiculously expensive gowns selected by the personal shopper Thomas had hired. They were all too... something. Too shiny. Too tight. Too long. Too expensive. Giving up after the tenth sequined concoction, she smiled politely at the tight-lipped woman and said insincerely, "We'll do this again soon when I get a better idea of the gala's theme."

Ducking out was a relief, even breathing in the sooty London air, Mrs. Thomas Williams smiled. She *was* getting more assertive. Chuck had the car magically by the curb in a moment, holding the door open for her. He inched one brow up slightly when Lauren shook her head. "I want to just, you know, stroll around for a little, okay?" Her bodyguard reluctantly nodded, waving off the car and following her.

It wasn't like Lauren to walk aimlessly, but she was rarely in this part of the city, and she was simply enjoying the watery sunshine and the beautiful old buildings. Chuck was close, almost at her elbow. Far closer than he usually was, but she didn't take offense. She was certain Thomas had ordered him to keep a close eye on her in case she cracked, or something.

Lauren was not going to crack.

It was a lot like how she'd felt when her mom died, she thought, pausing outside a flower store to admire a huge, beautiful assortment of hydrangeas. Except for being older made it easier, clearer. There wasn't a choice. She'd chuckled bitterly then at friends who dramatically wailed, "I'm giving up!" over a test, or a bad boyfriend, or losing their phone at the mall. Lauren never understood that. There was no giving up. It was not allowed.

So, maybe that's why her life with Thomas wasn't as unspeakable as she'd first anticipated. And her scary husband was unaccountably capable of moments of exquisite kindness, even occasionally tenderness. She hadn't decided whether that made her life worse, or better. Pausing in front of a little stone building, Lauren smiled to realize it was a Catholic church. She was lapsed, she had never gone back after her mother's funeral. A god who took the only person in her life that truly mattered - who was the world to her - was not a god she wanted to speak to ever again. But, it was a beautiful church, so she stepped in the old oak doors, Chuck close on her heels with a brow raised.

Smiling, Lauren ran her hand over the little wooden stand in the foyer, half-lit candles and a little arrangement of flowers. And then she started down the aisle. Feeling Chuck's breath lightly on the back of her neck, she mischievously stopped suddenly, feeling him recover a second before tripping into her. "Chuck? Dude? I'm not going anywhere. I'm just going to light a candle for..." swallowing convulsively, all her grief and loss over losing her mother came roaring back, and Lauren paused for a moment. "I'm just lighting a candle for my mom, okay?"

There was a moment, and she could almost hear the slightest lilt of regret in his voice. "Of course, Miss Lauren. I'll just sit here."

Continuing down the aisle, Lauren knelt before the altar for a moment before leaving a handful of pounds in the little collection box. Thinking about it, looking at the clean, but shabby velvet curtains and cushions, she dug into her purse and pulled out all the money she had, stuffing it in with the rest. Taking a taper and lighting a fresh candle, she bowed her head and tried to remember how to pray. Her lips moved, like muscle memory, but she couldn't seem to understand the words her mouth was shaping. Finally, feeling foolish and not sure what else to do, she sat in the front row, staring at the lovely stained-glass windows.

"Good afternoon."

Lauren nearly fell off the bench. "G- good afternoon, Father," she managed, pressing her hand to her chest.

The priest was a slight, older man, thinning gray hair and wire-framed spectacles. He had a kind, tired face and sat a respectful distance from her, hands holding a Bible in his lap. "I'm sorry, I didn't mean to startle you. You looked deep in thought."

She tried to give a dismissive laugh, but it turned out more like a gulp from someone who was trying not to cry. "I was, um, I guess I was thinking about my mom. She..." Lauren was silent again and so was the priest, calmly waiting as if he had all the time in the world. "She... died a couple of years ago. I just wanted to light a candle, but I'm not a big church-goer so I should just leave, I guess-"

"When I lost my parents, I didn't speak to God for a year."

Half-risen from the bench, Lauren awkwardly sat back down. "Oh, I'm really sorry, Father, that's-"

He patted her arm absently, "Thank you, it was twenty-five years ago, so my grief is not as fresh as yours. But you will always feel it." The priest smiled suddenly. "Everyone told you platitudes like, 'The grief fades in time,' and so on and so on?"

Almost giggling at the man's daring, Lauren nodded. "Exactly. It's all crap. I miss her even more now, it's-" her throat closed up again and she looked away.

Another respectful pause. "It's harder in times when her wisdom would mean so much, isn't it?"

Lauren looked at him, eyes wide. "How'd you-"

Shaking his grey head and chuckling, the priest said, "I know the look. Lost, looking for someone that's gone. It's difficult to figure out all the answers by ourselves."

Looking at him uncomfortably, Lauren asked, "You're going to give me the speech about how God hears our prayers now, right?"

But he shrugged. "Not necessarily." Taking off his glasses, he cleaned them on an old handkerchief before settling them on his nose again. "Have you read David Hume?"

A brow raised, Lauren said, "The Scottish philosopher? Oh, yes. Frank, my dad, kept telling me we were related somehow, in fact, my grandfather was named David Hume Fraser, so-" This time, she started crying, humiliated that she didn't know why.

The priest nodded, ignoring her tears. "A good Scottish girl, excellent! David Hume was a strong skeptic and empiricist. He claimed that our beliefs don't come from our reason but rather from our feelings and ideas of how the world should be. He was a passionate advocate of what he called, 'Accepting the Unacceptable.' Claiming that our insistence on believing what the world *should* be kept us from accepting and embracing what was." His visitor had stopped crying and seemed to be listening, so he continued, "Mind, this does not mean giving up and resigning oneself to one's fate if a situation is untenable. but it means not raging against what *is*. Do you see?"

Lauren nodded vigorously. "I do." Looking down at her fingers, she tried to think of what to say that wouldn't involve Chuck shooting the priest for Knowing Too Much. "But what if the unacceptable is truly - I mean, to God and most of society - truly unacceptable?"

The priest eyed her, frowning thoughtfully. Lauren did not look abused, her lively spirit was still glowing, undimmed by whatever circumstance she found herself in. "Then," he ventured, "perhaps one thinks about why one is in this place, this situation. Is there a role for them? A task? Room to do good in what seems dark and hopeless?"

Heart sinking, Lauren tried to picture even a corner of The Corporation or Thomas that could be changed for the better, that would melt at the promise of redemption. Shrugging and giving the priest a small smile, she said, "Then I'm thinking God has some unrealistic expectations." To her surprise, the priest burst out laughing.

"Have you heard what Mother Teresa said to the Pope when he complimented her on her work with the lepers in Calcutta?"

Lauren shook her head, her smile growing larger.

"His Holiness said," he continued, "that despite the unspeakable conditions that Mother Teresa worked in, that he had complete faith in her, saying that 'God never gives us more than we can handle.' Legend has it that Mother Teresa reared up like an angry cobra and hissed, 'Then I wish God didn't trust me so much!'"

They both burst out laughing at the same moment, Lauren still giggling for longer than the little joke deserved, but it felt so good to just *laugh*... "Thank you, Father," she finally gasped, "I haven't laughed like that in so long."

"Ah, laughing is crucial, my child. Every day if you can," the priest said sternly, but with a little smile. "You must make the effort. It pleases God to hear it."

Lauren's smile faded a little, but she held onto it. "I'll do my best." Standing, she uncertainly held out her hand. "Thank you so much for your time, Father."

Instead of taking her hand, the priest laid his on the top of her head gently, uttering a small prayer. *"Domine, benedicere puero hoc. Da fortitudinem ea invenire viam illam."* Lauren felt tears spring to her eyes again, but she felt the warmth of his hands and was still for a moment.

"Thank you, Father," she murmured, and he nodded again.

"I am always here if you need more advice from ancient Scottish philosophers," he joked, and Lauren chuckled as she walked down the aisle, looking back once to see him watching her go.

They were back in the car and heading home before she spoke again. "You heard our conversation, right, Chuck?"

There was a moment of polite silence, before her bodyguard agreed, "Yes." His glance flicked back in the rear-view mirror to see his charge's mouth tight and cold.

"Then you know there's no reason to hurt him." She could hear the faint sounds of traffic outside and the first pitter-pat of raindrops on the windshield.

When he spoke again, Chuck's voice was even more serious and grave than usual. "No reason at all, Miss Lauren. At all." He could see her relax visibly before returning his attention to the traffic, and they were silent for the rest of the way home.

Domine, benedicere puero hoc. Da fortitudinem ea invenire viam illam - Latin for: "Lord, bless this child. Give her the strength to find her way."

Chapter 24 – It Seems I Must Remind You Who You Belong To

In which we discover even the cool, collected Number Two of Jaguar Holdings can fall victim to feelings as passé as the Green-Eyed Monster.

"So, what was the final decision, Lauren?"

Arabella was smiling encouragingly at her, and Lauren smiled back gratefully. She knew this choice wouldn't be popular, the project was based in the poorest schools in London, not the "prettier" options the other committee members preferred. "Thanks, 'Bella. I selected the Genesis Project because of how much they've done with so little. Tracking their programs shows that students involved had a 220% higher chance of graduating than the rest of the class, they also scored consistently higher grades in math and science as well as art. This is important because it shows that the music education they're implementing tracks over to other course curricula." There was tittering from some of the other board members, and Lauren looked up, distracted. "What's so funny?"

It was the third wife of The Corporation's Mergers and Acquisitions Department who answered her. "And the fact the founder looks like a supermodel had nothing to do with your choice?"

Lauren shrugged, confused, "I don't know, I've never seen him." Unfortunately, the excellent secretary assigned to the board had promptly prepared a lovely presentation and had already passed them out to everyone at the table. Included was an 8x10 of founder Miles Rodgers who indeed looked like he'd just escaped from London Fashion Week.

"He certainly would have made up my mind..." sighed Kevin, the gay partner of The Corporation's top sales executive in gold and silver futures.

"Thanks for more or less terrorizing everyone into agreeing to the Genesis Project," Lauren gave Arabella a quick peck on the cheek as she gathered up her materials, stuffing them in her leather messenger bag.

Giving her friend a faux glare, Number One's wife stood lazily, stretching. "Those idiots wouldn't know a worthy project if it came up and bit them in the arse. You learn to herd the board like cattle if you want to get anything done."

Laughing, Lauren sketched a low curtsey. "I bow to you, my Queen."

"Let's go get a cocktail," Arabella suggested, "the afternoon is young."

"I can't," the girl said apologetically, "I'm meeting Miles down at one of the schools where the project is already implemented so he can give me a tour."

Leaning against the boardroom table, her friend looked her over, "My, my, are you sure all this money isn't going to Pretty Boy because he is so very pretty? A bit of a crush, perhaps?"

Lauren's jaw dropped. Arabella must be insane, saying something like that? In The Corporation's stronghold? Where everything was filmed and recorded and nuance and jokes were no excuse? "What are you thinking, Arabella?" her voice was sharp and cold. "That isn't funny. Not as a joke. Not at all." She felt a little sad to see the older woman's face pale, two red spots on her cheeks. "You... you want to come with me?" Lauren offered, "Come see the kids?"

Arabella shook her head briskly, "No, things to do. Enjoy."

Miles was everything she hoped he'd be. Funny, kind, animated - just as he been on the phone - and he was tall, nearly as tall as Thomas with blonde hair and warm brown eyes. "Let me take you to see our latest project," he said excitedly, gently pulling on Lauren's arm to bring her into one of the bigger classrooms.

It was an organized melee if such a thing existed, Lauren observed. Students were painting the walls with all kinds of fantastical figures. There were little groups gathered in a circle playing guitars and another section madly pounding away at keyboards. Someone was projecting all kinds of unusual, stark images of the sea and sky. Looking around, Lauren could feel a frisson of excitement going up her spine, responding to the feeling of creativity that was so strong, it made her shiver. "What is all this?" she asked, turning to Miles.

"One of our creation rooms," he explained sweeping out a hand grandly. "The students are hearing the music, and watching the images to put their own vision of what they hear and see, the musicians are creating music based on the art. It's an endless circle of creativity." Lauren nodded raptly, the feeling of excitement in the room was wonderful to witness, especially on the faces of usually blasé teenagers.

"It is amazing, Miles," she said sincerely. Turning to him, she asked, "How many more of these creation rooms can you make with one and a half million pounds?"

The man's jaw dropped. "I thought... I thought we were talking about say, 50,000 pounds," he gasped, "One point five *million*?" Running his hands repeatedly through his shaggy hair, he grinned.

"Not all at once," Lauren hastened to explain, "but it would start the foundation, and each year you could draw fifteen percent off the principal to use for-" She was cut off by a huge, enthusiastic hug from Miles who was still grinning foolishly.

"I can't begin to tell you–" he choked for a moment, "how many kids we can help with that kind of funding." He eyed her curiously. Lauren sometimes forgot how she looked to others: expensively dressed, certainly, but still with huge, innocent eyes and a friendly, unguarded smile. Lauren had always looked younger than she really was, and it was never more evident than when she was excited like this.

"How can you command that kind of fundraising when you're so young?" Miles questioned, "You still look like you should *be* in one of these classes."

Rolling her eyes, Lauren said, "One day I'm sure I will be happy to have my mother's good skin, but at my age, it's very annoying. And the money isn't commanded by me of course, it comes from The Corp-" Lauren thought of the dark, granite building that housed The Corporation and all its ugly secrets, and swallowed before finishing. "It comes from the generosity of Jaguar Holdings," she paused for a moment. "They're in finance, trust me, it will be good for their souls," even her inner self was rolling her eyes at that one, "and the ruthless fundraising is actually headed up by Arabella Kingston, the wife of the CEO of the company." Tucking a blonde curl behind her ear, Lauren shifted. "I am a very small cog in a very large wheel."

Miles instantly shook his head, putting his hands on her shoulders. "Not to me," he said sincerely, "to me you are the guardian angel for these kids." Smiling politely, Lauren stepped away from his grasp. She knew Miles was simply sincere and enthusiastic, but it would never do for Chuck to see it. "Come," Miles offered, "let me take you to lunch." To her amusement, they headed for the school's cafeteria, where the food was just as bad as she had remembered from her own high school experience. But they sat and talked for hours, animatedly discussing new plans of how far they could extend Miles's program.

Finally, Chuck rose from the adjoining table. "Miss Lauren," he said composedly, "it is nearly five o'clock, and I believe that Mr. Williams has plans for the two of you this evening?"

Lauren instantly rose from the table, grabbing her messenger bag. Miles stood too, with a rueful smile, holding out his hand. "I'm so sorry Lauren," he apologized sincerely, "I didn't mean to take so much of your time."

"Don't be!" Lauren protested, "It was wonderful to see this, to hear about your vision." She squeezed his hand and firmly pumped it up and down in a goodbye handshake. "I knew we had made the right decision with you."

Smiling, the man bent over and gallantly kissed the knuckles of her left hand, lips grazing her wedding ring. Looking down at it, as if for the first time, Miles released her hand and stepped away smiling apologetically. "Thank you again, Lauren. I will see you at the gala."

Thomas moved silently up behind Lauren as she was putting her keys on the hall table. Hands sliding around her waist, he pulled her firmly back against his hard chest. "Oh God!" she gasped, "you can't slink up on me like that! I swear you're part cat!"

He merely chuckled, placing slow, sucking kisses down the side of her neck, enjoying how her pulse raced against his mouth. "It is a rare thing when I return home before you do," he said. It was said without disapproval, but Lauren still felt the weight of it from his sonorous voice.

"I'm sorry," she instantly apologized. "I was taking a tour of one of the Genesis classrooms, it's amazing, Thomas!" Her husband looked down at her animated face with a slight smile. "Miles has done so much with so few funds," she continued, "he has over fifteen of these classrooms across the city, and with the funding, the foundation can bring he can expand it by another hundred in the next two years alone. Isn't that wonderful?"

Thomas paused for a moment looking his wife over carefully. Her excited lavender gaze was as wide and clear as always, her smile unrehearsed. "Then I am quite looking forward to meeting this musical genius of yours at the gala," he answered.

Lauren's smile faltered a bit at his cool, blue eyes. Shaking her head, she said, "Miles isn't mine," she shrugged, "I just picked him out of the selection of the candidates for the funding."

But by then Thomas was unzipping her dress – right there in the entryway! – and nothing more was said. Lauren found herself seeing her husband more at his place of business in the following week than she had for the entire time they'd been together. Many of the foundation's meetings were held there, and the intimidating Number Two would step silently behind her, taking her in a firm grip on her upper arms or hands landed heavily on her shoulders, pulling her back against him as if re-staking ownership. As if there were any need, Lauren thought, standing stiffly in front of him. Like anyone at The Corporation was the slightest bit confused about who owned her.

Because Lauren never did decide on a dress for the gala, Thomas had chosen for her and had the dress sent to their house the day of the event. Pulling the heavily beaded gown from its nest of tissue paper, the girl gasped. It was exquisite, a beautiful vintage 1920s dress in the style of the free-drinking flapper girls of the era. Sliding it on, she turned back and forth in front of the huge mirror in their dressing room. The skirt fell to just above her knee, with a saucy slit that ended higher up on her thigh than she was completely comfortable with. But the elegant design of the jade green and silver beading made her feel mildly sultry. Styling her hair and attaching a sequined headband, Lauren was just finishing her make up when Thomas stepped up behind her, hands low on her hips. "Beautiful," he approved with a husky tone, "I knew this would be the perfect dress for you." Lauren smiled shyly looking back at her husband in the mirror's reflection, admiring how effortlessly elegant he was in his tux.

"It's out of my comfort zone," she admitted, "but I feel quite glamorous, thank you."

Thomas didn't seem to be listening, running his long fingers along her exposed shoulders and the delicate ridge of her collar bones. "Beautiful," he said in the same tone, looking at her with totally filthy intent. "We'd best leave, darling, or I shall remove this from you now." Lauren laughed and nodded, taking his outstretched hand.

The newly refurbished ballroom in the old mansion they'd found could not be more perfect for the event. Lauren smiled, looking around at the elegant black and white decor and the white-coated musicians tuning up. "Everything looks amazing!" said Clara, coming up behind her and flushed and pretty in her own peach-colored dress.

"Doesn't it?" said Lauren, "I have a great feeling about tonight, we're going to raise the most money ever! The Genesis Project deserves it, you'll see." She grinned at Clara, squeezing her hand.

The gala was already crowded and underway when a sweating, nervous Miles sought Lauren out. "I feel ridiculous," he groaned, sliding a finger under his white collar and bowtie, "do I look like a complete ass?"

Laughing, the girl shook her head. "You look like a visionary," she assured, "that will inspire all of these wealthy people to pull out their wallets and just start throwing credit cards at you." They both broke into uproarious laughter, a little giddy with excitement about the potential for the evening.

It was then Lauren heard the voice of her husband behind her along with the irritating tone of the horrible Number One. "Ah," drawled Thomas, "and here he is, our honored guest this evening." Miles's big grin slipped as he looked up at Thomas, who was quite clearly looming over him.

Lauren hastily made the introductions to both men and Miles shook their hands, flinching slightly at Thomas's brutal grip. "I'll just take him over to Arabella," she interceded, "she'll get him ready for his speech. I'll see you later?" She smiled up at Thomas, who leaned down to give her a lingering kiss on the lips. Lauren was startled. The Corporation's cool, collected Second in Command was not prone to public affection, particularly at a Corporation event. But smiling up at him, she sheepishly swallowed her giggle before leading Miles away.

It all went as it had been rehearsed, she thought, watching Arabella introduce Miles, who spoke passionately and persuasively about the Genesis Project and the lives of the students it had changed. Lauren didn't realize how often the guest of honor's face turned to hers for support, reinforcement as she nodded encouragingly, but more observant souls did. Her eyelids drooped as her husband's beautiful voice whispered into her ear, his breath stirring the fine hairs escaping from her headband.

"Why don't you take a walk with me, little girl," he purred, "I do believe it's time to remind you who you belong to." Lauren was a bit confused, but obediently followed him out into the hall and down through another set of tall doors. Looking around, she realized it was the old library for the mansion. There were still hundreds of dusty books on the shelves, and her mouth actually watered, wanting to go through the titles and explore the collection. Thomas had other plans, leading her over to a tall reading table and hosting her abruptly onto it and her knees apart, stepping between them pressing his pelvis flush against her's. "My beautiful, incandescent bride," his voice was so deep with arousal that it ran against her throat making Lauren shiver and him chuckle approvingly, his lips running along the shell of her ear, "I've been longing to get you out of that dress from the moment you put it on."

Lauren suddenly tried to draw her knees together. "Oh, but

Thomas- n-not here, right? The party's just down the hall? Anyone could walk in?" His big, warm hands slid between her knees, pulling them wider again. She could feel the rasp of his calloused fingers travel up her thighs, snagging slightly against the gossamer-fine thread of her stockings. He was pushing the skirt of her dress higher, she realized, then pushing the slit on the side wider when the fabric bunched stubbornly by her hips.

One finger slipped past her silk undies to stroke along her center, Lauren gritting back a whimper and shifting anxiously as the offending digit circled her opening. "Now baby, don't be shy..." Thomas's voice ran along her nerve endings, sank into her senses, and blocked meaningless things like propriety and common sense. Thomas was always so controlled, he would never do anything that deviated from his perfect image, right? He was still murmuring beautiful filth into her ear, and Lauren shook, her thighs loosening shamefully as she felt the hard heat of her husband's cock pushing against her wet center. One of her beaded straps slid over her shoulder and down one arm, exposing a breast captured in Thomas's heated mouth.

"Thomas," she barely whispered, "you feel so... I..." his mouth was sucking on her nipple and she gasped, not able to think of what to say next. This felt horribly uncomfortable, perched on this dusty table with the music from the gala reverberating through the wood under her ass. But his sure hands were stroking over her skin and when Lauren heard the rasp of his zipper, she couldn't think of anything but the heat of him, his pulsing head pushing up her passage, slowly this time, ridiculously, gloriously, unfairly slow as each inch of him spread her walls, then pulled back to do it again, squeezing and kissing her breasts. Thomas teased his cock in and out of her, enjoying the tortuous slow stretch of him inside her before pulling it from her again, enjoying how her heels dug into his ass, the pleading noises from her mouth to do it again, come back in her again, and-

"Are you ready, my juicy little slut?"

Lauren froze at the crude phrasing, but she still felt the telltale shaking and clenching inside that told her she was about to come, and-

"Squeeze all those dewy muscles inside that tight cunt of yours, whore. Clench down for your Sir, now..."

They exploded together, Lauren gasping and sinking her teeth his thick shoulder and relishing his groan as she felt his heat flood her.

"Lauren? Are you in here? Mr. Kingston said you were heading in this direction and-" Miles stopped instantly as he caught the image of a taut, muscular ass stroking slowly into the girl he wanted so much. "Oh, god! I'm sorry! I'll just- yeah, I'll see you back in there so sorry and-"

Thomas pulled himself from her abruptly, making Lauren jump and gasp. They could hear the door slam behind them as Miles made a hasty retreat. Lauren's head jerked around as Thomas placed his fingers on her mouth. "Not a word, little girl." Irritably handing her a cloth, he ordered, "Tidy yourself," before straightening her dress and hoisting her inelegantly off the table.

Lauren was so sick with humiliation that she couldn't breathe. Her husband had just fucked her in front of someone else - a stranger, practically - as proof of ownership.

Thomas straightened his tie. "Pull your skirt down," he said, looking towards the door. "They will be announcing

the fundraising total soon. Collect yourself and get back in there."

Hands shaking in fury, Lauren did as she was told before heading for the door and leaving without another word.

Chapter 25 – You Are Whatever I Tell You To Be.

In which the cold, collected Number Two begins to question his wife's behavior, and his own.

Lauren was actually grateful for the following hours that kept her from having to be alone with the bastard who'd made her marry him, though she spent them in a nightmare of pretending everything was fine, while bitterly clenching her thighs together, trying to keep her cruel husband's seed from trickling down her leg. Because she was naturally shy, there were many embarrassing moments in her life. But never an experience so humiliating that even stepping outside of herself and pretending it was happening to someone else could not distance her enough from the shame she felt. To make matters more unspeakable, Number One was hovering close by, an ugly, knowing smile on his nasty face as he looked between her and an expressionless Thomas - and more worryingly - at Miles before running the visual circuit again. But Mrs. Thomas Williams completed her duties as a gracious hostess and co-chairman of The Corporation's charity, obediently applauding each new bid as the total contribution for the Genesis Project rose higher and higher, even outstripping her original estimate of 1.5 million pounds by a full million more. When the total was announced, Miles's knees actually buckled and he was hoisted up by the eager Kevin, the partner of their sales executive in gold and silver futures.

Lauren stood carefully away from the stage, clapping and smiling mechanically. The worst part of it wasn't the humiliation from being caught as Thomas fucked her - more or less - in public, it could almost have been seen as sexy that her husband wanted her too much to wait. She would have cringed but still felt a little daring as they walked out of the library. It was the misery of actually being shocked that Thomas would *do* such a thing to her. Deliberately. Treat her like a whore - he'd called her that at one point, right? - and being sent out still wet between her legs and seeing Kingston hovering in the hallway outside, clapping her disgusting spouse on the shoulder in an amused, "boys will be boys" way.

Lauren was angry that his act stunned her, knowing after all exactly who she was married to and somehow forgetting his monstrous acts because he'd been so sweet with her recently. Was that all it took? A bouquet of those huge hydrangeas from the flower shop by the church? (Because of course, Chuck told Thomas about the place and her momentary interest. Of course.) The hours of kissing her everywhere, murmuring bits and pieces of Shakespeare into her ear, enjoying her little, rapturous shivers?

Applauding again, Lauren refused to look in the direction of either Thomas or Miles. The former didn't deserve one second of her attention, and the latter did not deserve to be punished in some sick way if Thomas somehow thought she was interested in Miles.

Fortunately, their guest of honor seemed quite clear on the awkwardness, and kept away from her, finally waving goodbye with an uncomfortable smile on his way out the door. Lauren's heart sank. She had been so excited to see the new programs implemented in the lower-income schools. Now she knew she would never be able to step foot in another classroom if Miles was in it. Forcing a false social smile, she turned and cordially congratulated the rest of the committee, counting down the moments until she would be allowed to leave. She just managed to avoid a shudder when Thomas's hand landed on the small of her back. "Let's head home, darling," he said, leaning in close and not missing the way her head instinctively arched away from him.

The ride was silent, Lauren staring out the window and counting her blessings that the man beside didn't initiate conversation. She just wanted to get away from him and scrub herself raw in the shower. She had always felt a strange thrill when Thomas came inside her, enjoying somehow the proof of his attraction to her. Now, she just felt disgusting.
"I'm just going to go have a shower and go straight to bed," she said quickly as they entered the house, praying he wouldn't say anything. "So, good night." The cold Number Two was still silent as she hastily ascended the stairs and Lauren managed to hold the tears at bay until she got into the shower, not quite ripping the dress off of her and leaving it in a pile on the bathroom floor.

But it was only after a few moments of sobbing thatLauren felt her fury rise. *How fucking dare he?* she raged silently, she had never done anything inappropriate or anything to make him look bad. Did Arabella say something to Kingston? Did he see something on the feed from the meetings? Did Chuck exaggerate her behavior during the meeting at school? Angrily washing her hair, Lauren dismissed the last thought. She was quite clear that her bodyguard reported every second of her comings and goings to her controlling husband, but she didn't think he would deliberately try to get her in trouble. Lauren jumped and let out a little shriek when the shower door abruptly opened. Thomas was standing there bare-chested, still in his tuxedo pants and looking her over coldly.

"I'm nearly finished," she gritted out, trying to get the shampoo out of her hair as quickly as possible, "then the shower is all yours." Her goddamned husband still didn't say anything to her, merely leaning against the shower door and watching her bathe, his polar gaze traveling over her wet skin. Angrily turning her back to him and not realizing Thomas was just as happy with the vision of the suds slipping off her pert ass, Lauren snarled, "Could you please give me a moment? Some privacy?"

"No."

It was all Thomas said, but it sparked her fury into an inferno, and Lauren's arm clutching the soap raised back to throw it at him, but his hand shot up like a snake, grasping her wrist and holding her immobile. "L- let go of me, you-"

Instead, he pulled her out of their luxurious walk-in shower, still dripping and furiously thrashing in his grip. "Listen. To. Me." It was the terrifying emotionless delivery that made Lauren pause, still and alert like a cornered rabbit. One hand slowly reached out for a towel but Thomas briskly pulled her away and into the middle of the chilly room. "I expect you to take tonight as a lesson to the continued good health of that lovesick idiot."

Lauren stared at him, open-mouthed. It took her a minute to realize he meant Miles. "H- how does- well, you treating me like- like your whore have anything to do with the charity award?"

With a snarl, Thomas yanked her closer, her wet breasts brushing his chest. "Do not pretend to be stupid, little girl. I *own* you- and you will not disrespect me or my position by throwing yourself at infatuated boys, no matter how pretty they might be."

Lauren knew that her mouth kept gaping open, but she couldn't seem to close it. "Pretty? Wait, what are you-"

"Do you think it reflects well on you - on us - to have *Saint* Miles fawning over you in front of The Corporation's entire workforce? What kind of wife are you?"

She was furious, she was shaking with cold, and dripping naked in the middle of their bathroom. But the rage was clearing enough for Lauren to understand that she was the only rational one in the room at the moment. Her normally cool, collected husband was gritting his jaw so tightly she was amazed he hadn't cracked a molar. His eyes were burning with a cold fire and she doubted he knew how hard his grip was on her upper arms.

"I would never do anything that showed disrespect to you or your position at The Corporation," Lauren said evenly, precisely. "I have always been very well aware of the consequences of such a thing. It has never even occurred to me. I don't know why you think I've been flirting with Miles. That would be *insane*- I know Chuck reports everything back to you, and I'm sure you've reviewed the footage from the charity meetings." She laughed bitterly, "Believe me, I'm very aware that there's not a moment of my day that isn't reported back to you. So you know how I behave. You had no reason to humiliate me like that tonight, that disgusting Kingston leering at me-" her voice broke for a minute, and Lauren paused, furious at herself for not controlling her tears. "Treating me like a whore. Maybe that's who you're used to hanging out with," she said defiantly and unwisely, "but I'm not! I'm your-"

"You're whatever I tell you to be!" Thomas roared back, pushing her against the wall and to her shock, cupping her center with his other hand. "This is mine!" His face pushed close to hers watching her look away. "And you are mine! And you will do nothing that indicates in any way that you are not my dutiful wife." He couldn't understand why this stupid, ridiculous child was still defying him! Why Lauren wasn't crying and begging his forgiveness? Maybe a sound spanking from her Sir for this disobedient behavior was what she needed.

Thomas was halfway into hauling his naked bride across his lap when he stilled. She was trying to talk to him, make him listen. "T- t- Thomas, stop! Please stop! You're out of control and you're not thinking you know I didn't do anything wrong and if you hit me I can never forgive youwecan'tcomebackfromthatplease!" Setting Lauren back on her feet and backing off abruptly, he watched blankly as she grabbed a towel, wrapping it around herself and clutching it there with her arms tightly wound around her, like how she'd held her wedding dress to her body on their pitiful wedding night.

Ah.

It all came back in a searingly cold rush of clarity, his terrified, weeping wife and putting her to bed, feeling mildly nauseated that the new Mrs. Thomas Williams thought her husband was animal enough to rape her. And now tonight, backing away from him and angrily pushing tears off her face with the heel of her hand, lavender eyes gone gray and bleak as she watched him carefully, waiting for him to... What? Rape her? Hurt her? Running his hand distractedly through his hair, Thomas took in a deep breath, letting it out carefully. What the fuck had just happened to him? "Lauren, just go. Go to bed. I have work to finish downstairs." She nodded briefly but didn't move, staring at him until Thomas turned sharply on his heel and left the room.

Hearing the door to his study shut faintly, Lauren's breath left her in a rush, along with the strength in her legs, sliding abruptly down the wall and sitting on the floor, still clutching her towel. It was good, she nodded firmly, lips pressed together so that no sobs escaped, it was good to see the beautiful, composed mask peel off and show her the face of the monster she married. It was good to remember that.

To her deep relief, Lauren woke alone the next morning, the bed next to her cold and undisturbed. She'd laid awake most of the night, stiff and unmoving on her side of the bed, balanced just on the edge of the mattress to be as far away from her husband's side of the bed as possible without actually falling off. The house was silent as she hastily showered and dressed, not wanting to be caught bare or defenseless again. But the only person there when she finally, reluctantly descended the stairs to the main floor was her bodyguard, perched calmly on his uncomfortable chair in front of the stairs where he could see the entire house.

"Hey, Chuck." Lauren managed. "What's up?"

Putting his phone away and regarding her calmly, the older man replied, "Good morning Miss Lauren. Mr. Williams has tasked me with informing you that he will be away on business for some time."

Folding her arms awkwardly, Lauren huffed out sort of a chuckle, shocked that she felt equal parts relieved and heartsick.

It was, in fact, over two weeks before the Second in Command of Jaguar Holdings was set to return home again. Lauren did all the things she would normally do. Run in the mornings. Practice. There was plenty of time to practice, no distractions to interrupt her. Her sore undercarriage healed, no more little gasps when she sat down too quickly. Sometimes, she would get Chuck to sit with her at the cafe and drink his black coffee. Thomas only called once, about ten days after he'd disappeared "on business."

"How are you, darling?"

Lauren's hand tightened on her cellphone. He sounded just the same, her husband. Calm, composed, almost indifferent. "I'm fine. Where are- um, how are you?"

"Quite well, thank you," Thomas was politely distracted, she could hear the shuffle of papers and a few murmured instructions before he returned to their conversation. "Negotiations are taking longer than expected, I will be here another week or so."

Waiting a moment for him to mention where he was, Lauren's mouth tightened when she realized he wasn't going to tell her. "Oh. Okay."

There was silence, she could hear the faint crackle of their connection, his breath. "Your... performances," Thomas said finally, "the next series begins in a month or so, correct?"

Lauren thought of what she wanted to say to her husband, her beautiful, terrifying, unsettling, and addictive lover. "I miss you? I miss you in bed with me? Were you really going to hit me that night? Are you sleeping with The Corporation prostitutes?" Instead, she said, "Yeah, Rachmaninov. It's really beautiful work."

More silence, then Thomas let out an exhausted grunt. "Excellent. Chuck is looking after you?"

"As always." She just managed to keep the bitterness out of her tone.

"Very good." Another shuffling of papers. "Then I'll see you soon."

"Thomas? I..." it slipped out before Lauren could stop it.

"Yes?" his voice, his lovely, sonorous voice was flat, almost professional.

"Um... have a safe trip back." Lauren hung up the phone before Thomas could hear her cry.

Chapter 26 – How I Feel Safe

In which Thomas knocks some sense into his own, thick skull. Lauren meets the Grey Man. Arabella meets her reckoning. Chuck drinks coffee.

When The Corporation's Number Two did return to London, his first stop was not home, though to his chagrin, that was Thomas's immediate impulse. As the wheels of the jet touched the tarmac, his first thought was going home to undress Lauren, putting her on their bed and kissing her all over very slowly until she made those sweet pleading noises, lifting her hips shyly in invitation. He thought of where she would be at that moment- practicing at the rehearsal hall? Walking through another old section of the city? Firmly pulling himself back from his unseemly eagerness, Williams crisply instructed his driver to take him to The Corporation's headquarters.

Lauren didn't let herself think about why she woke early that morning, tidying up the already spotless house and trying on a couple of different outfits. She'd had an idea on when his flight was set to return, but when she didn't see him, she simply assumed he was running late. By that evening, she ate the carefully prepared meal she'd made by herself, finishing off the first bottle of wine and starting on the second. And by midnight, Lauren was in bed staring out the window and wondering if this was her life from now on.

Two days earlier...

Lauren never could have so successfully summed up her personality as well as Thomas had, but it was true. She was made to love, and her wide circle of friends and loved ones had shrunk to a narrow focus of primarily her husband, her bodyguard, and her now and forever absent best friend. The loneliness was crushing. It was one of the reasons she had agreed when Arabella had wanted to take her out to lunch a couple of days before. Even though it was to that same strange bar where the stares of the men had made her so uncomfortable that first time. In fact, a minuscule frown crossed Chuck's bland expression when she told him to take her there. But he merely grunted in agreement and started the car. Arabella stood and waved from their table as Lauren came in. As usual, the older woman was a drink or two ahead of her friend, bright pink spots on her cheeks, flushed and vivacious. "No martinis this time until I get some actual food!" joked Lauren, shaking her head at the martini cart and asking for a menu. After she ordered a tempting array of tapas plates, she raised her brow at Arabella. "You're not eating?

The woman raised her glass mockingly. "A liquid lunch," she said, "it's how I keep my girlish figure."

Lauren laughed. "You know you have a perfect body," she teased, "you could eat sixteen cakes and it wouldn't make a dent." Even carefully testing each word before it left her mouth for safety and blandness, it was nice to be out and chatting with someone. Lauren began to relax a little bit and tried a new kind of martini, sipping it blissfully. "I've never been one much for anything other than wine," she confided, "but this is freaking delicious." Arabella was her most sparkling butterfly-like self, her tinkling laughter making diners around them look up from their business lunches and smile. Lauren noticed one booth of men, in particular, spent most of their time staring at their table. Quickly looking back as one of the men caught her eye and smiled, Lauren asked, "Why do you like it here so much? It feels like such a boy's club."

"It is," agreed Arabella, signaling for another drink. "It took me a long time to be worth enough money to get a seat here. I'm not letting go of it. Let them stare. Some of these arseholes wouldn't speak to me for years, acting like I was dirt under their shoe."

"That makes sense, I don't blame you," Lauren said thoughtfully, "it's satisfying, isn't it? Rubbing their noses in your success."

Her friend paused, staring at her. "You mean my husband's money, don't you?"

"No..." Lauren finished her martini, looking sadly into the bottom of the glass. It would not do to have another. Chuck and whatever thug who was currently minding Arabella were seated quite close to them and she did not want Thomas receiving a report about his drunken wife. She shuddered a little. Especially not now. Bringing herself back to the moment, she finished, "It doesn't take just money, and you know that. It takes connections. Intelligence, and you're fierce, honey. I wouldn't cross you. I'm guessing a couple of these expensively suited assholes here have learned that."

Arabella was utterly still, staring at her. To Lauren's concern, it looked like the older woman had tears in her eyes. "You mean that. Don't you?"

Frowning, she nodded. "Of course. I was raised in a Fortune 500 company family," Lauren chuckled bitterly, "though I have no idea what Frank's done to my grandfather's business these days. But the money isn't enough. You can't buy your way to the top in circles like these."

Nearly knocking her off her chair, Arabella suddenly reached over, giving her a huge and awkward hug. "No one's ever said that to me before. No one's even thought it. I was just the whore who married well."

Flinching and hoping the woman's voice wasn't loud enough to carry, Lauren settled her in her chair again. "No, you're not. You're the woman who's handled Jaguar Holding's Number One for-" she tried not to shudder, "for what, ten years? A decade of Mrs. Ben Kingston? You're the queen, 'Bella."

Their warm moment was ruined when the men from the "staring booth," rose and walked by them, eyes fixed on the two women the entire time. The shortest, a grey-faced man with grey hair, and an expensive grey suit stopped next to Arabella, bending to take her hand. "You look lovely, Mrs. Kingston. I hope you are well." From the corner of her eye, Lauren could see her friend's "minder" growl and put his hand in his jacket. Chuck's arm shot out like a snake to block him.

"Easy..." Chuck murmured, and Lauren could suddenly see why Thomas had assigned the man to her. He was utterly lethal, body straight and leaning forward like an arrow, eyes moving calmly between her, a flustered Mrs. Kingston and the grey man currently kissing her knuckles.

"And this must be Thomas's new wife?" he turned to her, and Lauren swallowed. His eyes were dead. Like a rattlesnake's. "A pleasure to meet you, dear. I'm Colin Martinsson, an... associate of your husband's." One of the men with him chuckled but quickly turned it into a cough.

Lavender gaze moving between her suddenly shaking friend, Chuck, and the Grey Man, Lauren ignored his outstretched hand but favored him with an insincere social smile - she was getting good at those - and said, "I see. Well, a pleasure to meet you, Mr. Martinsson. 'Bella, honey. We need to get going. You know Thomas and Ben are expecting us."

"Oh, I thought they were out of town?" the Grey Man said innocently.

Her insides suddenly felt like they'd been shoved in a sub-zero meat locker. "They're just getting home," Lauren lied pleasantly. "Goodbye now." Pulling her friend up by her arm and Arabella's minder suddenly taking her other one, Lauren turned her back on the men and began walking an unsteady Arabella calmly out of the dining room. Looking behind her briefly, she found Chuck locked in a staring match with the Grey Man. She'd never seen that expression on his face, and she was grateful for it. "Chuck?" Lauren managed. He was at her side in a moment, following them out of the room. Bundling Arabella into her car with a hasty kiss on the cheek, she was about to pull back when the woman grabbed her hand.

"Colin. He's-" Arabella looked to see where their bodyguards were standing, "he's much nicer than he seems. Please don't say anything- no need to upset our husbands, correct?"

Lauren sadly shook her head. "Sweetheart, I'm pretty sure one or both of these guys has already sent a message. Maybe with video and audio, I don't know." Her heart twisted to see the look of terror on her friend's face. "'Bella, don't worry, it wasn't our fault. We didn't do anything wrong." Reluctantly releasing her hand as the minder shut the car door, Lauren stepped back, Chuck just to her left shoulder. "Well, that could have gone better," she sighed.

The car was silent on the drive home, under they were pulling up to the door. Chuck got out to briskly escort her inside while the other Corporation shooter - someone new - stayed in the car. After quickly checking the house, the big man came back down to the kitchen where Lauren was pouring her second glass of wine. "There is a reason," he finally intoned, looking out the window into the back garden, eyes moving restlessly, "that dining at Connaught Bar is ill-advised."

Swallowing a gulp of her pinot grigio, Lauren nodded, "Because the psycho Scandinavian guy hangs out there? Is that why everyone was staring at us?"

Chuck sighed slightly, folding his hands before him. "Yes, he is deeply out of favor with Jaguar Holdings. He holds court at the Connaught, and the wives of the two highest men in our organization dining there is unsuitable. It gathers the wrong sort of attention."

"You think?" choked out Lauren. "What was Arabella thinking? Jesus! Thomas and her creepy as fuck husb- Kingston will kill us!"

Stepping closer, he carefully took her shaking hand. "No, Miss Lauren. This was none of your doing. I will make that quite clear." Even Chuck's stone exterior cracked a little when she raised her heartbroken gaze to his.

"But what about Arabella? She doesn't deserve what-" she choked a little, "what that sick bastard will do to her."

"I'm sure she'll be fine," he replied mechanically. "Why don't you go settle your nerves, relax for a moment?" Nodding distractedly, Lauren climbed the stairs to the fourth floor, and he heard the frantic strains of *Ravel: La Valse* tearing from her cello. After playing for an hour, her nerves settled and her left hand painfully sore from the finger work, Lauren came back downstairs again to start dinner. Her bodyguard was just finishing a call. "Yes, sir. I'll tell her. Very good." Hanging up, Chuck nodded to her politely. "I have apprised Mr. Williams of the situation, and he is requesting that you do not associate with Mrs. Kingston until he returns."

Lauren froze, hand on the refrigerator door. "That was Thomas?" Instantly despising herself for being hurt that he spoke to Chuck and not her, she forced herself to nod. "Sure. Not a problem." Her back to him as she was pulling out some pasta, she forced herself to casually ask, "Did he mention when he was coming home?"

"Yes, Miss Lauren. He's returning Thursday, around 11am, I believe."

Hating that her bodyguard knew when her husband was returning when Thomas couldn't be bothered to tell her himself, she nodded again. "Okay. Thanks, Chuck, I'm in for the night, if you want to head out." Lauren wouldn't turn around and risk him seeing her hurt and disappointment, so she missed the quick flash of pity on his face.

"I have no other obligations, Miss Lauren, if you would prefer I stayed."

Lauren's brow rose. Chuck *never* offered to stay. He simply did as he was told with the same level of polite disinterest as he always had. Surreptitiously wiping her running nose, she mumbled, "Thanks, Chuck. I'm good. But... you know. Thanks anyway. Goodnight."

Currently...

And now, it was 2am on Friday morning, fifteen hours or so after Thomas returned to London and his bitter wife finally heard his key in the door, his quiet conversation with Chuck and his footsteps on the stairs to their bedroom. She closed her eyes, forcing herself to breathe evenly, her back to the door. She could see the faint light from the hallway under her closed lids, but her slow inhales and exhales didn't falter. Lauren could hear his deliberate tread come close to the bed and stop, Thomas likely examining her. Then in silence, he went into their dressing room, flipping on the light as he shut the door. Rubbing the tears seeping from her eyelids on her 1,200-thread count pillow, Lauren reminded herself. It was good that she knew who he really was. A monster. Nothing else, just a monster.

Waking late the next morning, she rubbed her crusty eyelids and groaned silently. Did she really finish off that second bottle of wine? Nonetheless, Lauren's nose twitched when she smelled bacon wafting up the stairway. Chuck never cooked. He had started their gigantic stainless coffee maker for her once but even that was clearly something that made him uncomfortable. That could only mean Thomas was still here. Sighing, she mumbled, "Let's get it over with," showering quickly and pulling on a dress. One she knew he didn't like. But a dress, as required.

"Good morning, darling." Her husband's back was to her as Lauren entered the room, but she still shivered a little to hear his voice, the Voice, warmer, the vowels almost caressing her. "Did you sleep well?"

Thrown off a little by the pleasantry, she awkwardly poured a cup of coffee, "Just fine, thank you. Um... don't you have to be at the office today?" He turned around then, and Lauren forced herself to look him in the eye. Goddamn him, he was so beautiful, her dark husband. Freshly shaved, in a crisp, light blue shirt and sapphire tie that matched his eyes.

"Not right away," Thomas said casually, "I finished most of the urgent issues that couldn't wait when I returned yesterday."

Cautiously, Lauren wondered if that was his way of explaining his absence all day. "Oh." Not sure what else to say, she took another sip of her sacred, life-giving coffee. She'd think more clearly when the caffeine hit. She would figure out why her husband was bothering to be nice to her, to explain things. Meanwhile, Thomas was plating up breakfast, the lovely, lovely bacon, waffles drowning in butter and far more syrup than was necessary - just the way she liked them - and sliced fruit. Puzzled, Lauren took her seat. Why was he bothering? "Thank you?" she said. His gaze was steady as he smiled at her briefly.

"Is that a question?" he asked as he took his seat, putting his napkin over his trousers.

"Um..." Lauren couldn't think of what to say. "I'm, um, sorry. Not enough caffeine yet. Thank you for breakfast." She really wished he'd go away so she could truly appreciate the waffles, eating in front of this man who was more or less a stranger again was very uncomfortable. But her unfairly handsome spouse seemed quite relaxed, finally finishing his food and sitting back in his chair, regarding her.

"How have you been, Lauren?"

She looked up, puzzled. "Excuse me?"

Thomas leaned forward, resting his elbows on the antique farmhouse table. "How. Have. You. Been?" Despite more or less spelling out the words, his expression was still pleasant, his eyes warm.

What did he want to hear? she thought, trying to come up with an answer. "I'm... fine, Thomas, thank you. Everything's been fine." Too late she realized he probably meant that disastrous lunch at the Connaught. "B- besides the lunch thing. You know, with Arabella."

"Ah," he said thoughtfully, "that." Thomas watched the top of his bride's head as she bowed it over her plate. She'd not looked at him directly once since walking into the room. Not that he deserved it. "I am sorry that happened to you."

Now, her head shot up, those lovely eyes wide. "What?"

Thomas spoke slowly, "You did nothing wrong, darling. You knew nothing about The Corporation issues with that arse Martinsson. But Arabella did." His expression hardened until he watched her tense up again. Forcing himself to relax, he continued, "Do you remember my trip to Denmark?"

"Yes, of course."

He nodded. "Martinsson's group was the one who lost the bid on the company takeover we negotiated there. It is not the first time this has happened. He is a fool, but he refuses to stop attempting to challenge us."

Lauren frowned, "He must be very dangerous."

Pleased that she understood, Thomas nodded. "He is not

someone I would have ever wished you to meet. I don't understand Arabella's carelessness, but-"

"Please don't let Number One hurt her!" Lauren burst out. "I understand why she wanted to go there- it wasn't to start something, I'm sure of it."

Leaning back and folding his arms, Thomas watched her, brow raised. "Explain."

"She... it's her 'screw you' move." Lauren tried to make her amused spouse understand. "Arabella didn't come from much - you know that - and it's her way of showing all the rich, snooty power types that she's just as good, on top of the heap." Waving her hands, she struggled, "You know, the 'screw you' move." Her spouse was smothering a smile, she could tell, but at least Thomas wasn't cold or angry at her.

"I see," he answered gravely, "but while we are dealing with the possible repercussions of this encounter, I would like you to avoid spending time with her." Lauren nodded, looking down again and fork making patterns in her little pool of syrup. "You, however," Thomas continued, "need to get ready. Your afternoon is a busy one."

Ah, now his girl was alarmed. "With what? Did I miss something? I'm sorry, I'll-" Lauren stopped instantly when his big, warm hand landed on her restless one, stilling her.

"You haven't neglected anything, darling. But the initial shipment of instruments and sound equipment is being delivered to the first primary school on the new Genesis Project schedule. I know you'll want to be there to help sort it out." Thomas felt the pain that had been twisting his gut for the last two weeks return at the look of shock, then anxiety on Lauren's lovely face. She could never hide her emotions.

"But... I... that seems like a very bad idea, Thomas, and I have lots to do... uh..." looking around the spotless, sunny kitchen, she finished lamely, "... um, here."

He took a deep sigh, "Lauren. You did nothing wrong that night. I was not..."

...in my right mind? Thomas thought, *Insanely jealous and a stupid bastard?*

"I was not being fair to you. I believe it is important for you to be there, at least for the start of this new chapter for the project. You deserve to see your hard work put into play." His sweet wife was staring at him as if he'd stripped naked and started rolling in the syrup while quoting the entire Coldplay music catalog. Thomas gave a rueful chuckle. "You think I've gone mad, darling?" Her pretty mouth open, Lauren tried to shake her head. "You do," he nodded. "But I am quite aware the music is your passion, not *Saint* Miles." Lauren still looked mildly puzzled, something he had not let himself see that night- her genuine confusion that he thought she'd be attracted to someone else. How had he not let himself see that?

Lauren felt brave enough to laugh a little. "Saint? The man never stops talking. But it's such an amazing project." Her wistful tone twisted the fist around his guts a little harder. When had she started making him feel... *things* again? He'd shot men with nary a twinge. And now her sad little face made him shift uncomfortably.

"Then it's settled," Thomas said calmly. "Chuck will be picking you up at noon, so you should get ready." His bride was still watching him cautiously as if waiting for him to revert to the furious lunatic he'd been that night. "Darling?"

She shook herself a little, "Hmmm?"

His beautiful face was set in its usual lines of urbane amusement, but Thomas's eyes were cobalt, almost twinkling. "Go get ready." Lauren was gone before he could blink, before suddenly rushing back into the room and taking her plate and silverware to the sink, smiling awkwardly and racing back out again, like an excited teenager.

It was bad enough that Thomas had conducted business in Costa Rica over the last eighteen days while drowning in self-disgust. His relief at getting away from his wife was palpable, shocked at his complete lack of self-control. What had made him act that way? Like a jealous, lovesick fool? And her humiliation... Lauren's face was pale for the rest of the night of the fundraiser after he'd sent her out from their tryst like a whore. Even in his anger, he'd admired her composure, calmly applauding and interacting and shaking hands with the wealthy who there to assuage their conscience with a fat donation. What he couldn't remember were the moments between her escaping for a shower at home and when he was hauling her over his lap to spank some sense into her. Lauren's desperate efforts to make him hear her. He was so shocked at his lack of control; he couldn't even bear to be in the same room with her.

He'd tried to throw himself into his work in Costa Rica, it was a sensitive deal and required a great deal of cunning. But his wife's alternate expressions of heartbreak and fury kept rising in his thoughts at the most irritating and inopportune of times. And her confusion when he'd accused her of wanting that lovesick idiot. Thomas knew Lauren would be appalled if she knew just how expressive and open she was- at least to him. Everything she felt fluttered across that lovely face of hers. It was clear she'd had no interest in the man. But he'd been so *angry*.

"You need to let off some steam, my boy."

It was eight days into negotiations and Thomas had nearly come across the table at the smirking CEO of the finance company they were buying. The company ostensibly focused on land development loans for most of the African companies, but their real expertise was laundering money for illegal diamond trading, used for funding military conflict in the Sudan, Congo, Sierra Leone, Liberia, and Angola. After eight days of dealing with the man's endless bragging, drug, and alcohol use, Number Two was ready to simply pull out his gun and shoot the arrogant idiot in the head.

Kingston was watching him carefully as everyone else filed out of the boardroom. "You are far too tense. There's a delightful club just full of obliging young ladies close to here. I've dropped by three times this week."

Thomas forced the mildly nauseating image of a naked Number One out of his head. With a filthy smile, he said, "Ah, I've found my own favorite dungeon. You know I prefer to work alone, Ben."

The older man burst into laughter, clapping him warmly on the shoulder, "It's good to have you back."

The first thought that went through Thomas's mind was, *I'm nothing like you, old man. Nothing.* But sitting alone in the dim boardroom, he frowned. But he was, that's what he'd always wanted, wasn't it?

Jaguar Holdings Second in Command did not go to a dungeon or sex club. He in fact went back to his hotel, as he had every night. Sitting in a chair on his balcony, one hand swirling a glass of Jameson, he found himself thinking for the dozenth time about what Lauren was doing at that moment. He pictured her glowing skin after he'd given her a string of orgasms, or her laugh when he'd chase her up the stairs. How her long legs looked while running. Sighing and rubbing his forehead, Thomas got up to head back to the hotel suite's desk and go through more company files for the closing.

It had all come together the night he finally returned home, standing over his wife who was pretending to be asleep in their bed. Thomas realized she would be just like Arabella in a few years if he didn't change. Dead-eyed, alcoholic because actually killing herself would hurt too many other people. He was never going to let her go. He knew that. Even if it was possible, he just... couldn't. But he couldn't let her become like Arabella.

So, rolling up the sleeves of his dress shirt, Thomas cleaned up the breakfast debris as his wife excitedly called from the door, "I'm leaving, see you tonight! Thank you!"

Lauren was still glowing when he returned home that night, a huge smile she couldn't seem to wipe off her face as she talked- at his urging- about the 8-year-old who'd picked up a violin and started playing an old French tune without a hitch, or her classmate from the Caribbean who immediately began teaching some of the other students how to play the drums. How she'd plopped a little 5-year-old on her lap and began showing her the fingering for a simple song on the keyboard.

"You should have seen them, Thomas! They're so smart, cheeky monkeys! Two nearly started painting on the wall before I managed to get the roll of paper put up..." she talked quickly, hands waving and laughing nearly every other sentence. His Lauren at her most lovely. Finally slowing down as she realized she'd been talking through the entire dinner; she flushed a bit. "Sorry, I didn't mean to talk so long."

"I enjoyed it," Thomas interrupted, "I'm intrigued by their response. I'd thought they'd be more hesitant at first."

"Oh, no," said Lauren, putting a chocolate eclair on a plate for him. "Children are naturally drawn to music, to art. If you give them the tools and stand back, they'll show you what they need. And you can learn so much about them by what they create. It's beautiful."

"As are you," he said without thinking.

She paused, looking up with an embarrassed smile. "Thomas..." But he wasn't teasing her. Thomas was leaning back in his chair, manspreading as usual and looking so handsome in his dress shirt and tie, one finger running over his upper lip, hiding a slight smile. Gathering the bit of self-confidence beginning to grow again that day, Lauren walked over to his side of the table and sat carefully on his lap, putting her arms around his neck. He smelled so good, her husband, his warmth familiar and comforting. After that horrible night, she'd never thought she would ever touch him willingly again. "Thank you," she whispered into his neck. As his arms went around her, Lauren drew in a shaky sigh.

Thomas gently kissed her neck, her cheek, his wife's mouth, and under her ear where she loved it so much. He finally allowed himself to say something he thought would never pass his lips. "I have missed you, wife."

"I've missed you too," Lauren managed to whisper, "how good

you feel. How I feel safe."

Thomas paused at that for a moment. Safe? She felt safe with him? He kissed Lauren's chest tenderly, right over her rapidly beating heart. It was in that quiet, perfect moment when he found the backbone to turn his face slightly, lips brushing her cheek and said, "I am sorry, Lauren. I'm sorry." And then she squeezed him even tighter.

Chapter 27 – I Wish We Could be Different People

In which Lauren is forced to see another ugly facet of the reality of life at Jaguar Holdings.

Trigger warning: aftermath of domestic abuse.

"Hey Chuck," Lauren called, "I need you this afternoon, please."

Her bodyguard/driver/hitman put down his phone and gave her his full attention. "Of course, Miss Lauren," he said. "And where might we be going?"

Lauren was attempting to sound unconcerned as if this was a social call, and there was nothing to worry about. But the words came out with a forced sort of breathlessness that made her sound like a teenager asking to stay out after midnight on a school night. Hideous. "We're going to pick up Clara," she said, "and go pin down Arabella at her place. She ditched the last charity meeting." She could tell as she grabbed a jacket and a messenger bag that the idea was not sitting well with Chuck.

"I see," he said slowly. "And is Mr. Williams aware of your social outing?"

Her eyes narrowed challengingly, "He knows that I'm hanging out with the wives today," she said evasively. Chuck stared at her for far longer than was comfortable, and she was reminded that the man had had a daughter before, and was apparently good at breaking down even the most well-crafted of evasions. Still, she was a grown-up and Mrs. Thomas Williams, and she wasn't letting this one go. So, with a sigh, the man stood and helped her put on her jacket.

Clara was, if possible, even more nervous than she was, and it helped Lauren calm down a bit. It wasn't until they pulled up to the palatial front door of the Kingston's that she turned to Lauren with wide, anxious hazel eyes. "You think she's... She's OK, right?"

Lauren nodded firmly. "Of course, she is! She has a lot going on outside of the charity branch, you know that. She's just been busy."

The man who opened the front door did not look like a butler. He stared at them both coldly, clearly indifferent to the fact that these women were attached to the other two in the power structure at The Corporation. "Yes?" he said in an extremely unhelpful way.

Lauren gave him her best insincere social smile. "We're here to see Bella," she said a little aggressively. "We haven't met. I'm Lauren Williams and this is Clara, Mr. Fassell's fiancée. So if you'll let Arabella know we are here, I'm sure she'll be delighted to see us." She leaned in slightly as she said it, attempting to look threatening. Looking back, she would realize how utterly ludicrous the attempt was, but the fact that Chuck stepped up behind her seemed to make the butler/thug give pause.

"Won't you come in," he said stiffly, "I'll see if Mrs. Kingston is available." And then he said the thing that Lauren had been dreading, the words that made her physically ill. "She hasn't been feeling well recently." As they stood in the hallway – Lauren noticed the butler/thug had not invited them to sit down – she tried to count back from the last time she had seen Arabella at that disastrous lunch with the Gray Man. Five weeks, give or take. She clenched her hands together tightly, trying not to shake. Clara couldn't see her freaking out; it would only scare the girl more. And Arabella was alive, at least they knew that. "Mrs. Kingston will see you now," the unpleasant man announced, clearly displeased they were bothering him.

Walking into the sumptuous living room, Lauren ignored the beautiful furnishings and a spectacular view of the lake behind the house. "Bella, we've missed you!" she started, "What's been-" Behind her, she could hear Clara try to swallow a startled gasp. Mrs. Kingston looked terrible: face bruised and heavily bandaged and more on her arms and wrapped around her chest, along with some kind of a brace. Lauren's eyes flooded with tears, oh God, that sick fuck Ben did this, he did this and she hadn't done anything to protect Arabella. She should've known that he would-

"Oh, stop with the dramatics, you two!" the chiding voice came from behind the bandages. Arabella attempted to smile and the effort was actually painful to watch. "I'm fine darlings, I just had some plastic surgery done over the holidays, just freshening up, you know."

"Freshening up?" repeated Clara doubtfully, still staring at the woman ensconced on the sofa surrounded by a multitude of pillows and blankets and her feet up.

"Yes," Arabella said firmly. "Why, what did you think? I'm not ready for a complete overhaul yet!" She laughed heartily.

Lauren forced her numb feet to move and headed for the sofa to very, very carefully kiss her friend on the cheek, squeezing her hand. "We really missed you, Bella," she murmured. She wanted to say more but both Chuck and the butler/thug were still in the room with them, watching everything carefully.

Squeezing her hand back, Arabella waved to her unwilling manservant, "Go get us some tea and some of those amazing little cheesecakes from yesterday."

Lauren was grateful she didn't call for wine, it was clear from her glassy eyes that the wife of Number One was still generously dosed with pain medication. She and Clara kept up a light patter, updating Arabella about the charity meetings and everything going on regarding the quasi-legal outskirts of The Corporation's activities. It seemed to take the older woman a bit of time to answer back, and Lauren could tell she had to think carefully about what to say. She wasn't sure if that was the medication or the awareness of their constant surveillance. Finally, she ventured, "When will you be um, unbandaged enough to come out with us? We could just take a few walks in a quiet stretch of the park until you're ready with your public face?"

Arabella's marked and bruised face lifted for a moment, looking right at Lauren with a suddenly lucid gaze. "Well, that would be-"

"Darling, I'm home!" To their mutual horror, the greasily fond tone of Number One echoed from the front hall. His expensive shoes clicked against the marble entryway as he headed unerringly for the great room in the back of the house. "Ah, there you are, Arabella. And with guests! The wives are always *so* loyal." His insectile gaze included them all as his mouth stretched in a terrifying smile.

Lauren watched Arabella shrink into herself as her fists clenched without her knowing. But Kingston did, his grin stretching wider to see her so angry. "Hello, Ben. How was your day?" Bella's voice was monotone, almost robotic.

"Good, darling, good," the vile bastard answered, the faux soothing tone almost nauseating to hear. "How lovely that your friends have *finally* come to see you."

Feeling a stab of shame, Lauren realized he was right. Despite Thomas telling her to cut off contact and let things settle, she should have pushed it. She should have insisted on seeing Arabella and asking Thomas to intervene on her behalf. What happened that day was no one's fault. Remembering the older woman whispering, "Colin. he's much nicer than he seems. Please don't say anything- no need to upset our husbands, correct?" *She called him by his first name...* Lauren shook her head, that didn't mean anything. No one deserved what she was certain had happened to Number One's wife at the hand of her twisted husband.

"You're right, Ben," she said clearly, "I should have been here sooner. Much sooner. I won't be so careless with my friendship with Bella again." From the corner of her eye, she could see Clara sitting motionless, like a rabbit hoping the hawk hasn't noticed it. There was the slightest hint of a throat being cleared behind her, and she knew it was Chuck. She had a feeling that if she turned around, her bodyguard would be wearing that same terrifying expression he had that day at the Connaught when things were so volatile that the slightest move could have sent guns blazing. "Well, we should get going, Clara," Lauren took a minute to make sure her voice wouldn't shake. Not in front of that black-eyed, black-hearted bastard. She would never give him what he wanted- her fear, her obedience. Leaning over to Arabella, she gave her friend a gentle kiss on the cheek. "But I'll be back. How does tomorrow sound?"

Number One's wife stirred briefly. "I don't- it depends on Ben's schedule. I..."

"No worries," Lauren stared at Kingston, whose fixed grin made him look even more terrifying, "I'll just keep checking back. And I'll ask Thomas to check in on Ben's schedule, too." She knew pulling her husband into this mess was an unwise decision, but she was using everything she had. "It won't be another five weeks, Bella. I promise."

As soon as the door closed behind them in the car, Clara burst into tears. "That wasn't a face-lift!" she wept, "He did something to Bella, didn't he? He hurt her, didn't he?"

Lauren sighed, putting an arm around her sobbing friend. "Probably a little of both, she-" swallowing down her breakfast that was trying to make its way back up her throat, she finished, "-she probably fixed some damage."

Clara was suddenly fierce, grabbing her by the arms and looking at her furiously. "How can you stand it? Why are we just accepting this? It's sick! It's evil and we're not doing anything and..." beginning to cry again, she didn't shrug loose when Lauren put her arm around her again, looking out the window as they left Kingston's long driveway and turned on to the street.

Back at home, Lauren found herself making that miserable circuit in the living room again. It was exactly twenty-one steps to the big, leaded-glass windows. Ten steps to the fireplace. Seven steps to the front entryway again. Absently counting out loud as she paced her erratic triangle, she tried to think of how to convince her cold husband to intervene in something that was really, none of his business.

Her eyes closed with inexpressible relief when she heard his deep, resonant voice echo in the entryway.

"Darling? I'm home. How was your visit with the wives?"

Lauren sighed silently. Of course, he knew.

"It..." fuck it, she thought. "It was horrible. Arabella-" she fought to control her emotions, "she was hurt. Badly. She was pretending she had some plastic surgery, she called it 'freshening up,' but Ben came home and she just sank into the couch and tried to disappear." Taking a moment, she swallowed and looked at her husband. Thomas was completely calm, watching her intently. "He did something horrible to her when you all got home from that trip, didn't he? A lot of horrible things."

Waiting for a moment to see if she had anything else to say, Thomas pulled off his jacket, laying it over the back of one of the wing-back chairs. He hadn't been looking forward to coming home and seeing the tearful anxious face of his wife after Chuck had called to notify him about the wives' little get-together, which had likely been right around the time Ben received a call from his wife's new "minder," and he'd headed out immediately with a cold glance at Thomas as he passed his office. That look had given Thomas a spiteful satisfaction that Number One considered his wife enough of a threat to head home- followed instantly with a chilling recognition that the vicious head of Jaguar Holdings considering Lauren a threat was a very, very bad thing.

Driving home, he was irritable with Kingston for treating Arabella so poorly that she retaliated in the most idiotic possible fashion- attempting a "friendship" with that arse Martinsson. And eating at the Connaught? Exposing *his* wife to that bastard? Lauren would appeal to him to help Arabella.

She would want to know more. This flare of concern and independence needed to be curbed immediately. His wife could not be in Kingston's cross-hairs. He'd never thought seriously about murdering the first in command, but it was appearing that it might be an expedient action.

"-help her?" Her lovely purple eyes were seeking his, wide with an appeal.

Irritated with himself for not paying attention, Thomas cleared his throat. "Do you remember me telling you about Colin Martinsson?"

"The Grey Man," Lauren agreed, watching him smile slightly.

"Then you see what an utterly suicidal action it was for Arabella to be speaking with him."

She shook her head, confused, "But- he came over to our table, she didn't-"

Thomas interrupted her coldly. "She should not have been there. She should not have brought you there. Arabella knew what she was doing, and she knew what would happen to her. I can't intervene. You should know that."

"This is insane!" Lauren burst out; hands clenched into fists. "No one- she didn't deserve- this is sick-" she sputtered to a stop, not knowing how to express her fury and helplessness. "So there was nothing you could do to protect her? What if he killed her?" Her eyes were filling with tears and Thomas made a sharp, impatient sound.

"You remember the world we're in, correct? You know your responsibilities, you've done well. Arabella's been in this life for over a decade. She *knows* better."

"You didn't see her, Thomas! She- I'm sure she had to have surgery to repair some of the damage that monster did to her! Can't we make him stop it?" Lauren stuttered, trying to find the right thing to say, "Can't you make Ben not hurt her?"

"This is not up for discussion," Thomas said with chilling calm. "Not another word."

His sweet wife ground her teeth furiously, "You want me to be friends with the other wives, you say they're the only ones who understand. But- but- but something horrible happens to one of them and I'm just supposed to drop her, just like that? No longer convenient?" She looked up, hoping she would see understanding or possibly even sympathy on her husband's beautiful face, but it was still set in its cold lines. In fact, she hadn't seen him look this unkind and forbidding since that terrible first night in his office.

Forcing herself to calm down, she turned to the kitchen. "I'll just... I'll..." Lauren made herself concentrate. "I'll just finish dinner." She looked at him one last time, searching for something she didn't find, and she left without another word.

Thomas growled silently, running his hand through his dark hair. This was The Corporation's reality. And like it or not, his sweet wife would have to get used to it.

It was around 2am when he heard Lauren slip from the bed. Thomas thought for a moment that she was heading upstairs to play her stress and fear away as she had many times before, but then he heard her in the master bathroom. He moved soundlessly to listen at the door. She was crying and clearly trying to keep it down. Lauren looked up, shocked when he opened the door and frantically scrubbing at her streaming eyes with the tissue. "I was just... I'm just coming back to bed now," she said in a dull, flat tone he's not heard before. Thomas looked down as she wiped her eyes quickly one last time before hastily discarding the tissue as if hiding the evidence. An unfamiliar pinch of sorrow twisted his insides from the sight. It was a rare emotion, and one Thomas disliked. Unfortunately, he found himself feeling it more than once with his wife.

"Darling..."

Lauren stopped her back to him and humiliated that she was so attuned to the sweet, caressing tone he used to an often-devastating effect that she obeyed, like a barn animal, or something. She stiffened as his hand came to stroke down her back.

Thomas's normally perfect, composed voice was a little hoarse. "I know what I've brought you into. Nothing can prepare you for this. But now I must keep you safe. Your safety is more important to me than- more important than I can express. I control many things. Life and death, occasionally. But not Arabella's." When he turned her to face him, Lauren was weeping those terrible, silent tears again.

She was shaking her head sadly, hopelessly. "I wish it could be different," Lauren wept, "that we could be different people." She felt his wide chest move as her husband sighed, and he simply held her for a moment until he steered her back to bed.

Chapter 28 – What a Conscience Can Bear

In which Lauren meets someone from her past. Someone even more horrible than her father. Though to make this the worst week ever, Frank shows up, too.

Trigger warning: remembered sexual assault. You can skip the chapter without missing too much if this would affect you.

"Your father's coming to London."

If Thomas had been attempting to destroy his wife's appetite, mission accomplished. It was just a shame, Lauren thought later because at the time they were enjoying some really spectacular Scottish salmon. Putting down her fork, she pushed down the nausea and anxiety this revelation caused. "Oh. How come?"

The corner of her husband's mouth quirked just slightly. "The annual board meeting for Atlantic Equities as a Jaguar Holding's asset. Since the company came under my division's personal supervision, ROI has improved. We're looking at moving Frank out of the CEO position. There are several more eager executives who could improve the company's profit margin."

A shard of grief twisted in Lauren's chest. "Atlantic Equities was my grandfather's company. He built it from nothing."

Thomas's chewing slowed, and he took a sip of wine. "This is hard for you to see it leave your family."

Hardening her heart, Lauren shook her head briskly, stabbing into a bit of salmon. "It left the family when my father sold it out from under us." A moment of confusion swept over her. If Frank hadn't run the company into the ground and then sold it to an international crime syndicate, she never would have met Thomas. Married him. Had her life change so dramatically? The girl waited to see how those observations would affect her. The sadness she should have logically felt wasn't there. Was this pleasure she was feeling? A sense of good fortune?

Thomas leaned back, idly swirling the wine in his crystal glass as he watched the rapid play of emotion over his guileless wife's face. He had a fairly good idea of the feelings it would spark for Lauren to realize she'd be seeing that worthless lump of flesh that sired her again. After Frank had walked her down the aisle and then promptly got drunk during the surreal nightmare that had been her wedding, she'd not spoken of him once. Knowing Lauren's sweet and forgiving nature, Thomas was quite certain Frank's instant capitulation to his demand for his daughter's hand in marriage was not the first time he'd placed his interests well above his daughter's. The twinge in the general direction of where a conscience might have resided - had he owned one - Thomas realized he *was* responsible for the final rift between father and daughter, though he didn't doubt it would have come sooner than later.

"Do we have to see him?" she asked abruptly, looking down at her half-eaten dinner.

Warmed by her use of "we," Thomas shook his head gently. "If you don't want to have contact with him, of course not. There's no reason to put you in a position that's bound to make you unhappy."

Lauren didn't look up, but she nodded. "Thank you, Thomas."

Nonetheless, Lauren viewed The Corporation's upcoming board meeting with dread. There would be entertaining "requirements," and since she didn't know how Arabella was recovering, the chances were good that she would be put in charge. While she hadn't come back the very next day, as she'd threatened to Kingston's thug/butler, Lauren was stubbornly back on their front steps the next week. Chuck's silent menace behind her kept the man's sneer to a minimum. "Arabella!" she said gratefully, noting that her friend stood this time to greet her. "You look much better, honey." Lauren was being truthful, Number One's wife was almost back to her elegant, polished self, though she could tell the older woman was still moving stiffly, carefully.

She didn't argue when Arabella airily waved her (no longer splinted) hand. "Plastic surgery! You'd think these procedures wouldn't take so long to clear up! But I'm feeling right as rain."

This time, neither Chuck nor the thug/butler stood in the room with them, though Lauren didn't doubt for a second that they were hovering right outside. In fact, she thought with a cynical twist to her full lips, there was likely plenty of listening devices around the room. So, she'd brought an iPad with her. "I was hoping you'd help me make some lists of things to do-" she scooted closer to the other woman. "I can take some of the weight off your shoulders if you can do the fine-tuning?" Meanwhile, she was rapidly tapping out, *"How are you, really? How can I help?"*

Pleasant social smile very much in place, Arabella airily answered, "That would be lovely. If you can call Carolyn at Elegant Affairs, she'll handle the menu and drink items if you just..." Nodding and typing rapidly as if taking notes on whether to serve the fish or steak dish, Lauren's stomach knotted as Arabella wrote, *"Don't trust anyone. Not even Thomas. Especially not Thomas. This upcoming meeting is going to be very bad."*

Finally, back at home, Lauren wandered the quiet, elegant rooms in their townhouse, staring at nothing as she processed everything she'd been told. People were going to be killed during The Corporation summit. It was possible her father would be one of them, despite her husband's promise to let Frank live. Thomas had told her she didn't need to see Frank, was that because he knew the man's demotion from CEO of Atlantic Equities included a shallow grave somewhere?

But... he'd told her the truth about Macie. Lauren had anxiously checked the Berlin Philharmonic's social media pages until she'd seen images of Macie playing during a performance. Alive, even if she could never see her again. Lauren knew that her husband usually simply refused to answer her, or he'd give her a look of terrifying chill that would intimidate her instantly if she asked something That Was None Of Her Business. She didn't believe Thomas lied to her, maybe because it wasn't worth the trouble.

But while Thomas did keep his promise about Lauren not having to see her father, she encountered someone much worse at the welcoming cocktail party.

Lauren's back was turned, chatting animatedly to a vice president from Atlantic Equities who'd been with the company since her grandfather ran it. Thomas smiled absently to hear the peal of her laughter more than once at the elderly man's stories from home. His wife was wearing a deliciously low-backed evening dress that stopped just around the dimples over her ass, and Thomas was enjoying the smooth play of toned muscle and skin. He'd selected that dress for her with this tantalizing view very much in mind. And then her entire body turned to stone.

"Well, how do you do! Is that sweet little Lauren, Frank's kid? You've grown up, honey."

She recognized the voice instantly, the nauseating, contemptuous tone of the scumbag who her father had sworn he'd fired after that- thing. And then his horrible fucking hand was on her bare back, low, near her waist and Lauren found she couldn't move. She stood utterly still, trying not to vomit into her glass of wine. The vice president she'd been speaking to, Alan Tarrow, looked concerned as he watched the color drain from her face. "Lauren, you look ill, why don't you come sit down, I'll get you some water-"

"Oh, hell Alan!" the bastard's voice was loud, boisterous. "I haven't even had a chance to say 'hi' to little Miss Marsh, here."

Lauren suddenly, violently arched her back away from his hand, stepping closer to Tarrow and shuddering. "Don't you- don't touch me. You shouldn't be here- you shouldn't-"

"Lauren? Darling, come with me." Thomas was behind her then, she could feel the heat from his body against her chilled skin, he was standing closer than usual as he slid an arm around her waist. "Excuse us, gentlemen," he said coldly, "my wife is needed elsewhere."

Lauren was walking away as quickly as she could without

actually breaking into a run, but she could hear the oily voice of that... *pig* suddenly change tone, sounding alarmed. "Wife? Fuck, Frank's little girl is married to *Williams?*"

Thomas quelled a rising fury as he looked at Lauren's face. She was sheet-white with two red spots burning vividly over her cheekbones. Taking a breath, he calmly asked, "Who upset you?"

Lauren was taking short gulps of air, vaguely aware that she was probably hyperventilating but trying to look calm as Thomas led her out of the room. "No- nothing, I just need-" another hitch of air left her chest and she tried to focus. She was aware she was being seated somewhere and a door was shut. Her cold hands were in Thomas's warm ones, and he was rubbing some circulation back into her fingers.

"Match your breath to mine, Lauren. Look at me, darling." Lifting her chin, his polar gaze found hers and held it, forcing her to breathe in and out slowly. When Lauren's chest stopped hitching, Thomas spoke again. "You were speaking to Alan Tarrow and Steve Meyers. Which one upset you?"

Lauren's heart nearly stopped again. She could hear the barely concealed fury in her husband's tone that meant someone was about to have a very bad night. No matter how much she hated that- that *thing,* she couldn't be responsible for his death. So trying to compose herself, she looked back at him. "I don't like Steve Meyers. He's a creep. All the women he worked with hated him because he's a misogynistic asshole. That's all. I just- I thought Frank had fired him a long time ago." Lauren cringed internally. Thomas's gaze had not left hers and it was clear he knew she wasn't telling the truth. After a moment, he nodded and rose, helping her up. "I will make certain," Thomas spoke precisely, another hint that he was hiding his temper, "that Meyers does not approach you again. Can you finish the night?"

Nodding, Lauren answered as if it was obvious, "Of course." Of course, she would. She would just be someone else, just watching like it wasn't happening to her at all.

But when she dreamt that night, that little trick didn't work.

Thomas had been forced to send her home with Chuck since the cocktail party turned into a spur of the moment meeting with the Atlantic Equities board when Number 3 produced some unflattering new information. Grinding his even white teeth, Williams had nodded at Charles, who moved to him swiftly. "Take my wife home, please. Do not leave her." Nodding the man glided away to collect Lauren, who greeted him with a relieved smile that did nothing to allay Thomas's suspicions.

In Lauren's dream that night, they were back at that horrible restaurant in downtown Manhattan six years ago and his hand was heavy on her forearm as he leaned in to tell her another disgusting joke. Lauren leaned away as politely as possible and said, "Excuse me, Mr. Meyer, I have to speak to my-"

"Relax kid! We're just having fun, remember?" The man was smiling, but his teeth were gritted. "Your dad's in such a great mood since I brought in the Diego de Luna accounts, let him celebrate!" With a weak smile, Lauren nodded but pulled away as graciously as she could. Hiding in the ladies' room for a moment, she washed her hands and the sweaty spot Meyers left on her forearm. Creepy bastard! And she knew her dad put him next to her at the table because he'd been staring at her all evening. He made her sick, there was something off about him and if her mom were here, she would have switched seats instantly and put him with the ancient Winkelmann twins who ran the accounting department.

But her mom wasn't here. Lauren swallowed down the grief and made her 17-year-old self smile. Mom was in the hospital getting another chemotherapy treatment, and she'd insisted along with Frank that she attend this business dinner as the "hostess." And she was capable of it- trained from early on when her earnest conversation and sincere interest was dubbed precocious, to now where she could deftly handle conversations with millionaires three times her age. Unfortunately, sometimes her graceful way of drawing out someone's interests and making them feel special was misinterpreted as something else. This creepy Meyers guy had to be in his late 40's! She kept away from her seat next to the slimy associate until the end of dinner and stood with Frank to greet everyone goodnight.

To her disgust, Meyers seized her hand, bending over to kiss it and Lauren's skin tried to crawl right off her body as she realized the disgusting troll was *licking* her hand under his lips. As she wiped her hand on her skirt, he shook her father's hand briskly, promising that "I'll see you both. Real soon," and chuckling as he left. Frank did not believe her when she complained about how disgusting Meyers was, how he kept grabbing her at dinner and put his disgusting tongue on her hand.

"Don't get so worked up, honey. You're misinterpreting his actions. You're a pretty girl - when you're dressed up, anyway - and he was probably trying to be, I don't know, gallant, or something."

Lauren thought she was being smart in her argument when she brought up the potential of a sexual harassment lawsuit against the company if Meyers behaved like this at work.

Frank irritably waved off her concerns. "He's a top earner in our South American division, honey. You know how it is down there. Everyone is flirty."

And two days later as Lauren was getting out of a cab, coming home from the hospital, the man was waiting for her outside her parent's brownstone. He stepped out of the shadow of one of the pillars as she opened the front door. "Hey, Lauren! Great to see you again. I've got some papers for your dad-" Meyers held up a couple of folders, "-and I promised I'd meet him here to sign them."

Lauren tried to slip through the door quickly while holding out her hand for the folders. "I'll give them to him for you. I don't know when he'll be back and you have other things to do-" She instantly realized her mistake when he shoved through the door before she could close it.

"You little flirt!" he chuckled, trying to look seductive as he pushed her further into the hall so he could shut the door and lock it. "If you wanted to get me alone, you just had to say so!"

She tried to swallow her sudden, sickening sense of fear and look coldly authoritative like her mother did when someone Got Out Of Hand. "Get out of here, now! I swear I'll-"

"You'll what?" Suddenly, she'd been shoved back against the wall of the entryway, knocking the breath out of her. The man in front of her had never been attractive, but now the ugly twist to his mouth and his red, sweating face made Lauren nauseous. "You'll call daddy? Do you think he'll care? Who do you think pays for your fancy fucking house and your fancy fucking education? Managers like *me*, bitch! And you need to start showing me some appreciation-"

"GET OUT OF HERE!" Lauren yelled back, "Get OUT or I'll call the cops, you freak-" A hard slap nearly knocked her over and she shrieked when Meyer's grabbed her t-shirt and ripped it nearly off her. Now she began to scream in earnest, terrified and trying to fight back but his bulk was already on top of her, crushing her chest and hurting her and then she was crying, trying to keep her knees together when he began yanking at the button to her jeans.

Suddenly his ugly face was yanked away from hers and a spurt of blood came from his temple where he'd been slammed across the face with a huge purse.

"Saia seu porco!" Beatriz, their housekeeper was there, slamming her bag against his head again, making the man let out a thin shriek. "I'm calling the police! Rapist! Bastard! *Eu deveria cortar seu pauzinho!"* She was still hitting Meyers when the door opened again, her father dropping his briefcase.

"What the hell is going on here! What the hell!" Frank was shouting at everyone, silver head turning as he tried to find the right person to blame. Looking down at his sobbing daughter, jeans wrestled halfway down her knees and pink bra showing under her torn t-shirt, he quickly averted his eyes. "Meyers! What are you doing here!" Lauren was crying so hard, trying to pull on Beatriz's offered sweater that she didn't get much of the conversation. Their housekeeper was holding her own, gesturing furiously at a bleeding Meyers and back at Lauren, still curled up on the floor. Suddenly, Meyers was scuttling out the door and Frank was yelling back at Beatriz to "Shut the hell up and let me think!"

The older woman stared at him furiously before turning to help Lauren up, who was still shaking and trying to pull up her jeans. "He tried to ra- to hurt me and he hit me, Dad! He wanted to-" she stopped for a moment, realizing that she really had been moments away from being raped without Beatriz coming back to pick up something at the house and saving her. "We have to call the police!"

"Don't be an idiot, Lauren!" her father shouted back, putting an arm around her shoulders and steering her rapidly into the kitchen. "Meyers wasn't going to assault you- he just misunderstood your politeness. He thought you were interested and-"

An enraged Beatriz burst into a rapid-fire round of Portuguese and Frank finally shouted over her.

"Is that what you want, Lauren? Imagine what this is going to do for the company's reputation!" Frank's hands were waving wildly as if trying to grasp some sort of persuasive argument out of midair that would make his daughter stop crying. "I'll just get a quote ready for the *Wall Street Journal* when they call asking about the rape culture at Atlantic Equities! Your grandfather's company, Lauren! To make your mother go through something like this while she's battling cancer? Really? Do you know what this will DO to her?" He was loosening his tie while he yelled at his daughter. "You know how sick she is- what the chemo is doing to her. How do you think she'll handle THIS?" He whirled and glared at the housekeeper, who still had an arm around Lauren. "We'll take care of this. You go home." When it looked like Beatriz would argue with him, Frank blustered, "I'm her father! I'll handle this!"

When Thomas got home early the next morning, Lauren was cycling through the worst part of the attack again, feeling the man's disgusting hands, his fingers trying to get past her jeans and yanking her hair. "Don't touch- you get off- it-

MOM!"

Lauren screamed for a moment as she felt hands try to hold her flailing ones and then she heard her husband's beautiful, soothing voice in her ear. "Shhh, darling. I have you. Shhh... you're safe. I'm here." Thomas heard the words come out of his mouth and wondered at how alien they sounded. Soothing a terrified girl and promising her safety was not his forte, but this was his Lauren, and when she stilled, he wrapped her in his arms and rocked her back and forth, whispering calm assurances and humming gently. When she could sit up, he went to the master bath and fetched her a glass of water, wiping her wet face with a warm washcloth. Settling her back on his lap and stretching out on the bed, still in his suit, Thomas ran his hand up and down her arm until she could talk again.

"Thanks, Thomas. I'm okay now, sorry. Just a nightmare." She smiled anxiously, trying to disarm him. It didn't work.

His eyes were still the color of the frozen sea as Thomas said calmly. "Tell me what Steve Meyers did to you."

"I-" Lauren's mouth gaped open like a fish, trying to think of what to say.

"He hurt you. This is clear. Tell me what happened, Lauren. Don't be afraid."

So, she did, finally looking down at her empty water glass and feeling sick again.

Her husband was silent for a moment. "Frank did not call the police and press charges?"

Lauren laughed bitterly, a harsh sound he'd never heard from her before. "No. He told me he'd fire him and make sure he didn't work in the industry ever again. Frank said..." she angrily pushed back her blonde curls, feeling so incredibly stupid. "Frank said it would kill my mom to think I'd almost been raped and that we had to protect her. That I'd never see Meyers again and he'd take care of it so that Mom wouldn't have the stress. So, I agreed." Clutching the glass so that Thomas removed it, worried she'd crack it and cut herself; Lauren shook her head. "He never fired him. Did he?"

Thomas's voice was emotionless, each word perfectly shaped and enunciated like shards of glass. "Meyers is vice president of the company's South American division. He's been in the position for six years."

Laughing a bit before she started to cry, Lauren gasped, "That would actually be a promotion, you know. In the company? A step up. Frank never fired him, he just moved him out of New York so I wouldn't see him again." Looking over at her husband's utterly still face, she started shaking. "Thomas, he's a monster but- you can't kill him. Please don't kill him. I can't have that on my conscience." Watching him as he took in a deep breath and let it out, Lauren knew that was exactly what he planned to do.

"Sweetheart, has it occurred to you that you are not the first, or the last girl he's hurt?" Thomas ran the back of his hand down her cheek. "Can your conscience bear it if he does this to someone else?"

"That's not fair Thomas! You're-" Lauren leaned back as his beautiful face darkened. "I mean, couldn't you just fire him? Ruin his reputation like Frank said he would? Killing him... I..."

Thomas took another deep breath, setting her down on the mattress gently and rising to remove his jacket and tie. "If that is what you want, I'll do so." Before she could thank him, he added, "Just after I beat him half to death. I will make quite certain he never touches another girl." He looked down at his wide-eyed wife. "It is the least he deserves, and don't pretend to yourself that you don't know that."

When he returned to bed, naked except for a pair of silk boxers, Lauren wondered if Thomas would attempt to soothe her the way he had so many times before. But instead, her mysterious spouse simply gathered her back in his arms and asked, "Can you sleep now?" At her nod, he tucked her head under his chin and rubbed her back until he heard her soft breathing. But Number Two in Jaguar Holdings didn't sleep for several hours later, watching the shadows from the trees outside moving on the white ceiling of their bedroom.

"Saia do porco!" - Portuguese for "Get away from her, you pig!"

"Eu deveria cortar seu pauzinho!" - Portuguese for "I should cut your tiny dick off!"

This is so important: if someone has forced you to perform a sexual act against your will - even if they just attempted it - it is not your fault. You did nothing wrong and you deserve help and support. The Sexual Assault helpline here in the US is: 1-800-656-4673
In England, it is: https://rapecrisis.org.uk/get-help/
In Canada: https://sexualassaultsupport.ca/support/
In Australia: https://au.reachout.com/articles/sexual-assault-support
In Europe: https://www.rainn.org/international-sexual-assault-resources

And if I've missed where you live and you need support,

please contact me privately on **Tumblr** and I will gladly help you find the right resources.

Chapter 29 – I Fell in Love with the Wrong Guy

In which justice is served.

Warning: graphic violence

The next two days were surreal for Lauren. She smiled and nodded and organized and directed, but all the while she wondered if Thomas had killed Meyers. At one particularly low moment, she wondered if he'd include her father in the execution. There were several other branches undergoing an examination at the same time as Atlantic Equities, so she saw very little of her husband, who remained his polished, urbane self even as she anxiously examined his expression when he returned home.

It was the third night when they were hosting a send-off for all the executives when she finally had her answer.

As fond as she was of Clara, she was driving her insane with her endless chatter about her wedding- a mere ten days away. "I just know Michael and I will be as happy as you and Thomas," Clara sighed with a dreamy smile as she sorted the guestlist for the third time.

Lauren stilled, staring at the girl who was obliviously humming. But… she *was* happy. Equal parts terrified and aroused, but happy. Her life was not what she'd expected, but what she had with Thomas, how he treated her... Forcing her confusion away, Lauren forced a smile and nodded, "I know you will be Clara. You're so sweet, everyone loves you."

"Just as long as Michael does," Clara giggled, and her friend nodded a little too rapidly.

Despite Thomas's promise to keep her from having to interact with Frank, Lauren was bracing herself for an appearance. He was still CEO of the company, right? Surely, he'd be required to attend the biggest evening of the year for Atlantic Equities. But as the evening drew out, she realized her father was nowhere to be found.

"One of the most inspiring elements of acquiring new businesses into The Corporation," intoned Kingston, "is watching them grow and flourish under our guidance." Lauren's gaze darted around the room, but not a single eye rolled. Everyone's expressions were frozen into a look of polite attentiveness. Returning to watch Number One, her stomach rolled a little at his look of avuncular fondness as he gestured to one of the younger men in Atlantic Equities' group of vice presidents. "David, come up here, won't you?"

A huge grin stretched across the man's face as he loped up to join Kingston on the elegant set of stairs they were using as a spontaneous stage. He briskly shook the hand of his new lord and master, and Lauren shuddered a little, wondering if he had the slightest idea of what he was getting into.

"Are you cold?" Thomas whispered into her ear as his arm came around her, stroking the skin of her bare arm.

"Where's Frank?" Lauren barely breathed, but she knew her husband heard her as his perpetual expression of urbane amusement didn't even ripple.

"I told you that you did not have to see him, darling."

Number One's voice cut in at that moment, "Congratulations to the new CEO of Atlantic Equities, David Monson!" The overeager round of applause buried Lauren's gasp as the new head of her grandfather's company gave a triumphant little fist bump with an amused Number Three.

Thomas ignored the sensation of his wife's body stiffening as if she'd received an electrical jolt. He noted with approval that Lauren's smile stayed constant as she listened to Monson's modest speech about "bringing more success to Jaguar Holding's already sterling record," and clapping mechanically afterward.

Was it possible to actually wear a path in her husband's antique oriental rugs?

Lauren wondered this as she continued the triangle of steps she could by now walk blindfolded. It was exactly ten steps to the big, leaded-glass windows. Twenty-one steps to the fireplace. Seven steps to the front entryway again. Thomas sent her home with Chuck, and she'd politely asked her bodyguard to stay in the kitchen. She needed to pace, or she might start screaming, and that would never do.

Twenty-one steps to the fireplace. Was her father dead? Not that she viewed him as one anymore, but saving his life was the reason she'd been forced to marry Thomas in the first place.

Ten steps to the leaded-glass windows, looking out on the

empty street. Did Thomas kill Frank himself? Did he use the gun or just order someone like Chuck to do it? Did he watch?

Seven steps to the entryway. If Thomas killed her father, he'd broken his promise to her. Lauren's feet stilled and she stood in the spacious entry, staring at her reflection in the mirror there. The fact that her husband had broken his promise hurt even more than the thought that he'd murdered her father. What had she turned into?

Chuck eventually couldn't bear his charge's obsessive pacing and forced her to go upstairs and attempt to get some sleep. At around 2am, she could hear the front door open and the low tones of conversation between the two men before Chuck left and her husband's steps sounded on the wooden stairway. There was a low sigh as he stood in front of the bed.

"I know you're awake, darling. Sit up."

Lauren's teeth gritted against the screams she wanted to let out, the hysterical, terrified questions. Carefully sitting up and putting her pillows behind her back, she looked at Thomas. He was unfairly beautiful, even at the late hour and a spray of stubble across his lean cheeks, tie loosened and hair cautiously beginning to wave from his strict style. He looked at her levelly, waiting for her to ask the question. But when Lauren spoke, it wasn't what he expected.

"You broke your promise to me."

One dark brow rose, but Thomas shook his head. "I did not."

The Second in Command at Jaguar Holdings was speaking truthfully. He did not kill Frank. Nor did he kill Steve Meyers, though it took more self-control than he'd expected. Frank killed Meyers.

Earlier...

"Here." Thomas turned and handed his gun to the man cowering in the corner of the room, who'd been sniveling and whimpering since he'd been dragged in.

"W- WHAT?" blubbered Frank Marsh, former CEO of Atlantic Equities, "Why are you handing me a GUN? What the hell is going on here? What the-"

Sighing, Thomas crisply slapped his father-in-law across the face, enjoying the older man's squawk. "You're going to shoot and kill the man who attempted to rape your daughter-" he stopped for a moment, taking in a deep breath and trying to control his fury. "-and my wife. You do remember, don't you, Frank? Your 17-year-old daughter crying in the hallway when you came home? Her face on fire from being hit repeatedly by this filth?" There was a barely audible growl from Chuck, standing behind the bloody lump tied to the chair. He took a fistful of the man's hair and yanked his face up.

"Fra..." Meyers's mouthful of broken teeth didn't allow for more precise speech, and Thomas flexed his fists, knuckles bloody from beating the man into a pulp. He'd actually offered Meyers the opportunity to defend himself, Thomas removing his jacket and rolling up his sleeves while the man put his hands up, waving them like a flag of surrender. But when he refused to defend himself, cowering and wailing, Thomas beat him soundly, enjoying the crunching noise of ribs breaking. And then he stepped back. Courteously inclining his head to a stone-faced Chuck, "Would you like to continue, Straker? I have meetings this afternoon and this scum has much to atone for."

When Lauren's bodyguard finally spoke, his tone was raspy. "It would be my pleasure, Mr. Williams." And so Thomas straightened his tie and smiled slightly at the first howl of agony as the man started his work.

It was several hours later when Thomas checked his watch, Chuck needed to be getting back to Lauren and he had one more subsidiary meeting before the closing cocktail party that evening. He held the gun out to the ashen-faced Frank again. "You can't redeem yourself for being the most worthless father alive, and believe me," Thomas chuckled, "I've seen some rather impressive candidates for the title. But I promised my wife that I wouldn't kill her would-be rapist. She didn't want his death on her conscience, no matter what he'd done to her." His attention turned to the mangled lump that used to be Steve Meyers, vice president of the company's South American division. "But you had to have known he wouldn't stop." Leaning in to stare at Meyers' ruined face, Thomas smiled slightly. "So it's time to put you down. Like a dog. And you-" he strode over to the terrified Frank and slapped the pistol into his hand. "You will finish him since you are responsible for all the women he raped when you promoted him and gave him free rein."

"I c- can't do that!" stuttered Frank, "I'm no killer!"

"Ah..." purred Thomas, "but you are quite capable of embezzlement, aren't you? Did you think being my-" he made a noise of disgust, "-being my father-in-law gave you immunity? You've stolen over eleven million dollars from Atlantic Equities in the last two years, most of it after I married Lauren. You must have felt quite confident about your safety. This was one of many mistakes. Now," he cruelly tightened Frank's fingers around the grip of the gun, "you will shoot this ex-employee. You will announce your retirement from the position of CEO, the money you've stolen has been returned to the company." Thomas's jaw clenched. "Fassell was the one who tracked down where you'd attempted to hide it. As your direct supervisor, I was required to repay the five million you'd already gambled away, you bloody idiot. Your assets have been liquidated and you will now live on a fixed income with a caretaker to keep you from fucking up again and requiring me to kill you." Thomas seized his father-in-law by the scruff of his neck, hauling him up and over to the sobbing Meyers. "Let me be clear," Thomas hissed into Frank's ear. "It is him, or you. But one of you leaves this room as a corpse."

The first shot was off, striking Meyers in the neck and making him scream shrilly. With a sigh, Chuck gripped his hand over Frank's, smiling as he heard a finger crunch and the next shot was through the left eye.

Currently...

And now here he was, looking into the wet lavender gaze of his wife. "I did not kill Meyers. I did not kill your father. Frank is alive, though a little unwell at the moment." Thomas chuckled unrepentantly at the memory of Meyers' blood spattered all over a shrieking Frank's face and expensive suit. Looking back at Lauren, he watched her begin to curl into herself. "Darling," he began to unbutton his starched white shirt. "You asked me about the scar on my back." Her head snapped back up, eyes wide.

"Yes?" Her voice was barely a whisper.

"There was a vile piece of shit at Eton - my public-school years - it was an all-boys school, but it didn't stop this bastard from harassing every girl within a twenty-five-kilometer radius of the school. He... there was a 19-year-old girl who worked in housekeeping, her name was Sally." Thomas paused for a moment, smoothing his hand over the back of his head. "She was very shy, easily cowed. He raped her. He bragged about it and she was fired. She needed that job, her mother had lung cancer and it was their only income. I beat the living hell out of him. Told him if he ever touched another girl, I'd kill him." Lauren was utterly still, barely breathing as if afraid she'd distract him. "MacGowen didn't like being made a fool of, everyone seeing him for what he was. So in the showers after soccer practice, he had four friends jump me. He stabbed me in the back repeatedly with a craft knife from the art department. Fortunate, that," Thomas said reflectively, "had it been a real knife I would have been paralyzed from the waist down, lost a kidney."

"What-" Lauren swallowed heavily. She would not cry; Thomas would never forgive it. "What happened to him? Did you press charges? Did the police-"

He cut her off, laughing harshly. "I was a scholarship student, darling. The Headmaster came to my hospital room and told me MacGowen's parents would pay for any recovery expenses and the rest of my time there."

Her full lips were thinned. "If you didn't go to the police. So their precious boy didn't get in trouble?"

Thomas nodded, pulling his shirt free from his trousers and unbuckling his belt. "Yes. I told him I would still hunt him down if he ever hurt another girl, but," he shook his head, "he was sent to a boarding school in Switzerland. I don't..." He felt the cool, soft hand of his wife's slide gently over his lower back, tracing the flex and pull of muscle there. She was stroking with her fingertips, gliding over smooth skin and ragged scar tissue. Then, her lips pressed to the scar and Thomas stood abruptly.

"Wait! Just... please stay." Lauren's sweet voice. That anxious, hopeful tone always weakened him, made him soft. "Thank you, Thomas. Thank you for telling me. Don't go." And then his wife was kneeling behind him, hugging him tightly.

It wasn't until she insisted on showering with him - Thomas standing patiently as Lauren carefully dried his wet skin - and they were back in bed when she finally asked what he'd expected when he came home.

"Where is Frank?" her voice was small. "What did you...?"

Thomas rolled to his side, wrapping a hard thigh over hers and keeping her facing him. "Frank embezzled millions from the company," he finally said, watching her eyes widen in horror. "He was allowed to retire and is now under supervision for..." he hesitated, "the foreseeable future."

"I'm so sorry. Oh, god."

It didn't occur to him that Lauren would be horrified, humiliated. "It's not your fault, you have nothing to apologize for. I made Frank offer recompense." This time, his wife was still. Thomas knew she understood. "He killed Meyers."

Lauren pressed her forehead into his chest and didn't say another word.

Clara and Michael's wedding was magnificent, of course, almost as spectacular as theirs had been. Thomas looked over at his wife, beautiful in silky layers of purple and blue that slid and moved along her thighs in a most distracting way.

Lauren took a sip of her champagne and smiled back at him.

They'd never spoken again about that night. She didn't want to know anything about Frank or where he was. Her heart and her conscience twinged when a glowing Clara came up to hug her. "I'm finally Mrs. Michael Fassell," she giggled a little bit. "This is everything I've ever dreamt of."

Searching for the right thing to say, Lauren finally smiled and hugged her tightly. "May you always be as happy as you are today, sweetie."

Meanwhile in Lisbon, Portugal...

"Ei vovó, isso veio para você?"

Beatriz looked up from the bread she was kneading, smiling at her grandson, who was waving a manila envelope with official-looking stamps on it. *"O que isso seria?"* Opening it and pulling out what looked like a deed and a cheque, the woman let out a shriek/gasp/laugh and read the paperwork, the check falling to the floor.

Picking it up, her grandson said, *"Vovó, este é um cheque de quinhentos mil euros!"*

Beatriz seized the cheque from the boy, shaking her head, beginning to laugh helplessly. Then unfolding the note attached, she read:

"Dear Mrs. Almeida:

I want to thank you for the care and protection you extended to my wife, Lauren Marsh, now Lauren Williams. You are an admirable woman and will always be in our thoughts. This is the deed to your house and funds to add to creating a comfortable re-

tirement. And my eternal gratitude.

Best, Thomas Williams"

"Hey Grandma, this came for you?" Portuguese: *"Ei vovó, isso veio para você?"*

"O que isso seria?" - "What would this be?"

"Grandma this is a check for five hundred thousand Euros!" - *"Vovó, este é um cheque de quinhentos mil euros!"*

Chapter 30 – This Merits Correction

In which Lauren is punished.

It was, Lauren thought sourly, as if the wedding for Clara and Number Three rang some starting bell that put them on a collision course with the Moscow Clusterfuck (as she called it to herself- strictly to herself) because her time with Thomas shrank accordingly. Some nights he returned grim; others perversely pleased. Either mood could spark a trip to the Fun Dungeon, though the grim mood was certainly less "fun." But those nights were still accompanied by a cascade of orgasms, albeit harder won.

The highlight of her day was when Thomas could run with her in the mornings, pacing his ridiculously long legs to match her stride. Her need for him was becoming worrisome to her. When he was late, the little voice began cycling in her head again, thinking of torture, dismemberment, capture- though this time she feared these things for her husband, even though he insisted on appearing bulletproof.

Even more uncomfortable was her time with Arabella and Clara. The new Mrs. Fassell brimming over with happiness and joy, and Arabella with a hatred so fierce towards her husband that she almost crackled with it when he walked into the room. Number One's wife hadn't said anything more about who to trust since their iPad conversation in her living room, but Lauren caught her eyeing all three of the men who ran Jaguar Holdings with the same look of loathing. It worried Lauren terribly that her friend seemed no longer able to hide her true emotions in the way she'd always had- under that veneer of sophistication.

"So you can see why it must be done," Thomas was saying and Lauren nodded without thinking.

"Of course," she agreed.

Her husband chuckled and she looked up, her cheeks already turning pink. "You haven't been paying attention darling," he teased gently. "I just suggested that you take a sledgehammer to your cello."

Lauren gasped in horror, both at the image and the fact that she'd been so distracted in front of her sharp-eyed spouse. "I'm sorry," she tried to smile, "I didn't mean to be such an airhead."

Thomas leaned back, one long finger absently rubbing over his lower lip as he watched her. "The question, darling," he said, "what is occupying you?" He continued to gaze at her as his wife's expressive face flushed and she shifted uncomfortably.

"I just..." with a sigh, Lauren gave in. She wasn't used to talking to her husband about her worries and fears, particularly because most of them were due to him. "I'm worried about Arabella," she confessed, "she has every reason to hate that bast- uh, Kingston." Thomas's eyes narrowed in amusement, but he said nothing, merely nodding at her to go on. "She doesn't seem to be able to control it, how she feels," Lauren tried to explain, "she so angry, and she should be! But..." The girl traced her fork through the crumbs on her plate. "I've never seen her not be able to keep it together, even when she's drunk. I'm worried she's going to snap and something terrible is going to happen." Lauren couldn't elaborate on what "something" would be, they both knew what that "something" would likely be. A quick execution and disappearance under the guise of Arabella "taking a long vacation" perhaps, or "retiring to the country." Staring down at the table, she swallowed miserably. She didn't even know what to ask Thomas to do. He'd made it clear he wouldn't interfere with that sick son of a bitch who was head of his precious Jaguar Holdings.

Thomas stirred; his beautiful face pensive. "I've known Arabella for over a decade, darling. Since her career in The Corporation brothel." He watched his wife's face as she simply nodded. He knew that she was aware of 'Bella's past. He admired her for not judging it. "This is the most serious mistake she's ever made. I do not know why she would make contact with Martinsson-"

"She didn't!" Lauren interrupted earnestly, "He was just there, and-" Her explanation broke off at his cold expression.

"Insisting on taking you there was not a mistake," Thomas said, his voice dipping to polar levels, "it was not a coincidence that Martinsson was there. There is a reason I have told you to distance yourself. I don't know what Bella is up to, but her actions thus far are foolhardy. But I believe she will regain her self-control. No matter what you think, she loves her position as Queen Bee." He watched as his wife drooped with sadness. "No matter what has happened to her darling, she will not let go of her place on the social scale. For this reason - if nothing else - I believe she'll pull herself together." He could tell Lauren didn't believe him, but she forced a smile and stood.

"I dropped by the Beau Boulangerie to pick up some of those chocolate eclairs you love," she picked up his dinner plate, and Thomas took her other hand, pulling her to a halt.

"Let's bring those upstairs with us, shall we?" With a high-pitched noise, Lauren hurried to do as he'd suggested.

Her worries about her friend came to a head the next week at a charity planning meeting. Arabella was dressed superbly in an alarmingly expensive suit. She was at her majestic best, presiding over the meeting, but Lauren could tell something was wrong. Her friend was moving stiffly, favoring her right side. And when everyone had filed out of the cafe where they'd met, Arabella side-stepped a confused Clara to drag Lauren out the back door.

"Bella?" Lauren was half-trotting, trying to keep up with the older woman as they headed down the alley. "What are you doing, honey? We need to get back- Chuck will be looking for me and whoever that mountain of muscle is, who's following you around isn't going to be that happy, so-"

"Relax!" laughed Mrs. Ben Kingston, "You're wound so tightly! Doesn't it feel good just to be free of everything for a minute?" There was a manic glint in her eyes as she looked back at Lauren teasingly, "Just for a moment, let's give them the slip."

She'd grown up in a city even larger than this one, but Lauren suddenly felt the buildings closing in on them as Arabella hauled her down a side street, looking behind them to see if they'd been followed. Her pulse sped faster, and she could feel sweat breaking out on her forehead, under her arms. This was a bad idea. A very bad idea. There were many people who didn't like their husbands. Lots of people. Any of those people could be... "Bella, I don't like this," Lauren managed, "it isn't safe, you know that. And we're going to get into a lot of trouble when-"

"Just for a minute!" The woman's voice pitched high, and she squeezed the Lauren's hand harder. "Just for a minute so we can talk without those apes hanging over us, listening to every word. Please, honey? Just for a minute?"

Shaking her head despairingly, she let Arabella draw her into a little bar. As her friend downed one drink and asked for another, Lauren watched her in concern. "How are you, really? You're moving kind of funny. Has he hurt you again?"

Arabella gave a little chuckle, gurgling a bit as it mixed with her recent swallow of vodka. "Again?" She put down the glass and took a deep breath. "This can't go on. I've tried to live with *him* - with what The Corporation does - but it must stop. And we must make it happen." The light flashed off the huge diamond on her left hand as she took another gulp of her cocktail.

Lauren's mouth dropped open. "Honey, you can't talk like this. It's nuts to even be saying this out loud. Let's go-"

"You're not listening TO ME!" Arabella drew in a breath as heads turned to look at them. "We can stop this, but I need you. There are people, friends who can help us, but-"

"No no no," Lauren shook her head, pulling away, "is this about the Grey Man, about-"

"Shhh!" hissed the other woman, "He's meeting us here in a moment, it's the only way we can talk safely."

Leaning in close, Lauren whispered furiously, "I can't believe you dragged me into this- you must be nuts, Arabella! Do you think that man gives a shit about you? I'm leaving and I don't want to ever talk to you about-"

"Mrs. Williams. It's time to go." Chuck's voice was emotionless as he stepped behind her.

Staring at his blank brown eyes, Lauren thought, "Oh, *fuck.*"

Back to wearing holes in her husband's expensive oriental rugs, Lauren numbly counted her footsteps. Fifteen steps to the fireplace... He would never believe she wasn't in on whatever mess the unhinged Mrs. Kingston was planning. She knew it looked terrible, sneaking off without Chuck and how he found them, how she was leaning over whispering like she was planning, plotting with her so-called former friend. Biting back a sob, she rubbed her hands over her bare arms. After everything he'd just done, Thomas thought he did it for her but it was for The Corporation, for him. But the controlled savagery of making her father kill her attacker? This would look like utter disloyalty. Would he even believe she didn't know anything about it? That Arabella was throwing her under the bus? What would even make that woman even *think* she'd go in on this suicidal plan? Lauren might be new to the terrifying world she lived in, but she was very clear after numerous business dinners and Corporation cocktail parties that there were worse monsters than the one she was married to. Far worse. What would Thomas be like when he came home? What would... stifling her moan, Lauren counted. Thirty-five steps back to the hallway...

"Is there anything you'd like to tell me before your punishment?"

Lauren whirled with a little embarrassing squeak. Thomas was standing in the entryway; she hadn't even heard him come in. Hands casually in his pockets, still looking as groomed and put-together as he had leaving the house that morning. "Thomas, I..." *My mouth is so damn dry,* she thought, *I wish I had a gigantic glass of wine right now- no, a jug of wine-* because it didn't seem like she could force the words out to explain to him that it was just a misunderstanding and that-

"Nothing, darling?" he bit the last word off as if it was distasteful.

"It wasn't my idea; I didn't plan it. Arabella just sort of dragged me out the back door of the restaurant and-"

In two long steps, her terrifying husband was looking down at her, his warm breath hitting her skin. "Dragged you. Did she drag you against your will, kicking and screaming? With no chance to alert Straker, who is there for your safety?" Thomas's voice rose into a sharp shout on the last word and Lauren tried to step away from him. One hand shot out and took her by the upper arm, long fingers wrapping around it as he turned towards the stairs, pulling her along.

Thomas had been on fire with fury since Straker had called to alert him that Lauren had slipped his scrutiny and was out somewhere, unattended, with that idiot Arabella. Who was concerned for no one's safety but her own. The looks of suspicion and amusement from Numbers One and Three, staring at him as Kingston also received a call to let him know his wife had slipped her chain. Fassell, that idiot had chuckled heartlessly. "Just got a call from my sweet girl. She's so very worried about her two friends just-" the man had the gall to put up his hands with two fingers, wiggling them mockingly, "-disappearing. Fortunately, I can always count on Clara to do as she's told."

His grip tightened slightly as he felt Lauren stumble on the stair behind him, and Thomas lifted her up effortlessly, pulling her along to the third floor and bypassing their bedroom as he opened the door to the room that held so many options for discipline.

He'd called out several employees to start the search until Straker had called back within five minutes. Of course, the tracker on his wife's phone. And the one sewn into her messenger bag. So really, just three hundred seconds of what Thomas realized had been bone-searing terror ripping through him. Three hundred seconds of wondering who'd kidnapped his Lauren and what they were doing to her. Three hundred seconds as he'd raced from the top floor of the office and down to his car to picture her lifeless eyes, her broken and bleeding body. And the fifteen-minute drive home to realize just how terrified he'd been. How weak. And how angry he was now. But Thomas refused to leave the Jaguar for another twenty minutes until he was sure he had his temper under control, and his rage at the panic he'd felt at the thought of Lauren gone.

"This merits correction. You can't be surprised by this."

She let out a sob, he could hear her voice waver as Lauren attempted to plead with him. "Thomas, please just-" the words were cut off as he flipped up the leather-padded benchtop of the long ottoman and lifted her swiftly, putting her inside the barred enclosure.

"Bad girls do not receive the privilege of speaking. You will have to earn back your freedom, one step at a time." He saw the shock in her lavender eyes, her mouth open as he shut the top of the bench and locked it. Walking over to the armoire and pouring a drink from the bar there, Thomas counted down, waiting for her scream of outrage. *Five... four... three... two... one...*

"WHAT ARE YOU DOING? ARE YOU INSANE? GET ME OUT OF HERE!"

Even though his eyes were a polar frost blue, Thomas's mouth quirked up on one side.

The Corporation's Second in Command was reading a book and sipping from his scotch comfortably, legs feet propped up on the padded ottoman that contained his wife. He ignored her thrashing and kicking in the narrow enclosure and even grinned when her hands made it through the bars, trying to slap at his legs. This was actually the first time he had used the ottoman for this purpose, and Thomas was quite pleased with its functionality. His feet were comfortable on the leather-covered bench and the bars were wide enough that he could see his wife and she could see him, even the space left very little wiggle room for her.

He'd been enjoying the book, a series of essays by philosopher David Hume that he found in Lauren's stack of volumes on her side of their bed. He had a similar pile on his side as well and they often exchanged books to enjoy something the other had read to them. In fact, there had been several very pleasant winter nights when the fireplace was crackling and Lauren's head was on his lap, smiling as he read to her in his beautiful sonorous voice as his fingers idly combed through her hair. His smile disappeared and his jaw firmed. He'd been too lenient with this girl. Too soft. Telling her about his scar! "Thomas?" He turned a page, taking another sip. "Thomas?" she persisted, "How long are you keeping me in here?"

He knew she was listening carefully, there was utter silence beneath his propped feet, so she could hear another page in his book turn. "Each time you speak," he said calmly, "an additional hour will be added to your containment time."

As he expected, this set off another round of bar rattling and kicking at the bench's seat as she screamed at the top of her lungs, "This isn't my fault! I didn't run away! I wasn't plotting anything and Arabella-"

With a sigh, Thomas moved his feet, lifting the lid and rapidly chaining his bride's wrists to the bars above her and her ankles to the bars at her feet. When she opened her mouth to scream at him again, he pointed a finger at her. "Take responsibility for your actions. You knew it wasn't safe. You ran off with Arabella like a child and put your life in danger. You terrified Straker, who has come to care for you like a daughter. You made yourself a target and a potential liability, just as she is, to Kingston and Fassell. And you..." Thomas could feel his fury and his fear heating up again, and he took a deep breath. "And you have deeply disappointed me. You have lost my trust."

Slamming the lid shut again, he gritted his teeth shut, wanting to shout at his foolish, irresponsible wife for terrifying him, furious that he *was* terrified for her. He listened, waiting for her to plead with him again, writhe in her handcuffs like a demented eel. But Lauren was silent. Thomas stood, stretching a bit. "You have another hour in containment because of your outburst, as warned. I'm going downstairs to order dinner."

"Wha-" the query shut off instantly as his footsteps slowed. With a dark smile, Thomas left the room, shutting the door behind him.

Lauren could not know, of course, that he monitored her on his phone, making sure she didn't injure herself in her thrashing. Lauren started kicking at the bars the moment shut the door, setting off a furious string of profanity that made one brow raise in amusement. After idly examining some takeaway menus, he ordered something to be delivered in a couple of hours. Just enough time for the next step.

There was no way to tell time in the goddamn fucking Fun Dungeon, Lauren thought, angrily kicking at the bars again. She hated that mean son of a bitch bastard! Locking her in this cage like a dog? That's right, she'd asked him during her first foray into this room if this was a cage for an animal. She stilled as the door finally opened. "There's my sweet pet. Have you been a good girl?" Thomas tilted his head to look through the bars of the bench. His wife was staring back at him, lips firmly pressed together. "Ah. You may speak now, darling. Choose your words carefully."

"May I please come out of here, Sir?"

Good girl, Thomas thought, remembering the right words for her role in this room. "Are you prepared to take responsibility for your own actions?"

Her voice was a little strangled this time. "Yes, Sir."

"Very well." Flipping the lid of the ottoman up, he deftly unfastened the handcuffs around her wrists and ankles, holding his hand out to pull her from the box. Lauren's hands tightened on the edge of her cage, sitting up. He knew she didn't want to touch him, didn't want to accept help. So that clever mind was analyzing whether there would be a consequence for refusing his assistance. Just as Thomas was about to issue another punishment, she gingerly took his big, warm hand and rose to her feet. He held her elbow for a moment as she regained her balance and hastily stepped from the cage. Thomas moved to sit on the corner of the bed. He'd removed his jacket, and she watched apprehensively as he rolled up the sleeves of his pale blue shirt. "Come here."

Lauren's brow furrowed and she looked at the door and then back to him. He wouldn't make her do something now, would he? When she hated him so much? Slowly moving to obey him, she stood between his spread legs. "Kneel." Staring at him, the girl could feel her insides turn to ice. This was a different Thomas, cold and withdrawn from her. There was still an alarming look of genial amusement on his face, but it was nothing she'd seen directed at her before. Maybe he showed this face to people he killed? Legs shaking from that thought, she knelt quickly and gracelessly. Pulling off his tie, Thomas held it in his hand, watching her gaze turn fearful, staring at it. "Look at me," he ordered. When Lauren obeyed, he put his other hand under her chin, lifting it.

"What did you do today, pet?" Her lips tightened at the new nickname, but she answered.

"I left the restaurant without alerting Chuck. I made him worry."

Thomas's head tilted. "What else?"

A bitter tone crept into her speech, but Lauren remained composed. "I made you look bad in front of the rest of management. I put myself in danger for not sticking with Chuck." She clenched her hands into fists in her lap, trying to stay composed. Her husband didn't look angry, or disgusted, or concerned. He just looked... indifferent. Slightly indulgent like she was a poodle begging for scraps.

"That's not all, is it?" His deep voice was like granite.

"I..." horrified, Lauren could feel herself start to cry and tried to swallow the tears down. "I disappointed you. You don't trust me anymore."

Thomas nodded. "You will have to earn that back. One step at a time." He could tell she was forcing down her tears and her resentment was poorly hidden. "Very well, let's continue." He patted his lap. "Lean over my legs."

The look of furious shock onher face was almost comical. She knew this position, though she'd not had a punishment spanking since her first week here. "I..." her mouth opened and closed a couple of times as Lauren slowly got to her feet. She glanced at the door again, and Thomas mentally added it to her growing list of bad behavior.

Bending over his lap, she settled her hips into one long thigh as her breasts rested against the other. She closed her eyes as Thomas yanked her skirt off, and then her lace underwear. But then he briskly gathered her wrists together and bound them with his tie. It was tight against her skin and the position he used pushed her hands up between her shoulder blades. Trying to move them only hurt worse. "You have committed three major offenses today. You'll receive twenty strikes for each offense." Lauren sagged in horror? Sixty? He'd *never* spanked her like that. And then the words she hated the most. "You will count each time I spank you and thank me for it."

The first slap of his hand on her ass made Lauren give a shocked little shriek. It hurt- so much more than any other- "OW!"

"You will count each one and thank me for it," her monstrous husband's voice was implacable.

"O-one," Lauren gasped, "thank you, Sir."

By the seventeenth slap, her ass was already a glowing red and Thomas showed no signs of slowing down. By the twenty-fifth, Lauren was sobbing. Suddenly his equally crimson palm was lifted in front of her face. "This won't do," he said, "ah, I know..." Lauren started crying harder when he slipped his leather driving gloves on.

"Ah! God, ple- twenty-six, S- sir," she hiccupped. By the fiftieth slap, the lower half of her body was a medley of purples, reds and searing pink. Lauren wasn't capable of counting anymore, so Thomas took over for her. She wasn't crying anymore when he finished, her body limp over his lap.

Untying her wrists, Thomas spoke, "You think this was a cruel punishment. You have no idea- NO idea-" he yanked her upright on his lap, ignoring her pained yelp as her brutalized skin met his hard thigh. "No idea what would be done to you if the wrong person found you. Do you think that piece of shite Martinsson would help you?" He felt her stiffen and his suspicions were confirmed.

"That's who-" Lauren painfully cleared her throat, "that's who Arabella was trying to meet."

"Yes," Thomas agreed, then slipped her underwear and skirt back on. The lace was acutely painful against her ass, and she moaned in protest.

"Can I please have some of the lotion, the-" Lauren began.

"No," was all he said before standing. "Come downstairs, it's time for dinner."

Lauren nearly started crying again when it was clear her husband expected her to sit on one of the wooden kitchen chairs. She thought of asking for a pillow, but if he said "no" to cooling cream, she wasn't going to set herself up to be denied again.

The food tasted like ash in her mouth, but she mechanically ate the amount she thought would be enough to keep him from ordering her to eat more. The room was silent, Thomas ate quickly, efficiently while Lauren moved very carefully from one hip to another, trying to find a resting spot that didn't torment her blistered ass. When he was finished, the man leaned back and looked her over.

"Go upstairs and take a cool bath. I'll be up shortly."

Grateful for the noise of the water, Lauren dissolved into tears again in the privacy of the bathroom. She *hated* him. She hated Thomas so fucking much. She wouldn't be in danger if *he* hadn't placed her in it. Then he had to drag Chuck into it, which really was awful and made her feel terrible, especially since her husband had said: "You terrified Straker, who has come to care for you like a daughter." Did he? Did Chuck really care about her like that? God, he didn't get in trouble because of this, did he?

"Oh, shit..." she whispered. Lauren could totally see The Corporation having some kind of scary-ass consequence for something like this. Thomas walked in as she floated in the tub, tears running down her red cheeks. "Did you hurt Chuck?" she burst out, "You didn't do- it was my fault, not his! He wouldn't expect me to run off, I've never done that he wouldn't expect it this isn't his fault please don't-"

Pleased that his wife was finally beginning to understand the seriousness of her actions, Thomas put up a hand to stop her anxious flow of words. "I did not. Had he truly lost you, he would have been killed for his stupidity." Watching her fresh flow of tears for a moment, the man finally walked over, kneeling beside the tub and his sobbing wife. "There now," his voice could not have been smoother, more soothing, "no more tears." Taking the washcloth, he liberally soaped every inch of her front, gently wiping her face free of tears and makeup.

Chapter 31 – Saint Margaret and the Dragon

In which Lauren finds her inner Badass Saint, and Thomas learns about this thing called Expressing Your Feelings.

Waking up the next morning, Lauren felt exactly like she had on her first day as Mrs. Thomas Williams. Hauling hauling herself stiffly out of bed, pressing her lips together. She was - as she expected - alone, but if that son of a bitch bastard was still in the house, he wouldn't hear *her* crying. No fucking way. Brutal spanking like the first day? Check. Terrified of the man who made her marry him? Check. Very carefully pulling on her softest underwear, she looked at her backside, twisting her neck awkwardly to see at the blooms of purple and grey blossoming like an ugly garden on her bottom and thighs. Lauren's mouth trembled before she firmed it. This wasn't like the first day. Along with the fear and the fury was hurt. Her hurt and sadness were much stronger than the other two emotions- enough to make her feel like her heart was bleeding in her chest. "I should probably go running..." Lauren mumbled, staring at her closet door blankly. "Stretch my legs, get the blood flowing..."

With a sigh, she finally pulled a lightweight jersey sundress on and wandered downstairs. She hadn't brushed her hair or teeth but seriously, Lauren thought, who cares? Who fucking cares? Her stubborn Scottish nature was trying to prod a little righteous anger out from under that lead blanket of sorrow, but it seemed like too much effort.

"Good morning, Miss Lauren."

To her embarrassment, she let out a screech that sounded a bit like a barn owl's and whirled around. Oh, thank god. Chuck. Chuck!

"Oh, god, Chuck!" Lauren gasped, "Are you all right? You didn't get like... whatever happens if something goes wrong? It wasn't your fault, I'm just so sorry, I would never mean to-"

Her bodyguard quickly and efficiently cut her off. "Miss Lauren, it is behind us. No harm came to you, but I trust you understand that your safety is my singular purpose?"

His brown eyes were warmer this morning, and Lauren nodded rapidly, "I'm so very sorry. I wouldn't want any harm to come to you, either." They nodded together, each understanding the other.

While her apology to her ominous, armed shadow made the girl feel better, she refused to think of giving one to Thomas. He *was* a monster. Why did she keep pretending otherwise? "He took his apology along with the skin off my butt," Lauren muttered bitterly, low enough to make sure Chuck wouldn't hear in the other room.

But she did remember the alarm that swept over her as Arabella dragged her down the sidewalk. She knew the feeling of being exposed, unprotected. Why did she follow along like the woman's pet sheep? Sitting down abruptly, Lauren fought the sense of desolation threatening to swamp her.

Was Number One's wife really her friend at all, or was Lauren just "useful" as Number Two's wife? Was she manipulating Clara this way?

Absently rubbing her hands on her thigh, she realized she didn't have any friends at all, not really. Her friends back home received the most careful possible messages, nothing trackable on social media and when anyone suggested flying over for a visit, Lauren had to find a new excuse: on vacation... traveling with the orchestra... she didn't dare expose any of them to the scrutiny of The Corporation. Clara. Maybe? But the girl felt more like someone to protect, not confide in. Macie was gone. Forever. Thomas was her husband. Sometimes her lover, most times her Sir. She had thought for a while he was maybe coming to love her a little.

After last night and that cage and the spanking? Lauren shuddered. God, that was mean. Irritably pushing the heel of her hand against her eyes, she tried to keep the tears from welling up again. She'd been trapped in this luxurious, deadly prison to keep her father alive. The man who'd proved quite decisively that he didn't give a shit about her. Staring at the green of their little garden outside the kitchen window, Lauren wondered what she was going to do for the rest of her life. What would happen when she was no longer skilled enough to play in the orchestra? Music was who she was. And at this point, the only thing keeping her sane.

"Chuck?" she called, "We're going out."

Pulling up in front of the old stone church again, her bodyguard hesitated for a moment before getting out to assist her.

Lauren looked up, puzzled. "I need you to open the door, remember, Chuck?" It never failed to infuriate her that the man engaged the child locks in the back seat when they traveled as if she was an untrustworthy toddler who might squirm free from her booster seat and try to escape. "Dude?"

Hands still on the steering wheel at positions ten and two, the man flexed his fingers. "I only wished to determine if you were in a... fit state to speak to the priest."

Her brow furrowed. "A fit state?" Oh. Mouth firm to keep her from hissing, Lauren nodded. "I see. No, I'm fine. Despite yesterday's, uh, stuff. I would never say a word. There won't be any reason to do anything. To anyone."

"Of course," he agreed politely and moved to open her door for her, trailing along as her ever-present dark-suited shadow.

Lauren had no particular intent when she wanted to return to the little stone church that had once sheltered her. It just seemed like the only place that would hold any peace on such a miserable day. She wouldn't even talk to the nice priest. She'd just... sit there for a while. But of course, Lauren lit a fresh candle for her mother and stuffed another fistful of notes in the donation box, and there he was, right behind her.

"Ah, you've returned, my Scottish friend. Here for more philosophy from the homeland?"

Despite his quiet, calm voice, Lauren jumped and put her hand over her heart again. "You would think I'd be less jumpy in a church right, Father?"

The older man chuckled, "Not necessarily. People come here seeking calm, but that doesn't mean they arrive with it." His gentle gaze observed the bitter twist to her mouth before she nodded politely. He swept a hand toward the pews. "Would you like to sit for a moment?"

Eyeing the hard, wooden pews as the bruises on her bottom throbbed ominously, Lauren sighed. "Yeah, not today, thank you." She was intrigued by the fact that the priest had to know Chuck was with her, but he seemed to ignore the bodyguard's existence. Not rudely, more as if Chuck was simply part of the scenery.

"All right," he nodded. "Are you interested in Gothic era architecture?"

Lauren's mood lifted slightly. The man was so kind but so quirky. "Actually Father, yes, I think I am."

So they circled the little chapel, the priest narrating, "You'll notice the ogival, always in threes... You look a bit unwell today, my child."

Shrugging awkwardly, Lauren mumbled, "Oh, I didn't get much sleep last night."

"Ah. And the flying buttress, a classic element from this era. You'll see that the stone setting denotes..."

Chuck, sitting in the precise center of the chapel so he could watch them at any angle, smothered a yawn with one battered fist.

Head cocked, Lauren was trying to determine the identity of the subject of a brilliantly colored stained glass window. "Who is this, Father?"

"One of the more cunning female saints," he was beaming as if she'd complimented his cooking or the color he'd selected to paint the dining room. "Saint Margaret of Antioch. Her singular beauty attracted the attention of a Roman noble who pursued her relentlessly. She refused his godlessness and fled."

"What happened to her?"

The priest smiled, almost apologetically. "She was eventually caught and tortured to death."

"That seemed to happen a lot with the female saints," Lauren observed sourly, still enjoying the sound as he burst into laughter.

"When I speak of the saints," he mused, "I suggest that instead of thinking of their inevitable and often grisly deaths, think perhaps of the characteristics one might share with them." The priest smiled slightly at her skeptical expression.

"For instance..." he gestured at the stained glass window, a magnificent image of a female saint battling a dragon. "Saint Margaret. The story is familiar; abandoned by her parents, but as she refused the suit of the Roman Governor, her story grew. Various miracles occurring through her efforts to evade the evil that followed her, bringing more and more people to Christ from her example. At the height of her struggle, we are told she is swallowed whole by Satan in the form of a massive dragon- who was forced to spit her out because the cross she carried irritated its insides dreadfully."

Lauren looked at the stained-glass image again. "The girl was hardcore, Father."

He laughed delightedly. "Indeed. While it is easy to assume a magic cross was responsible for her victory over Evil, I choose to interpret the cross as her unflinching belief that what she was doing was right. And that in the end, it would save the countrymen she loved."

The sun shone through the pale blues and greens of the window, lighting Lauren's eyes. "I don't have that," she said sadly.

The priest shrugged, straightening his collar. "While I know this is only our second meeting," he observed, "I would disagree."

Eyeing Chuck, shifting in the uncomfortable wooden pew, she said, "Thank you for your time, Father. I..." Lauren laughed a little, "I actually feel really... good, right now?"

He chuckled, eyes brightening approvingly. "Excellent. May I offer a blessing?"

"Thank you," she bowed her head, appreciating the gentle weight of his hand on her hair as he spoke soft Latin phrases. As she was walking out, Chuck at her shoulder, Lauren turned back for a moment. "I'm sorry my memory is so faulty on my saints. What was St. Margaret of Antioch the patron saint of?"

Somehow, she was not surprised when he answered almost gleefully, "The patron saint of impossible cases."

Lauren was standing in the doorway of the Fun Dungeon, a room she no longer characterized as "fun" at all. She was staring at the long, low bench where her dark and confusing husband had imprisoned her the night before.

Of everything Thomas had done to her as "correction," that was the worst. It was cruel. Even for her husband at his most enraged and terrifying, it was unnecessarily cruel. Degrading. Thomas enjoyed her obedience. Her submission. But he'd never humiliated her for pleasure.

"So eager for another round, darling? I suppose I could clear my schedule."

Her eyes closed. Of course, that smooth bastard would sneak up on her. He probably didn't even try to. "How was your day, dear?" Smooth over fear and hurt with sarcasm. Thomas leaned in to lightly kiss her cheek, not missing her flinch when his lips touched her skin.

"Oh, business is such boring talk," her husband's voice was still so damnably beautiful, deep, almost purring as he leaned in again. "And what has my sweet wife been doing all day?"

She couldn't stand it, couldn't bear him standing so close to her so Lauren pushed off the doorway and stepped around Thomas. "I'm sure Chuck and your various surveillance systems will have a full report for you." Thomas stiffened slightly, eyes narrowing. But her tone wasn't angry, just flat, resigned. "I'll go start dinner."

"Don't bother," Lauren stopped as he spoke from behind her. "I have a business dinner tonight." Thomas turned and walked into their bedroom.

Playing furiously on her cello, then her bass guitar, moving to her piano, and finally rotating back to the cello, Lauren sawed mechanically through her practice session, her conversation with the priest at the little stone church going round and round in her head. She was no saint, that was certain. Lauren snorted a little at the idea. She'd developed a mouth that could make a sailor blush. She knew that clever, kindly priest was trying to guide her into some kind of heroics, some genius move that would perhaps save Thomas from committing more evil, prevent his inevitable transformation into the murderous, repellant Number One. The priest couldn't know exactly what kind of evil she was battling against, but he somehow knew she was in the middle of something dark.

Her bow slowed to a stop on the strings as she thought it through.

The Corporation was the dragon- ready to swallow Thomas whole. There was more good in him that her husband was prepared to admit. He was capable of tenderness, passion, protectiveness... at one point, she'd dared think capable of love.

Could she save Thomas? Did he *want* to be saved? Would he ever be willing to picture another path in life than the deadly one he walked?

Lauren rested her head on the neck of her cello, unaware that the rosin on the strings was painting white stripes across her cheek. The concept of turning into the warrior saint that the priest seemed certain she could be seemed ridiculous. She'd gotten by in life by being her mother's "good girl," a loyal friend, a hard worker. But "fierce" was not a word ever used to describe her. And if she tried to battle for Thomas's heart, could he ever be capable of loving her?

She thought back to the night on the dance floor where she knew she'd never leave him. So would she just... stay leashed in a collar, clipping the chain on herself? Lauren chuckled mirthlessly, pouring another glass of wine. Even with the need she felt for her husband, that sounded pathetic. But in her past life, if she'd ever asked herself: "What's the worst thing he could do?" it would have involved a breakup or some minor humiliation. she shuddered in spite of herself. The "worst that could happen," by Thomas Williams's definition was utterly terrifying to contemplate.

Thomas was swirling his glass of Jameson, looking attentive

with a light, sardonic smile while in reality having no idea what Monsieur Boucher was talking about. The French arms dealer was visibly disappointed that Lauren did not accompany him that night. Williams hadn't been surprised that Arabella was "ill" as well, leaving the tremulous Clara to attempt to act as hostess at the dinner. He looked at her and smiled warmly with a nod, which the girl seemed grateful for. Michael had mainly ignored his bride during the dinner to exchange in filthy banter with Boucher's adult son, who was well on his way to becoming as blood-stained as his father. Forcing himself to look chagrined, Thomas bowed out after the last small cups of coffee and Creme Brule were consumed. "Forgive me, I have a series of conference calls with Moscow in the morning, and there are still files I must go over."

He and "The Butcher" were standing a bit apart from the rest of the increasingly raucous dinner group, politely shaking hands.

"Of course," the man said, before hesitating a moment. An expression of concern crossed his plump face, making the arms dealer look even more like someone's grandfather. "This... partnership," he said with a frown, "it is as you expected?"

Thomas arched an elegant brow. Discussing dealings with other criminal organizations was Simply Not Done. "I have no idea what you're talking about, my friend." His tone dropped to a lower register, making his smooth tone sound vaguely threatening.

But Boucher was unwilling to let the matter drop, and his expression almost made it look like the man cared. "Loyalty is not constant with that organization," he said quickly, aware the others were rising from the table. "I would not like to see you surprised by this."

Number Two at Jaguar Holdings eyed the Frenchman thoughtfully. "I appreciate your concern?"

"Ah," Boucher said, his genial expression returned and in place, "I do have a gift for your bride." He gestured to an assistant, who brought out a small white box, wrapped in a pretty purple ribbon. Thomas looked at it, a little confused. The man who sold surface to air missiles to both sides on several different conflicts had thought to bring a gift to Lauren?

"It's lavender honey from the nunnery she and I discussed when we dined last. I traveled there this winter, just to visit. It sounded so enchanting, as described by Mrs. Williams."

"And how did it appear to you?" Thomas inquired, interested despite the oddness of the exchange.

The Frenchman looked a little sad. "I suspect all things are more beautiful as seen through the eyes of your bride."

Thomas gingerly took the box, oddly conflicted as he thanked Boucher for the gift. "I am certain Lauren will be very touched and pleased, thank you, Phillippe." Driving home, he circled around the odd conversation with the arms dealer. "The Butcher" being troubled about their association with Bratva? His grandfatherly fondness for his wife? It was... irregular. Something Thomas disliked. He spent most of his existence analyzing every move and reaction for variables. This entire night had been an unseen variable, from Lauren's coldness to this old man's warmth. A little confused, he let himself into the house, letting Chuck go for the night.

"Any problems tonight?" he suddenly asked.

Chuck, his hand on the front door handle, turned slightly

with a look of polite inquiry. "Not at all, Mr. Williams. Mrs. Williams stayed in her conservatory all night, practicing. The London Symphony Orchestra series for this next month seems to have some rather fierce-sounding pieces of music." He waited politely at Number Two frowned at him thoughtfully until the man collected himself and sent him home. Walking down the steps, Lauren's bodyguard allowed himself a very small smile, really just a curve upwards of one side of his mouth. Rare to see his employer looking... unsettled?

Climbing the stairs to the third floor, Thomas paused on the landing. There was silence from above, so Lauren was likely asleep, or even more likely pretending to be. He'd always been amused by her favorite method of avoiding him. But the bed was empty, still neatly made and no telltale shower steam from the bathroom. Brow furrowed, Thomas stepped out into the hall again.

The door to their 'playroom' was still open, but he was still surprised to see his timid bride seated in one of the big leather armchairs. Leaning against the door and folding his arms, he gave her his most infuriating expression of urbane amusement. "Darling, I do believe you're attempting to send me a signal here, lounging in our "special" room like this."

Lauren stared at him with an unreadable expression. Thomas felt a small twinge of tenderness to see the rosin marks across her cheek. His musically gifted wife always seemed to have those white bits smeared somewhere on her person. But he could tell she was attempting a forbidding expression, so the man kept himself from smirking.

"I was just looking around," Lauren finally said, deliberately placing her bare feet on the long ottoman she'd be trapped in the night before, "wondering how it felt for you to have me thrashing around and begging you to let me out of this dog cage. Wondering if you enjoyed it."

"It's not a dog cage, darling," Thomas strolled into the room, running a hand along a length of rope hanging from a ceiling hook. "It's a 'pet' cage. Quite a different thing." He could tell she was fighting to keep calm.

"That's not what it felt like!" It was the angriest he'd ever heard his sweet bride, and his eyes narrowed.

"Be careful, pet, you will want to think now, before you speak." Thomas's voice was always beautiful, elegant, rich. But when he lowered his already deep tone, it was ominous.

Lauren rose from the chair, walking to him. "You asked me there - in the hall - if I had anything I wanted to tell you before my 'punishment,' but then you had no interest in what I was trying to tell you."

He rolled his eyes irritably. "You had nothing to say but excuses, reasons why the whole idiotic adventure was not your fault. Like a child."

Her lips pressed together angrily. "Arabella was my friend!" Thomas noted the past tense in that sentence. "She'd been beaten within an inch of her life, and she was desperate when she dragged me out the door. I thought if she could talk to me freely without anyone listening to report back, I could maybe..." Lauren hesitated, her pretty face turning sad. "Help her?"

Thomas made an irritable noise, brushing past his bride to pace, hands on his hips. "I made it quite clear you were not to spend time with her! You chose to disobey-"

"Haven't you ever had a friend?" Lauren interrupted him, for the first time she could remember and feeling both terrified and giddy. "Someone who needed you? Maybe the only friend they could count on?"

His first thought was to throw his outrageously insolent wife over his lap and spank some sense into her, and then Thomas was chilled by the memory of Lauren trying to get through to him in their bathroom that night, how it made him feel disgusted with himself. Weak. So Thomas took in a deep breath and waited until he was calm again. "My actions - my friends - have no bearing on your behavior or what I expect from you.
"My requirements are always quite clear, and they are in place for your continued survival, little girl! Do you really think Arabella gives a *second* of thought in that apparently empty blonde head for you? For your *safety?* That is my task, and Straker's. How dare you question-" And she did it again, his suddenly, *clearly* insane wife interrupted him *again*.

"You care about my safety?" Lauren pounced, "Not just that I'd die and make you look bad as a scary Crime Lord, but that you really care?" He was staring at her as if she'd grown a tail, and the incongruous image of the three tails attached to plugs she'd spotted in the armoire accosted her, and the girl had to swallow down a hysterical giggle.

"I..." a frown crossed her husband's beautiful face, and she held her breath. Thomas growled and took her by the arm, hustling Lauren from the room. "You're a grown woman, and you know that your safety and that of your admittedly worthless father's rests upon your good behavior." Thomas shut the door to the room with a loud "thunk!" of the heavy door. "Nothing has changed from my original requirements for you as my wife."

"Thomas, just-" Lauren started, but he cut her off.

"I have work to do in my study. Go to bed." He turned on his heel and headed for the stairs, and she almost shouted the next words.

"WE CAN BE MORE THAN THIS! We ARE more than this! I'm not a dog that you have to discipline- I'm your wife, Thomas! Don't-" his back was to her, but he could hear the hitch of her breath as she tried not to cry, "don't turn me into Arabella. We're not them."

He hesitated for a moment, his broad shoulders stiff, then her husband calmly descended to the next floor, and she heard the click of his office door.

It was an hour before Thomas climbed the stairs to his bedroom, tie loosened and even another liberal application of Jameson failing to restore his cool equanimity. Lauren was not as instructed asleep, she was curled up in the window seat, staring out to the darkened park across the street. She stiffened as he opened the door, but she didn't turn her head to look at him.

"I put you in the cage because I was furious you ran away. Because I was terrified that I didn't know if you were alive or dead. Because I could not believe I was still capable of terror. Because all I could think to do was to lock you in a cage and just... keep you." Thomas couldn't seem to stop the words from flowing from him but Lauren turned and those huge lavender eyes were wet.

She gave a little, watery laugh. "Don't you see it, Thomas? I hold the door to my cage closed without you ever needing to lock it." His dark brows drew together in a little confusion, but she rose, taking small, cautious steps toward her husband. "I'm not trying to run away. But you can be so beautiful to me, and then- that stuff. Making me ashamed, making me feel worthless. You don't want an Arabella. And I can't be one. Because-" Lauren started crying but she got the words out, "because that would make you Number One."

Thomas felt like he'd been punched in the chest. "Come here, Lauren." She let him wrap her in his arms and simply stood, rocking slightly as she forced herself to stop weeping. "I shamed you. I intended to. Because I was disgusted with myself for feeling terror. I'm sorry. This is the second time I have apologized to you, and the second time in the last twenty years that I have apologized at all."

Her voice was a little muffled because his sweet wife's face was buried in his chest. "I'm sorry for terrifying you. But I'm glad you care enough to be terrified. But I won't do that to you again."

She felt the deep chuckle from his chest. "My sweet bride. So fierce tonight." He was kissing along the thin skin of her temple, sliding his lips down to her cheekbone, making soothing noises as he rubbed her back. Lauren surreptitiously wiped her nose on the back of her hand before raising her face to him.

Then, Thomas's mouth was on hers and her wet cheeks cupped in his big, warm hands and they were kissing, a little sloppy but urgent. "Lovely, beautiful girl..." It was hard to believe after how he'd made her feel the night before that she would ever want to feel his hands on her again, but the slide of the zipper on the back of her dress made her press closer to his chest, feeling his pleased rumble. Then they were on the bed, Lauren on her back with her fingers clutched in Thomas's curls as he kissed along the smooth skin of her stomach. "No one can hurt you," he murmured between kisses, "no one can be allowed to touch you. I must keep you safe."

Chapter 32 – I Won't Forget

In which Thomas and Lauren prepare to enter the Lion's Den.

Lauren was sore again the next morning, but cautiously stretching each arm and legs against the cool cotton sheets, this time, she didn't mind. Especially when the raspy cheek of her husband brushed against her smooth one. "Good morning, my bride," Thomas's voice was mesmerizing at any time - but in the morning, deeper, with a bit of a gritty edge - it was almost enough to make her come just by listening to him. He chuckled darkly when he felt her little shiver. "So sensitive this morning, little girl. I thought I might have rubbed you raw last night."

Making a bit of a groan, Lauren buried her face in the pillow. "You and your... sexy talk. And that Voice. You're giving me chills, Thomas!" She wiggled helplessly as his long fingers trailed down the curve of her waist and over her hip.

"Hmmmm..." he grunted, "you seem quite limber for a girl begging me to stop last night."

"That was this morning," the girl laughed helplessly, "and it was the third time. I don't know how you have any fluids left in your body." Lauren shivered again as he made that growling noise as he slunk down to her pelvis, looking very much like the animal The Corporation was named for.

"Poor darling," Thomas soothed mendaciously.

When Thomas finally dressed her quite some time later, he handed her a pretty white box while he zipped up her dress.

"What's this?" Lauren was turning the box over, looking for a notecard.

"It's from Monsieur Boucher," he answered, kissing the back of her neck. "He was quite disappointed that you weren't there last night."

She smiled, shaking her head at the thought that the man with the face of a grandfather and the soul of a monster thought to bring her a gift. Thomas put his chin on her shoulder as she unwrapped it. "It's from the nunnery in Italy!" she marveled, "The one we'd talked about at that business dinner last fall."

"Yes," he dropped another kiss on her shoulder and turned to dress. "He said he wanted to go back and visit after your description of the place."

Lauren carefully put the little jars of honey back in their tissue nest in the box, smiling to herself. If she could touch a man like Boucher - even a little bit - maybe she could find a way inside Thomas's hardened heart for good.

A mere handful of days later, and Mr. and Mrs. Williams were packing to head for St. Petersburg.

Lauren couldn't crush the feeling of intense anxiety- it all felt wrong. Though her husband was as calm and confident as ever, she couldn't shake the feeling that they were walking into the lion's den. Thomas watched her, mouth set and her lovely eyes the grey-purple shade of a sunset on the edge of a storm.

"What worries you, sweetness?"

She dipped her head and smiled then, still a little giddy every time he used that tone- tender and patient.

When he pulled the dress she was folding away from her and drew Lauren on to his lap, she leaned into him. "This is- it all feels wrong, Thomas," she sighed. "I know I don't know all the workings of The Corporation, but this feels... off. Did you see Kingston's face last night?"

Granted, it had been a rough evening, the "End of Season" cocktail party for the LSO, with the musicians scattering for a couple of months of freedom before rehearsals began again. To Lauren's deep relief, in her review with the LSO Board, they had lauded her first season with the group and even gave her a small raise. And she was warmed to sense that it was solely on her merits.

She was beginning to see the "tells" now when people were speaking to her but thinking about her deadly husband. There had been none of that during her board review. So naturally, Lauren's happiness as Thomas escorted her into the party was immediately crushed by the alarming interest from Number One.

"Well, here's our little musical prodigy!" he praised with a shark-like grin that didn't reach his black eyes. Arabella was standing next to him, weaving just slightly and staring off to the side. It was clear that Mrs. Kingston had been medicated. Heavily. "Such good timing to be finished with all..." he made a dismissive wave at the rest of the orchestra members, "...this, so you can concentrate on your role with The Corporation in Moscow." The man's grin stretched impossibly wider, ready to swallow her whole, "As a good, supportive wife. Like my Arabella."

Lauren's eyes darted to her friend, who was humming something under her breath, a melody, over and over. With a chill, she realized the polished wife of Number One was humming "Mary Had A Little Lamb" in a tiny, childlike voice.

Putting her head in the warm space between her husband's shoulder and his chin, Lauren sighed as he squeezed her tighter in those long arms of his. "This has been far more..." she could tell Thomas was struggling for the correct, safe phrasing and she smiled a little. "more complicated than I'd foreseen. But I studied the Bratva for years before I made the overtures for partnership. I am quite aware of what to expect. I will keep you safe, darling."

Thomas frowned as she burrowed her head into his shoulder. "I just want you to be safe. That's all. Please promise me you'll be careful." He could tell Lauren was near tears and he rocked her back and forth.

"You never need worry about me, sweet girl," he soothed her, kissing his bride's suspiciously wet cheeks, then her neck and back to her lips, making comforting noises. When Lauren began returning his kiss, opening her mouth and sucking his tongue inside, Thomas groaned and gently pushed her back on the bed.

Afterward, Lauren drifted in a warm, comfortable daze for some time as Thomas gently bathed her and rubbed away sore muscles. He made her drink some water and then put her head on his lap, gently brushing her hair until she managed to gather her scattered brain cells back together. "I'm going to miss this," she said sadly.

He sighed, still silent for a moment as he finished brushing her hair. Placing his lips against the thin skin of her forehead, Thomas said, "I am sorry that I will not treat you as my beloved in public. But you understand why we're doing this."

Nodding against his lap, Lauren sighed. "I do. Let everyone think my bad behavior by running away-" she stopped, scowling. She hated that phrase; she didn't run away that day! "-that you're punishing me by showing I'm not to be trusted."

"Exactly," Thomas praised her, a little sadly. "Showing any softness after your disobedience is dangerous. It must appear that my first loyalty is to The Corporation. You must appear shamed, cowed by your punishment. I am sorry, but I will make up for it in private, my darling. You won't forget that I l-" There was silence for a moment, Lauren held her breath, praying he'd just *say* it, but... "That you are my sweet, most precious wife."

Rubbing her cheek against his thigh, Lauren forced herself to sound confident. "I won't, Thomas. My Sir. I won't forget."

Later, dressed in cream trousers and a lavender silk top, she handed the rest of her luggage off to Chuck, who nodded as he carried it out to the BMW waiting to take them to the airport. Thomas held her face in his warm hands, smiling down at her. He was so beautiful, her husband, with those Mediterranean blue eyes and a smile that could almost be characterized as tender. "It's time to go, darling. You won't forget?"

Lauren's teeth worried at her lower lip. "I won't forget."

She watched as all the warmth drained from his perfect features, his gaze turning polar. "Very well," even his voice was chilly, clipped. "It's time to go. Come along." Without waiting for her Thomas turned and left the house, striding to the idling car.

Chapter 33 – Mine

In which Thomas gives Lauren the best of all gifts. Jewelry. And surveillance.

Thomas was busy going over reports on the way to the airport, so Lauren simply sat with her hands folded properly in her lap, looking out the window. She was still terrified about this trip- some unknown part of her raging and pounding on the walls of her subconscious to, *pay attention goddamnit!* But she couldn't stop it, so she had to be watchful. Lauren sighed, crossing one leg over the other while looking merely pretty and ornamental. She had a sudden, intense longing for a big fat bottle of wine and a sincere prayer there would be one on the jet. But given that Arabella was supposedly dry, she wasn't sure what would be available to the wives.

Wives.

Oh, shit. Lauren realized she'd have to keep an eye on Clara. This was going to end the honeymoon between her and Michael in a big way, and not for the first time Lauren was oddly grateful that Thomas never hid what he was, what he wanted from her. Her heart hurt, thinking about the expression on her sweet friend's face when she finally realized the handsome monster she'd married.

By the time they boarded the jet, however, Arabella was deeply asleep in one of the reclining seats with a sleep mask and what suspiciously looked like a shackle on her right wrist, leading to the armrest. Kingston's "assistant" quickly pulled up the fur lap robe on Arabella's legs to cover it. Once the jet had left London, Thomas and the other two men disappeared into the jet's boardroom to go over papers, leaving Clara and Lauren alone. While Michael gave his bride a lingering, pointed kiss first, Thomas left the cabin without a backward glance. "I won't forget," Lauren repeated silently, "I won't forget. I know he was going to say 'love' today."

"Are you nervous?" The question in Clara's pretty voice made Lauren look up and pay attention.

"What do you mean?" she hedged.

The other girl looked out the window, staring at the clouds. "This feels... bad, I guess. Of all of The Corporation's business contacts, these people are the scariest-" Clara shuddered, "remember that awful strip club?"

Lauren was a little startled to hear the shy Mrs. Fassell bring it up, given what they'd both had to do there. "Oh," she agreed bleakly, "I remember." She couldn't stop herself from blurting, "I didn't think I'd speak to Thomas for a week after that."

She watched as Clara cringed, "I don't ever want to have to do something like that, ever again." While she'd known they'd both been required to "perform," it still made Lauren terribly sad to hear it. Especially because she was certain that the new Mrs. Fassell didn't get a picnic and Shakespeare in Hampstead Hill Garden the next day as an apology, the way she had.

With a sigh, she reached out and squeezed Clara's hand. "Well, we'll look out for each other, all right? We already know our men can take care of themselves." She spotted a bottle of Riesling in the small glass-fronted fridge and rose with an unseemly haste to fetch it.

Being packed into the same huge, black SUV with the rest of The Corporation's management meant Lauren couldn't dart back and forth between the car windows, trying to see everything. Her high school friend had told her so many exciting things about St. Petersburg and she was dying to explore. But instead, she sat sedately, legs crossed properly and hands in her lap, squished between Thomas and a barely conscious Arabella. It could be worse, she thought, looking at a miserable Clara wedged between her husband and the noxious bulk of Number One, who insisted on deliberately leaning over her to address an amused Number Three. Even so, their malevolent presence couldn't quell her excitement when they pulled up to the Grand Hotel Europe, where she just barely stifled a "squee!" when she and Thomas were escorted to the Tchaikovsky suite.

"This is amazing!" she gushed, trying not to bound from room to room like an excitable gazelle, "Can you believe that Tchaikovsky wrote the *1812 Overture* here? In these very rooms!"

Thomas leaned against the bedroom door, smiling as he watched the way her joy lit Lauren's face in a way he'd not seen in a long time. He felt a painful twinge in his chest as he realized how closed-down and careful his bride had become. "This is The Corporation's way," had become less and less of an acceptable justification.

Then the smile faded away as his wife faced him. "When we go out to dinner tonight with the Bratva's hosts, are we going to have to...?" Her conversation with Clara rose up again and Lauren remembered the soiled feeling she'd had after leaving Semion Mogilevich's nightclub. "Do more... stuff... to accept their hospitality?"

Thomas sighed, straightening to walk over to her. "No, love. Fortunately, at these kinds of events in Bratva's territory, the wives and families attend, so there are no side trips to a Gentleman's Club."

Lauren snorted inelegantly. "You, Sir, were no gentleman."

One dark brow raised, her husband began edging her back against the wall, "And you, darling, were no lady." Thomas grinned rakishly as she blushed a painful scarlet. Leaning close to whisper in her ear, he growled, "And though it was not how I would have planned it, I very much enjoy the idea of taking you against some club wall, or in a darkened corner again. Very much indeed." His bride was still, and for a moment he wondered if he'd brought the memory back too vividly for her. Then Lauren stretched up, slipping her hands under his suit jacket as she made a sharp little bite on his neck, just barely where his shirt collar would cover it.

"Next time no listening devices," she hissed and bit him again. With a groan, Thomas picked her up as if she weighed nothing and simply threw her on the bed, grinning at her stifled shriek as she bounced rather high before landing again, her demure dress hiked up to show her white silk undies.

Pouncing on her before the girl could catch her breath, Thomas whipped his tie off and rapidly tied her hands to the headboard. "And what," he said with a deeply satisfying growl, watching his sweet wife shiver, "would Pyotr Tchaikovsky think of me eating you out on the very bed where he perhaps composed *Swan Lake?*"

His dark head was between her thighs in seconds and Lauren sucked in a huge breath as Thomas pulled her panties aside to attack her center. "A- actually," she whimpered, "it's said that he composed it for Vladimir Petrovich Begichev, as the intendant of Moscow's Russian Imperial Theatres, and oh! Oh, my god, Sir, please do that again!"

Putting his forehead against her soft stomach he breathed her in, the scent of her that was curiously, always like vanilla when she came. "Mine," Thomas breathed out like a prayer. Finally, someone who was his. And he was hers, even if he couldn't say it yet. Though the man was quite sure his beautiful bride already knew that.

They were getting dressed for the Bratva welcome party, having showered, soothing scratches and bites with tongues and fingers. Zipping up her black Vera Wang dress, he admired the plunging back and the smooth way it slid over her hips. "You're beautiful, darling." His voice was huskier than he liked, but really... As he expected, she blushed and dipped her head.

"Please," Lauren laughed, "you're the beautiful one in this relationship." She laughed harder at his perplexed expression. "You don't think men can be beautiful, too?"

He made a noncommittal noise, running his hands over her waist. The dress was more demure in front. Elegant, unfussy. Like his Lauren. Finally, with a sigh, he pulled away. "Straker will be by to collect you in half an hour. We'll drive to the party together, but I must meet with One and Three first." His big, warm palm slid down her stomach again, pressing gently. "Are you all right?"

Lauren wondered if her face would eventually just freeze in its beet-red flush since her terrible husband insisted on making her blush all the time. "I'm fine, Sir," she managed. He was sliding his hand over the flat planes of her belly with an unfamiliar expression on his face. "What are you thinking?"

Thomas pulled back, he'd been thinking the strangest thing, how beautiful her stomach would look, swollen with his child, her breasts fuller and plump. Shaking his head, he assured her, "Nothing, darling. I shall see you soon." With a tender kiss, he was gone.

Ready and waiting when Chuck knocked on the bedroom door, Lauren gave a grin to see her unflappable bodyguard well, composed as always. But he was holding a small white box. "Miss Lauren, Mr. Williams requested that I find a security feature for you."

Confused, she took the box, looking it over. "What kind of feature?"

Removing the lid, he pulled out a silver chain with delicate links. "This is platinum, very difficult to break. There is a microscopic GPS tracker inside that will not be spotted by a traditional security scanner. I will always be able to find you when you wear this."

It felt like a sliver of ice suddenly plunged into her stomach, making her shiver. "This is more dangerous than anyone's going to admit, isn't it, Chuck?"

With a most un-Chuck-like gentleness, her bodyguard removed the necklace from the box and fastened it around her neck. "Let's go slay the dragon, shall we?"

Lauren looked in the mirror, tears springing to her eyes. The platinum charm holding the tracker was a St. Margaret's medal. She should have known. With a determined smile, she turned to him. If Chuck thought she was strong enough to be a saint, she was going to try. Grabbing her purse and taking a deep breath, she nodded. "Let's go fuck that dragon up."

She heard a low grumble to her side as she laughed, "Now, there's no need for that kind of talk."

Chapter 34 – In the Belly of the Beast

In which Lauren and Thomas find a warm welcome, cold vodka, and an ugly revelation in St. Petersburg.

The car was silent as they headed to the Bratva-owned restaurant where they'd be "meeting the family," as a grinning Number One put it. Lauren looked wistfully out the window at the city and hoped Chuck would be willing to explore with her tomorrow. When they pulled into the winding driveway leading to where their Russian hosts were waiting, everyone was a little impressed. Fairy lights twinkled harmlessly in the trees and shrubs along the drive and up to the massive ivory building, built in the Imperial Russian style. In fact, Lauren thought with a little grin, it bore a striking resemblance to the Menshikov Palace on the other side of St. Petersburg. When the fleet of black cars turned into the circular driveway, the girl got her first taste of The Corporation swagger on someone else's turf. They had quite the impressive entourage, she thought cynically, watching multiple dark-suited men step out and flank them in a procession to the restaurant.

For a moment, Lauren forgot her role and moved to take Thomas's hand, her heart thudding painfully when he moved his away. Gritting her teeth, she forced a pleasant smile as they walked through the towering doors. Inside was a cacophony of sound and light and delicious smells: roasting meat, the sweet scent of baking bread, and more. Further down the hall, a group of musicians was tuning up, and Lauren vowed to make her way over there once they started.

Lauren had thought a great deal about the Bratva Clusterfuck (again, never a phrase said out loud) but she'd anticipated it either being a surprisingly not-horrible evening, like the one they'd shared with Karl Romanoff. Or, what she secretly feared was another terrifying and sordid night like the one they'd endured with the Bratva chief, Semion Mogilevich. She'd thought about it a lot- what to say, how to handle the endless potential pitfalls. As it turned out, the night was not like either experience.

"Dobro pozhalovat', druz'ya!" The woman who stood before them as they walked into the huge restaurant had her arms spread out in a hug, radiating good cheer, and motherly charm. She was tall, nearly as tall as Thomas and a shamelessly brassy blonde. She wore an incalculable wealth of diamonds on her fingers. The woman simply glittered. Effortlessly herding the three Corporation wives away from their spouses, she dragged them over to a group of laughing, chatting women. Looking them over with shrewd brown eyes, the woman turned to Lauren. "Welcome, darlings! We have been so curious to meet the families from The Corporation!"

Lauren grinned back at her. "Thank you for your hospitality, I'm Lauren Williams- Thomas's wife. Nodding at Clara, she added, "Clara Fassell, a newlywed and Michael's bride." There was a chorus of well-wishes from the little gaggle of women and Clara's smile became more natural. "And- and this is Arabella Kingston, Ben's wife and the head of Jaguar Holdings charity division." The gaggle was quieter, looking at Bella, who'd been seated by her handler and given a bottle of water, an absently pleasant look somehow frozen on her pretty face.

After a polite silence to see if Arabella was going to respond the blonde said, "It is good to meet you all. I am Yehvah Mogilevich, Semion's wife but you will call me Eva and..." Of course, thought Lauren, the Queen Bee. It unnerved her that the woman had gone straight to her instead of Arabella. She was quite sure Eva knew who they were well before introductions.

Forcing herself to focus, she nodded and smiled as she met the rest of the female power structure. Lauren was relieved to meet Zia, the surprisingly young wife of Karl Romanoff. "Oh, this must be the little one whose pictures are stuffed in her papa's wallet," she cooed, bending over to smile at the baby.

"Really?" Zia looked shocked, "Karl- he showed you pictures?"

Lauren wondered if she'd done something wrong. "Oh, at a business dinner when he was in London last fall. He showed pictures of the boys, but he seemed quite proud of his first little girl." A huge smile spread over the other woman's face, and she sagged in relief.

The Russian wives neatly encased The Corporation spouses and it actually took a moment for Thomas to find Lauren again. He finally spotted Straker, on the periphery of the group of laughing, chatting women and upon closer inspection found his wife bouncing a baby on her lap while teaching a toddler how to make a paper airplane with their placemat. The crowd between them separated for just a moment and she looked up with a sweet smile when she caught his gaze, and without thinking, Thomas smiled back. They lost sight of each other again in the movement of so many bodies, but there were three men who didn't miss the exchange. Apparently, Number Two's weakness for his wife was more pronounced than they thought.

When the head of Bratva stood, so did everyone else. The laughter and chatter cut off instantly, and Lauren could hear herself swallow in the silence. Semion Mogilevich could be quite the showman when he wished, and he was in rare form tonight. *"Dobro pozhalovat', druz'ya!"* he roared cheerfully, *"My rady, chto vy zdes', v nashem dome, posle vashego gostepriimstva v Anglii. Tost za Jaguar Holdings i nashikh novykh partnerov."*

Looking around, The Corporation group raised their glasses with the others in a shout. *"Ваше здоровье!"* Lauren smiled warmly and tipped her glass to Eva and threw the shot back, grimacing despite her best effort. But her hostess merely laughed and filled her glass again.

The night was turning into a bit of a blur, but Lauren laughed and talked with the Bratva wives, mentally adding in translations from her grasp of Russian when their English slipped and they all understood well enough to enjoy the conversation.

"No children?" Zia said sadly, looking at Lauren and Clara's flat stomachs.

"Not yet," they answered together, which apparently was the signal to push another glass of vodka in their hands.

When the endless table was groaning with food, Eva called everyone over, and The Corporation wives found they were sequestered with the women again. Lauren looked longingly up the table a few times, but Thomas never caught her eye. Clara leaned in close, "I guess we should be grateful they let us sit together, huh?" Squeezing the girl's hand, Lauren looked over to see Arabella sitting quietly, playing with her fork.

The meal started with a wonderful, thick soup. "*Solyanka,*" Eva explained as her guests hummed in pleasure. Next was *Pelmeni,* which Lauren had enjoyed several times at her friend's home in Manhattan. She shamelessly took three, biting into the crisp pastry blissfully, enjoying the dumpling slathered in butter. Each course was more delicious than the last, though the most popular with the children crowding the table was the *morozhenoe-* which Lauren savored. More texture than American ice cream, but with a lovely body and flavor that even gelato couldn't boast. When no one could contemplate another bite, the musicians began tuning up and Number Two's bride was on her feet, eager to see their instruments.

Thomas had forced himself to focus in on Mogilevich all night, the sly Russian had been making strange little jokes about "family" that really made no sense. But he watched the interaction between the Bratva chief and Number One, who were toasting each other and laughing. There was an undercurrent that he couldn't recognize, but he had to stay focused and trust that Straker was watching over his wife.

This was not as easy as Lauren's bodyguard might have hoped. She was darting excitedly from one musician to another, examining their instruments and asking questions. When the group launched into *On the Murom Path,* Lauren's hand was seized by one of the children and she entered the circle to dance. When the circle finally became a blur after a few more songs, she held up her hands in appeal and sat down for a minute. Her eyes were closed, enjoying the sweet sound of the domra and the balalaika when she heard the two men behind her.

"That's the musician? Williams's wife?"

Lauren forced herself to stay relaxed. They were chatting

away in Russian with confidence that she wouldn't understand them, so let them talk.

"Yes, pretty thing." She recognized the voice of the lieutenant who'd been shut down by Romanoff that night when he was rude to her. "The silly thing unpacking all those instruments for the schools, thinking she is a saint helping poor children."

Oh, please, she thought. *Please, not the one good thing. Not the one thing that matters to me...* But Lauren sat and listened anyway, to every word.

The ride back to the hotel was livelier, everyone - even Kingston - was more relaxed after lavish applications of vodka. While Thomas didn't touch or look at her, he was close enough for Lauren to feel the soothing heat from his body and it was comforting. After setting guards around the suite, Thomas walked into their lavish bedroom, loosening his tie and looking forward to getting inside his wife. She'd been such a good girl all night- charming Mogilevich's wife and the rest of the Bratva female leadership. The sight of her dancing with the children, face flushed, laughing and blonde hair flying everywhere had made him dangerously soft in the middle of a discussion that required his complete attention.

"You behaved beautifully tonight, darling," Thomas said, tossing aside his tie and pulling his shirt loose as he unbuttoned it. "The Bratva wives were quite taken with you."

Her back was to him, she was slumped over the dressing room table, removing her jewelry. "Were they? That's good."

The steel nerves of Thomas Williams suddenly twinged like guitar strings. His sweet girl's voice was flat, almost lifeless. With a huff, he put his hands on her shoulders and turned Lauren around to face him, one hand under her chin, lifting it. "What did you hear?"

It was fortunate the walls between the suites in the Grand Hotel Europe were old and thick, or the guards outside would have been treated to the first full-fledged battle between the intimidating Number Two and his furious wife.

"The charity? You're laundering money through it? Of all the things The Corporation turns to shit, you couldn't-"

"Who do you think you're speaking to, little girl? How dare-"

"It's the charity, Thomas! The one thing that redeems all the filth that-"

"None of this is your concern! Your precious school program is still getting its instruments, so why are you behaving as if your very virtue has been violated?" Thomas shouted over her, fury at the stupidity of the Bratva lieutenants and irritation at his wife's heartbreak making him even less able to attempt to calm her.

"Are you kidding?" Lauren screeched, "What the fuck does that matter when you're pumping drugs into the same schools? How sick is that? Really? Your precious Corporation doesn't have enough blood money?"

Even a furious and crying Lauren knew to stop when her husband growled, and his hands reached out to grasp her upper arms.

"What drugs?"

It was a couple of hours later when Thomas had ruthlessly questioned his wife over and over to make sure she had given him every scrap of information. Lauren was exhausted, wiping her swollen eyes and wishing she could fall asleep and pretend this night never happened. "So Bratva and someone on The Corporation side have been running drugs through the shipments. On top of laundering how many millions?"

"Quite a bit," Thomas answered, staring out the magnificent window in their sitting room. His eyes closed briefly as Lauren made a bitter little noise.

Rising to strip off her pretty red dress, the girl tried to focus. "This is bad, isn't it? You not knowing about the drugs. Is there any chance it's someone lower on the management ladder, running it without the Big Three knowing?"

In his heart, he knew it was very unlikely. "Go to bed, Lauren. I have calls to make." Thomas knew his voice was colder than he meant it to be, but his wife's heartbroken face was, it was itching at him, somehow. Irritating him and making him feel unsettled.

"What are we going to do?" Lauren asked, ignoring his order, "I mean, we can't let-"

"And what is this 'we' nonsense, little girl?" his voice lowered to a growl and she knew she was on thin ice, but she stayed put.

"It's my project too, Thomas! You can't let-"

Furious, he cut her off, his voice dripping ice. "I can allow anything I like and it is not your place to say a word about it. I *own* you, little girl! You do not dictate to me!" Thomas noted with a certain uncomfortable satisfaction that her tear-stained face now held the proper fear. He began walking toward her, gliding like a panther, deadly. "Did you forget who you married? I'm a bloody criminal, you stupid child! I run a multi-billion pound organized crime empire, you do remember that? It is not your place to be disappointed, with your heartbroken purple eyes and your crying. This is what I DO, LAUREN! This is who I AM!" Thomas sucked in an enraged breath, he'd been shouting into his wife's face and she'd just stood there, refusing to back down.

For one terrifying moment, Lauren had wondered if he would hit her, if Thomas would hurt her. But he didn't. He pulled back, staring at her, almost puzzled that she wasn't crying or cringing away. "I know. But that's not all you are," she finally said, "there's more to you. There's good. You are more than this." He was staring at her, shirtless and still beautiful, even in his fury. But she could see it, just under the permafrost of his glare. There was dismay, shock. Maybe even some guilt. He probably didn't know what that felt like anymore. "I know you now, Thomas. I'm your wife and I know there's more."

There was one moment where it almost looked like he would take her in his arms, bury his face in her neck and kiss her, soothe her fears. Then the impassive lines settled back over his face. "Go to bed, Lauren." He watched as she turned and walked into their palatial bedroom, shutting the carved doors behind her.

"Dobro pozhalovat', druz'ya! My rady, chto vy zdes', v nashem dome, posle vashego gostepriimstva v Anglii. Tost za Jaguar Holdings i nashikh novykh partnerov." Russian for: "Welcome, friends! It is our pleasure to have you here at our home, after your hospitality in England. A toast to Jaguar Holdings and our new partners."

Chapter 35 – New Friends and Old Enemies

In which Lauren is played. Like a finely-tuned instrument.

Lauren was on her side, watching the first golden streaks of light creep across the polished marble floor of their bedroom. After Thomas left her to "make some calls," she stalked back and forth, hands on her hips and getting angrier and increasingly frightened to accompany it. Thomas not knowing something happening at The Corporation meant either someone...

A: Was so stupid they thought they could pull something off right under his nose or,

B: Numbers One or Three or both were involved.

Why leave out Thomas? It was a huge blow to his status if they were behind it. For the hundredth time, she wished her stupid, stubborn and unreasonable husband would just fucking talk to her! Who else could he trust more? She was the only one who would be completely behind him and his survival at The Corporation, even if she hated him being there.

So, she took a bath. Brushed her hair. Tried out at least six of the adorable little bottles containing lotions and powders and something that smelled alarmingly like mothballs. Put on a pretty little nightie that she'd been hoping would be used for more salacious purposes and paced some more. When he still didn't come back, Lauren defiantly pulled out her cello and practiced for another hour until her eyes were drooping too much to see the music. With a final, spiteful twang, she angled the bow incorrectly and her furious movement broke it at the tip. Lauren stared aghast at the shimmering length of wood and fine strands of horsehair flying loose. Her second-best bow...

"God-DAMNIT! My bow? My fucking BOW? Russia hates us!"

It was in the middle of her diatribe when Thomas came back into the bedroom, locking the doors and slipping his phone into his pocket as he watched his demure bride charge angrily up and down the oriental rug, madly waving her bow. There was something so fetching about his girl in her sweet lingerie and her stomping and temper-tantruming. He frowned, when on earth would a woman's tantrum be considered adorable? When you felt... things for them? Angrily closing off that line of thought, he cleared his throat.

"Darling. What happened to your bow?"

Lauren stopped abruptly and glared at him. "I broke it."

Naturally, Thomas looked composed and perfectly put together, leaning against the wall. "May I ask how?"

"Because," she drew out insolently, "I was playing... angry. It was angry playing and now my goddamn bow is broken and my husband doesn't seem to realize the only person he can trust in this world is in the same room with him!"

He'd just been about to take her over his knee for snappishness and cursing until her last sentence stopped Thomas in his tracks. He stared at her, utterly silent and Lauren braced herself with a scowl as his frosty gaze conducted that slow head to toe circuit he used to unnerve her. "You are still worried about last night's revelation."

Lauren's jaw dropped- an expression that made her look remarkably simple-minded but couldn't be helped. "Worried? *Worried,* Thomas? Something is happening at The Corporation that you're not aware of and the only good thing, the-" humiliatingly, her voice broke, but she continued, "the charity is laundering money and running drugs. These all seem like things to worry about."

"I told you, little girl," his voice was ice again, meant to freeze his wife in her tracks, "this was none of your concern."

She was waving the bow around again like a rather sharp and aggressive baton. "I know you're my scary crime lord husband and I'm just your dutiful arm candy. But we're in Russia and deep in the Bratva clusterfu- uh, the Bratva stronghold and stuff is going sideways. I don't know who you have on your team here, but you have me. Let me help. Women talk, tell me what to listen for." Lauren waited for Thomas to terrify her into submission with a cruel glare and some cutting remark. But he didn't, standing there with his hands in his suit pockets and staring at her as if she was something exotic he couldn't quite put a name to.

With a sigh, Thomas took off his jacket and tie, unbuttoning his dress shirt. "You are correct. I did not know about the drugs. I guided The Corporation away from the drug trade four years ago. Too... messy."

Biting her lip, Lauren fought to not scream at him about

there being far more serious issues than 'messiness.' "That's where those idiot Texans come in, right? With that psycho shoot up?"

He nodded, a slight smile on his thin lips at her description. "He wasn't happy that I'd cut off our association with his cocaine cartel. But this development..." Thomas paused for a moment, thinking and she was struck again with how beautiful her evil and apparently drug-dealing crime lord husband was. "Lauren, did any of the wives last night make odd references to 'family?' Something that didn't quite make sense?"

Frowning, she shook her head. "There were toasts to our two families coming together, but nothing too weird." He walked over, looking down at her as he ran the back of his hand over her smooth shoulder. "Can you be my clever girl tonight and listen?"

"Of course," Lauren said instantly, "what else can I do?"

Thomas fought off a sense of unreality as he stared at the determined blonde. His wife hated The Corporation with an almost cellular intensity, he knew that. Yet here she was, insistent on helping him because she knew something just turned sideways. She was helping *him.*

"Such a good girl," his voice was huskier than he'd expected, and Thomas irritably cleared his throat. "Arabella does not look to be in any kind of shape to talk, much less answer questions. But see if you can get anything from her tonight. Don't ask Mogilevich's wife anything leading. She's much too experienced. Listen to the other wives. See if the men guarding you talk to each other. But do not-" he took her upper arms and shook her slightly, "do *not* look in *any* way as if you're attempting to gather information. Do not draw attention to yourself, do you understand?"

Her eyes were wide but not frightened. "I understand."

Thomas made an irritable noise. "It is my responsibility to keep you safe," he began pacing the room, hands on hips, "not allowing you to help." He drew the last word out in a sneer, which Lauren forced herself to ignore. She stopped his circuit around the bed by putting her arms around him.

"I'm here to help you, Thomas. Not The Corporation. But I'm here." For a moment, Lauren was worried he'd angrily pull away from her, but with a sigh, her husband's long arms wrapped around her, too.

"Yes, my lovely Valkyrie, I'm quite aware of your budding savagery," his chest rumbled in a chuckle as Thomas fastened his lips over hers. "My fierce little bride."

Tidying each other under the elaborate shower afterward with giggles from her and a conspirational grin from him, Mr. and Mrs. Williams tried to tone down the giddiness of what really, was a spectacular round of orgasms. Lauren knew she was a little cock drunk, but she felt back in sync with her husband, a sense of partnership that was rare and precious. "Where are we going tonight?" He was zipping up her silvery dress with a skirt shorter than she preferred.

Straightening the back of her dress, Thomas said, "One of the Bratva nightclub properties." Seeing her look of horror, he chuckled and shook his head, "No darling, as I told you, the wives are along on this trip. It will be nothing like last time." He ran one finger over the slight slope of Lauren's breasts as she heaved a sigh of relief. They both stepped reluctantly to the closed bedroom door. When they opened it, he would once again be the icy, indifferent husband and she would be the shamed, cowering bride. "Listen, but do not look as if you're attempting to get information," he warned, dipping his head to kiss her.

Lauren forced a smile and nodded back. "And I won't forget." There was a flash of something in his Mediterranean eyes, and her crime lord husband kissed her again.

"Don't forget."

By any jaded New York or London standards Lauren might have had, the Bratva nightclub was spectacular. Four levels of swooping industrial style steel and oak, elaborate (and likely, wildly uncomfortable) seating and DJ's that switched from house music on one floor, then to dubstep, trance on the third and by the fourth, it was clearly the VIP section and the DJ looked suspiciously like Dutch star Tiësto. When he looked up and smiled at her, Lauren was certain of it. "Damn..." she mumbled.

As expected, she, Clara, Arabella were instantly cut from the herd of The Corporation's black suits and sent to sit with the Bratva spouses. They looked quite different than the night before when everyone was dressed elegantly. Tonight, the Bratva women's dresses were plunging and slit high, makeup darker and their laughter louder. Lauren sat next to Zia; Romanoff's timid bride who seemed very different. She was briskly puffing on a joint and offered it to Clara, who shook her head with a nervous smile, then to Arabella, who took it in a matter of fact manner and smoked it down to ash. The Russian woman merely laughed and lit another one. Lauren waved it off with a smile and bent in to ask about the nightclub.

"This place is amazing, Zia," she said, "how many of these clubs does the company have?"

"Oh-" the girl coughed, waving the lit joint around dangerously close to Lauren's face, "dozens through Eastern Europe, fifteen here in St. Petersburg. We make the rounds to show the peasants who is in charge." The wives around them laughed, and Lauren forced a smile. Zia was darker tonight, sharper and when she laughed it wasn't pleasant. Deftly intercepting another joint being passed to Arabella, she tried to engage the women in conversation about the city, their children, what they enjoyed. A couple of wives leaned closer to chat but most grouped up to giggle and sniff elaborately, letting her know there were other party favors floating around the VIP lounge.

Looking over to her right, Lauren stiffened. Thomas was in a circle with Romanof, Mogilevich and Number Three. As she watched a small mirror moved around to her husband, who bent and sniffed the white powder elegantly, tilting his head back with a chuckle. A cold fist felt like it was winding her stomach and intestines into a knot. She'd never seen Thomas do drugs, never seen him display the slightest interest. Why would he snort coke at a crucial time like this? When they needed to be sharp and clear-headed? Chuck was the only one allowed to bring her a cocktail, so she knew what she was drinking was safe.

Thomas's indifferent gaze swept over the wives for a moment in response to something one of the other men said, barely landing on her before moving on. Suddenly, Lauren was nearly sweating with the need to suck down her vodka and ask for another one. Clenching her hand around her glass, she moved back into the conversation again.

Something new blared out from the speakers and some of the younger wives shrieked with delight. "We are dancing!" Zia announced, yanking Lauren and a startled Clara out of their seats. This apparently only involved the other girls, none of the men made a move to join them and Lauren was suddenly pressed firmly between Romanoff's bride and another wife, writhing and gyrating enthusiastically against her.

Looking around the dance floor for Clara, Lauren found Chuck hovering on the periphery of the lit platform with the look of a father who just found out that his daughter had stripped off her prom dress and was dancing in her underwear. His faintly appalled expression was suddenly hilarious, and she burst into a round of giggles as the other girls joined in. "You're so pretty," Zia purred, sliding her hands over Lauren's swaying hips, pulling her closer, "You and me? We should give our men something to see tonight. There are rooms here..."

All Lauren could think was, *God-DAMNIT. I knew I was right! A sedate night out with the family my ass.*

His head was buzzing a bit from the bump he'd snorted. Thomas rarely indulged in drugs and only in social situations that required it, such as here. To refuse a sample of Bratva's purest product was an insult, but it fueled his impatience. Looking over at his wife, he could see Lauren was attempting some kind of movement while trying to keep the girls with her from rubbing up against her. His eye twitched as that silly girl - whose wife was she? - attempted to cup his wife's breast. Karl Romanoff leaned in. "The girls are getting along," he rumbled, taking a drink and watching Thomas over the rim of his glass, "so pretty together, eh?"

Despite himself, Thomas found himself agreeing absently with Romanoff. Despite his wife's clear anxiety and her attempts to keep the other girl's hands within at least PG-13 rated territory, the three of them together were arousing. The lights flashed off Lauren's silver dress and her toned legs were shown off beautifully by the short skirt. He knew he would kill any man who ever touched his wife, but another girl? Kissing sweetly, hands running over Lauren's lovely body? With a start, Thomas realized that coke was stronger than he thought. Lauren would hate that. And this was not his pleasurably long and sordid past. This was his wife. And what they had was between them alone.

It hit him then, illuminated him, went through him like a bolt of lightning. He loved Lauren. He loved his wife. More than his power. More than his money. More than The Corporation. And as Lauren neatly slid around one girl and looped her arm with Clara's to pull her out of her sandwich of undulating Russians, Thomas chuckled. She was magnificent. "Very pretty, Karl," he agreed. "Beautiful."

Clara's grip was a little tighter than was comfortable, but Lauren patted her back as they swayed together. "I went out on a double date with my friend who was dating a Navy guy in New York? So, they came into port after six months at sea and I thought the sailor they set me up with was going to try to get my dress off with his teeth before I slapped him. That guy was a complete gentleman compared to these girls." As she'd hoped, Clara burst into laughter.

"I'm beginning to think 'Bella knew what she was doing," the younger girl confided, "she's too stoned to sit up, much less dance." Clara's smile faded. "I feel like she's gone."

Impulsively, Lauren wrapped her arms around her for a hug, which merited a cheer from the watching men. "Keep dancing," she said, "we stick together. Everything will be all right."

Aleksei, the oldest of Mogilevich's sons and the most vicious, joined them, sniffing compulsively. "No shortage of beautiful women in London, I see," he was already tapping out another line on the curve of his thumb. Absently offering it to Thomas, who waved him off politely. Mogilevich Jr. hoovered the powder. "Ah," he groaned, throwing his head back. "So then, our three? We have a big, big bed, comfortable chairs and vodka just down the hall. You like my girl?"

"She's beautiful," Thomas said mechanically, watching another wife slide her arm around his bride's waist. He didn't know which girl the Bratva brat was talking about, only that his Lauren was briskly herding Clara in and out of the mix, still dancing to avoid insulting the other women without letting them actually feel her up. When did that crying, shaking girl in his office that night turn into this deft and courageous woman?

"So?" prompted Aleksei.

Thomas turned to him just as a flash of white light from the club's elaborate display illuminated his face, sharp features set in forbidding lines. Mogilevich Jr. saw for the first time the killer that lurked under the expensive suit and smooth manners. "I do not share," Thomas said. "With anyone."

Finally pleading exhaustion and heading for the bathroom after seating Clara safely with a dozing Arabella, Lauren headed for the VIP bathroom, feeling itchy and irritated from having so many hands on her. Leaning on the counter, she rubbed her eyes, trying to keep some of the mascara on her lashes. What the hell? The friendly wives from last night who talked about their kids and swapped stories about terrible labor and delivery stories turned into sharp-faced glittering harpies who were predatory in a way she was not prepared for. Hearing the females chattering outside the bathroom, she hastily moved into a stall locking the door and without thinking why, drew up her feet so they weren't visible. It was Eva and Zia. *The Queen Bee and her... uh...* she was just tipsy and tired enough to zone out for a moment, wondering what the next in line for Queen Bee would be called, Lauren almost missed hearing her own name.

"You bad girl, playing with Williams's pretty wife right there on the dance floor!" It was clear Eva was not scolding.

Zia giggled, "She's adorable. I want to keep her after..."

The door opened and they quickly greeted the newcomers. Lauren numbly crouched on the toilet seat until she was sure they were all gone. She'd had to keep one hand awkwardly twisted to cover the sensor on the tank to keep it from flushing and alerting the other women and her wrist was killing her. So when she finally limped out of the restroom, the girl groaned as an ankle twisted and she more or less fell on the man walking past her.

"Ah- are you all right?" The voice was British, and for a moment Lauren almost leaned on him in gratitude, just for hearing a voice from home before hastily righting herself.

"Oh, my god! Please excuse me. I wear spiked heels about as gracefully as combat boots, so sorry-" Looking up, she flushed to see a handsome man grinning down at her. He was shorter than Thomas, with warm brown eyes and a fuller mouth. He was also holding her elbow in a respectful way, helping her get her balance.

"Not at all. It's not every night I get a beautiful girl falling into me," he was laughing, but it was said in a kind, polite way, not meant to embarrass her. Once she was back on her feet, he held out one hand. "Duncan, but my friends call me Mac, and here on business. And you?"

Shaking his hand, she answered, "Lauren Williams, also here on business. Well, my husband is."

Sweeping out his hand, Mac ushered her back to the lounge before pausing to briskly kiss her hand. "A pleasure, Lauren Williams, here on business. I hope to meet your husband as well."

Making her way back to the grouping of couches where the wives were chatting, Lauren smiled. A British gentleman. A nice thing after everything that's happened tonight.

Thomas was finally beginning to feel like he was getting his footing again, after the unpleasant revelations of the night before. After a day of reports from "his" people in The Corporation, and some skilled questioning tonight, he was sure he knew who authorized the drug shipments and he fully intended to put a bullet in the stupid bastard's skull. Kingston and Mogilevich joined his group, greeting Romanoff and Aleksei as the head of Bratva signaled for another round of shots. "Ah, you are here, boy. Come and toast with us to a new partnership." Thomas's back was to whoever Mogilevich was greeting, but as he accepted a vodka glass, he recognized the voice instantly.

"Oh, your friends from Jaguar Holdings, Semion?"

"Yes, take a glass and join us. Gentlemen, this is one of my most trusted associates in Europe-"

It took every ounce of Thomas's self-control to not smash his fist into the grinning face of the man in front of him, winking at him as if they were sharing a private joke.

"Oh, I went to school with Williams. How do you do, gentlemen? I'm Duncan MacGowen."

Chapter 36 – For Better or for Worse

In which Lauren Takes A Stand. And Thomas revisits belonging to the vilest family in England.

"How bad is this?"

Lauren's voice was flat. Thomas was rigid with fury, face pale as he ushered her into their suite and she carefully leaned on the table, arms folded as he made himself a drink.

Earlier...

The minute MacGowen introduced himself at the party, Lauren fought the urge to vomit on his shoes. She'd shaken this man's *hand*, she'd *liked* him- and this was the psycho who raped girls and stabbed her husband in the back. Literally, and now her fear was figuratively as well. He'd tauntingly shaken the hands of Numbers One and Three before holding out his hand to Thomas with a grin. "What, Williams? No hug after all these years? I thought we Eton men were forever comrades?"

Lauren watched, paralyzed with horror. What would

Thomas do? This creep stabbed him, the son of a bitch! But her husband was made of sterner stuff. With his usual indulgent, indifferent smile, Thomas looked the smirking intruder up and down, before clearly finding him lacking and turning away. *Nice...* Lauren thought with misty admiration. No one could be as cuttingly dismissive as her spouse. Thomas walked away calmly, leaving MacGowen with his hand out and smirk beginning to slip. Taking her elbow, Chuck followed after his boss.

Various members of Bratva attempted to stop the couple as they left the nightclub- to say goodnight, or for the wives, another chance to fondle Lauren, and most movingly was Clara, who hugged her hard. "We'll talk tomorrow," she whispered in Lauren's ear, "we'll talk and figure things out. We stick together, no matter what." Kissing Clara's cheek in gratitude, Mrs. Williams ignored the giggles from the Bratva wives.

Currently...

Now watching her husband sip elegantly at his glass of Scotch, Lauren bit back a growl. "I know this is bad, Thomas. But how bad? Bad like we need to get the jet fueled and leave tonight bad?"

"Don't be silly, darling." Yes, Thomas Williams, the terrifying Number Two of Jaguar Holdings was at his most arrogant and infuriating. "I do not 'run' from anything. I brokered this partnership. And I will not allow that stupid bastard to interfere." But he was pacing the room, one hand loosening his tie.

"Thomas. Please." Lauren knew that her tone was irritatingly yearning, that the fact that she loved the man who made her marry him was likely humiliatingly obvious. But they were together in this, and she wouldn't let him shut her out. "How could that little troll possibly be here? Associated with Mogilevich and the whole St. Petersburg leadership for Bratva. This is a setup; we both know it. What am I missing here?"

For a moment, she was certain her cold, composed husband would order her to go to bed, but then Thomas paused in his pacing with a sigh.

"MacGowen is my brother."

Lauren knew her mouth was open and closing like a goldfish, but she couldn't help it. "WHAT?"

Making an impatient movement with one hand, Thomas clarified, "My half-brother. My father's legitimate son," he added mockingly.

"Oh, god," she whispered, "your own brother stabbed you? What kind of a sick-?"

Thomas steamrolled over her, apparently intent on getting the conversation finished. "My mother was a secretary in MacGowen Equities and apparently caught Mitchell's eye. She was soon pregnant with me, and he pensioned her off into a little flat with a monthly payment. My mother," his mouth twisted, "was quite content with this arrangement. Mitchell came by every now and then, primarily to fuck her." Lauren winced, she couldn't help it, and his eyes narrowed. "Crass, I know. But accurate."

"So, your father," she wanted to throw up again, "knew what that little bastard did when he stabbed you and he still covered for him? Against his other son?"

"Ah, darling. You are incorrect," Thomas smiled mockingly, "I was the bastard. Mitchell paid for my education at Eton, but insisted it be delivered under the guise of a scholarship, which earned me quite a bit of scorn from the wealthier students. Educating me as agreed, but punishing me for it."

"What a son of a bitch," Lauren whispered, so angry she wanted to stomp out of the room and punch someone. Anyone. "So that's why he hates you so much? Because you're the smarter, better son?"

"Well," Thomas allowed, "there is more."

"Of course," she mumbled, ignoring his stern glance. "What happened?"

"When I graduated from Cambridge," Thomas continued, "I rose to the second position in The Corporation quite rapidly. One of the first moves I made in our Mergers and Acquisitions Department was buying out MacGowen Senior and Junior from their own company using a shell corporation. The two thought they had a fat payoff, and never mind who was left to pick up the pieces. Neither ran the company well, they were relieved to be free of it before it collapsed." He took another drink of Jameson before continuing. "They also had incompetent attorneys, who did not read the purchase agreement thoroughly enough. A few small, insignificant clauses that seemed to mean nothing until they were in default. Senior and Junior both lost everything, I broke the company apart and paid off the employees well. They were most supportive of the sale."

Lauren grinned; she couldn't help herself. "Is it wrong that I'm like, incredibly happy about this right now?" Thomas paused to kiss her, smoothing his hand over the back of her head.

"I do believe you have a savage streak that I was unaware of," he said approvingly, pressing his lips to hers again.

Kissing him back, Lauren let herself just feel for a moment, enjoying the movement of his heartbeat against her cheek, the scent of her husband's cologne and his big hand stroking through her hair. "So, Junior has a lot to be bitter about. But from the way Mogilevich talked, it seemed like they're best buddies- like he's known MacGowen for years." Lauren swallowed heavily, wishing she could have a gulp of that glass of Jameson. "Does this mean that your creepy as fuck half-brother somehow..."

"Engineered this partnership?" Thomas finished her thought. He rubbed his forehead. "They did approach us first. I took point on brokering the deal."

"This also explains the weird jokes about family," Lauren said dismally. "And you said that Number One was part of that conversation?" She felt a chill as her husband's beautiful eyes turned polar blue, like a sheen of ice had frozen over him.

"Indeed," Thomas said thoughtfully. "And Ben insisted I take a wife." For a short, hysterical moment, Lauren almost burst out laughing at his peculiar phrasing, though it was quite accurate in their case. "Another bit of leverage to hold over me." He looked down at her sweet face and the heart he was certain did not exist cracked painfully. "I have put you in danger in a way I could not have anticipated. I was so certain I could protect you from anything, I-"

Rising on her tiptoes, Lauren kissed him, one of the few times she'd ever initiated kissing the beautiful, scary man who'd made her marry him. "For better or for worse, Thomas," she reminded him. "None of that... anyway, it doesn't matter now. We're in this together and you have to count on me, all right?"

Then, the strange thing that the Bratva wives said in the ladies' room came back to hit her full force and her stomach dropped like she been punched. "There's more I have to tell you though," she said regretfully. It wasn't bad enough that her husband had just had the worst revelation in history, now she had to add to it? "When I was in the restroom, a couple of the wives came in- Romanoff's wife and I think the Queen Bee." She swallowed as his eyes narrowed in that 'get on with it' kind of way he had. "They said something strange about me, Zia asked if they could keep me afterward."

She didn't think her husband could be more frightening than when he was angry but now the permafrost that seemed to cover him was terrifying. "They dare- *my* wife?" Thomas growled. All of his exquisite enunciation and polish was gone, and he sounded more like a street thug ready to stab someone in the throat.

Lauren forced herself to not back away and answered, "I don't know, that's all they said before someone else came in. I hid in the stall until they left, hoping someone would say something else." Despite her best efforts to remain the cool, focused wife of an international crime lord, tears rose in her eyes. "This is really bad, isn't it, Thomas? They want to hurt you, or-" Her voice chopped off in a sob. Of all of the times at the beginning of their married life that she had imagined the man dead in various horrible ways, the stark reality of it was something very different.

Thomas blinked and seemed to come out of the polar state that had held him immobile for the last few minutes. Putting one big hand on each of her wet cheeks, he smiled down at her. "No, darling they will not hurt me. This is not the first time I have been in a double-cross, and there is always another plan."

Running one hand anxiously up and down the starched cotton of his shirt, Lauren asked, "But this time that asshole-uh, Kingston is in on this. He knew about the family connection, all those weird jokes?" Thomas was silent for a moment, and she could tell he was struggling with what to tell her. It was against his basic DNA to release any information other than what was absolutely necessary. But she was looking up at him with such faith, when had anyone ever looked at him like that, once they knew what he really was? "What can you tell me, Thomas? Let me help."

Taking a deep breath, he began pacing again. "I have a group of men I brought into The Corporation that I know are loyal to me. Or-" Thomas smiled cynically, "loyal enough that if one intends to betray me, another will kill him."

"That..." Lauren floundered, "seems like a tidy, uh, safeguard." She could tell he was trying to smother a smile, but at least he was talking to her.

Thomas paused, hands on his suited hips, and looked down at her. "The first step is getting you out of here."

"What? No! No, Thomas, I'm here and I can help! I-" Lauren protested, a little angry because she was scared but trying to cover it up with bravado.

He interrupted impatiently. "Darling, do you understand what those women said? They want to keep you. Like a pet. The wives were putting on a show last night on the dance floor so their husbands could arrange group sex. There were several requests for you." His wife's face was sheet-white and the significance of the Bratva "socializing" episode was clear.

Lauren seized his glass and took a healthy gulp of Scotch. Thomas was doing that dismissive expression thing again and despite her own sense of self-preservation, she blocked his way. "You know if you smuggle me out of here, you're ringing the dinner bell. All the bad guys will know you know they're coming for you. Surely, we're not at DefCon 5, right?"

He was staring at her, her beautiful husband, his expression a mixture of amusement and exasperation. "When did you become so obstinate, darling? I thought I'd spanked all that out of you."

Rising on tiptoes, Lauren gave him her best giddy smile. This whole thing was fucking nuts. This couldn't possibly be happening. But she was bringing out her Inner Badass, just in case she still woke up in the Tchaikovsky Suite the next morning and this was actually real. Holding his tie, she whispered, "And then you spanked it right back into me."

After carefully showering her and washing away the smoke and smell of alcohol from them both, Thomas carried his wife and put her to bed, sliding in behind her and wrapping his long arms and legs around her. "I'm meeting Clara in the morning," Lauren said finally, "she was very upset tonight about MacGowen as we left. I have to think she knows something." She felt him take in a deep breath, holding it for a moment. "For better or for worse, right?" Lauren said in a small voice.

His arms tightened for a moment, then Thomas kissed her ear. "For better or for worse."

The next morning, Thomas held her longer when Lauren released him to head toward the door for breakfast with Clara and hopefully some information. When his arms tightened, she looked up in an inquiry. It looked like he wanted to say something, but didn't have the words. Then a huge smile spread across her face. "Do you know that's the first time I stopped hugging you before you stopped hugging me?"

He promptly placed a kiss on her neck, straightening her dress. "Stay in Straker's sight at all times. Do not count on the tracking device, they may have a way to jam it. Learn what you can but do NOT put yourself in danger."

Lauren nodded solemnly. "I promise. I-" she wrestled with herself, then looked up at her tall, formidable spouse. "I love you," she said clearly. "I don't expect you to say it back, but I wanted- I needed to tell you." Kissing him quickly, she turned without looking at him again, afraid that his expression would be irritation, or worse, indifference.

Clara was already seated at the little bistro's patio they'd agreed on, just down from the Grand Hotel, but she rose quickly and hugged her. They spoke about general things and plans for the evening, but Lauren was writhing with impatience inside. She needed to see if Clara had heard anything- anything at all from Number Three. But her infuriating friend was happily prattling on about her wedding china and how someone sent her a setting that was the wrong pattern. Only the glorious cheese blintzes she was devouring after heaping them with sour cream kept her from leaping over the table to the sweet girl and shaking some sense into her.

"Let's go." Clara was scooting back her chair, looking at Lauren expectantly.

"Um, what?" Her friend's light peal of laughter made the little man with the sledgehammer inside her skull swing harder.

Lauren rubbed her forehead.

"Oh, someone's got a hangover from all that vodka last night!" Clara giggled, "You agreed to go shopping with me today." Chuck was holding the open to another black SUV and Lauren sighed and got in.

Once the doors were shut, Clara pressed the privacy screen to move up between the front seat and the back. When she turned back to look at her friend, Lauren blinked. Gone was the sweet, shy smile and this Clara's eyes were narrow and focused. "Thomas's half-brother MacGowen is planning to kill him and take over his position as Number Two at Jaguar Holdings. The deal is to move The Corporation back into drugs and human trafficking. But I'm guessing you know that?" Clara smiled slightly at Lauren's stunned expression, looking much like she'd just been hit in the back of the head with a tennis racquet. "C'mon, Lauren," she teased, "no one can be this sweet and gullible! I'm MI:6, and this mess is so much bigger than we thought."

"I KNEW IT!" Lauren didn't quite shout the words, but she slapped her hand over her mouth, staring at her friend. "You WERE too good to be true!" Sobering suddenly, she realized sweet Clara was an intelligence operative in Her Majesty's Secret Service and she wanted information about Thomas, the Number Two in one of the deadliest organized crime empires in the world. Taking a breath, she tried to focus. "How do you know about MacGowen's plan to kill Thomas? Do Kingston and your hu- uh, Michael know this?"

Nodding grimly, Clara squeezed her hand. "Neither were happy about Number Two moving them out of the sex trade and drugs in the first place. Kingston hates him because he knows it's a matter of months - if not weeks - before your husband will take his place."

"Oh, shit... shit shit shit!" Lauren groaned. "When are they going after Thomas? I have to tell him-"

"Listen to me!" Clara interrupted. "We have to make a plan first. MacGowen and Semion Mogilevich both want this to be big, with lots of celebration with the change in power." Her pretty face sobered. "And you're part of the bargain, Lauren. MacGowen gets you in the deal. And when he's used you up, you go back to Bratva."

Chapter 37 – 'Til Death Do Us Part

A cello case. An escape. A murder.

"You can do this, you can do this..." Lauren chanted as she knocked on the door to the hotel suite occupied by Mr. and Mrs. Kingston

She'd given Chuck the slip by taking off her St. Margaret's medal and leaving it in her bedroom after telling him she was going to take a quick nap. Hopping one balcony to the next was not as terrifying as one might expect, although she knew Thomas would have lost his mind, seeing her dangle from one balcony to the other, where Clara was waiting. "If I'd wanted to do this shit for a living," Lauren gasped, "I'd have booked us the James Bond suite."

The little redhead started giggling. "It's not available. We are actually staying in the James Bond suite." They burst into laughter before remembering the seriousness of what they were about to do.

Clara rapidly gave Lauren her final instructions and she nodded, slipping an item into her pocket and heading for the suite of the man she hated most in this world. The thug who answered Kingston's door merely grunted at her, which sent a chill up her spine. Disrespect from The Corporation goons was another bad sign that Thomas's authority was shaky as Number Two. Narrowing her eyes, Lauren leaned in. "I'm here to see Arabella," she said haughtily. She was rather impressed with the sneer with which she delivered it, but the bodyguard merely raised an eyebrow. After a muffled conversation with someone behind the door, he swung it open to reveal Kingston.

"That will be all," Number One dismissed the thug with a regal wave of his hand, insectile eyes fixed on the hated bride of his second in command. "Come in, Lauren dear."

Taking a deep breath, she stepped into the den of the beast. "Where's Bella?"

Kingston, as she expected, merely grinned at her unpleasantly, folding his arms. "My wife is resting at the moment. And why are you here?" Consulting his watch, he said, "I don't have long, we have a meeting with Mogilevich in a moment."

Lauren gave a dismissive sniff and moved bravely toward the bar at the other end of the room. "Do you have any of that good stuff- that Scotch you have in your office back home?"

He looked disgusted. "I do not wish to waste another drop of a twelve-year-old vintage on you, you ridiculous child." Finding the bottle herself, Lauren glanced back at him triumphantly.

Pouring them each a glass, she hesitated. "Wait. Do you take ice with this? I can't remember."

Kingston took the glass and the bottle away from her quickly. "Ice dilutes the flavor. Didn't your father teach you anything?" It was a low blow, even for him, and he enjoyed the flinch on the stupid child's face before she tightened her jaw.

Raising her glass, Lauren managed to say, "To Jaguar Holdings." It was the only toast she knew the bastard would drink to. And smirking, Number One did.

Meanwhile...

Thomas walked into the private dining room where they'd be meeting with Mogilevich and his head captains. His brow rose elegantly to see he was the only upper management present from The Corporation.

"Where are your associates, Thomas?" Semion Mogilevich's pale blue eyes were blank in his hardened face, his bald head shining and squat, powerful body encased in expensive workout clothing.

Thomas smothered a smile. *Business casual, I see,* he thought sardonically, wondering what the allure of $900 tracksuits was to the Bratva. Nonetheless, he seamlessly launched into the meeting. Number One and Three not being here was both a mystery and a blessing. It gave him time to work with the Russian and see what had to be done to sway his favor back to Thomas. "They'll be along, I'm sure," he said casually. "In the meantime, let us discuss the many surprises The Corporation has discovered here in St. Petersburg..."

The meeting was going surprisingly well, Thomas noted with some surprise. Mogilevich's shrewd little eyes were examining him carefully, looking for a weak point after the revelation of his loathsome half-brother the night before, and Number Two was damned if he'd give him one. Instead, he worked through the power structure at The Corporation and made subtle but clear references to the profit from financial games and arms trading vs. drugs and prostitution. Casually addressing the increased scrutiny through Europe and the more savage retribution from government prosecution and rival groups in the Middle East, he began to watch the Russian's posture change. He'd apparently been sold a much rosier picture about the opportunity for growth.

His confidence rapidly shrunk when MacGowen slimed into the room moments later. "Looks like talks are going well," he said, the expression on his face varying between a smirk and a sneer.

"My friend," Mogilevich nodded slowly. "And what have you to add?"

"Well," drawled the man Thomas had hated with a steady intensity for most of his life, "it seems strange that Williams here talks about the close relationship Bratva has with Jaguar Holdings when he's trying to smuggle his wife out from under your nose."

Now, the stone-faced Mogilevich turned a furious red. "What do you mean, MacGowen?"

"Yes," Thomas hissed between gritted teeth, still managing to look calm, "What *do* you mean?"

It was a tense ride to the private airstrip where The Corporation's jets had landed, and Thomas spent most of it in a staring match with the worthless bastard bound to him by blood and nothing else. Though admittedly, MacGowen's current position with one of the most vicious organized crime empires on the planet spoke to some skill on the wrong side of the law. His half-brother was grinning openly, and the Bratva head was smoking furiously, the thick haze of smoke from his cigar darkened the limo's interior.

Thomas had tapped out rapid messages to both Lauren and Straker's phones, and the lack of an answer was making the fist currently tightening in his gut twist tighter. Had there been an emergency? Did the Bratva wives try to take Lauren? Did Straker remove his wife for her own protection? Both knew better than to not answer his texts immediately. Which meant something was very wrong. The thought of Lauren missing, perhaps hurt- his chest clenched and he found it impossible to draw a full breath.

Lauren was safe. She had to be. Or he would set the world on fire.

They pulled into the private hanger housing the jets and Thomas stepped out, frigid blue gaze scanning the massive building. His stomach dropped when he spotted a terrified Clara and Straker, jaw clenched and clearly ready to shoot someone. And then his stomach fell to his ankles. Lauren's huge cello case was sitting on the concrete.

"What is this?" Mogilevich barked, "Where is the girl?"

MacGowen was almost giggling with excitement. "Right there, Semion," he said, nodding at the cello case.

"What?" Thomas and the Russian said together.

Strolling over to the trembling Clara and leaning in, MacGowen continued, "Apparently your boy there-" he nodded to Thomas- "isn't as confident as he'd like you to believe if he's desperate enough to try to get his wife out of the hotel and on to the jet in her own cello case. Doesn't speak to a lot of faith in your new partnership, Williams."

Thomas strode forward, huge fists clenched and of all the

people he would not have expected to stop him it was Straker.

"Now hold on, Mr. Williams," the bodyguard intoned, "no reason to upset yourself." And before Thomas could speak or move, two Bratva goons stepped up and started firing at the cello case, lighting up the hangar with a shower of sparks.

"NO! FUCK NO NOT LAUREN DON'T-" Thomas screamed until he was hoarse, trying to lunge for the case and held back by his wife's bodyguard and three other men. He was still screaming when the gunfire stopped, and MacGowen kicked the scraps of the case open. Inside was the body of Number One, Kingston's body more holes and blood than skin. And clearly, decisively dead.

"Hush, Sir," whispered Chuck under the shouts and furious questions rattling through the hanger, "Miss Lauren is fine."

"What is the meaning of this!" Thomas snarled, quickly regaining his composure, and both Mogilevich and his shaken half-brother turned to him. "What kind of a sick game is this? You have slaughtered the president of *Jaguar Holdings!* We came to you in good faith and you murder Kingston? How DARE you?" He was at his most formidable, his tall figure looming over the others. But if Straker had not whispered that his wife was safe, he would have pulled his gun and started shooting until the clip was empty.

Mogilevich was at his most menacing, growling like a dog as he turned to MacGowen. "What is the meaning of this, boy? You dishonor us? You murder our most respected guest?"

"Shite, oh shite, I didn't- I don't-" His customary sangfroid deserted Thomas's half-brother and he ran a shaking hand through his hair.

Clara of all people spoke up. "Is this why you and my husband were talking all night? Where is Lauren? Where is Michael? What is going on here?" She began sobbing uncontrollably, and Thomas put his arm around her, still staring at the other men with a white-faced fury that made even the impenetrable head of Bratva shift uncomfortably.

"You have a great deal to explain," Thomas hissed. "Are your people completely without honor?"

Coming to his senses, Mogilevich jerked his head at the bloody cello case and what was left of Kingston stuffed inside. "Clean that up. Bring everyone back to the compound."

Thomas drew himself up to his most intimidating height. "I will be riding with my people in a separate car. It seems we have much to talk about. And you, Semion, have much to explain."

Once the SUV's door shut behind them, Thomas whirled, grabbing Straker's suit with both hands. "Where the fuck," he enunciated with exquisite precision, "is my WIFE?" The bodyguard's face was turning red, but he did not attempt to dislodge the man's grip.

"She is safe, Sir," he managed to croak.

Clara's pretty face was red and tear-stained, but she explained, "I overheard Michael saying they were coming for Lauren. That Number One ordered it. Lauren drugged him and we put him in the cello case. She's hiding in my suite. I don't know where my husband is."

Thomas rubbed his forehead. "You two are geniuses. It now looks as if MacGowen is behind Number One's murder. Wait- how DID Lauren manage to drug Kingston? *Kingston?*"

Straker glowered. "She slipped my notice by taking off her St. Margaret's medal. She visited Number One's suite under the guise of looking for Mrs. Kingston. Miss Clara enlightened me just before the Bratva lieutenants broke in. We were able to hide Miss Lauren first."

"I would shoot you right now, Straker," Thomas said, "but for the fact that Lauren's outrageous behavior is not at all surprising to me. Do we know where Number Three is?" Looking at Clara's red, swollen eyes, he apologized, "Sorry darling."

"No need to apologize," she sniffed, "this has just been a really terrible day so far."

Absently patting her hand, Thomas looked out the window, his mind moving through all the options at the speed of light.

As they drew up to the massive restaurant they'd dined at their first night in St. Petersburg, they could hear the shatter of glass and the furious bellow of Mogilevich. Thomas smiled unpleasantly. This was a huge loss of face for Bratva, violating the accords of meeting with international partners. It made the Russians look weak before the multiple organized crime empires that had dealings with both parties. How could you negotiate with someone who would murder the president of a partner corporation, and under their hospitality? He knew the man would be half-insane with rage, and he intended to take advantage of it.

Stepping out of the luxury SUV, Thomas turned, blocking the other two. "Straker, take Clara back to the hotel. Make sure everyone is looked after. I have enough people with me, and you have other responsibilities."

As his keen grey eyes viewed the dark-suited men piling up

behind Number Two, Chuck nodded his head. "Of course, Sir. Do..." he hesitated, not sure if it would insult his employer. "Do be careful. Miss Lauren will never forgive me for leaving you." As he watched Thomas stride off, not quite rubbing his hands together with eagerness, he sat back with a sigh. The man would somehow come out on top of this. Number Two was quite the slippery bastard.

Once back in the James Bond Suite, Clara scampered for the complicated series of doors holding the bathroom and walk-in closets. "Lauren honey? Are you okay?" She rapped on the door three times, and Lauren opened it, falling out into the other girl's arms.

"What happened?" she gasped, "Is Thomas all right? What about Kingston?" Looking over the redhead's shoulder, Lauren viewed the seething stare of Chuck. "Oh, shit," she mumbled, before stepping away from Clara. "I'm so sorry, Chuck. I'm so sorry I did that to you. Clara's with MI:6, she's going to help us..." her apology died off as the man she'd come to love like a father stared at her silently.

Finally stepping up, Chuck raised his hand and slowly, he opened one battered fist, displaying her St. Margaret's medal with her GPS tracker. As she bowed her head, he placed it back around her neck. "Never," he managed, "never do that again. Not to me. Not to your husband. Do you understand?" His voice was like broken glass, and he watched her eyes fill with tears. But when she looked up, she realized his were glistening as well.

It was several hours later when Thomas finally called, and Lauren dived for her phone. "Areyouokaypleasesayyes!" she blurted, both relieved and terrified.

Rubbing his eyes, he sighed at the sound of her voice. "Darling, I intend to spank you until you cannot sit down for a month for terrifying me. But not just now. Are you all right?"

"Yes," Lauren's voice wavered, trying to sound like a strong organized crime boss's wife and not like a newlywed who was about to burst into tears at the sound of her husband's beautiful, cultured tone. "I'm fine. Kingston is gone and they... wait, can you talk?"

"Yes, darling," he answered, "my line is secure. The organization is in disarray, this has been a disastrous day for Bratva. Kingston is quite dead and they are certain MacGowen and Number 3 are behind it. Fassell is also the idiot who attempted to negotiate the new contracts for the drugs and human trafficking. I'll be quite happy to give him up. Is Clara all right? She's so fragile."

Laughing, Lauren stretched a little, not having moved for the last hour as she'd stared at her phone. "Don't worry about Clara. I knew that no one could be that sweet! She's MI:6, Thomas. She's going to help us, and it was her idea to drug Number One and-"

Thomas felt like he'd just been punched in the throat. "Did you just... did you say Clara told you she was working with the British Secret Service?"

"Yes," Lauren agreed, "she's been brilliant, really-"

"Darling," Thomas loosened his tie. "Darling, that is not possible. I have been feeding information to MI:6 for the last six weeks. Clara is not an operative. Where are you now?"

Swallowing the scream of frustration and terror about to rip from her throat, Lauren answered, "In... h- her suite."

Chapter 38 – It Was All So Simple When They Planned It

In which Lauren and Thomas discover that old allies become new enemies. And vice versa. Also, Kingston is still dead.

Earlier that day...

It had all been so simple when Clara and Lauren planned it.

"I'm... going to murder someone," Lauren said numbly, not quite believing it.

Clara gave an un-Clara like snort. "No, you're killing the monster that wants your husband dead and has beaten and drugged our friend into a coma. If we don't do it, he'll kill Thomas. Or you. And me. Can you do this? He'll never even let me in the door."

It was the threat against Thomas that galvanized her, and Clara knew it. "Give me the stuff. I just have to get him to drink it, right?"

Handing her the pill in a tiny vial, Clara nodded. "Drop it into a drink, it'll dissolve instantly."

And it had worked just the way it was supposed to, and Lauren watched Number One rub his forehead in a confused manner, then drop like a bag of dirt. When she let Clara into the suite, she glanced out into the hallway. "Wait, where's the bodyguard?"

"Taken care of," Number Three's wife said succinctly, "now help me with your cello case- how do you drag this thing around?" She puffed, blowing a red curl off her forehead.

Laughing, Lauren took it from her. "Years of taking it on to the subway and climbing endless flights of stairs at Julliard." They turned to Number One, limp on the floor. Gingerly, Lauren took one arm, hauling him awkwardly into the case. "I can't believe I have to touch him."

Shoving the man's feet into the bottom, twisting them awkwardly to make them fit, Clara shuddered. "Imagine being Arabella and having to... ugh, you know."

Panting as she stood up, Lauren stifled a gag. "Don't. Just don't even put that in my head." Some rational part of her was screaming at her casual treatment of another human being. She was participating in someone's murder. But then a terrible thought occurred to her. "Oh, shit! Bella! The bodyguard said she was in the bedroom?"

They both hurried to the bedroom door, but the room was empty, the bed made and no drugged wife.

Clara shook her head. "She has to be somewhere close; Kingston wouldn't risk his image by doing... well, anything. Here, bring in the bellman's cart and I'll shut the lid." Watching her friend head for the door, the redhead knelt down by the case, slapping the monster that was stuffed within it like a boneless chicken. "You're not going to enjoy this, Ben. But I will. You'll be awake for the whole thing. Able to feel, but not move. Not a muscle." She slapped some tape over his mouth and smiled pleasantly. "By the way, your wife and Colin Martinsson say hello. It's going to be a whole new era for Jaguar Holdings." Clara knew he heard her, the frantic sense of rage and helplessness clear in those insectile black eyes.

Shutting the lid, she sat on it to get the latches to close as Lauren wheeled in the bellman's cart. Handing her the key to the James Bond suite, Clara instructed her on where to hide. The suite, named after the legendary spy, of course had a secret closet. Then wheeling the grisly load to Lauren's suite, she took a deep breath and knocked, smiling as Chuck knocked on the door. "Chuck? Lauren's fine, she's safe, but we only have a couple of minutes to get set up before the Bratva guards are here-"

He was already moving towards the bedroom, not quite sprinting, and Clara heard his growl before he stormed out again, holding the St. Margaret medal in his fist.

And from there, it was pretty much as the new Mrs. Fassell predicted, until Chuck had to hold Thomas back with all his strength as the cold-hearted Number Two screamed his anguish, believing his wife was being shot to pieces inside her cello case. And Clara was hiding a smile, picturing Kingston's utter helplessness and acute horror.

The present...

Now back in the James Bond suite, Clara pulled out a bottle of water, watching Chuck, who was pacing in front of her closed bedroom door where Lauren was talking to Thomas.

"Lauren," Thomas said urgently "open the door and ask Chuck to come in. Do not allow Clara to enter- let me speak to him."

"Sure," Lauren whispered, padding to the door. Would Clara or Number Three be there with a gun? Would Chuck be all right? Opening the door, she breathed a little easier to see him standing right there while Clara was sitting on the couch. "Chuck," Lauren said, attempting to sound cheerful but pretty sure it was coming out as more of a gargle, "Thomas needs to talk to you for a minute, something about tomorrow?" Her bodyguard raised one well-bred eyebrow but followed her into the room, shutting the door.

"Yes, Mr. Williams?" Lauren watched as his face turned to stone. But he listened for a few more minutes before nodding and answering with a crisp "Yes, sir." Handing the phone back to the girl, he murmured "He would like to speak with you before he hangs up."

"Sweetheart?" Thomas sounded calm, but urgent. "Chuck is going to take you back to our suite. I have three more men on the way to stay with you. I will be there within twenty minutes. Do not open the door to anyone, do you understand?"

"Yes," Lauren managed to clear her throat and say it more firmly, "yes, Thomas. Everything will be fine. I'll be waiting for you."

But when she reluctantly pressed the button to end the call and opened the door, Lauren was beginning to strongly doubt her last statement. Clara was standing there with her usual sweet smile. Holding a gun. Sitting on the couch was Arabella, looking much more alert, and the scary blank-eyed guy from the bar- Martinsson?

It was the recently widowed Mrs. Kingston that broke the stalemate. "Lauren honey," she said calmly, "do come over and sit down. Nothing bad is going to happen here. No one wants to hurt you."

Giving a short and bitter laugh, Lauren shook her head. "I'm having trouble believing that after the last 72 hours, Bella." She very slowly crossed the living room, Chuck at her side and his hand inside his suit jacket.

It was exactly seventeen minutes later when Thomas found his suite empty and with a red haze distorting his vision, he led the men loyal to him to the Bond Suite. He didn't care who died in the next few minutes as long as his wife was unhurt. If she was... Well, then death would take much longer. Much longer than any of them could imagine. He barely stopped himself from violently kicking the door open- a wise choice since Clara was already greeting him with a happy, chirping tone.

"You made good time, Thomas! Come in, there's so much to discuss."

She was not quite shouldered aside by Lauren, her lovely eyes made violet by the sheen of tears she was trying to control. "You're all right," she barely breathed, "you're here." The chilly demeanor of Jaguar Holdings' Second in Command collapsed as Thomas yanked his bride into his arms, burying his face in her silky hair.

"Sweet girl, I thought- I watched them shoot up your cello case, I thought-" his voice choked and Thomas couldn't speak. So instead he assembled his most terrifying Number Two expression and eyed the group. "Martinsson," he drawled, "you do have a knack at turning up unwelcome in the most unexpected situations, do you not?"

The Dane attempted a smile, but with his lizard-like stare, it was acutely unpleasant. "Now Williams," he scolded amiably, "is this how you thank the man who saved your sweet bride's life? Not to mention tidying up the mess Kingston had made?"

"And what would you know about 'messes', Martinsson?" Thomas had a death grip on Lauren's hand, but he seated her on a couch, crowding her into the corner, and turning slightly to shield her with his big body.

"Certainly enough to know you had no idea that Kingston was negotiating with Bratva and your long-lost brother? My goodness, he does carry a grudge, doesn't he?"

Lauren leaned forward, ready to snarl at the smug bastard but her husband's long fingers slid to the back of her neck. "Well, one can't pick one's family, but one can kill them, " Thomas smiled pleasantly. "But I am quite willing to enlarge the circle of corpses."

Shockingly, Martinsson laughed. "No need. I believe we can assist each other. There are portions of The Corporation that I believe are not of interest to you. I, and my dear Arabella," he paused to smile fondly down at the glowing blonde next to him, "will be happy to take them off your hands,"

"Really," drawled Number Two, "and what portion would that be?"

Martinsson's rattlesnake gaze sharpened. "All of it."

The tense silence in the exquisite room was broken by

Thomas's hearty laughter. "Really," he tried to control his mirth. "You're forgetting that you never had the reach to compete for the Bratva contracts before? And you're ready to plunge into human trafficking and the heroin trade?"

Arabella leaned in. "No need to expand Corporation reach from what we do best. And once your idiot brother and Number Three are out of the picture, that new push is out of the way. But we're sure there's room for negotiation." She smiled up at Martinsson fondly, and for a startled moment, Lauren saw her friend look at the terrifying Scandinavian in the same way she looked at Thomas.

I guess anyone's Prince Charming after Kingston, she thought, choking down the semi-hysterical bubble of laughter. The verbal sparring between Thomas and Arabella's bizarre new beau continued until Lauren realized with a certain amount of shock that they actually seemed to be making progress? Seriously? Whatever was left of Kingston barely cold in his, uh, cello case and her husband was negotiating the future of Jaguar Holdings with the murderous and extra creepy Martinsson? She leaned against the solid frame of Thomas, closing her eyes for a moment. The repeated bursts of adrenalin had worn off and Lauren was grateful just to feel his warmth and strength. Just for a moment.

Her eyes fluttered open when she heard her name. "...and Lauren is exhausted. I suggest we all take a moment before we see what new surprises Mogilevich has for us tonight." There was a murmur of agreement and Thomas helped her to her feet.

Surrounded by Chuck and several of her husband's men, they walked down the opulent hallway to their suite, and she caught a glimpse of her face in one of the gilt mirrors. She looked like someone else. Someone who would kill a human being and not care.

Much.

Back in the Tchaikovsky Suite, Thomas sent her to the bedroom while he spoke to the bodyguards in low tones. Lauren took off her high heels and just stood there for a moment. She couldn't seem to make her brain work and her thoughts darted back and forth like a hummingbird, unable to really land on anything long enough to examine it. *Is this shock, maybe?* she thought, but even that seemed like too much to examine. The door opened and as Lauren turned, she was already in Thomas's arms and he was kissing her. Desperately, violently while yanking at her pretty green dress.

"I thought you were dead," he groaned, "I stood there and watched them murder you and all I could think was that I'd failed. Failed to protect you, failed to tell you that I..." he hesitated, pulling away from her lips and staring at his wife a little wildly. His hands went back to pulling away her dress and then he suddenly squeezed her tightly, his dark head buried in her neck. "I should have told you that I loved you. Before you honored me with your statement. I should have. I have known for so long and you could have died today-" His beautiful, resonant voice choked off and Thomas simply stood there, still clutching Lauren and swaying slightly.

"I love you," Lauren said back, arms tight around his neck and on tiptoe to reach his face, "I love you. I do. I-" she would have said more, but Thomas had her face between his hands and he was kissing her with a rather delirious level of desperation, which led to a mutual rendering and tearing of clothes. And when they fell back on to the bed, he was already inside her, making Lauren give a breathy little shriek. But her arms and legs were still wound around him and Thomas hitched her up, arms looped under her knees and spreading her wide.

She could feel the hollows on the side of his ass tighten as he pulled out once, then thrust back in. All the way to where he pressed painfully against her cervix and held.

Lauren's legs began to tremble with the need to push against him, to urge her husband to *move,* damnit! But Thomas did not, instead rotating his hips and keeping tight inside her, making little sparks of red pain and blue pleasure cycle along her slick channel and behind her closed eyelids and she moaned. Her dark husband cupped her breasts, stroking one while sucking the other, then switching sides when Lauren felt wound so tight that she nearly came.

The size of him inside her was pervasive, with no glide in and out to ease the girth of his cock, Thomas's slowly rotating hips making sure he brushed against every sensitive bit of her. "I'm in you to the hilt, little one, and I only wish I could stay buried inside you forever." His precise, cultured tone was slurred with lust. He chuckled, and it made small reverberations inside her and Lauren's back arch, trying to make him move, make him let her come! But he felt it and whispered into her ear, "No darling, you may not come yet, not until your Sir allows it." His long fingers slid down and spread her nether lips open, leaving her tender clitoris bare against the wiry curls at the base of his cock, adding to her stimulation, but it still wasn't enough to let her come.

Thomas rested on his elbows, cradling his wife's face and smiling down at her, enjoying her irritable little groans as she tried to adjust to the intense pressure and weight of him inside her. She was writhing, feeling like she was so close but he wouldn't let her come- Thomas was keeping her in a perpetual state of arousal and desperation for that last bit of something from him that would let her finish.

Pride finally forgotten, Lauren pleaded, "Please Sir. Please, my dear husband please let me come! Please! I'm so close and you won't help me-" she choked as he somehow found another inch to slide inside her.

"Not yet, lovely," he murmured soothingly, "not just yet. I cannot leave you. If you are pinned beneath me, if I am buried inside you, you can't disappear. You must stay safe under me." Another rotation of his hips. More whispers of love and bits of Shakespeare, Thomas knowing he was driving his beloved Lauren insane. He surrounded her in every possible way, caging her in and holding his wife- his stubborn, unreasonable, wayward wife who threw herself into the path of danger under him, inside her. "So sweet and slick, darling, aren't you? I feel you clutch me from inside, I know your tender cunt wants to keep me right where I am."

Lauren was nearly insensible with desperation. Each slow cycle of his hips pressed that giant cock against something that flared red- pain blazing in the soft tissue until the next brush, a smooth slide of blue and the pleasure canceled out the pain again. The rotation of red and blue behind her closed eyelids started swirling faster and faster until she was shivering uncontrollably.

Then, drawing his knees up against the mattress, Thomas went back on his heels and gripped the soft globes of her ass in each hand, squeezing tightly, lifting her up until the tip of him rested inside her and then dropped Lauren down on his shaft. He watched every perfect moment, his Lauren made so beautiful. Her back snapped into an arch and she let out perhaps half a scream before her orgasm roared over her and into his, sweeping through him and tightening every muscle as if he'd been electrocuted. His release inside her was almost painful and the terrifying Number Two managed to gasp "I-god, I love you. Forever." It was as he was gently putting her back against the pillows that Thomas realized his wife was blissfully unconscious, a tiny, dreamy smile on her lips.

It was some time later when Chuck began politely knocking on the door, reminding them of their next meeting with the Bratva leadership. Carrying his wife into the shower, Thomas washed the dreamy, limp girl until she was able to come back to herself a bit.

"How do we handle tonight?" Lauren asked, watching him in the mirror as he brushed her hair.

"Martinsson and that surprisingly cunning Arabella now have a stake in getting this mess resolved with the Russians," Thomas said dryly. "But there are other resources on the way."

"Politics isn't the only thing that makes strange bedfellows," she shook her head, accidentally pulling on the hair her husband was brushing. "Wait - that reminds me - you said you knew Clara wasn't with MI:6 because you've been feeding them information for the last six weeks!" Lauren's eyes were wide, staring at her unperturbed spouse. "You? British Intelligence? Seriously? How could this possibly happen?"

Thomas sighed, fighting again with his resistance to tell this sweet girl anything that could harm her. "I've known for some time now that Kingston and Fassell wanted to return to the flesh trade and drugs. I've been sending information and data transfers between them and the three groups responsible for most of the activity through Europe, the US, and the Middle East." Lauren looked like she wanted to be sick, but she nodded for him to continue. "There are always ways to single out data that does not impact The Corporation as a whole but gives a clear look at where this activity is happening."

Frowning, Lauren watched him give the last few strokes to her hair. "But your half-brother was a surprise- do you think Number One was trying to replace you?"

He gave a thoroughly upper-crust sneer. "That was the most foolish and desperate thing he's ever done, but I had intended on retiring him within the next year."

Pulling on a black sheath dress that made Lauren look rather sophisticated, she asked, "How, uh... how does one retire senior management in Jaguar Holdings?"

Tilting her head up with a finger under her chin, Thomas smiled. A dark and terrible smile that made her grateful it wasn't really directed at her. "Not quite in the spectacular fashion you managed, my savage little bride. But just as permanent."

Chapter 39 – About 50% of St. Petersburg Seems to Want Us Dead

In which we throw up our hands and ask: really? Is there anyone in St. Petersburg who doesn't want to screw over Thomas and Lauren?

Thomas pulled a giggling Lauren into the bathroom with persuasive kisses, intending to debauch his wife one more time before facing down the unfriendly faces of Bratva, but the insistent buzz of his cellphone broke the mood. Growling under his breath, he walked into the living room to answer the call while Lauren tried to restore her hair into some appropriate shape. Staring at her reflection in the mirror, she shook her head. If anyone had told her a year ago where she'd be right now, she would have laughed politely and then asked if they'd forgotten to take their meds. But here she was. In love with her crime lord husband and apparently, about 50% of St. Petersburg wanting them dead. No one was who she thought they were. "Including me," she mused. Hearing a rustle behind her and embarrassed that Thomas caught her talking to herself, Lauren turned. "Sorry, I'm almost rea- MMMMMPH!"

It was not Thomas.

It was, in fact, his disgusting half-brother who had a Glock jammed hard against her cheekbone. "Shut your whore mouth!" MacGowen hissed, shoving the gun harder as if he could split her skin with it. "Come with me quietly and I won't have Fassell kill your husband."

Lauren's mind was racing as she was dragged toward the balcony- the same one she'd slipped over in her bid to escape Chuck. *Oh, Jesus, she thought wildly, Chuck will never forgive himself if I go and get killed! And Number 3 had disappeared, he actually could be pointing a gun at Thomas-* ow! MacGowen had a fistful of her hair and one hand on her arm, yanking it up painfully behind her back as he half-shoved her over the railing to an angry-looking man she recognized vaguely as belonging to the Bratva contingent. Lauren desperately kicked off a shoe, hoping MacGowen wouldn't notice. Given his eagerness to pull a syringe out of his jacket, her lost shoe was the only thing she had going for her. And then the needle plunged painfully into her neck and the world went dark.

"You have to help me, this is insane!" Listening to Number Three whine, Thomas bit back a growl. It was infuriating enough that the idiot had conveniently disappeared for the last what, 36 hours? - while he'd been dealing with Kingston getting shot up, Martinsson and Arabella suddenly dropping in as serious contenders and his Lauren in danger. And Fassell was whining that he needed protection? Thomas was beginning to question how Number Three had risen as far in The Corporation as he had.

"Shut the hell up," Thomas said crisply, "take a stiff drink and show up for the meeting tonight. Keep your goddamn mouth shut until we find out who the players are, here. Do you understand, Michael?"

There was a silence on the other end as if Fassell was covering the mouthpiece and talking to someone. When he returned, the whine was gone and his standard smug tone was back. "Oh, Number Two. We have something we must take care of, first. Namely, your wife."

Feeling like a giant hand was squeezing the top of his head, Thomas clenched his teeth, moving swiftly to the bedroom. "What are you talking about, Michael? This game has been played and you know what happened to Ben." The room was empty, and he strangled the roar that wanted to erupt from his throat. Moving swiftly to the terrace, the only place she could have been taken, Thomas noticed her shoe, lying on its side on the next balcony.

"I'm sure you've noticed Lauren's absence?" Now, it was the ugly, gloating tone of the unmitigated piece of shite with whom he unwillingly shared blood.

"MacGowen," Thomas's voice was so cold that it felt like frostbite, just to hear it. "Even as stupid as you are, I did not think you suicidal." Straker chose that moment to poke his head in the door and stilled, seeing his employer's white face.

His half-brother laughed, sort of a donkey-like chortle that didn't sound like Mac really found anything amusing. "You've lost your touch, Williams. I snatched her right behind your back. There will be no mix-ups with cello cases this time."

Thomas tapped his throat looking at Straker and mouthing the words *'tracking device?'* Yanking out his phone, the bodyguard opened the app and nodded. It was amazing how much he could gather from several violent gestures from his boss including, *Get all the people loyal to me in cars with guns, and tell Martinsson if he wants a deal he better have every armed thug he owns following you within 10 minutes.*

Returning his attention to the phone, Thomas's tone changed, crueler and more indifferent. "If you think that holding a pretty little girl over my head is going to make me give up The Corporation that I've built for over a decade, you're even more of an idiot than our father thought." There was a silence, McGowan for once not having an instant retort. "He did say that you know," Thomas purred maliciously. "You do know that he came over to visit his second family every week," he lied easily, "most of his complaints centered upon what a dimwit you were. Is that why you tried to carve out my kidneys McGowan, that day in the shower? You weren't really angry about being taken to task for one little sexual assault, were you?"

If this had been any other time, Thomas would have truly enjoyed delivering this vicious monologue, but now all he could think of was Lauren tied up under this rapist's control and possibly hurt. But he knew making his half-brother furious would make him sloppy. Careless. Thomas was also quite certain that Fassell was supremely self-interested, rather than insane like his loathsome half-brother. He wouldn't let MacGowen hurt Lauren as long as she was useful as a bargaining chip.

Thomas continued on inexorably. "True, it would be a touch awkward if I showed up without my wife tonight, but finding another pretty girl to take her place is hardly a task." Here, his hand shook as he disconnected the call, breathing deeply and trying to push down the nauseating rise of terror in his stomach. Straker already had the men in the SUV and Thomas slid in the passenger seat.

For the first time in his career, Straker questioned his boss.

"Do you think it was wise to antagonize him so?" he said, his hands gripping the steering wheel as if choking the life out of it.

Thomas drew a deep, shaky breath. "He couldn't have risen so far in Bratva without some self-control," he managed between gritted teeth. "In addition, that idiot Fassell knows how important my- my wife is to me. He's too self-interested to let her be hurt." Thomas barked directions, following the app tracking his wife and beginning to flounder in the fear that for once, maybe he wasn't right.

"Wake up, bitch!"

Lauren groaned, rolling over on what turned out to be a rather lumpy couch trying to bring her hands up to rub her face and finding them handcuffed. Opening her bleary eyes, she found the malevolent countenance of MacGowen glaring at her. Whatever he'd jabbed into her neck was making her dizzy and sick. "Hey, could I have a glass of water? This feels-"

He shoved her, hard, into the arm of the couch. "Shut up!" Leaning closer again, MacGowen grinned. "Do you know, we tried to ransom you off to Williams? He said, and I quote, 'finding another pretty girl to take her place is hardly a task.' You're not as valuable as we thought."

Rolling her eyes, Lauren found this was a mistake as her nausea spiked and she found herself throwing up on MacGowen's pants and expensive loafers. This earned her a hard slap from the vomit-covered man, who raised his hand again.

"Put your hand down, Mac! Are you mad? Thomas will pull your fingers off with pliers for that. No harm, remember? She's bait." Lauren's eyes narrowed as Number Three hastened into the room, glaring irritably at the other man.

MacGowen grabbed a bar towel, trying to wipe off his pants. "Williams said he didn't want the whore back. He said she wasn't worth The Corporation."

Fassell sighed, rubbing his neck. "Trust me, he's lying to you. Go... ugh. Go clean yourself off and we'll make a little video for Number Two. Something with Lauren all pretty and crying." He smiled down at her unpleasantly as the other man stormed from the room. When MacGowen was gone, his expression changed abruptly. "Lauren, stop making trouble! Just keep your mouth shut until we make a deal with Thomas. His brother wants his position more than killing you, but let's not give him an excuse."

Lauren wiped her unpleasantly wet chin on her dress, "What is wrong with you, Michael? You're teaming up with this rapist asshole?"

He shook his head irritably, but still rose to fetch her a bottle of water. "This is a period of change; I have bigger things to pay attention to. Now just shut up so we can get this deal over with."

She cocked her head incredulously. "Dude, are you serious? You really teamed up with MacGowen? Against THOMAS? Are you suicidal? And where's Clara in all of this?" At this point, Lauren was quite clear where Clara was, but she wanted to know what her husband seemed to think.

Michael flapped his hand dismissively. "She's back at the hotel, like a good girl. An obedient wife. Not like you and Arabella. Jesus, she turned out to be a loose cannon, eh?"

He really believes his own bullshit, Lauren marveled silently. Casting an anxious look at the door, she focused on Fassell again. "Look, you know this is nuts! Just get back with Thomas and hand me over. This can't end in any way but bad. Are you remembering Kingston? The cello case?" He really did look a little green around the gills, but before he could speak, MacGowen was stomping back into the room and over to her, grabbing her hair and yanking her upright.

"You shut up! I should beat you bloody for soiling my clothes- those were Gucci Braxton's! But I'll take it out of you the hard way." He advanced on her threateningly, as Fassell's voice rose, trying to calm him down.

"Where are they!" Thomas turned angrily from one direction to the other. The tracker stopped here, in a green space between two old buildings.

Straker groaned, "Oh, lass..." The St. Margaret's medal was lying in the sparse grass, the chain ripped apart. He picked it up, turning it over and over in his big, rough hands. Thomas's phone rang then, and he almost dropped Lauren's necklace.

Numbly clicking the Facetime button, Thomas watched as the grinning face of the monster he shared blood with showed up in the screen of his phone. "Ah, did you just find the wifey's necklace? Nice effort, Williams. Really. A little amateurish, but..."

Thomas was composed, wearing the same expression of urbane amusement as always. "Yes. I'm guessing that Number Three actually thought of sweeping her for a tracker, but we'll just pretend it you," he winked confidentially, watching as MacGowen's face darkened again. "So, now that you've been terribly clever, just tell me where my wife is, and I'll let you live. I won't even carve off any souvenirs."

Lauren's face was pulled into the tiny screen, and she smiled at him. "Hi honey, sorry about the hotel. Are we gonna be late for the party? Those Bratva wives get so mad when we're not there for the appetizers."

"It's fine darling," he soothed, "I'm sure Clara is making our excuses." There was a sudden yelp of surprise from behind Lauren, and she turned her head to smirk at the man, clearly Number Three.

"Yeah, Michael. Not so obedient now, huh?"

"Shut UP, you sow!" MacGowen had ripped away the phone and there was a sharp sound of a hand hitting skin.

A low growl from Thomas made him look up. "That just cost you a hand, brother dear. Shall we continue?" For the first time, his father's other son looked uncertain. "Just tell me where we're meeting," Thomas said impatiently, "and yes, I'm sure the next thing out of your mouth is the overused phrase 'come alone.' So dramatic. That's the whole point of this pathetic little stunt, isn't it? So, get on with it. We have a party to attend."

It was Fassell that barked out the address, not even bothering with the tired warning of, "Come alone."

Lauren twisted her wrists again, wishing she could just have her hands free so she could rub her eyes, maybe gently pat the stinging red mark left on her cheek. MacGowen was pacing back and forth in front of her, spinning a knife absently in his long fingers. He was good, talented, she had to give him that.

He caught her watching him and grinned at her. "Yes, I've

been practicing," he agreed, as if she'd asked him a question. "That little craft blade - it was sharp mind you - but not nearly effective enough." He spun the knife on his palm again, fascinated by the play of light on the steel. "This, however, is as sharp as a Masamune Katana. They used them for slicing through diamonds, rock, human bones as easily as tissue paper." He smiled up at her, and for a moment, she could see Thomas's expression in his dark grin. "Maybe I should start on you?" MacGowen offered nastily, "Give your dear husband something to scream about when he shows up? You're so pretty..." he was coming closer, and Lauren gritted her teeth, picturing tearing off his finger in a single bite.

The scrape of a shoe made them both look up, and Lauren sagged in relief. Her beautiful husband looked her over, carefully impassive but she understood. No distractions, he had work to do. "Showing off, MacGowen? How childish. But you still are daddy's little man-boy, aren't you?"

There was a groan as Number Three came from behind him, grabbing Lauren's handcuffed wrists and dragging her over to a hook, lifting her to hang her there, high enough that her toes barely touched. "Williams, for once in your life, just do the sensible thing. Keep your mouth shut," he pleaded, stepping back as his partner approached Lauren again. When Thomas moved too, Michael shook his head, lifting the Glock to point it at him. "Ah, ah," he chided. "I warned MacGowen you never listened to common sense. Don't make me hurt her."

Every step the loathsome MacGowen took closer to her made Lauren try to edge away, eyes fixed on that vicious knife. She knew perfectly well Thomas had a plan. He probably had dozens of plans. But- all it would take is one swipe from his blade and her throat would be opened, ear to ear. He circled behind her, tilting his knife back and forth teasingly.

"Your guards are busy right now," MacGowen said casually, "trying to hold off my Bratva lieutenants. You're alone, Thomas. Just like at school. No one wanted anything to do with a penniless bastard. That hasn't changed, has it? Your people turned on you so easily, *brother*," he emphasized mockingly. "I'm going to dump your carved-up corpse at the foot of Mogilevich, right before I graciously accept control over Jaguar Holdings-"

"As *we* accept control over Jaguar Holdings!" hissed Michael and as the two men glared at each other, Lauren saw Thomas's hand move slowly to the small of his back. She knew no matter how well they frisked him they'd never get all his weapons.

As Number Three and MacGowen leaned into each other's orbit, Mrs. Thomas Williams remembered a certain trick her husband had taught her in the Fun Dungeon, one that required quite a bit of core strength. Eyes darting once to Thomas's suddenly concerned ones, her legs swung up, spread wide, and then wrapped around Fassell's neck with the intensity of an anaconda, swinging furiously from her hips to knock the man off balance. She was already cringing, waiting for his gun to go off, likely into her leg to loosen them and then right through her heart but instead Mssr. Boucher was there, shooting Michael in the head and waving his hand to a bodyguard to lift her shaking body off the hook. The arms dealer put a grandfatherly arm around her.

"Are you all right, dear? Are you hurt?" He was carefully turning her, trying to keep her back to the room, but she forced herself under his arm and whirled to look for Thomas. "Non, non, Lauren, you must not..." Boucher's voice fuzzed out like a bad radio signal turning silent as she watched her husband cut his brother to pieces. A hand, as he'd promised, a vicious strike through the heart. An ear...

When the impeccable Thomas Williams looked up, there was a spray of blood across his white shirt, up his neck and over his left cheek. His eyes were glittering and there was a flat set to his mouth, like he'd forgotten how to look human. Then his gaze landed on her, he sighed and rose to his feet, stepping across the room in two big strides and holding her with his face buried in her neck, whispering, "I love you, I'm sorry. I love you, I'm sorry. I love you, I'm-"

"Shhh..." Lauren tried to sound soothing, but it came out more like a croak. "It's all right now. It is."

Chapter 40 – I Know the Oddest People

In which there is blood and retribution. Answers, but more questions. Because life in The Corporation can be like that. Incredibly irritating.

Even though Lauren knew her husband could barely contain his impatience, she continued to dab compulsively at the blood sprayed heavily across his beautiful face. He was attempting to speak with Boucher, who seemed amused by the couple's efforts to Handle The Situation. Simply the fact that there *was* a dead body - in several pieces - on the floor and Number Three from Jaguar Holdings was sporting a bullet wound in his forehead would seem to be a cause for concern. But Lauren noted that the grandfatherly Frenchman didn't seem the slightest bit perturbed by the grisly scene, meaning it wasn't the first time he'd been involved in one.

I know the oddest people, she thought, trying to decide if that was amusing or horrifying.

Chuck was holding her hands, squeezing them gently and looking into her eyes. It occurred to Lauren that he was checking to see if she was in shock. Clumsily clearing her throat, she forced a smile. "I'm uh... I'm good Chuck. It's all good." He gave her his professional smile, the one she secretly called the "You're full of shit" smile, but he simply nodded and kept close. "Did you find my shoe?" Lauren asked suddenly, "I kicked it off on the other balcony so you'd know what direction they took me?"

"Yes, Miss Lauren," Chuck agreed sedately, "of course, we also had your GPS tracker in your necklace."

"Oh, yeah..." she nodded, feeling ridiculous.

But then his rough hand opened and her necklace was there, her bodyguard pressing it into her hand, closing her fingers over the torn clasp. "They ripped it from your neck," he said, pausing for a moment. His throat worked as he swallowed. "I was not there for you."

Lauren absently pressed her hand to the side of her neck, feeling the abraded skin there for the first time. "Well Chuck, I was in the bedroom, Thomas was right there. Number Three screwed us over. It's not something you could have predicted-"

"But I should have," he interrupted her, eyes a bleak gray, "I should-"

It had been some time since Lauren had had the nerve to interrupt Chuck, but she did, figuring this was a conversation that was going nowhere. "Hey, did you see my thing with knocking over Number Three? That was pretty good, right?"

As she hoped, Chuck's face cleared and he squeezed her hand holding her St. Margaret's medal. "Fierce and savage. Like a dragon."

Suddenly, the room seemed full of people. Clara was there, along with Arabella, Martinsson, his men, Thomas's men,

Boucher's men- it was crowded and the groups eyed each other coldly. Thomas broke the ice. "Clara darling, I regret to inform you that you're a widow. I apologize, it couldn't be helped."

The sweet-faced girl who had shocked Lauren so many times on this trip shocked her again. Clara walked over and put her coat over her husband's ruined face. "Poor Michael." It was all she said, but Lauren could tell - for a moment at least - that the girl was sincerely sad over Number Three's brutal end. Looking up at Lauren, she smiled wryly. "It wasn't a real marriage, but sometimes, it felt like one. Just for a bit." And then she was all business. "Since we're all here," she nodded at Martinsson, "perhaps, Sir, this is a good time to discuss your approach with Bratva tonight?"

As Clara moved back to stand by her, Lauren mumbled, "Daaaamn, girl. Who the hell are you? I'm liking badass Clara."

The girl's suggestion was a good one, and the main players pulled closer, discussing how to handle the upcoming affair.

"They won't be expecting me alive," Thomas smiled unpleasantly.

Boucher nodded to Martinsson, "Nor will they be expecting us at all. So, the surprise is on our side, yes?"

Lauren tried to follow the rapid-fire negotiations as well as she could, still a little woozy from whatever knockout cocktail MacGowen had stuck her with. Absently rubbing the handcuff marks on her wrists, she wondered how they could walk into yet another meeting with the terrifying and effusive Bratva wives. She wasn't feeling particularly tough at the moment, but she was pretty sure she didn't get to head back to the hotel for a hot bath and a nap. Turning back to Clara, who was following the discussion, Lauren whispered, "Okay, out with it. Who the hell *are* you? Seriously? Because you deserve an Academy Award right now."

Laughing soundlessly, the other girl gave her a one-armed hug. "I'm just Clara. But I'm also Clara Martinsson."

"GET THE HELL OUT!"

Lauren forgot where she was and what was happening for the sheer astonishment of the moment. Cringing a little as everyone turned with a frown, she waved weakly. "I apologize. There's a lot of big revelations right now. I'll just... uh...." Sitting down, she dragged Clara with her. "That's your *dad?*" she whispered fiercely, nodding to the grey-colored Scandinavian.

Clara nodded, clearly amused. "I take after my mother's side of the family. But I always did love Pappa's business sense. And I can play the long game, as you see. Arabella didn't know who I was until this trip, but I was the one who managed to introduce her to my father in the first place. Their thing happened on its own."

Shaking her head, Lauren still discreetly stared at Martinsson, who was standing very close to a sober and pleased-looking Arabella. "Your dad..." she mumbled thoughtfully. "So, this was all a plan to get into The Corporation's inner circle?"

There was a low chuckle. "Well, you know how men get after an orgasm. Michael was very chatty." Lauren felt a chill when she looked at her (former?) friend's eyes. They were as flat and blank as a rattlesnake's. Just like her father's.

Lauren was quite correct that there was no time to head back to the hotel and recover, but suddenly there was a complete outfit waiting for her and a bag of cosmetics. Thomas drew her to the bathroom, wetting a cloth and gently wiping her face and her hands. "I know this has been an unimaginable day," he said kindly, pressing his hand against her sore cheek and gently stroking it with a careful thumb. "But do you think you can be my brave girl a little longer?"

"Of course," Lauren looked at him as if it was obvious. "But, how are you? This has been..." she floundered for a moment, not sure how one asked one's husband if he was okay with cutting his half-brother to pieces and seeing the last remaining member of The Corporation's management team shot to death.

But her husband gave her the most charming smile, leaning in for a moment to press his forehead against hers. And then Thomas started humming. Lauren's brow furrowed. Humming? What the hell was he- she burst out laughing. He was, in fact, humming the tune of *99 Red Balloons.* Getting dressed in her new outfit, she giddily sang along.

It was Deja vu of the worst sort to step back into the Bratva's gigantic restaurant, bracing for another round of hugs and kisses from the poisonous mouths of the Wives.

But Lauren gritted her teeth, feeling curiously comforted by having Clara and Arabella at her back. In fact, she watched with some amusement as Number One's "grieving" widow took point, smoothly inserting herself into the conversation between all the women. Even Clara, who still played the guileless newlywed since the Russians didn't know yet what happened to Fassell or MacGowen, moved between Lauren and some giggling, grabby maneuvers from Romanoff's pretty little wife Zia. It all gave her some breathing room and a moment of spiteful satisfaction seeing quickly concealed shock from Mogilevich and his men as The Corporation's new Number One strolled in, flanked by the unlikely pair of Martinsson and Boucher. To his credit, the Bratva head knew when he was being outmaneuvered. "Gentlemen," he rasped, "a quiet meeting before dinner, yes?"

"This is ridiculous!" growled Arabella, enjoying a brimming glass of vodka - her third - without any seeming ill-effects. "The men clustered together and making the 'big' decisions-" she mocking made quotation marks with two fingers on each hand, an impressive skill when still holding the vodka, "while we're out here and being mauled by the lipstick lesbians."

"I think they're more bisexual," Lauren volunteered. She leaned in, nudging her older friend. "So... you and Martinsson?"

Arabella examined her, an amused pout to her Juvaderm'ed lips. "He sees me as a partner. Shocking, I know. Everything they're discussing in there-" she nodded towards the double set of doors the men had disappeared through, "was put together by the two of us. Equally."

Stealing more dumplings from a passing waiter, Lauren shoved one in her mouth, chewing thoughtfully. Eyes turning to Clara, she suspected the redhead also had a pretty good idea of the negotiations. Which made her the odd one out. The dupe. Still, before her insecurity could rise and make her feel like nothing, the girl straightened her spine. It might not have happened until here in St. Petersburg, but she and Thomas were partners now. For real.

"So," she swallowed the dumpling. "What's Clara going to call you? Mum? Or Mother?" The slitted-eyed glare Arabella gave her almost made the whole fucked-up day worth it.

Part of the subtle power change was clear when Thomas made for Lauren, taking her arm and seating her next to him at the vast dinner table, rather than with the Bratva wives. And there she stayed, listening to the conversation with a secret smile, enjoying how much they were giving away without realizing she could understand them. And after dessert and tiny cups of coffee as black as coal and as thick as tar, they all piled in the luxury SUV's and made their way back to the hotel.

"You must be exhausted, love." Thomas held Lauren's drooping head in his hands, looking down at her tenderly. "But I am so proud of you."

Smiling up at him, she nodded, "When we get back to London, we're going to sleep for a week straight, and I personally, will shoot the first person who wakes us up." Enjoying her husband's somewhat startled laughter, Lauren sobered a bit. "Tell me. Please. I need to know what happened."

To her surprise, Thomas didn't smoothly brush her off or herd her quickly to bed. Seating her on the couch where he'd made love to her so forcefully just a few days before, her husband took off her high heels and began rubbing her feet. "Mogilevich was not happy. But he had the grace to be embarrassed at such an amateurish stunt."

Lauren forced a smile. It was easy to call it that now, but she knew her husband- who was never, ever caught off guard, had not seen any of this coming. Or had he? "Wait. Did you know something was off when we got here? Is that why you got Mssr. Boucher to come to St. Petersburg?"

He frowned, the fingers massaging her sore toes slowing, Lauren noticed to some regret. "The first night. Everything was going wrong, even though we- *you* discovered the drug trade. Clever girl," Thomas said fondly, leaning in for a kiss. "But I knew The Corporation power structure was disintegrating. Boucher is the only partner strong enough to engage in negotiation with me, allied against whatever games Kingston or Fassell were attempting. Though they both had their own plans, as it turned out."

"Yeah, you didn't see Clara coming, either, right?" Lauren shook her head, "And Arabella and that crazy-eyed Dane? Seriously!"

Thomas laughed. "Well, Martinsson's grandiose plan of taking over Jaguar Holdings was almost as unrealistic as Michael's and-" his mouth thinned, thinking of what MacGowen had done to his wife. "But Boucher and I were willing to... share. He will accept his part."

Taking a deep breath, Lauren braced herself. "And what is everyone's uh, part?"

He didn't answer her right away, staring at her wide violet eyes, still seeing her trust. Her faith in him. "We are breaking The Corporation apart and creating new divisions. Martinsson will be taking over the illegal financials and money laundering." Thomas paused; he knew that his wife liked the Frenchman. "Boucher is absorbing our arms trading and chemical weapons."

Lauren's smile faded. She remembered that night when she and the grandfatherly man had spoken of the convent, of the nuns and their beehives. And then she pictured the horrors he could unleash on the world with sales to any radical cult. Nodding in a short, jerky fashion, she asked, "And what do we take over?"

Thomas picked up her foot, kissing the tip of each toe.

"I began passing information to an MI:6 agent months ago, framing Fassell and Kingston for the new turn into sex trafficking." His mouth twisted contemptuously. "They weren't interested until I threw in some large-scale bank fraud. But it was part of a plan."

He pulled her onto his lap, ignoring her startled yelp. "I had a plan to remove you and me from the illegal part of The Corporation. From The Corporation entirely, in fact." Thomas enjoyed her stunned expression for a moment, then continued. "I still have enough information to feed them, pinning quite a bit of the activity on my dear, late half-brother, that will satisfy MI:6. They'll have to find new ways into Martinsson and Boucher's syndicates, but we will not be part of them. I have carved out the legitimate financial division of Jaguar Holdings, including your grandfather's company."

Lauren was utterly still for a moment, then surged forward to kiss him greedily, hands gripping the tailored shoulders of his expensive suit.

For a moment, Thomas just allowed himself to love his wife, to treasure the feel of her kisses. But then he gently took her wrists and pulled her away when she tried to loosen his tie and unbutton his shirt. "Love, tomorrow, when you've rested, I must ask you a question. Because we're moving into the legal portion of Jaguar Holdings does not mean we are... we are safe. You might need a bodyguard for life. There are other intelligence agencies aside from MI:6 that might come for us. Boucher or Martinsson may run into difficulty and attempt to drag us back into their net."

He paused for a moment, gathering courage, kissing her hands. "I am not a good man, Lauren. But for you, I want to be a better man." Her eyes were glossy and Thomas gave her a tender smile, carrying her to the bed and carefully undressing her, kissing each new bit of skin he revealed. Watching her fall asleep, he wondered how she could possibly stay with him.

He remembered every moment vividly after being pushed into that hotel room, Lauren handcuffed and her face swollen from his piece of shite brother. How he pulled his knife before MacGowen could wield his. Cutting until what was left beneath him was unrecognizable, and he looked up to see Lauren staring at him. Staring at the bloody monster she'd married.

Gathering his sleeping wife in his arms, Thomas spent the night staring at the ceiling, enjoying the feeling of the only pure thing in his life.

Chapter 41 – I am not a good man. But I am in love with you.

In which Thomas does things properly.

Waking in the morning was blissful for Lauren. Somewhere along the way in her strange marriage, finding her husband still in bed with her gave the girl a huge surge of joy. And on this morning, it was a great relief to see Thomas asleep next to her, his beautiful features relaxed for the first time in... weeks, really. So, Lauren simply watched him, feeling the warmth of the sun rising over St. Petersburg and creeping over her skin. The first rays to light his face woke Thomas, she mourned a little to see his eyes open abruptly, instantly alert. Then finding her next to him, her mysterious husband relaxed again, one long finger stroking down her cheek.

"Good morning, lovely. Have you been staring at me while I sleep?"

"No," scoffed Lauren, lying through her teeth.

Thomas bared his own in a rakish grin, gaze drifting down to her barely-clad breasts. "I see. May I say I have never been greeted with a more beautiful sight? Here you are, quite calm. Most women..." His big hand was sliding over her hip, inching her nightie up at the same time. "Most women would have disappeared into the night by now."

Lauren's soft foot was smoothing along his calf. "I'm not most women," she said boldly, a little amazed at herself.

This time, his face lit with his smile, warm and caring. "This, I am quite clear about, darling. Quite clear." Then his mouth was on hers, and Lauren gave that little, shuddering sigh she had when Thomas was about to gift her with a string of orgasms. But this time, he stopped. His grin was suddenly the cool, knowing one she was used to.

"Aren't we going to... uh..." she floundered. There was never not a time that her dark husband didn't carry on when he placed those talented hands on her. But he sat up, so awkwardly pulling up a strap over one bared breast - an action he regarded with some disappointment - Lauren did the same. She watched with surprise as he abruptly rose from the bed, stalking back and forth, one hand running absently through his hair.

"No, Lauren. First, I-" she watched as he paced the bedroom some more. It was such an alien behavior from her cool, collected spouse that she began to squirm anxiously. Was there something else? Good lord, what else had Bratva managed to turn to shit in the last eight hours?

"Who's attempting to murder us now?" Lauren asked, aware that she sounded a little dispirited. But really- this has been the creepiest week of her life, and given her existence within The Corporation, that was saying something.

Thomas paused at that, heading back to the bed and running his hands up and down her arms. "Poor darling, it wouldn't even surprise you, would it? No one is planning our imminent demise- no one *new*," he corrected with an expression that almost looked embarrassed. "No one new," Thomas repeated. Seating himself next to her, he took her left hand, absently stroking her soft skin. It was then Lauren realized her wedding ring was missing.

"Oh, crap!" she groaned, "Where did my ring-"

Holding up his other hand, Thomas wiggled his ring finger at her. Perched above his much larger ring and not even fitting over the first knuckle was her wedding band, the lovely, large diamond twinkling in the early sun. "The first time I put this on your finger," he mused, "it was a shackle. You would have never willingly married a monster like me."

Lauren opened her mouth to object, but slowly closed it again. At the time? No, she would have run as fast as she could in the opposite direction. Screaming. A lot. Thomas gave a wry smile and was about to speak, but she bravely put two fingers to his lips, surely the first time anyone had ever "shushed" the terrifying Number Two. "Then?" Shaking her head, she gave a helpless little chuckle. "But... this isn't then. This is now. And it's hard to remember those days, knowing what I know now about you."

There was an odd sheen to those crystalline eyes of his. Lauren couldn't decipher the emotion but she watched as he held up her ring, still perched at the tip of his finger. "I want to be a better man for you, darling, and I-" Thomas paused as his wife watched, wide-eyed. She'd never seen her spouse so hesitant, unsure even. "I believe if I were truly a good man, I would set you free. Insist on it. Send you somewhere far away from me, where the repercussions of my actions would no longer affect you. But... I am not a good man. But I am in love with you. I am in love with the woman who held off a herd of lustful Bratva lesbians."

"I really think they're bisexual," Lauren said absently.

The firm mouth of her husband curved slightly before continuing. "The woman who outwitted Number One and held her own against two men bent on doing harm to us both. The wife..." Thomas was pulling her on to his lap at this point, and she was giddily allowing it. "the wife who stood in front of me and demanded to share my burden. To stand with me." He shook his head, bemused. "I do not deserve you, but..." Slipping her wedding ring off his finger and holding it between his thumb and forefinger, Thomas took a deep breath. "I would like to ask you to marry me, Lauren. Properly. As a man who loves a woman would."

Every girlish instinct left in Lauren gave out a huge internal "squee!!" as her husband placed her on the bed and knelt before her. Lauren Marsh-" he gave a little chuckle, "-Williams, would you do me the very great honor of being my wife?"

All things considered, Lauren thought a little wildly, it was absurdly romantic- there in the beautiful old hotel, her husband only his sleep pants and thick, dark hair askew. And on one knee, like a proper proposal would be. And Lauren blurted out, "Does this mean I can start saying 'dude' again?" One dark brow rose, but he nodded his head. "What about jeans, can I start wearing my jeans-" His smile was becoming a bit tight and Thomas's eyes were narrowing, so Lauren hastily backpedaled, "Well, we'll just negotiate that later." He bent to kiss her knuckles, so sniffing a little already, she croaked, "Yes, of course, Thomas. Of course. We're a team, now."

His sudden grin and the way it lit his eyes to the blue of the Mediterranean made Lauren tear up in earnest, wiping the moisture from her cheeks as Thomas gently, carefully slipped her wedding ring back on her left hand.

So, when the new Number One of Jaguar Holdings and his

two de facto partners swept into the final meeting with Bratva, Lauren accompanied him, not surprised to see Clara and Arabella shouldering their way past the Russian security as well. Mogilevich sat back and watched the procession, his bushy grey eyebrows drawn together. But nothing was said of it as Thomas rapidly moved into the first order of business.

Sitting back and watching her husband decisively cut through the Bratva blustering with a calm, polite ease, Lauren was alarmed to feel her treacherous center getting wet. Shifting uneasily and pressing her thighs together, she chanced a quick glance around the room. Everyone was focused on the negotiations, and she breathed a sigh of relief. It was humiliating to be getting almost visibly aroused by Jaguar Holdings' new Number One- but she'd never seen him in action before. Not like this, forceful, controlled.

Shifting again, Lauren wiped her perspiring brow. God, he was hot. They really should have had sex that morning because she was so turned on right now. She looked up just as Thomas glanced over at her, his gaze dropping lower to her peaked nipples. One corner of his mouth turned up, just slightly, and it was almost enough to make her come on the spot. Praying the fabric of her suit was thick enough to hide her nipples, the aroused Mrs. Williams blew a blonde curl off her wet forehead and tried to concentrate.

"Are you quite well, darling?" Thomas slipped a hand around Lauren's waist as they left the meeting, and she stifled a groan.

"I'm fine!" she hissed, "I just didn't expect you to be so..."

He was clearly fighting a filthy grin, but her husband inquired solicitously, "So what, lovely?"

"Forceful and, you know, really gorgeous," Lauren admitted, face already flushed and her embarrassment making it worse. "You're crazy hot when you're in action."

Thomas made a thoughtful, humming sound. "'Crazy hot'. That is not a term I've heard used before in my professional life."

Retorting before she could think, Lauren snorted slightly, whispering, "Yeah, because you were usually killing the guy at the time." She stopped short in horror, realizing what just came out of her mouth. Putting a shaking hand over her lips, she looked up at her silent spouse. He was expressionless, but his hand tightened slightly at her waist.

Pulling her over to a quiet corner, Thomas stared down at his trembling wife. "This is often correct," he allowed, "will you truly be able to accept being married to me, knowing what I was?"

"I..." Lauren floundered for a moment. "I just joked about you... you know. I made a joke!" Her hands waved around anxiously, the restaurant's bright lights sparkling off her ring. "That's so horrible of me! I'm a horrible person! But... if I'm joking about it, then I think it means I already have?"

His mobile mouth fought to avoid a smile, but Thomas finally gave in, leaning down to kiss her behind her ear, enjoying his wife's little shiver. "You surprise me every day, my lovely virgin bride," he purred, knowing how the depth of his voice aroused her.

Angling her chin up hoping for a kiss, Lauren groaned softly. "Can we get out of here soon?"

"Ah," Thomas took her hand, pulling her into the dining area.

"I fear not. The final night is a feast and party with incalculable amounts of vodka. We will be here for some time, I suspect."

Lauren was trying not to pout. "Oh, okay."

Lifting her chin, her diabolical husband brushed his lips over hers. "Also, since we are newly affianced, it would be inappropriate for me to take advantage of you before the wedding. I respect you, darling."

"What?" It came out as a whine, and Lauren tried to keep her voice down. "What does- what are you even talking about? We're married!"

His smile was pure sin as Thomas smiled down at her tenderly. "Oh, my lovely girl. I promise the wedding night will be worth the discomfort of our wait." Enjoying the look of horror on his lovely wife's face, he continued towards the head table.

"You're totally fucking with me right now, aren't you?" Lauren's voice was small and dispirited, and it took everything in him not to laugh.

Chapter 42 – Taming the Dragon

In which Lauren is given the wedding of her dreams. And the wedding night of her nightmares. Because life in The Corporation is often like that. A total fucking buzzkill.

To Lauren's genuine shock (and to Thomas's as well, though he'd never admit it) nothing bizarre or threatening happened during the Bratva group's farewell dinner. Romanoff's wife Zia did corner Lauren, clasping her face between her heavily ringed hands as the Russian gave her a lingering goodbye kiss. "I will miss you, sweet girl. We would have been so pretty together."

Lauren was longing to kick her husband - who was watching the "tender" scene with poorly-concealed amusement - but she simply gave her would-be paramour a weak smile. "Uh... yeah."

There was more dancing, but fortunately, Russian folk dances this time that the children gleefully taught Lauren. She danced once with Mssr. Boucher, but his alarmingly red face made her guide him back to a chair and fetch him a drink.

The Frenchman thoughtfully sipped his wine - a delightful Muscat Ottonel Brut from the Fanagoria vineyards - and watched Lauren as she hummed along with the tune, watching the musicians play. "How do you feel about the changes that have been made today?" Boucher finally asked.

Looking up, she smiled slightly. "I'm still waiting for the other shoe to drop." At his raised eyebrow, Lauren huffed a little. "Nothing's ever this easy in this... you know..." she awkwardly waved her hands around. "This world."

The grandfatherly face of the man with her fell into a hundred soft wrinkles as he chuckled. "Mon Dieu! You do not think to discover murderous long-lost relatives, the being kidnapped, and also seeing the Jaguar management shot before you are not difficult enough?"

Lauren's eyes widened as she watched him chuckle before she dissolved into laughter, too. "Well, Mssr. Boucher, when you say it like *that-*"

He patted her hand absently, still watching the children sidestep each other, giggling in the twists and turns of the dance. "It would honor me if you called me Jean-René, or perhaps even Grand-père." The old man turned to look at her shrewdly, noticing her surprise and maybe just a touch of fear. "Or, not. It is perhaps too soon, eh?"

It was simply another facet of her unreal life, Lauren thought, in a world where a man could save her life and ask her to call him grandfather and the next day be selling machine guns to rebels in Syria. But she could only work with what she knew. Smiling at him, she murmured, *"Ce serait mon honneur, grand-père."*

Nodding, Boucher gave her hand a little squeeze. "Good. This is good."

He seemed a little misty around the eyes, but she pretended

not to notice.

Driving back to the hotel, Lauren fell asleep on her husband's shoulder. It had been one hell of a day, but when Thomas gently woke her when they arrived, she still intended to do her seductive best to get him into bed for a round of "Holy shit I can't believe we're still alive!" sex. Unfortunately, she was aware that she had zero seduction skills and traditionally, they were unnecessary because Thomas usually swept her off her feet and onto the nearest horizontal surface when the mood struck him. Which was often, but apparently not tonight.

Her hopes were unfairly inflated when Thomas tenderly undressed her and put her in the shower, running a soapy sponge over her with many kisses and compliments.

But when Lauren put her hand on her husband's cock, he gently removed it. "No darling, be my good girl," Thomas smiled sweetly, but she could see the devilish grin fighting to surface.

"But..." she protested weakly, "shouldn't we uh... you know, celebrate?" Lauren pressed her wet breasts against his chest, feeling his pectorals ripple a bit in response. "We kicked ass today, right?" She could feel it- the beautiful, hateful, unreasonable man was inches away from lifting her up against the tile and briskly pounding into her. But then, Thomas drew in a deep breath, forcing another smile.

"The wedding night, my darling. It will be worth it, I assure you." Kissing her on the nose, the new Number One pulled her from the shower, dried her tenderly, and put her to bed with a gentle pat on her bottom, which made her want to crack the lamp from the bedside table over his head.

It wasn't until they were leaving for the airport the next morning when the realization of The Corporation's galactic shift hit the girl. Martinsson's group was heading for their own fleet of SUVs, and that group now included Clara and Arabella. Lauren's step slowed, forcing the men around her to unwillingly slow their steps, too.

"Clara? Bella? You're heading back to London, too?"

The two women approached her with their usual friendly smiles, though they could tell she was not quite ready for the standard Corporation Wives hug and air kiss just yet.

Everything she'd known about them - everything - had collapsed within the space of forty-eight hours. And being a Corporation wife herself, Lauren intended to use caution with all things Jaguar Holdings, including her former friends. *I keep losing friends right and left,* she thought a little dismally.

"We are," Bella said, her smile was brighter than Lauren had ever seen it, and it was nice to know that the absence of her late, unmourned husband was responsible. "Not on The Corporation jet, of course." She beamed up at the gray man speaking on his iPhone, "We're taking Colin's jet." Bella leaned in a bit closer, "It's an Embraer Lineage1000E, quite comfortable."

Lauren smiled blankly, unaware that Bella was pointing out that the scary Dane's jet cost around $55 million, about ten million more than Jaguar Holding's Dassault Falcon 5X. "I guess... we'll see each other at some of the events?" she finally asked, not quite sure what would happen now.

It was Clara who took pity on her. "This is all very strange, isn't it?" Her tone was sympathetic, almost like the old

Clara - but this new girl, the corporate spy, and daughter of the Scandinavian mobster - carried herself with more confidence, looked around them with a sharper gaze. "We'll talk when we're back in London." Lauren felt a chill prickle on her arms when the other girl smiled darkly, "I'm looking forward to seeing Miles again and seeing how the music program is going in the new schools."

Throat dry, Lauren tried to swallow. Clara didn't want to... A vision of Miles and his open, honest face, his tentative interest in this extremely alarming girl - it made her indrawn breath turn into a wheeze. "R- really?" she managed, "I thought that would all be disbanded now, with the splitting up of The Corporation's assets?"

The redhead simply smiled at her, using a few too many teeth, and walked away, trailing her father to his car.

"I knew it couldn't be this simple!" Lauren mourned to Chuck, standing guard, as always.

But when they arrived back in London and headed home, after the bodyguard had seen Lauren settled in, ordered the disbursement of luggage and such, he found Thomas. "Mr. Williams? A word?"

Frowning, Thomas nodded, ushering him into his office. "What is it, Straker?"

His employee pulled out his gun, removed the clip, and offered it to him. "I am certain you would wish to sever my employment, sir. I failed in my duty in St. Petersburg, more than once."

Number One stared at the man, who was meeting his eyes

with a steady gaze. Straker knew what "terminating employment" in The Corporation could mean. It certainly didn't involve leaving the building with a cardboard box of personal possessions and desk supplies.

"I do not wish to accept your resignation," Thomas finally replied. "My wife certainly aided and abetted in the first incident, and the second..." he swallowed his disgust, "during the second episode, she was under my care."

Charles was undeterred, blocky fists opening and closing. "I failed in my duty."

Sighing, Thomas slapped the clip back into the pistol and offered it back to Lauren's bodyguard, handle first. "I know you would give your life for my wife if it was required. There is no one else I could trust with her safety more than you." He nudged Straker with the gun's handle. "And you know, Chuck," he emphasized a touch gleefully, "Lauren would never forgive me. Now kindly accept your firearm and let's get back to work."

Lauren watched as her husband walked the man down to the front door and slapped him on the shoulder in a manly fashion, bidding him goodnight.

"What was that about?" she asked as the tall, beautiful man she'd married ascended the staircase toward her.

Kissing her fondly, Thomas shook his head. "Just business, darling. Now, to bed. We have a busy day tomorrow."

Walking into the bedroom in a dispirited fashion, Lauren began shedding clothing. "Oh, yeah. A bunch of big board meetings to let everyone know what's going on? Big changes in the Corporation..." she cheered up slightly, thinking of a couple of lethal and unpleasant managers who were about to be very disappointed in the power shift. Nonetheless, the girl held out hope that Thomas would still want to share a little victory sex with her, but the infuriating man simply kissed her goodnight and fell asleep with one arm resting heavily over the curve of her hip.

Yeah, she thought bleakly, *he's totally fucking with me.*

"...Wake, lovely... wake up now..."

The rich, resonant tone of her husband woke Lauren the next morning, and she smiled, turning her cheek into the hand that was cupping it. When she was finally alert enough, her heart sank to see Thomas already garbed in a dark blue suit, wearing her favorite tie that made his eyes glow like the Mediterranean. "Oh, you're going into the office already?" Lauren asked, trying to keep the disappointment from her tone. Of course, he was. There was a lot to do...

"Not just yet." Thomas gave her a curious smile, tender but still slightly off. "I need you to accompany me to a meeting."

Yawning, Lauren shoved her wildly disordered hair back. "Sure. Just let me get dressed-"

Thomas interrupted her, "I've selected something for you to wear, it's hanging in the bathroom." She eyed him suspiciously as she walked across the large bedroom. He looked... strange. Aside from a few, notable, recent moments, her husband was always calm, his expression of urbane amusement very much in place. But right now, he looked younger, excited and anticipatory like it was, what, like Christmas morning?

When she entered the elegant bathroom, her heart started pounding as she found the dress her husband had left for her, white, edging into palest pink, with simple swooping lines and a gauzy overlay covering the long white slip.

Touching it carefully with one finger, she mumbled, "Maybe he's not fucking with me..."

It was funny, Lauren thought as she pulled her hair up into a simple twist and adding a light layer of makeup. She'd thought she would be shaking from nerves or excitement at a moment like this. But... she was calm? There was a certainty here that made her smile and step carefully into the dress after putting on her prettiest underwear.

"Thomas? Could you zip me?"

Lauren felt just a bit of nervousness stir until he came through the door, and Thomas's expression changed. Unguarded, emotional, delighted.

"You are so..." he paused for a moment, long fingers fumbling as he reached for the zipper. "So beautiful, my darling. I should have given you several gowns to choose from - it should be your choice this time - and I..." Thomas was babbling, he knew it but couldn't seem to shut up. "It just... seemed like you," he finished lamely.

His wife turned to him; her sweet face alive with happiness. "It's beautiful, husband. It's perfect."

Thomas shook his head before giving her a tender kiss. "No, it is merely a dress, my darling. *You* are beautiful and perfect."

Chuck was, of course, waiting at the curb and helped her into the car, carefully tucking her dress inside. As he moved to shut the door, Lauren grabbed his sleeve. "You're- you're coming too, right?"

His lips compressed with unseemly emotion. "Of course, Miss Lauren. Nothing could keep me from being there."

"Good," she nodded decisively, "that's good."

Lauren somehow did not find it unexpected when Thomas turned the Jaguar into the little parking lot of the Catholic chapel she'd visited during some of her lowest moments. She wasn't even remotely surprised when the priest was waiting for them, garbed in a more formal cassock and standing by the altar, surrounded by flowers. Chuck stepped up as Thomas left her, giving the girl a rakish wink as he headed toward the priest and shaking his hand.

"This is for you, Miss Lauren," the bodyguard intoned, handing her a beautiful little bouquet of peonies - her favorite! - in the palest shade of pink. Wrapped with the ribbon was a pretty silver locket, and Lauren could see her mother's photo was inserted there. "Mr. Williams-" he cleared his throat, "Mr. Williams thought your mother should be present."

Now, Lauren was pretty sure she was about to lose it, and since her mascara wasn't waterproof, it took a heroic moment to regain her composure. "This is perfect," she managed, "just perfect, thank you." Straightening her St. Margaret's medal around her neck as she smiled at the stained-glass window of its namesake, she nodded. "I'm ready." Chuck extended his arm graciously, and she took it as he walked her down the aisle.

The elderly priest's words were beautiful, and he smiled upon them both with great warmth and approval. Lauren knew perfectly well that he shouldn't be marrying a lapsed Catholic and - good lord, whatever Thomas could be considered - but he did, the simple ceremony making her feel like her heart was ready to burst from her chest. The man holding her hands and reciting his vows in a clear, confident voice, the solid bulk of his employee who'd come to feel like her father, and the warmth and safety of the tiny church and the priest who'd given her the courage to fight was all-encompassing, overwhelming in a perfect, wonderful way.

"It seems you have tamed the dragon," he smiled kindly, admiring her wedding ring.

Lauren shook her head, laughing. "That dragon is untamable, Father. But he is willing to accept a mate."

They drove home with Chuck following them, the Jaguar wobbling slightly when the passenger attempted to climb over the stick shift to get at the driver.

"Lauren- darling-" Thomas was attempting to drive through London traffic while enjoying the eager kisses of his bride. "I have an exquisite little wedding cake and champagne waiting for us at home- be a good- darling, I love your kisses, but you must-"

Even with his bride's most determined efforts, Thomas Williams, the intimidating new Number One of Jaguar Holdings managed to get them home without driving his sportscar right into a light pole every time her clever little hand stroked over the zipper on his dress pants. And they managed to bid a civil "thank you" and "we won't be needing anything else today," to a carefully expressionless Chuck and the other four men on their security detail before stumbling through the front door and locking, kissing each other desperately.

Thinking back on the afternoon later, Lauren was infuriated with herself, why she didn't see that the perfection of the day was the warning? A screeching siren clamoring that everything was about to turn to complete crap?

But since she wasn't thinking clearly and even willing to overlook the cake in order to get those pants off Thomas, it was a genuine shock to the new Mrs. Thomas Williams when the gunshot sounded from behind them, a fiery streak tearing through the skirt of her gown and angling upward to lodge in the chest of her new husband.

Chapter 43 – Twelve Hours

In which Lauren and Thomas do not spend their wedding night celebrating their union with the kind of top-shelf sex you would expect from Thomas. But instead, covered in blood on the concrete floor of the Panic Room.

Everything slowed down, the blood pouring from her husband's chest, the *"crack!"* of someone trying to shoot the front door open (it would take a while, it was steel-lined) and the sound of footsteps thudding down the hall to them.

It felt like her hearing was muffled, steel wool scraping over her senses and muting them.

Except for Thomas's voice. That first day when he showed her the panic room. "Once the locks are engaged, they do not open for twelve hours, darling."

The memory of his voice, the expression on his face, even his position in the doorway of the panic room were crystal clear. And that particular room was only six feet away. Six feet. It was an incalculable distance when she knew the footsteps belonged to whoever shot Thomas and was about to finish them both off. That's when Lauren's hand slid into his expensive jacket's inner pocket and pulled out the gun she just knew would be there. And when the man rounded the corner to the entryway, Lauren's shaking hands were pulling the trigger.

Once. It missed him, but the assassin's blocky face showed surprise to see Mrs. Williams with a gun.

Twice. The second shot struck him in the shoulder and spun him around, and as he whipped back around again, gun raised to finish this stupid, interfering bitch off-

Three times. This bullet nicked the contract killer in the neck. Just enough to tear through the artery there and Lauren's eyes widened to see the spurt of blood shoot out into the room and spraying the wall.

Dimly, she could still hear Chuck's shouts and the sound of his gun trying to shoot out the lock. But more alarmingly, she could hear another set of footsteps tearing down the stairway. *The third-floor landing?* Lauren thought, grabbing Thomas under the arms and digging in her heels, teeth gritted. *Almost there almost there almost there...* it was a desperate childhood chant that told her there was only a little more to be endured if she could *just hurry up-*

Thomas groaned, "Get in there, Lauren! Get in and lock the door! Leave me-" But he was pushing hard with the heels of his Berluti Scritto dress shoes, trying to move them along. She shrieked as a bullet went into the wall by his head, plaster puffing out from the impact and showering his suit. But with a heave that she was pretty sure ripped the cartilage off her ribs, Lauren rolled the two of them through the door and managed to slam it shut with a desperate, bare foot.

"Where's my shoe?" she mumbled as she slapped the button that activated the locks.

For a bit, there was nothing but the frantic heaving of their chests, his head on hers and both Mr. and Mrs. Williams trying to get enough air back into their lungs. But when Lauren finally felt something wet on her arm, she looked down to see his chest wound was bleeding with an alarming level of volume.

"Sh- shit!" she gasped, trying gently to put Thomas flat on the floor but wincing when the back of his skull bounced off the floor as she leaped up. The gigantic and well-supplied medical kit was easy to yank off the shelf and her shaking hands unzipped it as quickly as she could. Outside the door, someone was pounding viciously against it, already the meaty "thunk!" of bullets had slammed against the exterior with no effect.

"Oh," Lauren took a deep breath, "okay, sweetheart, we're going to get you taken care of, okay? You know Chuck is outside, totally kicking ass but we have twelve hours in here and I have to get you patched up, so..."

His long fingers clasped over hers, calming her frantic movements. "My good, sweet girl," Thomas said hoarsely, "I am so very proud of you."

Biting her lower lip to keep it from quivering, Lauren smiled at her bleeding spouse.

Thomas could see the moment when it hit her, his sweet wife. Lauren's face went sheet-white and for the first time, it looked like she might burst into tears. While the panic room was a life-saver in one way, if he bled out in here because there was no way for medical help to reach them, Lauren would be cradling a corpse for however many hours were left.

Then she pressed her lips firmly together and yanked open

the medical kit, grabbing a package of gauze before turning back to Thomas. "Do you think you can make it to the couch?" she asked, trying to get his jacket and shirt undone at the same time.

"I don't... believe so," he managed, and the girl looked up, terrified. Thomas was deadly pale, cold sweat dotting his forehead and lips compressed with pain. Nodding rapidly, Lauren finally got his blasted shirt open and looked for the wound. *Fuuuuck!* she moaned internally. Even her sketchy knowledge of human anatomy could recognize the bullet tore somewhere through his rib cage and possibly nailed his lung. Putting the big wad of gauze on the bloody hole, Lauren forced a smile. "Sweetheart I have to roll you - just a bit - but I have to see if there's an exit wound, okay?"

Her husband gallantly attempted to roll himself but fell back. To her terror, the red spot on the white gauze was widening and she swallowed a sob. Moving him to his side as gently as she could, Lauren felt desperately for a matching wound and found it. "Th- that's good. Okay, we can work with that," she was babbling a little, but she couldn't seem to stop trying to make reassuring sounding words that would ease Thomas's torment. Ripping off the top of the package of antiseptic spray, she squirted it liberally over his back and into the bullet hole, cringing at her husband's stifled moan of agony. Packing more gauze over the spot, the girl gingerly rolled him again.

"So, you know the funny thing here, sweetheart?" Lauren wasn't quite crying, but she quickly wiped her eyes before Thomas caught her. "So..." she continued, holding the bloody gauze with one hand while searching for an item in the first aid kit with the other. "The funny thing is that your exit wound is like, right by your stab wound, but just above the kidney. You have the luckiest kidneys in the whole world!

Really, I mean..." yep, she was babbling again. But her patient's attention was suddenly directed at the door as something heavy slammed against it.

"Darling," he groaned, "please go over to the communications board and press the two red buttons. One s- ah! Fuck!" Sweat dripped down Thomas's face as he gritted his teeth. He didn't completely remember how painful his half-brother's stab wound was, but he'd certainly taken a vicious beating or two before rising in the ranks at the Corporation. Nothing- *nothing* had ever felt like this, like his chest was on fire, like a fist had a grip on his lungs and was twisting them casually.

"Go on," Lauren was clenching her teeth, but he felt a rush of love at her effort to be strong for him. "Who am I contacting?"

She was already crawling over to the section of the wall devoted to lights and buttons and video screens. Flicking them on, she could see that Chuck was standing over the man collapsed just outside the door of the safe room. *That must have been the other shooter guy.* Lauren nodded disjointedly and punched the button for the Corporation and searched for a phone. There was a keypad set into the glass front, so she started to dial Chuck's number until she realized she didn't know it. It was stored in her contacts, for fuck's sake! And her phone was somewhere on the floor in the entryway, likely smashed by a lot of angry feet.

Scampering back to Thomas, Lauren put her lips against his cheek, chilly with sweat. "Sweetheart? Thomas? Please open your eyes, okay? Chuck is just outside the panic room; it looks like he killed the bad guys. He's waving his arms at the camera. Is there a speaker to talk to him?"

Opening his eyes with some effort, he tried to breathe more

shallowly. "Just call him, darling."

"I don't remember his phone number!" Lauren wailed.

Thomas panted out, "020 7946 0430."

"Wha-? How do you remember stuff like that?" she gasped, leaning down to lift his head a bit higher. "Never mind, okay, okay, um... I'm calling him and then he's going to get a god-damn doctor on the phone for us, okay?"

"Language..." he grumbled.

"Chuck!" Lauren had him on speaker as she was putting more gauze on Thomas's chest. "He's been shot in the chest - just over his left kidney - we need a doctor!"

"Miss Lauren." She almost wept at Chuck's calm, emotionless voice. "Everything will be all right; you must be very brave. I know you can do this. Are you packing the wound?"

"Y-yes," she sniffled, suddenly feeling like a child who knew that Dad just got home and everything would be all right. She'd never really had that feeling with Frank, but she was sure this was the right description.

"Very good, you're doing well. I'm patching in a doctor and we'll walk through this. There should be a small camera on one of the shelves there. Is Mr. Williams stabilized enough for you to get it?"

Lauren looked down. Thomas's eyes were closed and his breathing was rapid. "Sweetheart? Thomas?" He just opened his eyes enough to squint, and she sagged in relief. "I've got to get the camera so the doctor can look at your wound. Don't move, okay?"

Even knowing that was the stupidest possible thing she could say, Lauren ignored the small curl of his lips as he whispered "Fine..."

Suddenly, there was also the calm voice of a doctor looking at the images she was sending and asking questions and then instructing her and then things weren't quite so terrifying. *Still terrifying as fuck,* Lauren thought feverishly, *but I won't let Thomas die.*

When Lauren finally even thought to search for the time, the red digital readout on the control board told her four hours had passed since she'd dragged her bleeding spouse through the door of the safe room. She'd gotten a small dose of pain meds through the unwilling lips of Thomas and carefully cleaned him up and sterilized as much as possible. With the doctor's precise instruction, she'd used the suture gun, which she could tell put her poor husband through even more suffering. But there was no way her hand was steady enough to try stitches. Laying down next to him and turning on her side, Lauren smiled as she ran her hand over his cheek. "We have the worst wedding nights ever. I don't think we should get married anymore."

He smiled briefly, but a look at her bloody wedding gown made his expression turn sorrowful. "Your pretty dress..." Thomas mourned.

"It's just a dress," Lauren shook her head. "Just a dress." Looking down, her heart stuttered as another bloom of red spread over the gauze on his chest. "But you have to breathe slowly for me, okay?"

"Mmmmm." It sounded like an agreement, and his lids fluttered shut. Absently admiring his unfairly thick lashes, she stroked his hair back.

"You asked me once how many people I've killed..." he murmured at one point.

"I don't need to know that, Thomas." Lauren was so terrified of missing a single breath that she was nearly nose to nose with her patient. She thought about it. "Do you regret any of them?"

"Hmmm..." he groaned, taking in a deeper breath, "No." His eyes opened, and she nearly drowned in the beauty of them- clear, like the pond near her grandfather's cabin where she'd swam every summer, leaping from the dock so her toes would touch the sand on the lake bed. His eyes were like that, clear blue where she could surely dive to the bottom of him.

"Every one of them deserved it, Lauren. I don't take a life carelessly. They were monsters. Every one of them."

"Do you see their faces? When you dream?"

Thomas gave a weak chuckle, and she sucked in a breath as some blood decorated his lower lip. "Never. I slept with the rest of an untroubled conscience. Until you, of course."

Gently checking his pulse and feeling the thready motion of it, Lauren starting praying silently to the God she'd not spoken to for so long. "What do you mean, until me?"

"I dreamt of you."

She felt flushed, "You dreamt of me? I mean, when?" Lauren very carefully dabbed at his mouth, not letting her husband see the red on the cloth. But he was still staring at her.

"The first night... when we met. Your job interview." One eyebrow quirked humorously as he watched her eyes widen.

"Nothing specific... just how-" Thomas coughed and she nearly screamed in terror when he wet the cloth she hastily put to his mouth with another red stain. "-how beautiful you were. You were sitting in our garden - my garden then - in the sunshine. Looking up at me and smiling. I'd never had anyone at home to greet me. It..." another cough, no blood this time, "...never occurred to me that such a thing would be desirable. Until you."

Lauren used every ounce of self-control she possessed to speak calmly. "My beloved, I have to get Chuck to link us to the doctor again - just, you know, checking in - so just relax, okay? I would like to hear more about the dreams."

He seemed to be in a light doze, so she cried silently as she dialed her bodyguard, who already had the poor physician on the line.

Eight hours gone by. Four more hours. She just had to keep her husband, who was in terrible pain and bleeding sluggishly, alive for four more hours. Then the medics would take over.

"They're already here, Miss Lauren." Chuck was trying to soothe her as he watched the tears pour down her reddened cheeks. "Just ready for the door to open and take care of your husband."

"He's..." she was trying to choke down a particularly loud sob. "Everything's been taken away from me-" she laughed mirthlessly, "-mostly because of him. But I can't lose Thomas. I can't. I... I know this is all nuts. But he's mine. He made me more. Better. He's better too, now..." She regretted the words almost instantly because, for a moment, her stoic father figure almost looked gut-shot himself.

"I... Miss Lauren," he finally answered, "you will not lose Mr. Williams. You are doing a fine job."

"So did that fucking bullet tearing through his chest," she sobbed in a whisper. "Could you just, you know, call me Lauren? Would that be okay? Like... family?"

For the first time, it seemed that Charles Straker had thrown caution utterly to the winds, behaving in a ridiculous, almost madcap sentimental fashion that was so utterly alien to him. He smiled. "We are family, Lauren," he finally answered, "and I see you as my daughter. And as my daughter, I could not be prouder of who you've become."

Wiping her cheeks with the back of her hands, she smiled at the video screen in a watery fashion. "Thank you, Chuck. I wish you had been my dad. I bet I wouldn't have been such a wimp growing up."

"Ah, Lauren," he said gently, "but then perhaps you would never have met Mr. Williams. Never married him. Never fallen in love. Even knowing what you know now, would you have rather had that other life?"

Angling the video screen so she could watch his face when she laid back down with Thomas, Lauren shook her head. "No. No, I wouldn't. I just wish... it wasn't so brutal. People keep getting hurt. I wish it wasn't like this."

He looked rather sad, but Chuck nodded. "All those in this position wish the same. But that is not for us to decide. What we can do, is decide what to do with the time gifted to us."

There was a comfortable silence between them as Lauren stroked Thomas's forehead. "Chuck?"

"Yes?"

"You totally stole that whole line from Gandalf in *Lord of the Rings*, didn't you?"

It was the first time she'd ever seen the man laugh.

"Thirty minutes, Thomas," Lauren whispered, both hands cupping the gaunt cheeks of her husband. "Thirty tiny minutes and we're out of here and you get better. I love you so much. Just thirty more minutes, okay?"

For the first time, he didn't answer her back, and Lauren began to sob in earnest. "You don't get to go away! T-Thomas I will say 'fuck' three hundred times a day! I'll wear jeans! I'll-I'll not only say 'fuck' at your funeral, I'll totally lie and tell everyone you liked polka music and only drank boxed wine at home! I mean it!"

There was the faintest smile on his face as Thomas rasped out, "I intend to live primarily for the satisfaction of spanking you for that outrageous threat."

Curling around him like a desperate strain of ivy, she whispered, "Yeah, okay."

The electronic buzz and the crisp "click!" of the door opening was drowned out instantly by the stampede of feet. The doctor Lauren recognized as the man who'd been coaching her for the last twelve hours. Paramedics. And Chuck, who immediately wrapped his arms around her. Lauren's knees finally gave out under her when the physician looked up.

"He's alive, Mrs. Williams. You did a good job. Let's get him to the hospital."

Chapter 44 - If you try to pull out that IV, I will sit on you.

In which Lauren makes it clear she is Not Fucking Around.

When Thomas woke next, it was in a hospital bed.

This was the worst possible position for a man in his, well, position to be in. But as his bloodshot eyes scanned his room, he spotted Chuck and another trusted man by the door. Lauren's bodyguard was just inside it on a chair, and the other man sitting in the hallway, glaring at everyone passing by. And then, with half her little body slumped on his covered legs was his wife. Smiling tenderly, Thomas attempted to reach out and stroke her hair, but the IV in his hand stopped short. Lips curled back in a sneer, Number One of Jaguar Holdings was about to rip it out of the vein it was puncturing when the flash of light from Lauren's wedding band stopped him. Her left hand was covering his, and his sweet bride was wearing a thunderous scowl.

"Don't you even think it, Thomas!"

His dark brow rose elegantly in a challenge, but Lauren actually growled. It was more like a cat than a panther, but her fierce little "Grrrr" was adorable. Until she leaned in a bit on his bandaged chest.

He gave a deep groan, which made Chuck look up but not move.

"Do you know what I've been through, husband?" Lauren wasn't backing down, and really, his little wife was quite heavy when she was leaning on a chest wound.

"Now, darling, I..."

Swooping forward, she placed a kiss on his lips before whispering, "If you try to pull out that IV or even move another inch, I will sit on your handsome, muscled midsection. Right at the level of your kidneys, in case you were wondering." Her pretty eyes were a cold lavender-grey, and it was clear his gentle spouse was Not Fucking Around.

Looking over at Straker, Thomas could see he would be no help. The big man simply settled himself more comfortably in his hard chair and ostentatiously looked away. The intimidating Number One was torn between outrage and a sudden desire to laugh. Aware that the latter would hurt terribly and that the former wouldn't go over well with his beloved wife, who indeed looked like she was ready to sit on his chest, Thomas simply put his head back on the pillow and sighed. "How long...?" his question was interrupted by a cough, and he watched Lauren's body go rigid, her gaze focused on his mouth. She snatched a tissue from the box on his bedside table and held it, hand shaking slightly. "Darling?" Thomas started again, "It's all right, why are you so-"

"When you coughed, in the room," Lauren interrupted, "when you coughed there was blood on your lips. I don't- when you cough, I grab a tissue just in case-" It was his eyes that made her start crying, Thomas's blue gaze was terribly sad. She'd never seen the expression on his face before.

His other hand - the one without the IV - grasped her shaking one and brought it to his lips, kissing it gently. "I'm sorry, my sweet girl. I'm terribly sorry you were in harm's way yet again. That you were forced to care for me."

Lauren laughed- more like an angry little huff. "You still don't get it, do you? Thomas, I was terrified because I thought you died! Thirty goddamn minutes before the door would open and a doctor could save you and I thought you were gone." She used the tissue she was clutching to wipe her nose. "*Forced* to care for you? I'm so glad I was there. If that was going to be our last twelve hours, I wanted it to be with you." Lauren put her wet cheek against his.

"My beautiful Lauren," Thomas whispered, "I will move heaven and hell to stay with you. I am yours, as you are mine."

The two stayed together, face to face and whispered until the doctor came in, smiling at seeing the couple together on the hospital bed. "Mrs. Williams, thank you for not pulling out the patient's chest tube this time." Thomas took one look at his bride's mortified face and choked out a laugh. "It's good to see you alert, Thomas, I'm Dr. Giles." The doctor was beaming at him approvingly as if he'd done something more talented than simply regaining consciousness. "Your wife has been quite determined that we keep you alive. When an unidentified nurse walked into the room, your associate-" the doctor nodded at an expressionless Chuck, "-drew a gun on him while Mrs. Williams here jumped on top of you, shielding you from an attack. Hence, the chest tube." Thomas pressed his lips together, almost feeling the heat of Lauren's painful blush.

"My wife is very fierce when provoked," he managed, "as you have seen."

Dr. Giles simply chuckled, "Indeed. I consulted with her while you were in the Panic Room. Lauren was admirably courageous. She saved your life."

Smiling up at his teary-eyed wife, Thomas kissed her hand. "Of this, doctor, I have no doubt."

Limping back into their townhouse a couple of days later, Thomas could smell the fresh paint. Everything looked perfect and undisturbed- even the walnut wainscoting that hid the door to the Panic Room looked unmarred. Lauren had hastily put together a comfortable bedroom on the main floor to keep him from climbing the endless flights of stairs in their home. Finally, resting in bed while she arranged the pillows behind his back, he gave a huge exhale of breath. She looked up immediately, eyes wide. "Are you all right? Are you in terrible pain? I can get a pill-"

"I'm fine, darling," Thomas assured her with a tight smile. It was a lie of course, and they both knew it. He'd stubbornly refused most of the pain medication, wanting to stay as alert as possible. "But I would be grateful for some water, and a moment to speak with Chuck?"

Lauren's brow furrowed, but she nodded and gave him a kiss before heading out the door. Straker passed her, giving her a completely unrecognizable smile, one with warmth and fondness. Thomas shook his head. Of course, she'd won over the most unemotional man in his organization. Of course. But when the bodyguard paused before his bed, he was all business.

"Sir," Straker noted gravely, "you look much better."

"Thank you," Thomas replied. He took a deep breath, refusing to flinch at the corresponding flare of agony in his chest. "You have completed your investigation into the attack?"

Now, Straker wore the unkind, forbidding expression he was used to before Lauren. "I have, Mr. Williams."

Thomas waited until after the dinner he didn't feel like eating, but he forced himself, knowing every bite removed one of the little lines furrowing Lauren's formerly smooth brow. She'd kept up a cheerful commentary about the music program in the schools, looking gloomy only once when she mentioned Clara.

"Yeah, she's been there with Miles a lot. I can tell he's totally getting into her, 'grieving widow' or not." Lauren made the little quotation gesture with her fingers, another vulgarity he would not have allowed before everything changed in St. Petersburg. In fact, Thomas found himself smiling a little, enjoying his wife's quick wit and occasional sarcastic asides. She shuddered. "I don't see that going well. And there's not a word I can say to the poor man."

Looking at her worried face, Williams felt a surge of tenderness for his wife. Even after a year now as a Crime Lord's Bride, she was still empathetic, still sweet and caring. "Perhaps it's his innocence that attracts her," he mused, "but since she's Martinsson's daughter, I can't imagine her keeping it up for long."

Shrugging as she sipped from her wine glass filled with water, Lauren sighed. "I don't know, she kept up the innocent fiancée thing for what- a year and a half?" Collecting her thoughts, she took his now-empty tray from him and settled his blankets again. "Can I ask what you and Chuck talked about?" Her eyes were on the pillow she was fluffing, but Thomas could hear the anxiety in her tone.

"I rather suspect you know, darling," he answered. The weight on his chest felt heavier than the bullet that had torn through it, but Thomas forced himself to continue. "He was heading up the investigation into who sent the assassins. Straker kept the second shooter alive long enough to question him."

Lauren's full mouth was drawn into a tight, thin line. "I would imagine that was a smart move," she agreed. "What did Chuck find out?"

Thomas took her hand, smoothing out her clenched fist and resting it on his lap, admiring his wife's long, slender fingers. So gifted in coaxing beauty, unlike his, which were gifted in bringing death. "The man who ordered the hit." he sighed and forced himself to continue. "It was Frank. Your father."

He heard her stifle a sob but Lauren looked up, dry-eyed. "Go on."

"He thought if I was removed from the picture, The Corporation assets I controlled would go to you. Frank believed he could manipulate you into signing everything over to him in the middle of your grief and confusion. He would then have a controlling share in Jaguar Holdings and regain his position and millions of dollars. He-" Thomas stopped for a moment, clenching his teeth and feeling such a flood of rage that his pulse surged. "Frank intended to then marry you off again to another rising star in The Corporation, strengthening his position." Thomas continued to hold her hand, running his thumb gently over his wife's soft skin as he watched her bowed head. When she finally looked up, Lauren was livid. And heartbroken.

"I knew it. I just... somehow, I just knew it was Frank. That chickenshit bastard. Everyone would think he was too cowardly to do something like that but he's always been ruthless when it came to getting what *he* needed." Lauren shook her head, laughing harshly in a way that pained Thomas more than his chest wound. "He always thought I was pathetic, a pushover and that I was nothing unless I was *useful.*" She drew out the word furiously. "What are you- wait. I don't know if I want to... shit!"

Lauren angrily stood up, and he watched her pace back and forth across the room. "You know, I was looking back over a couple of scrapbooks my mom had made me- stuff like birthday parties?" He nodded carefully. "I looked for any pictures with Frank in them and I realized- the only birthday of mine he ever celebrated was one where the *New Yorker* was doing a story on him. I didn't realize at the time how mad mom was at him for bringing in a photographer. Frank put me on his lap and helped me blow out the candles on the cake. I was so excited he was there. I remember wishing that he would be there for my birthday the next year. That was my wish." Taking a deep breath, she sat carefully on the bed next to him, her warm leg brushing his thigh. "And now he tried to murder the person I love most in this world. Once again," Lauren hissed, "for his shitty stocks!"

Thomas was still, other than gently running his hand up and down her shaking arm. "He is still your father, and this is terribly painful. I am sorry." But her answer stopped his attempt at comfort.

"Is that how you felt about your father?" Lauren's tone wasn't as angry, but it required an answer.

"I..." he floundered for a moment. He didn't even remember uttering any thoughts about the man who'd given him life out loud. "He was a name. I'm sure- I do remember being excited when he'd come to visit us when I was a little boy.

My mother would attempt to list my accomplishments- she knew that was the only thing about me that would catch his interest, but..." Lauren squeezed his hand, then bringing it to her cheek and holding it there.

She laughed bitterly. "Our taste in dads totally sucks."

Thomas slid his hand from her cheek to her chin, pulling gently to make her look at him. "I will tell you that you did not deserve Frank as a father. I suspect you would say the same to me. But at this point, my only concern can be for your safety. I will not tell you what I intend to do. I do not wish you to ever ask me." He leaned in closer, forcing her gaze to his. "Do you understand, my sweet wife?"

For the first time when discussing the harsh and serious reality of this side of their life together, Lauren didn't cry, didn't give him a look of painful heartbreak. This time her gaze was level, expressionless. When she nodded, he realized with a painful twinge that she looked a bit like Clara. And then he vowed she would never have a reason for that expression again. "Yes, Thomas," she said calmly.

Pulling her closer and ignoring the corresponding surge of pain in his side, Thomas kissed his bride lingeringly. They sat together, watching the sun set over the park just outside the windows.

Finally, he asked, "Did you really yank out my chest tube?"

Chapter 45 – I Shall Wait, Darling. But I Fully Intend to Ravish You

In which consummation is not quite as easy as Lauren and Thomas might hope.

"Be sure to forward the Italian stock reports before you..."

Lauren sighed, moving the tray to her other hand to open the door to her husband's temporary bedroom. While the new Number One of Jaguar Holdings' financial division was in no shape to be heading back to the office, it didn't stop him from Zoom meetings from his bed. For hours. In fact, she had to smother a smile at the sight of her stern-looking spouse in a dress shirt and jacket hiding his plethora of bandages and pajama bottoms. Waiting until he ended the meeting and disconnected the call, Lauren placed the tray on his lap.

"Thank you, darling," he pulled gently on her hand until she bent to kiss him. "And where is Straker?"

"Chuck," Lauren playfully popped the "k" at the end of the bodyguard's name, "is sleeping in the guest bedroom upstairs for the first time in like 48 hours. But Aimes is in the hallway and your guy who looks like a boxer?"

Thomas suppressed a smile, "Michaels?"

"Yeah, he's cruising around outside and intimidating the neighbors," she laughed. "Here..." Lauren busied herself, laying a cloth napkin over his lap and pillow behind him. "Will you please take a pain pill with dinner?"

"Don't need it," Thomas grunted, painfully moving higher. He growled as his insolent wife rolled her eyes. "Careful little girl, I'm quite capable of heating your shapely bottom."

Leaning forward with a saucy grin, Lauren murmured, "Just as soon as you can catch me... Sir." Instantly darting out of reach, she gave him a wink over her shoulder as she headed for the little cluster of pill bottles.

Truth be told, Thomas was healing much faster than any men with an abdominal gunshot wound should be- especially since he drove himself relentlessly. In fact, they'd indulged in a make out session that morning that was far too steamy, given that he was pale and a little clammy when she made him let her go. But it didn't change the fact that every time the light sparkled off her wedding ring, Lauren was suffused with need for her beautiful husband. And the unabashed hunger in his cobalt gaze told her he felt the same.

"It's been three days, you slut!" Lauren lectured herself while filling a glass of water, "Control yourself! What the hell kind of wife are you?" But taking the water and medication back to the bed, she melted as Thomas looked up at smiled at her, the real smile that deepened the fine lines around his eyes.

"How are you, darling?" Thomas took her hand again, "You are eating with me, do get comfortable." He patted the bed next to him with a mischievous wink, and Lauren nodded, forcing a smile.

"I'll sit with you, but I've- I ate already."

Now, her husband put down his fork and stared at her coldly. "You're lying to me."

"What? No!" Lauren gasped, "I'm-"

"I've not seen you eat once since I've come home from the hospital." Thomas's voice was calm, edging toward cold. "And I've seen you thrash in that recliner-" he nodded at the chair she slept in by the bed, "when you're asleep so it's either extremely uncomfortable or you're having trouble resting."

He relented slightly as he viewed his wife's head, bent and looking at the tray in his lap. He hated to see her misery when he scolded her like this, but it couldn't be more obvious that the only one getting care in their home was him. "Lauren. Lovely girl, look at me." Thomas despised the unfamiliar feeling of guilt that suffused him when his sweet wife looked up at him, faking a smile with a trembling lip. "Sweetheart," he said kindly, "I'm getting better. I'll be fine."

"I know," she answered, surprising him a little. As if it was obvious that he, Thomas Williams, Number One of Jaguar Holdings could do nothing less than completely recover. "I just... I know that. You're too stubborn to do anything else." Lauren managed a watery little smile.

He frowned, one arm lifting - still with a tremor, she noticed - to run his thumb along her cheekbone. "Then what is it, lovely? Aside from all the obvious possibilities," Thomas added with a grimace.

Her wet purple eyes finally met his. "I killed people. I murdered Kingston, and the shooter."

"You didn't-"

For the first time in his memory, his wife interrupted him. "I did. He wouldn't have died if I hadn't drugged him. I hated him; I totally hated his guts but I..." Lauren shook her head helplessly. "I see his face, the way he looked when we stuffed him into my cello case. I keep having this nightmare where he opens his eyes just as we're shutting the lid. Sometimes..." She was crying now, hating herself for looking so pathetic and upsetting him when he was still so weak. "Sometimes, I see myself in the case."

Thomas let out a long, pained sigh and pulled on her hand. "Come here, baby. Come here now."

"I don't want to hurt-"

"Shhhh," he soothed, "come here." Lauren crawled on the bed and carefully arranged herself against his long body, shuddering a little in relief. Even with the crinkle of his bandages and his slightly labored breathing, her husband was solid, comforting. "I cannot force you to see the reality of this," Thomas murmured, rough fingers stroking up her arm, "but you know I am correct. Ben would have died. Likely within the next few days, and most probably by my hand, if not one of his numerous enemies. Indeed, knowing what we know now, I'm a bit surprised Arabella didn't insist on ending him herself." He chuckled before realizing Lauren would not find it as entertaining as he did.

She was quiet for a while as he softly kissed the top of her head, holding her a little closer, even though it really did feel like someone was driving a spiked glove into his ribcage. Finally, Lauren raised her head to look at her beautiful husband, his eyes so kind, as she'd so rarely seen them before. "I would do it again, if it meant saving your life. Just like that man in the hall. I'd do it again. To both of them." She buried her face back in his neck and they sat together in the sunny quiet of their home.

Now, it wasn't Thomas fucking with her, Lauren miserably thought. It was the entire goddamn universe. Seriously! Because her stubborn husband refused to stay down, he developed pneumonia, a terrifying development with his chest wound and unbearably painful when his illness set off a round of coughing. Naturally, he still conducted business, furiously sending off emails and reports and issuing orders in his scratchy, croaky voice.

But, sick or not, it had been so long since he'd laid hands on his lovely wife that the doctor walked in on Mr. and Mrs. Williams desperately kissing each other with his hand in her undies. After her horrified little yelp and his barking at the poor physician to "Get the HELL out!" she had firmly refused to get within reach of Thomas's alarmingly long grasp.

"I'm *not* going to be the person who ends up killing you after everyone else who's tried!" Lauren snapped when he attempted to "Sir" her. This set off a few days of cold, clipped communication from Thomas, who she knew was suffering as much as she was from their enforced chastity. Still, it chipped at the new intimacy they'd created and it was all wearing her down.

Chuck found her one afternoon, weeping in the garden while she tried to water the new wisteria vines she'd planted. "I'm not sure I've ever seen growing instructions that included a woman's tears," he remarked blandly, looking off into the distance to allow her a moment to compose herself.

"It's my stupid husband," Lauren finally managed, "and his stupid Number One thing that means he can't even recover from a fucking gunshot wound to the chest when there's The Corporation business to be done."

Dusting the leaves off a bench, he seated himself, listening attentively. "I can imagine this is an issue of discord between you," Chuck finally offered. "Mr. Williams is mulishly stubborn. Much like yourself."

"I am not," she mumbled, wiping her nose awkwardly on her sleeve.

"Hhmmmm..."

It was classic Chuck, Lauren thought crossly. Noncommittal, simply observing, well, she could be that way, too. All calm and- "We didn't even get our wedding night!" she burst out, "We finally get married for the right reasons and we get exactly nothing! Well, Thomas got a bullet but damnit! This is so stupid and I'm being unfair and childish..."

Aaaand, she was crying again, Chuck noted, placing an arm gingerly around her shoulders and offering her a clean handkerchief. "Use this," he said, "your sleeve is getting sticky."

They talked for a while- well, Lauren burst out in a series of grievances and he listened, making more of those encouraging sorts of noises.

"Hey, honey." Lauren looked up with a smile as her husband stepped gingerly into the kitchen. "Do you want to eat with me in here, or in the bedroom?"

"Here, please darling," Thomas shuddered, "when I am able to climb the stairs and leave that sickroom for good, I am going to brick over the door and pretend it doesn't exist." She laughed, a pleasing sound, he thought. One that he'd not heard for a while.

They talked about the results of his latest chest x-ray and the big summit for all the businesses - the legitimate ones - under the Jaguar Holdings umbrella that would be held next week.

"Do you have your speech in mind?" Lauren asked, clearing the plates and bringing over a pink pastry box, one her husband eyed with some interest.

Selecting a lemon tart, Thomas nodded. "Of course. They need to hear a firm vision for the future to dispel any concerns - or more importantly - any stock fluctuations from the news of the split."

"Of course," she agreed with a little smile, and his brow rose at her tone. "I think we should just..." Lauren sighed. She couldn't believe she was saying this! "Let's just take the pressure off of us until after the summit. We're both so stressed out and -"

"Deprived? Denied? Desperate?" Thomas offered.

"Yeah," she sighed, "that. Let's plan our night the way it should be, without worrying about dislodging the tube in your chest or you getting- god, what else *is* there? The Bubonic Plague? We'll wait, and it will be perfect. It's what you wanted for us back in St. Petersburg, even when I begged you, so let's... not. You know, do anything." He was leaning back in his chair, tart forgotten in his long fingers. "Besides," she shuddered, "I'm going to kill myself if Dr. Giles walks in on us again."

"Hasn't the man ever heard of knocking?" Thomas snarled, but he nodded reluctantly. "All right. You deserve the perfect wedding night."

"Let's not call it that," she disagreed, shaking her head vehemently, "wedding nights never work out for us. It's our... oh, my god! I just realized it's going to be our first wedding anniversary in ten days! You know, from the first time we got married? That would be perfect!"

Her husband gave a sigh that sounded more like a groan, but he nodded. "I shall wait, darling. But I fully intend to ravish you."

Thomas leaned forward and a delighted little chill went up her spine. He looked so *hungry*. Starving, in fact.

"I shall stretch those long, lovely legs of yours on the softest bed I can find, and tie your pretty hands to the headboard," he promised, his voice deep from his illness and his sheer need for this woman. "I will feast on your tender, soft pussy until you come for me over and over until you beg me to stop. And then I shall force you to come once more on my tongue before I slide my cock into you and it all begins again."

Lauren vaguely heard something dripping, but it wasn't until her devilish husband deftly plucked her sagging wineglass from her hand that she realized it was drooping sideways in her numb fingers.

The next week was torture. Thomas had generously offered to at least make his desperate wife come, but she stubbornly refused. "Together or not at all!" Lauren insisted, groaning as she turned the shower handle to "cold." She was aware that he'd made plans, renting a beautiful beach cottage in Brighton on a lonely, windswept little spit of sand that was utterly isolated.

"No one will hear us," he promised in that terrible, purring voice, "no one will hear what I'm doing to you." Thomas grinned as she gave that nearly silent squeak that he found utterly adorable.

The Jaguar Holdings summit was quite the affair, Lauren thought. She'd reluctantly realized that as Number One's wife, she was now the one who needed to help put together these events and oversee the social side of the summit. Fortunately, it kept her busy and she found that several of the spouses helping her were pleasant, more fun and relaxed now that the group operated with a decisively different aim. Most of the boring and haughty members of the old charity committee, fortunately, ended up with one of the two new companies. There was more laughter and offers of help in this group, and she cautiously began going to lunch with one or two of them, maybe getting a cocktail after a long meeting. One, she reminded herself firmly, with a bit of a chill, just one cocktail these days. So, standing backstage with Thomas at the large and luxurious ballroom they'd prepared, Lauren could feel the excitement; from the audience, from her husband, who looked magnificent in a perfectly cut navy blue suit that outlined his spectacular ass so nicely. Realizing she was staring at that portion of his anatomy, she looked up guiltily to see him smiling in that scary, meaningful way.

"How do I look, darling?" Thomas purred, enjoying the fact that he could still make his wife blush such a pretty pink. Almost the color of her luscious little ass when he'd spanked her, perhaps three or four swats when it turned such a delicious shade of-

"They're just beginning the introductory video, Mr. Williams." Chuck was at their side, still scanning the area around

them.

"Thank you, Straker," the new Number One said in a stately way, "is there a spot with a mirror around here?"

"Of course," he intoned, leading them both to a little closet of sorts that was apparently meant to be a dressing room.

Uncomfortably wedged into the dusty space, Lauren managed smooth her husband's tie and smile up at him. "You look so handsome. You're going to rock this." Her hands wandered to the strong column of his neck as she sighed a little. "Yeah, you're going to be..."

The big, warm hands of her spouse were sliding along the light silk of her dress, and Thomas's voice was suddenly hoarse again. "And you, my darling, so sweet. Your beautiful face smiling up at me..." His hands were drawing the soft folds of her dress up without really being aware of what he was doing, but he suddenly groaned. God, this woman- she smelled so fucking good, so delicious, he wanted to *devour* her and-

His mouth slammed down against hers, swallowing her grateful little whimper as her hands went to his belt, feverishly yanking and trying to free it from his dress pants. The tenuous thread of control he'd been hanging on to for weeks and *weeks* snapped and Thomas growled, reaching under his wife's clothing to yank down her underwear. He briefly noted they were her plainest cotton ones, the "laundry day" type she'd been sporting recently to discourage herself from letting him see her scantily clad. Number One chuckled darkly against the wet mouth of his pretty bride. She could be wearing one of Kingston's suits and he'd still not be able to resist her.

Wedging one polished shoe against the door and bracing with the other, Thomas hauled Lauren upwards, grinning at her stifled shriek and greedily gripped the soft globes of her bottom in his hands, squeezing and massaging them.

"I fear I cannot wait, lovely," he growled, running his tongue against fluttering pulse in her neck. "I must fuck you right now or walk out on stage with the largest erection of my life."

To his pleasure, Lauren burst out laughing, strong thighs tightening against his hips and awkwardly perched against the rickety table under the mirror. "Please don't wait, oh, god, Thomas! I've been waiting and waiting - I've been so good, Sir!"

The smooth and urbane Number One groaned. "Oh, god!" he managed, before diving back in, slanting his mouth harshly against hers and sliding his tongue between her lips, smothering her moan. Bracing her pelvis against his thigh, hitched up to hold her then left one of his hands free to grip her hair, yanking it back to bare her throat to him. He could dimly hear her gasping breaths, hands digging in to his shoulder, the other in his hair, nails scraping pleasurably along his scalp. "Beautiful, perfect girl," Thomas managed, "you're rubbing yourself against my thigh, riding me like the dirtiest, greediest little girl. I can feel your swollen clit brushing my trousers, darling."

Diabolically, his other hand shifted to help her move against him, the soft lips of her center swelling and slick as Lauren rubbed helplessly against the lean muscles bulging in his thigh, braced perfectly for her. Only the tips of her pretty high heels touched the floor, pushing desperately to give her more traction against his thigh. Her back was arched, long lashes fluttering and that pretty mouth open and gasping as his lovely bride brought herself to her finish, Thomas hastily slamming his mouth against hers to stifle the rather loud trill she gave as she came.

There was a fairly urgent knocking at the door and Chuck enunciated, "Mr. Williams, they have introduced you and are now applauding to welcome you-"

"One moment!" Thomas not quite shouted, inelegantly heaving his moaning wife to the left and grasping his cock, sliding it along her lusciously silky slit.

Putting his mouth to her ear, he diabolically whispered, "You must be quiet, my darling. You don't want everyone to know what a delightfully dirty little girl you are, now do you?" Unfairly, he'd wedged the tip of his cock at the entrance of her passage, and as Lauren attempted to answer him, he thrust. Thomas dimly felt her nails sinking into his neck and could only enjoy the sting along with the overwhelmingly intense pressure of being inside his wife. "The heat of you, darling," he hissed, "the way you're gripping my cock, I can barely move-" He did heroically manage to begin force himself in and out of her spasming channel, enjoying pushing her through her orgasm and extending it as he forced her open.

Sweat was beading on their foreheads as they pressed together, Lauren desperately trying to smother her whimpers as he moved faster inside her. It had been so long- he thought disjointedly, and she was very slick and sweet, her body clutching him inside her, heels pressed into the small of his back and he could feel the moisture between them making it easier to thrust harder and faster.

"I am not a gentleman, darling," he groaned, "I'm sorry this is a bit-" he thrust hard, enjoying how his wife desperately bit into his neck to keep from screaming, "abrupt and harsh, I'd intended to-" another vicious thrust, and another sharp sting from her teeth, "-to seduce you and prepare you slowly, it has been so long and darling, oh-" Thomas thrust up so hard he moved her up the wall, which was fortunate because the little table underneath her ass cracked, one leg dropping and tilting the whole thing sideways.

More urgent knocking and Chuck's voice, beginning to lose its constant composure. "Sir! I must insist that you-"

"IN A MINUTE!" shouted Mr. and Mrs. Williams together, both gasping as his cock swelled impossibly harder. Really, Thomas thought, he was amazed he hadn't come the second he'd managed to get inside his wife, but it all felt so unbearably good that he almost dreaded finishing. But he could feel her slick walls beginning to flutter, and he knew she was ready to come again, and not even the vaunted self-control of Thomas Williams was enough to resist the moans and gasps from the woman he loved as her cunt clamped down hard enough to strangle his cock. So with hastily smothered groans, they exploded together, Thomas feeling every ripple of her body against him and feeling his throat hitch back a sob because nothing would ever feel as tight and beautiful and perfect as his wife and-

"MR. WILLIAMS!" shouted Chuck, "The audience is waiting and you are wearing a mic!!"

Lauren froze in horror, hands batting against his suit jacket to find the tiny electronic device that so effortlessly delivered his voice to-

One big hand covered hers, smothering the lapel microphone. "It's not on, lovely," Thomas crooned, "don't worry." They both strangled back another moan as he pulled reluctantly from her and she yanked over a box of tissues from the broken table to dab helplessly at the shiny wet spot on his expensive trousers.

"Oh, god, honey," she moaned, "oh, shit, I'm sorry!"

"Language," Thomas corrected absently, hastily stuffing his cock in and zipping up, tucking in his shirt and fastening his belt. "No one will see a thing," he soothed, "I shall be behind a podium, now give me a kiss." His deliciously cringing bride did as she was told and he licked the traces of her mint-flavored lip balm from his mouth.

Such was the stern gravitas of the new Number One of Jaguar Holdings that there was not a single giggle, not the tiniest of titters as he strode into the lights, calmly gripping the stand and mesmerizing the crowd with his speech. And if his mic had been on before he took the stage, there was not a soul in that vast room suicidal enough to tell him.

Three days later...

"Happy anniversary, my dear husband." Lauren shyly handed Thomas a glass of champagne, blushing as his gaze dropped to her bare breasts as he accepted it.

"And happy first anniversary to you, my sweetest and most lovely bride," he returned, kissing her lingeringly, enjoying the tart sparkle of the wine on her mouth. They were resting against a mountain of pillows - something he'd requested specifically when he booked the cottage, knowing how much Lauren loved them - and looking out at the surf, the moon shining on the ocean and the salt breeze drifting through the open window. He looked down into the shining eyes of his wife, this beautiful, impossible, courageous woman who chose to love him against all good sense. And he thanked the god he'd not spoken to for decades for it. "I love you, Lauren," Thomas blurted without any of his calm or measured speech.

Her arms went around his neck and he could smell the lavender and honey warmth of her skin. "And I love you, Thomas," she kissed one high cheekbone and then the other, "Sir... with all my heart."

Rolling over on to her back and smiling up at her spouse with an utterly mischievous leer, for the moment Lauren pushed away all the requirements of being The Corporation's new Queen Bee. Including planning a funeral for her father Frank, who'd apparently perished during a fishing trip off the coast of Cape Cod. Sadly, there was not enough left of him for an open casket. But that was all right. She was good at handling those sorts of things. She was, after all, Mrs. Thomas Williams.

Afterword

Thank you again for joining Lauren and Thomas on their adventures! If you enjoyed the story, would you mind leaving me a review on Amazon.com? I would deeply appreciate it. Here's an easy-peasy direct link: Amazon.com/review/create-review?&asin=1477123456

If you have suggestions or insights, feel free to contact me at ariannafraser88@gmail.com

About The Author

Arianna Fraser

Working as an entertainment reporter gives Arianna Fraser plenty of fuel for her imagination when it comes to writing stories about Norse Mythology - Loki in particular - and current-day romantic tales. There will always be an infuriatingly stubborn heroine, an unfairly handsome and cunning hero - or anti-hero - romance, shameless smut, danger, and something will explode or catch on fire. It's clear she is a terrible firebug, which is why her husband has sixteen fire extinguishers stored throughout the house.

When she's not interviewing superheroes and villains, Arianna lives in the western US with her twin boys, obstreperous little daughter, and her sleep-deprived husband.

Books By This Author

I Love The Way You Lie - A Dark Loki Paranormal Romance

A nameless princess: innocent, damaged and very lethal. A ruthless king with the power of a god. And trouble, lots of it. When King Loki of Asgard takes the daughter of the Dark Elven Queen captive, he not only strips an enemy of a powerful weapon, but gains for himself a wife. Now the newly named and wed Queen Ingrid must learn to survive the perils of court life, the wages of war, and most dangerous of all, her seductive husband's bed.
I Love the Way You Lie is a dark romance and for 18+ only

The Reluctant Spy - A Dark Mafia Romance

Maura MacLaren - mousey, dowdy, and very, very good with technology - is a perfect Corporation employee. Brilliant at her job, smart enough to know to keep her head down, and in debt to the criminal enterprise that gave her a chance when her past left her with nowhere to turn. But this puts her under the watchful eye of the Corporation's diabolical, gorgeous, and utterly unforgiving Second in Command, James Pine.

Pine has been sent by the head office in London to be sure nothing will go wrong with the Corporation's largest deal to date. The last thing a man in his dangerous position needs are feelings, or surprises. Especially feelings for a nerdy underling who is turning out to be full of surprises, including a sensually submissive nature that Pine finds too compelling to resist. But Pine is as cold-hearted as he is handsome and he never denies himself what he wants.

But when Maura's darkest secret puts her life and Pine's deal in danger, they both find themselves shocked at the sensual depths he will drag her to for revenge. And the lengths he will go to in order to save her life.

The Reluctant Spy is a dark romance and for 18+ only.

The Reluctant Bride - A Dark Mafia Romance

Lauren, freshly arrived in England, is looking forward to starting a new career with the London Symphony Orchestra, and a new life away from her indifferent, foolish father. But she finds that an ocean is not enough to separate her from his mistakes. After letting his company be taken over by the infamous Corporation, one bad choice after another has left him afoul of its ruling body. Only Thomas Williams, The Corporation's powerful Number Two, can save him. For a price, of course. His daughter. Thomas had never wanted a wife, a family, or anything conventional in his life. His demanding sexual predilections and violent past had always made such things seem out of his reach. But The Corporation has just made a deal with a devil even more dangerous than they are - The Bratva Crime Ring. The Bratva are old-fashioned monsters, and they believe that marriage and children make a man - or at least make him easier to handle. So a seemingly docile, innocent young woman like Lauren, who owes him her father's life, seems to be the perfect choice. But soon, what was just an expedient arrangement turns to passion, loyalty, even friendship. And maybe more. Maybe a real future together. If his past doesn't get them killed.

The Reluctant Bride is a Dark Mafia Romance and is 18+ only.

Printed in Great Britain
by Amazon